HALLOWED

SOUTHERN WATCH
BOOK 8

ROBERT J. CRANE

OSTIAGARD PRESS

HALLOWED

Southern Watch, Book 8

Robert J. Crane

2nd Edition

PROLOGUE

THE DRIFTER

Franklin, Tennessee
Four Weeks Ago

"Lafayette Jackson Hendricks, you look like something ate you up and shat you out," Frieda Winthrop said. She was a handsome, dark-skinned lady, and one that reminded him distinctly of someone else. Slight graying in her black hair, not a wrinkle showing even though she was in her fifties. She stared out the open screen door, her husband Micah glaring beside her on the porch. Glaring at him. She looked slightly more kindly disposed – worried, almost. Motherly, perhaps. Which made a certain amount of sense.

After all...he had married their daughter.

Hendricks stood shaking beneath his black drover coat and cowboy hat. It wasn't that cold out; maybe fifty-five Fahrenheit, but it felt like freezing-ass temps to him. There was something hot burning beneath his collar that made his boots threaten to clack together, made him pull the coat closed, hands stuck so deep in the pockets that he couldn't dig any deeper into them without reaching China. "Something maybe did," he said to Frieda. Her eyes were wide with concern, an emotion he was not used to seeing these days, hadn't been used to seeing in a long time except–

Maybe from Erin. Or Alison, before she died. Or Arch.

"Where you been, Staff Sergeant?" Micah Winthrop asked, his voice big and booming. Just like a Gunny's voice ought to. Felt like he could use that voice to push Hendricks right off his porch, out of his town, maybe right out of this state.

"Town about three hours from here," Hendricks said. Were his knees knocking together? Felt like it. "East. Past Chattanooga."

"Well, what were you doing there?" Frieda had a dish towel stretched limply over her shoulder, and she was fiddling with it nervously, like she wanted to throw it down or something.

"Killing demons," Hendricks said, and saw the flare of impatience, annoyance, sheer dogged pissed-off-ness in Gunnery Sergeant (Retired) Micah Winthrop's eyes. "Killing lots of demons. Of all kinds."

"You still on that bullshit?" Gunny asked. Never had believed Hendricks about his daughter dying at the hands of demons.

Hendricks just shrugged. He didn't have it in him to argue about it with his former father-in-law. Not anymore.

"You look like you're freezing," Frieda said. "Come in out of that cold. Supper's done, and we got plenty enough for you." She caught a glare from the Gunny. Or not; he sent it, but she either didn't notice, or didn't give a fuck. Which Hendricks worried a little about, because it felt like the sort of shit that would blow back on him later. Like eating five cans of Hormel chili and beans while staying in that shitty little room in the Sinbad.

"Come on, now." She had a hand extended, beckoning him forward, while Gunny's eyes were threatening to roll up in his head from rage or cussedness or both.

Hendricks listened to Mrs. Gunny over Gunny any day. He knew who the boss was at home, regardless of who had bossed his ass around over in Iraq. "Yes, ma'am," he said, shaking as he made his way up the three steps from the porch. He didn't have to be told twice to come in out of the cold.

At least, not in a literal sense. But metaphorically...his ass was still in the cold. And it had been ever since Renee died.

ONE

WHEELS IN MOTION

MIDIAN, TENNESSEE
NOW

Archibald "Arch" Stan awoke in the darkness of a back room in the sheriff's station off Old Jackson Highway to the sound of something chirping in the distance. He'd been in one of those thick sleeps, the kind that wraps you right up and takes you off to Never Never Land – not the kind in Peter Pan. The kind where you just wish you Never, Never have to wake up.

He sat up on the old military-style cot, head heavy from the sudden, unexpected wakening. Dreamland faded unpleasantly; he'd been in an opiatic haze, the light touch of a hydrocodone pill having pulled him into a painless sleep.

But he wasn't painless now. The back of his right hand bore an ugly bit of stitching, crusted blood dried along the ebony skin. He felt a little nauseous, too; he didn't like using painkillers, but

Dr. Darlington had insisted before she'd started stitching him up. It was stupid – the pills, the stitches, the fact he'd gotten himself ripped open at all, and by some little demon that looked like an iguana dipped in tar. It had slithered around with about a thousand of its fellows, rushing through the streets of Midian, and Arch had gone after it with his sheriff's car consecrated by Barney Jones – tires, bumper, doors.

But not the windshield. That had been a whoopsie.

So the demon iguana had busted right in when he'd been driving through them at high speed. And he'd managed to plunge a holy dagger in the thing, but not before it had ripped up his hand first. The interior of the car had looked like a slaughterhouse afterward. Blood everywhere, ripped stuffing from the seats, and a dadgum mess for whomever drove it next to clean up.

And here he lay in bed, drugged out of his mind for who knew how long, recovering from the dumbest injury in the history of the Watch.

The consequences, they did bite. And it felt like he was paying on the installment plan for things he'd done years ago, the consequences of which were all coming due at once.

Staggering out of bed, still wearing his khaki uniform (which could have used an ironing), he threw open the door to the station hallway. He could hear a tide of chaos down the way, in the bullpen, and he headed in that direction. Surely something was up. It always was these days.

"I NEED A LITTLE MORE CLARITY," Erin Harris said, leaning over the shoulder of Benny Binion, the Watch's dispatcher. He was thin, and so was his hair on top, Erin noted. Just a small-town guy in his mid-thirties who'd taken up the job as a dispatcher when they'd asked for help. Gone, though, were the days when he'd send out a horribly misspelled group text informing the Watch that daemons were running amok at Hairy Poons. Which was actually Hardcastle Point. Or that fire sloths were tearing through Ass Bristles (Anson Boulevard).

Because not a soul in this town still had internet, or cell phone coverage, or even so much as a land line to make a call on. It was all gone, and had been for about a month. Just after that big earthquake had reduced the main roads in and out of Midian from twelve to eight. And just after they'd discovered that the town water supply was dry, and being fed by trucks coming surreptitiously from the federal government.

And not FEMA, either. Some unregistered demon welfare program designed to keep Midian limping along, inhabited, so that people wouldn't leave, they'd stay and be human Happy Meals for the burgeoning demon population. Like the worst fucking USDA program ever.

"I got nothing more for you, Erin," came the voice of Yuval Simon. He had a squad on the far side of town, right where Oak Street ended and the national forest began, a wooded rough that had seen the disappearance of those damned tar iguanas that had come through last night. "All I can tell you is there's motion on the sensor we set up, but none of us can see what's moving in there. Could be tree branches swaying in the breeze, could be a pack of demon cyclists running a spin class out there. I ain't going in to find out without force of numbers behind us, y'know?"

Erin sighed. "I know, Yuval. That's smart." Yuval was a smart guy. Smarter than most of the crew she relied on. Not that they were dumb, it's just there were more than a few of them who'd go charging in dick first, not realizing they were rushing into a set of spinning blades that would turn their fucking salami into a summer sausage.

Ugh. Thinking in terms of dicks again. She mentally flogged herself.

"I'm not sure we want to go out there in force, Yuval," Erin said, relying on Benny to trigger the mic for her with a gesture of her hand. At this, he was minimally competent. And she leaned in close, smelling the scent of Benny's sweat, aftershave, and a beyond-liberal application of deodorant. He had to be on day three without a shower, and she could only sort of tell. He actually didn't smell bad. It made her want to lean in closer, so she did, and felt a mild surge of concern shock through her and land in her belly. "We might want to let this sleeping demon lie for a bit, y'know?"

"Your call, boss," Yuval said. "It won't break my heart not to go tromping into the dark, scary-ass woods after demons that may or may not be in there. I sense my guys are fine with leaving this one alone, too."

Erin rubbed the bridge of her nose. How much harm could be hiding beneath those boughs?

Answer: based on past experience, a lot. A whole fucklot. There was a tension in her neck that caused her to throb a little right at the base of her skull. And in her back. There wasn't much other than a pharmaceutical intervention she could do about those. And...lower, and in a very different way, though there was even less she could do about that at the moment.

Erin was dimly aware that it had been months since the last time she'd gotten laid, probably the longest stretch in Erin's life since she'd lost her virginity, and it was driving her fucking nuts that her town was sliding straight to hell and all she could think about other than demons is how much she wanted to catch a high quality dick. It was perhaps the most maddening part of all this; demons, she could deal with. But she was leader of the Watch, and she found herself thinking about sex an annoying amount. Was this what men dealt with all the time?

Who could function thinking about getting it on every two minutes?

A sound behind her made her turn, and she watched Arch come staggering in, shirt truly rumpled to hell and gone, like no iron ever made by man – or maybe by God himself, if she went by Arch's reckoning of the universe – could put it right again. His eyes were half-closed, and he looked like someone had dragged him right through the turd patch. Never a bad-looking guy, he looked so pitiable now as to render him almost unrecognizable as the Arch from the before times.

Before the death of his wife. Before the fall of Midian.

And it was the fall of Midian. Sure, it extended out toward the smaller towns elsewhere in the county like Culver, almost forty minutes away, but it was centered here. It was landing hard, here. It was fucking them, here, and not in the way Erin was ready to spontaneously combust in the crotch to experience.

"Sounds like it could be serious," Arch said, voice ragged as hell, too. Why should he sound any different than he looked? "Maybe we ought to call everyone out, hit it hard."

Erin hesitated, really mulling that one over. "My big fucking worry is," she said, checking first to make sure Benny's dumbfuck ass didn't have the mic's transmit button held down, "we are ragged as hell, Arch. Ragged as you, and if you could find a mirror, you'd know I'm saying something there. What are we gonna do, pull everyone out in an all-call for maybe nothing?"

"What if it's not nothing?" Arch asked. "Can you live with that, then? If it turns out to be something, and something tears somebody up?"

She wavered. It was always something. Always some demon tearing somebody up. This had been the way it was since last summer, and it was January now. The one-way ratchet had continuously advanced toward Armageddon, too, at least for Midian, without a fucking centimeter of reversal. "Okay," Erin said, maybe against her better judgment, if she had any of that left beneath her dick-starved exterior. "Let's call 'em out."

"GARY," someone said, stirring Gary Wrightson out of a deadass-sleep in his wheelchair. It wasn't a subtle voice, which was good, because Gary wasn't a subtle person. It intruded on his pleasant dream, one in which he was riding high, rolling down a damned hill with a sword in one hand, a machine gun chirping off in the other, and a bald eagle perched on his shoulder screaming the national anthem like a metal band as he ran over the fucking demons who'd ruined his business, his town, and his life for the last few months. He watched them pop as the wheelchair tires dragged them under, like he was the Killdozer and they were the interfering-ass bureaucrats in that Colorado town. Sure, Killdozer hadn't actually kill anybody, but Gary had. And Gary would kill more, because fuck if he wasn't dreaming about it at night, watching those piss-pot demons pop, black essence exploding out of them with that rankass sulfur stink that followed.

He'd known when he'd gotten into this thing that he was going to kill every last one of these motherfucking demons. Kill 'em all, him and his team. How could they not? They were asskickers and hard dickers, every last one of them. Even Marina. He dreamed of her sitting astride his dick bouncing up and down as the eagle sang, the machine gun burst, the tires screamed, and he rolled down that hill.

"I'm awake," Gary said, leaving the bliss of his dream behind and slapping his hands down on the wheels of his chair. He was in a darkened room, in a one-story house a block off Main Street and the square in Midian. He didn't sleep much these days, and when he did catch shut-eye it was here, in this place, rather than his fucking place, which had been burned down by goddamned government fuckers who'd come to kill him the only time he was vulnerable. But he'd showed those pigs, turned one of them into sulfur stink and pissed off the other one. Then he'd made his escape through sheer fucking will while that fed cunt burned his house down around his ears.

He'd showed them, though. He'd skullfucked the demon servants of Uncle Sam. And he hadn't felt a thing except the triumph inherent in any proposition where Gary Wrightson pitted himself against a problem. They lose, Gary wins. That was how shit worked in his life. Every fucking time.

Or at least, that's how it had worked.

"What do we got?" Gary was already rolling, skinning his knuckles as he passed through a too-narrow door from the bedroom of the abandoned house and into the main room. Abandoned houses in Midian were more common than occupied ones these days. They even had squads move from house to house turning off the water and draining the pipes for a while there. Get the last drops of water out, kill a few nesting demons. It had been win/win. Til they got too busy, and the water had started to turn.

"They're calling out the Watch," Larry said, his dark-haired, dark-bearded ass looking like he was shrouded in shadows. They had a few candles burning – smelled like goddamned key lime pie, because they'd been raided from the abandoned houses, and apparently they were taking from some middle-aged fucking Karen who presumably had LIVE LAUGH LOVE tattooed on her tramp stamp, and maybe even across her waxed-smooth pussy lips just so her life philosophy couldn't possibly be missed on the rare occasion she found some simp pathetic enough to go down on her joyless cooch. "We got movement in the woods near Oak Street, where those lizards disappeared last night."

Gary grunted. The lizards had been some shitty little fuckers. He hadn't even gotten out of the van for them, just drove its holy tires and grill straight through the bastards at high speed. The Watch had a shit ton of consecrated vehicles now that he'd shown them how easy it was to turn an instrument holy. Father Nguyen had revealed himself to be a little bitch in heart, spirit, and body the day that had come out. So what, he wasted months of his life doing some long-ass consecration ritual when Barney Jones could whisper over something for ten seconds and bless it to the destruction of the demons from hell. There was no need to be a fucking pussy about it. Honestly, the little father seemed less like a man and more like a little girl all the time. Did they still make eunuchs? Because he might have been one, Gary figured.

"What do you want to do, boss?" This from Ulysses, the old gray-bearded bastard. Gary had never thought much of him as an employee, but then Gary hadn't thought much of anyone as an employee other than Marina, long may she ride his dick. He saw her rubbing her eyes as she came out of the bedroom behind him. No dick riding tonight, though; they'd both been too knackered after the stupid fucking lizards.

"I want to find a way to cast a holy fucking fire spell that runs over everything demonic in this town but spares the good folks that are left," Gary said with a real rumble in his voice. Angst – yeah, some, maybe, but not like bitchboy Nguyen. They'd been at this for months, and while Gary hadn't expected instant victory, there'd never yet been a thing he couldn't turn his hand to in life – sports, back when he could walk, the plumbing trade, now, or even bowling – that he couldn't make into a winning situation for him. He *veni, vidi, vici'd*, didn't these demon cocksocks understand that? When Gary Wrightson came to work on a problem, the problem got fucking *solved*. Thus ever it was.

Until now. Until these demons. And somehow, with all his

focus, all his will, all his powers of mind, and his whole fucking family plus his employees...

Shit had gotten worse. Measurably. Specifically. Ugly...ly?

And this was simply not a state of affairs that could continue. Not while Gary was applying shoulder to fucking grindstone.

"Well, absent that, though?" His brother Paul asked. Of all his brothers – and there were three – Paul was his favorite. Not his mother's, but his. "Since I don't think fire spells are a thing at present?"

He didn't give Paul the look. He didn't need to. "We fucking saddle up, of course," Gary said, sweeping his gaze over them all, keeping it mild, keeping it cool. There was Terry, and there was his mom, nodding at him. All accounted for, he spun the wheelchair around and headed for the ramp out the front door. He'd be the first one out. Because that's what leaders did.

THE HOUSE WAS quiet when the radio woke Dr. Lauren Darlington out of a half-sleep. That was all she got nowadays, a half-sleep. Not the slumber of the righteous, not the sleep of the just, only a pale, waxy imitation of sleep. Like her residency all over again, but with more demons and less impacted bowels.

"You hear that?" Molly was there, hovering above her. Molly was her daughter. Sixteen years old, and here, in the war zone that was Midian, Tennessee. She was bright-eyed and bushy-tailed – or at least bushy-haired, because hair care was the first thing to go in a water-parched war zone – and had a mug of beautiful-smelling coffee steaming over her. "They're calling."

"That's what they do," she said, with only enough dexterity to catch the coffee and shove it in her mouth like a hungry baby catching a tit. She didn't know why she thought of it that way; she hadn't breast-fed Molly, after all. Too time-consuming, and she was still in high school. "They call, and they call, and we roll out with our holy water squirt guns and consecrated vehicles, and we drive through whatever nasty-ass demon infestation is currently roiling what remains of the town." Lauren pulled her knees in close, wrapping her arms around them, cupping the coffee like a lover. Certainly it was the closest thing she'd had to a lover in many moons. It was hot and it was inside her regularly, and what more could she ask at this point?

"Well, they're calling," Molly said, already dressed in her cute jeans and warm sweater with a watch cap clutched in her fingertips now that she'd conveyed the coffee to Lauren. "So it's time to roll out."

"Right, right," Lauren said, with a quick look around her room. Her room. Her bed.

Her town.

Had she really left behind Chattanooga for this? The safety of Chattanooga. The prosaic job at Red Cedar hospital treating patients in the ER? Forgone it all so she could wrangle demons in her FedEx'd-to-hell-in-a-handcart hometown?

And dragged her daughter with her?

"I can see the wheels turning in your head," Molly said, standing over her.

"The wheel cannot turn," Lauren said. "The hamster is dead." She sipped the coffee. Perhaps the hamster could be resuscitated, but only through an mg of atropine directly to the heart. Or a cup of coffee straight to the soul.

"We came back to save this town," Molly said, sitting down on the bed as if to encourage her. Wasn't this Lauren's job? Encourage the teenager? To go to school, to get good grades, to go to a fine college and repeat cycle so she could have a wonderful life? Possibly with a lover of her own at some point, and then a daughter, and repeat cycle again? Maybe keep the father this time, though. Mostly so Lauren didn't have to do the raising she'd mostly skipped out on with Molly. That had been a real raw deal, and she was glad her mother had taken it up. She did not feel she would be as willing as her mother in the same situation.

"Yeah," Lauren said, tracking back to the conversation, "but it's not exactly going our way, is it?"

Molly nodded slowly, that bushy-wild hair moving up and down around her pale face. "I have come to a conclusion."

Lauren took another sip. "Proceed."

"It's okay to leave town," Molly said, drawing a breath as if in preparation to say something harsh, something foul, something in the realm of gossip about Andrea Gronhoy, that slut. It was scandalous to talk about her now; she was dead, after all. So was her husband, and her kids. "But on our terms, not theirs, or else they're pushing us out."

"Yes," Lauren said. "They are. With murder, which is a compelling argument, because I don't want you to be murdered by demons."

"And yourself?"

"Ehh," Lauren said, running a hand over her thigh through the sheet. Time was, her legs had been her most attractive attribute, in her opinion. With the right moisturizer, and a proper shave, with a good pair of heels with a nice skirt, she could clip-clop her way down a street, through a mall, or up to a stool in a bar and know that a healthy swath of the guys in the place were watching her do so.

Now? She hadn't shaved those bad girls in many moons. She wouldn't dare wear heels in Midian now, for fear she'd die while attempting to flee from a demon. And forget about a skirt in this cold. No power meant no heat; everyone was wearing layers and using generators and space heaters. However many of them were left. Which was not terribly many.

Shaving her legs had never been a joy, even in the best of

times. She did it because of how she felt once it was done, how it felt when she could parade around and catch some quality male attention. Sure, she got some bad male attention, too, but you had to take the good with the mediocre and the shitty on these things.

Killing demons was just like that, wasn't it? "Ughhh," she said, and threw off the sheet, the comforter, and the quilt. Molly blanched at the sight of her unshaven leg hair. Pretty soon Lauren was going to have to braid it. "Let's get this over with," Lauren said, throwing her hairy-ass legs over the side of the bed. She had a pair of pants here somewhere. "Oh – and give me more coffee. What is this? A kiddie cup?" She drained the last of the little mug. 16 ounces? Pfeh.

"That's the last of the coffee," Molly said.

"What?" Lauren asked. *"What?!"* Her daughter just shrugged, and left her there, wallowing in her horror.

DARLA PIKE AWOKE ENVELOPED in sensual, silk sheets draped across her naked body. No light streamed in from behind the blackout curtains that covered every window in the rented house's bedroom. The smell of brewing coffee came from another room, somewhere far down the hallway where she rested her blond head. There was no clock in the room, for why would she need one? She was on no schedule, on no one's timetable. She had no appointments today, tomorrow, or the day after, so far as she knew. In fact, there was only one appointment on her calendar, but it was for an indeterminate date in the future, one she would know when it arrived.

It was the day when the world ended, and she would claim her eternal reward.

That was the day she'd been working for since she was old

enough to know what demons were and what they wanted. She'd started young, making deals with daemonic players. Gotten burned a few times, too, especially early on. One of them had gone so wrong she'd wondered if she'd even be able to get pregnant naturally afterward. These were the pitfalls, she'd learned, of being willing to trade with beings who were powerful and utterly devoid of morality and compunction. She was lucky she'd survived those early fuckups. And gotten pregnant afterward. Four times, with two successful births. The other two she didn't know whether to chalk up to simple biology or what had happened to her with the demons.

She shuddered a little as she lay in bed, thinking about the course of her life, the way it had curved and wended like a river in these fucked-up hillbilly lands. She'd met Jason, someone as grasping and power-hungry as herself – well, almost. And it had been good. Exciting. They'd constructed their perfect family, with the little boy and the little girl, one for each of them. Little Jason Jr. and Mera. She was ninety percent sure that Mera was Jason's. Less so on Jason Jr., which made her laugh when she thought about that little secret she'd kept under peril of – well, some sort of vengeance. When your husband was regularly making deals with powerful demons, you kept your infidelities very quiet.

He'd been fun, though. Not everything she ever hoped for, but probably the most she ever thought she could get out of a fellow human being. But then he'd had to go and get himself killed, the dumb fuck. And it had left her in a hell of a place.

Still, his death had been the end of their little family. And this place had been spiraling toward the apocalypse. What was a single, savvy, widowed mother of two supposed to do without a big, strong, wheeling-dealing-demon man to watch out for her interests?

Watch out for her own, of course. Because one could deal

more powerfully than two. Especially if that one didn't mind making a few sacrifices.

The first had been Jason's mother, Marischa. Darla had slit her throat and caught some of the blood in a cup, then used it in a proper ritual. After that...

Well...she wasn't a mother anymore. But her quality of sleep had gone through the roof since. Why, she slept like the babies she'd killed.

Darla stretched over the silken sheets. Okay, maybe the sleep wasn't so great. The naked thing wasn't even for sensual reasons; it was supposed to make it easier for you to fall sleep and stay asleep. Same thing with keeping the bedroom extra cold, and the blackout curtains she'd installed. She was even taking magnesium because that was supposed to help.

Yet she was still waking up at all hours of the night, smell of coffee coming from the kitchen or no.

It was almost as if the little fuckers were reaching out from beyond the grave – or the basement of that shitty house out in the country, as the case might be – and tugging at her the way they had when they were still alive. *Mommy! Mommy!*

Darla Pike shuddered. She'd never hear those words again, at least not in this life. And if her pacts all held, she'd never hear it again in any other. Her day of ascent was coming, her means of ascent were secure, and now all she needed to do was wait for things to fall into place.

With a yawn, she threw the sheets off her naked body and slid into a silken bathrobe. Her hired servant had fixed coffee anticipating her rise; she might as well go begin her day. After all, what was sleep to a soon-to-be immortal?

Four Weeks Ago

HENDRICKS WASN'T THAT HUNGRY, a fact he discovered only three bites into the meal. Everything smelled solidly good – chicken-fried steak with white pepper gravy, mashed potatoes, sweet baked apples, and homemade biscuits, because his mother-in-law believed in cooking a feast for everyday occasions – but when the rubber met the road, or rather the food met his mouth, he just couldn't get it down.

Gunny ate in silence, keeping a fiery, resentful silence even as his dark eyes were locked on Hendricks with an intensity and purpose that he had generally reserved for shitass recruits at basic. "Food not to your taste?" he asked with an impressive amount of resentment oozing off the collection of words.

Hendricks just met his glare blandly. "I don't feel right," he said, and he didn't.

"Because you ain't right," Gunny said, taking a big ol' bite of biscuit. He had grown around the waist since his retirement, but there was zero chance Hendricks was going to mention that to him. Not if he wanted to live.

"Lafayette," Frieda asked gently, "you don't look so good, honey. Have you not been eating well?"

Hendricks tried to remember his last meal. It had definitely been before he'd left Midian. Before he'd had his last argument with Erin and Arch. Probably before he'd gutted that peckerwood County Administrator Pike, which had been yesterday at around midday, and which had prompted the argument. Had he eaten breakfast yesterday morning? He couldn't remember anything about the morning – had he fucked Starling before he killed Pike? Those experiences were all blurring together, too, and the memory of the redhead's naked body made him feel even sicker, suddenly.

"Lafayette?" Frieda asked again. "Honey?"

Hendricks didn't even feel it coming. The change in his blood pressure wasn't subtle, but it was sudden. It was a rushing sensation in his head, and the world turned over on him, sending him sideways out of his chair.

He hit the dining room rug cheek-first, but he was already out before it happened, and thus did not feel the sting, nor hear the screams, that followed.

TWO

THE VOID STARES BACK

"You're going to be a good boy, and keep your mouth shut again today, aren't you?" The middle-aged black woman stared at Duncan with penetrating eyes that were as fake as the rest of her. Full lips, fake. Black curly hair, fake. Slightly moving breasts beneath a stylish red blouse, faker than silicon-loaded titty bags out in Cali. Because at least those had real nipples and some hint of breast tissue larding the surface. Amanda Guthrie's – as she was now called in this world – had none. Beneath the blouse was demon shell, and beneath that, demon essence, and beneath that–

Well, the demon known as Duncan wasn't sure, exactly. It was a question for a higher power, and far outside his purview. To Guthrie he made his answer simple, and the same as every day that had passed since she'd given him the burden of knowledge he was now holding onto like some poor innocent fuck who got handed a bloody knife while sirens were blaring and red and blue lights were coming visibly closer: "Yes."

"Damned right you are," Guthrie said. Her name? Also fake. But then, so was Duncan's. Giving out real names in the demon world was like giving a serial killer your home address. Unwise, to say the least. Inviting calamity would be another way to put it. A better way, in Duncan's opinion. Smoother. Grander.

Not that Duncan was all about being grand. He was actually fairly modest as these things went. He sat silently as Guthrie steered the car. The all-call for the Watch had gone out, and they had left their beds in the crappy hotel downtown – it had shut down weeks ago, the employees had all stopped showing up, leaving with the rest of the rats smart enough to get the fuck out of the sinking ship that was Midian – and were now driving the short distance to the rendezvous point.

"Who do you serve?" Guthrie asked, as though it were a mantra, or the Walmart chant. Like they were starting their fucking shift, and trying to remember that excellence was part of their business or some shit.

"I serve the Pact," Duncan said. "I am an Officer of Occultic Concordance." He didn't bother to inflect the words. He usually didn't.

"Fucking right," Guthrie said. Duncan couldn't decide if he liked her better like this or back when she'd been a pasty white fellow named Lerner. In the end, he supposed there wasn't much difference. The real change was soul-deep – or essence-deep, since Guthrie was a demon.

And all those changes had happened when Lerner had cracked a shell fighting demon cyclists up on Mount Horeb, and been sucked back to hell to enjoy the brisk torments therein. One did not usually come back from that, even if one was an OOC – an Officer of Occultic Concordance. A demon cop.

But back Lerner had come, with new flesh, still no blood, those peculiar things they called breasts, and so much more. Bells and whistles, really, including a remarkable new ability to hide her essence's feelings from Duncan. Had that put a damper on their relationship? Duncan didn't think so. He thought it was the deeper thing.

The secret. The one Guthrie had come back with.

The one she'd shared.

The one that had fucked up Duncan's ability to concentrate ever since.

"Keeping your mouth shut is the mark of a good boy," Guthrie said, so condescendingly. If Duncan didn't bother to inflect most of the time, Guthrie made up for it for both of them. "And good boys are rewarded when the time comes." She sent him a glance pregnant with meaning.

"This the spot?" Duncan asked, because Guthrie was slowing the car. This was Oak Street, and even in the darkness, with the lack of street lamps, the moon shone down on swaying boughs overhead. The street was tree-lined, beautiful, really, and not among the areas of Midian that looked like a disaster area.

Yet.

"Probably up there, huh?" Guthrie nodded ahead, where two cars were already parked, lights shining into the woods past a vacant lot that had been left to overgrow. It needed the touch of a lawn mower, and probably a gardener. Maybe a ditch witch, too, or a flame thrower.

No, a flame thrower would be a bad idea. It was almost January, and the air was dry, the wind was cold, and there hadn't been a proper rain since last summer. But under normal conditions, a burn would have done it good. The grasses were waist-high, and underbrush was stretching out like a thicket from the edge of the woods. New growth, the old forest trying to assert its dominion over this abandoned piece of land.

"Remember," Guthrie said, checking her baton, "you're going to be a good boy, right?"

"Stop asking me," Duncan said, doing a function check of his own. Though there were no demons in sight in the vacant lot or beyond, though he could sense...something...out there. He exited the vehicle and tromped off through the brush with a growing sense of unease, telling himself it was just from what was ahead of him, and not from what was behind.

WHEN ARCH GOT to the end of Oak Street, his head was mostly clear. He rode with Erin anyway, because he didn't need to be hit in the face with a blustery wind while he drove himself. He was proud, but not too proud to admit that his car was in rough shape, and he himself was in rough shape. Operating heavy machinery wasn't out of his realm of possibility, but neither was it first on his list of things to do while still lightly impaired by the painkillers Dr. Darlington had plied him with.

But fighting demons under the influence? Well, he had to.

The Explorer's tire bumped against the curb, and Erin blanched. "We probably ought to do...what?" She was already looking out the window toward the dark woods. Someone – Casey Meacham, if Arch wasn't mistaken – had parked a truck across the sidewalk looking into the brushy, overgrown lot, and its high beams were aimed at the woods. "Form a skirmish line and walk through until we find something?"

"Or don't find anything," Arch said, his mouth cottony, dried out. It was a thoroughly unpleasant sensation. "Maybe we'll find nothing." He felt oddly hopeful about that. Over half a year of this demon fighting, and now two months past his wife's death, and the allure of constantly mixing it up with these servants of darkness had faded. Maybe it was the hydrocodone talking, but he found the appeal of returning to his cot in the back of the sheriff's station much more gratifying than slogging through the dry brush at this unholy hour like they were forming a search party to look for that Wellstone kid again.

Arch felt a pang at that. He'd seen more than his fair share of losses during this fight, but that one still stung. The boy had lost his father to demons on a hunting trip, then his mother to a roadside ambush...then he himself had just disappeared. As though he evaporated into the trees above, became part of the branches and twigs on his way up to the sky.

"Okay," Erin said, and she was chewing her lip. Probably feeling it like he was. Endless wars tended to grind one down. Or so Arch suspected, and had some evidence to back it up. After all, what was Lafayette Hendricks if not a soldier with a neverending war under his hat? Half the cowboy's problem had seemed to be that slow descent into nihilism that came from no victory, and no hope of it. When everything around you only gets worse, but you have to keep fighting, how do you even maintain a pretense of hope?

Arch sighed. He was past trying to manufacture hope out of horse puckey. He opened the door to the Explorer and felt a chill seep over him as he left the warm, comfortable environs of the police cruiser behind him and followed Erin into the spotlighted darkness.

LAUREN LET Molly drive for reasons of safety and reasons of enthusiasm – as in she wasn't safe until Lauren finished her coffee, and Lauren had zero enthusiasm for life or keeping herself from whipping the wheel ninety degrees into a power substation until she finished it. Molly, on the other hand...

"I feel like I'm really getting the hang of this," Molly said, her head bouncing a little. Her grin was infectious, probably, but only in the sense that if it spread to Lauren, it would mutate in the process and become a deep and festering loathing.

"Great," Lauren said, still suffering that lack of enthusiasm.

How many calls had it been in the last month? How many times had they shown up at midday or morning or late in the night to combat whatever demon had shown its ugly, toothy face? Whether calf-high like the damned lizards last night or big as a house the way that fire sloth thing had been a couple months back, it was all blurring together, all becoming the same: kill demon, repeat ad infinitum. Watch ever more spring up, in a never ending cycle.

Molly bumped the curb with her tire as she brought the car in just behind the Sheriff's Department Explorer. Arch Stan got out of the passenger side ahead of them, and Erin out of the driver's. Which was good, Lauren thought dimly. Arch was on the painkiller she'd given him, after all – she'd made him take it in front of her before she'd stitched him up – and would be woozy, probably. "Whoops," Molly said.

"It's fine," Lauren said, because she had no care for the condition of the whitewalls, or the hubcaps. Plopping the now-empty coffee cup in the cup holder in the center console, she reached for the massive squirt gun that took up half the back seat. Molly's took up the other half. She checked the tank, then got out and went through the unruly process to get it on.

"I always feel like a Ghostbuster in these," Molly said with a bit of a waddle as they followed Arch and Erin to where they waited just beside Casey Meacham's oversized, jacked up, micro-penis-compensating truck. Or so she'd always thought, until she'd seen his trouser snake in outline while they were living at Melina Cherry's whorehouse for a spell.

"Well, you're way prettier than one," Casey Meacham said with a broad grin, turning to look at them as they approached. His face was shadowed by the high beams on behind him, but Lauren could see the customary leer.

"So good to see you again, my darlings," Melina Cherry said. There were lines at the edges of her eyes, and she was wearing something a bit more conservative than her usual attire at the whorehouse. Brothel. Whatever. She gave Molly a peck on the cheek and then the same to Lauren. A whiff of her perfume left hanging in the air after she did so, and Lauren had to blink a couple times for fear it might be burn her eyes, it was so strong.

"So we've got Yuval's squad right at the tree line?" Erin asked, squinting into the shadowy dark. "Who else?"

"Jim Leighty's crew is two minutes out," Casey said, clutching a walkie talkie tight in his hand. "Also, Gus Terkel and Keith Drumlin are coming with that group. Mike McInness is a little farther out. And I see Duncan and Guthrie skulking over there." He waved the antenna down Oak Street, and everyone turned to look and observe that, yes, there was a pasty, slightly overweight white guy and a thin, serious black woman making their way over. "Oh, and the Wrightson crew is right there." He pointed again as a plumbing van seemed to take the corner of Oak hard enough to slide, and came to a thumping stop just behind her car five seconds later. The doors were immediately thrown open, and a ramp clanged against the sidewalk a second before Gary Wrightson was disgorged at high speed, rolling toward them.

Erin was squinting hard. "Anyone else?"

"Oh, yeah," Casey said. "Braeden Tarley and Barney Jones, right there." He pointed at an old Buick cruising quietly along in the Wrightson plumbing van's wake.

Erin's squint was pronounced now, and she seemed to be staring at Jones's Buick almost blindly. "I could have sworn we had more people than this yesterday."

"Last week we definitely did," Molly bubbled. "But that was before Tony Kelhauser's crew got half-wiped out, with the rest running for the hills after Tony died. Metaphorically, I mean; I think they actually ran to Knoxville."

"Terri Pritchard stayed," Casey said, looking into the darkness by the wood's edge. "That fine slice of aged heat joined up with Yuval's crew." He waved into the darkness, and from the shadows Lauren saw a somewhat shapely female figure flip Casey the bird. Yeah, that was Terri, all right.

"What happened to Marie Mulligan's bunch?" Erin asked. She seemed...overwhelmed? Not good, that was for sure. Lauren wondered if she needed a quick exam. Had she hit her head last night during the demon iguanas thing? Or was she just running on fumes? Which, to be fair, so many of them were by now.

"They died on Christmas, Erin," Arch said. "Remember? The–"

"The outhouse thing," Erin said, shaking her head. "Right. With Medford and Hoskins and..." She trailed off, staring into the middle distance.

"And Ted Bailey's group left right after," Arch said. Who could blame them, though? In fact, just listening to this list was making Lauren nervous again, like...why was she bringing her sixteen-year-old daughter, who she loved, on these missions where so many grown-up people, people in some cases who had military experience, were dying?

Lauren gulped. Couldn't help it, she just gulped. Because suddenly she was feeling so very, very stupid.

Then some words came back to her again from a man now dead, and she felt no better: *The gates of hell await.*

Because, hey, what better place for her daughter was there than where the gates of hell threatened to open to eat them all?

"ALL RIGHT," Erin said, because she really couldn't justify waiting any more. Braeden Tarley and Barney Jones were hustling down the sidewalk where they'd parked; the Wrightsons were out of the van and streaming toward her now. "Let's saddle up and do this." *I guess*, she didn't add. But it was how she felt.

"SHIT, this is actually in the woods?" Gary rolled to a stop at the curb.

Erin Harris looked over at him dully. "Yeah. We're forming up and sweeping ahead in a line until we confirm there's something in there or...or not." She seemed a little out of it. Probably just tired. Weren't they all, though?

Paul stopped beside him, clutching a holy machete. "You want to try and buck the odds, bro? I could carry you, maybe? Or you could try and roll?"

"I ain't rolling over fucking uneven forest ground with no idea how long it's gonna go," Gary said. "It could be a hundred feet or two miles." A cold wind blew through, and he resisted the urge to shudder. "And no offense," he added, almost always before he knew he was about to say some shit that was guaranteed to offend, "but you look like you could carry me from the tub to the toilet and that's about it, forget about backpacking me through the fucking woods."

"He's right, Paul," their mother said, clicking the bolt closed on her AR. No one had said no guns, but the Watch tended to be pretty careful with using them, given how many of these events tended to turn into absolute clusterfucks with little demons swirling in between their legs and shit. "You got a sunken chest, boy. Need to spend some time in the gym. Maybe get on tren."

"I'm not getting on steroids," Paul said, his voice rising.

"Maybe a course of TRT, then," Terry said. "I had to stop because it made my prostate swell up and my balls shrink, but you don't have balls to begin with and no one's gonna stick one up your backdoor to pluck the male g-spot, so you should be fine."

"I just want to say on the record: fuck all of y'all," Paul said. "And I'm glad I don't have to carry your ass." He looked disdainfully down at Gary. "You can go ahead and spin your fucking wheels right here."

"You will be all right, Gary," Marina said, pausing at him to drop off – yeah, the M60 and belts of ammo. Why did the little eastern European chick carry the big belt-fed machine gun and all the holy ammo? Because she fucking wanted to, and no one had the balls to tell her no, that was why. She gave him a kiss on the cheek, too, and a pat on the leg he didn't feel. Then she stole his consecrated Stratocaster guitar, which he'd killed at least a hundred demons with, and off she went with the rest of them.

Sure, no one had promised going to war with demons would be wheelchair-accessible, but it still burned Gary's ass to be left behind like this. He thought about throwing down the M249, but thought the better of it. He'd wait here instead, stew in his own juices, mostly self-pity, and sweat the bitch out of himself. Come out stronger and better while they just dicked around in the woods.

Hopefully it was just dicking around. Hopefully.

"YOU SENSE ANYTHING?" Guthrie asked as they stood at the edge of the woods, their backs to the cars. Headlight beams flooded past them, casting person-shaped shadows across the overgrown field.

"No," Duncan said, because he couldn't. "You?"

Guthrie just shrugged with a slight smirk. "Why would I if you can't?"

Why would you ask? Duncan wanted to say. But he didn't, for reasons he didn't really understand.

"LET'S MOVE IN," Erin said blearily.

Arch stared at her, wondering how long she'd been awake. But he didn't stare long, because he moved with the rest of them, one foot after another, trying to shake off the last, dull effects of the painkillers as he walked into a world of shadow and dimming light, staring into the dark and trying to discern the truth of what waited for him within.

Four Weeks Ago

HENDRICKS WOKE to the steady beep of medical machinery, the kind he'd heard on hospital dramas and in the infirmary in Ramadi. Heart rate monitor. Steady tone, beep, beep, beep.

"You awake, fuck head?" Familiar voice, too. Hendricks could have picked it out coming out of a deadass slumber fifty years in the future. Probably because it had wakened him out of a number of deadass slumbers only a few years in the past, and much less politely.

"I'm awake," Hendricks said, realizing for the first time he had points of stinging at places around his body: back of his right hand, where medical tape held an IV into his vein, his nose, where some kind of tubes had been shoved up there and plastic was resting on his upper lip. His voice was scratchy and his clothes were gone, replaced by one of those medical gowns that didn't quite shut in the back. His ass was touching sheets and the edges of the gown, and for a second he wondered if they'd stuck something up there, too. He squinched his cheeks and realized nope, but there was a plastic tube rammed up his dick. "The hell did they do to me?"

"Saved your life – for now," Gunny said roughly. "Or so they said." He was sitting beside the bed, a window outside providing a fine view of a brick wall and windows that seemed similar to the one he was looking out of. Below, a parking lot, filled with cars. Hospital. Yep. "Me, I'm wondering how fucked up you are, that you passed out at my table?"

"So am I dying?" Hendricks smiled bitterly. "Cuz I kinda been half-suspecting I might be checking out."

"We're all dying, dumbass," Gunny said. "Some of us just quicker than others. The best they could say is they don't think you're going to die today – but you got some kind of organ damage they can't explain." He leaned closer, actually got closer for the first time since Hendricks had seen him on the porch. "What the hell is going on with you, shitheel?"

"Probably took some stuff I shouldn't have," Hendricks said. He was thinking of those stupid vials that Wren Spellman had given him. There were going to be consequences for them at some point, he figured, but hell, his life expectancy had been falling by the day, and he'd needed to get back in the fight. Who cared about the future?

Especially since Hendricks hadn't really had a future. At least not for about five years.

"You been snorting down gas station dick pills?" Gunny asked. Impossible to tell if he was serious.

"Exactly that," Hendricks said, trying to hit that same irreverent, guess-if-I'm-joking timbre. "See, I've been juggling this perky blond and this insatiable redhead, and it gets hard to stay hard all the time. I know you know."

Gunny did not look amused. The only one who was

supposed to make jokes in Micah Winthrop's world was him. "Back on the white girls again, huh? That's a bad habit, Hendricks. I did warn you it'd kill you."

"Well, I figure if I made through kicking doors in Ramadi, a blond and a redhead were going to be pretty tame comparably. Who knew I was wrong, wrong, wrong? Other than you."

"Dumb fuck," Gunny whispered, and boy was there some heat behind it this time. He rose, and though he was not a tall man, he was damned imposing. "I did everything I could for you, boy. Took you home with me when you lost everything. Let you marry my daughter – my only baby. I didn't even blame you when things went wrong in New Orleans. Because it's New Orleans, and things go wrong in New Orleans, and life, but mostly New Orleans. I wanted nothing but the best for you – you shitheel – because it's what my daughter would have wanted. But this shit you are doing, this shit you have done – it dishonors the hell out of her memory, it dishonors the hell out of whatever you felt for her, and it dishonors your own damned spirit, son."

At the word 'son,' Hendricks felt an almost physical impact in his guts.

And Gunny just left. Walked right out, leaving Hendricks in the bed with a tube in his dick, up his nose, a needle in his arm. Left him with that thought, and away he went. Hendricks sat in the dark for a long time after that, and sleep never came back.

Neither did Gunny.

THREE
INFLAMED

Flashlight in one hand and her consecrated baseball bat with the nails through it in the other, Erin stepped carefully over the crunching leaves and occasional downed tree branch. Looking down one end of the line to the other, she saw familiar faces.

And she also saw a line that was significantly smaller than it had been a few months back, when everyone started pulling together after Halloween.

Wind whistled through the trees, shaking the boughs above her and dislodging an oak leaf that fluttered down in front of her flashlight. It cast a weird shadow across the forest floor as it did so, like a hand in front of a projector in the old days.

"Where's Father Nguyen?" Erin asked, looking around.

"Back at St. Brigid's," Arch said from about six feet to her left. "With the supplies, with the folks that are hunkering down there, with the injured." His eyes were front, he wasn't overthinking.

So why was she?

It was like a voice in her head, casting these annoying

doubts. When was the last time she'd slept? It felt like it had been a while. Too much going on. She took another step, the crunching, dead leaves becoming like a soundtrack. She imagined stepping on bones, hearing the crack and crunch–

That jarred her ass back awake. Stepping in a pile of bones was a real thing that had happened to her not that long ago. Human ones, too. Which time had that been...?

"Hey, Erin, you sure you're all right?" This from Casey, who was on her right. He had his tomahawk in one hand, giant beam flashlight in the other. Looked like he was carrying a 55-gallon drum with a light mounted in it. Thankfully, he kept it pointed ahead, not at her. On the other side of him, Miss Cherry was leaning forward, looking at Erin.

"Just a few things on my mind at the moment," Erin said. Not lying. Not quite.

BRAEDEN TARLEY HAD TAKEN his place in the line beside that demon OOC, the white one, the man one, if that applied to demons. He still wasn't quite sure what to make of the guy, with his broad, pasty face and cheerfully bland inoffensiveness. There wasn't much that could offend Braeden, not before Halloween, but now...well, a demon probably could come the closest to tripping his damned trigger, and trip it quick.

Because he'd lost his little girl at Halloween.

It was hard not to blame himself. If he'd believed in demons beforehand, he'd have run from this town, just like everyone else with half a brain. But Midian was the place he'd buried his wife, and now Midian was the place where he'd lost his girl...

...And if he'd had one ounce of hope left, he'd have got the fuck out, too. But Braeden wasn't all about the hope.

He was about bloody fucking vengeance – minus the blood,

because demons didn't have any. He was about sulphuric, shell-smashing vengeance, and he had a consecrated wrench that he'd done a fair amount of it with.

Braeden looked left; two down from him was Barney Jones, pastor of one of the two Methodist churches in Midian. The black one, in this case, because that was the difference between them, the parishioners. It wasn't segregated or anything, there was a mix, but there was definitely a predominant group at each.

He hadn't gone to church before Halloween. Hadn't been much of a believer. Now he was living with Barney ever since, and the man's wife Olivia. She was a damned saint. They both were.

But Braeden didn't really go in for that forgiveness stuff. Maybe for him – he sure needed it after how bad he fucked things up – but he wasn't going to go giving any of it to the demons. No slack for these fuckers. Not the ones who took his baby. Or any others.

Except maybe this bland, pasty, tastefully inoffensive fuck. Braeden looked him over again, didn't bother to disguise it.

The demon noticed. "I'm still sorry for your loss," he said.

Braeden didn't feel shame for looking. Didn't feel relief at what the demon – Duncan – said. "Just watch my back and I'll watch yours," Braeden said huskily. No malice. But no camaraderie, either.

Then, to his left, he looked, just to avert his gaze before shit got awkward with Duncan, and he noticed: "Oh. Hey, Terri."

"How's it going, Braeden?" Terri Pritchard asked. She had a real low, husky voice. She also had about ten years on him, and he knew this because she lived down the street from him growing up, and she was in high school when he was in elementary. Though he doubted she remembered that. She probably just remembered him from skinning his knuckles working in his shop. She'd brought hers in sometimes, after all. Almost everybody did if they didn't drive to the shitty dealerships to get ripped off in Chattanooga, Knoxville, or Cleveland.

Not that any of that mattered now, two decades removed, along with a swath of Braeden's hair, years of his life, and a river of damned pain separating him from that moment. Still, it stuck out like a nail in the middle of a fresh two-by-four.

"It's going," Braeden mumbled, because he couldn't think of anything else to say. Lucky it was so dark, she couldn't see him blush. "How 'bout you?"

"It's not been the greatest week ever," Terri said. Talent for understatement. "Or year."

Braeden just grunted. Hard to argue with that.

WHAT ARE YOU THINKING, *bringing your daughter into the demon-infested woods in the dead of night?* Lauren wondered, that small voice in her head screaming at her. *With so many dead, including your own mother? What kind of mother are you?*

"Mom, are you okay?" Molly asked. The faint of hum of the water pump in her backpack was fairly muted compared to the sounds of fifty or so people shuffling through the December leaves into the eerily quiet woods.

"Just pondering the similarities between me and Casey Anthony," Lauren muttered. That prompted a look from her daughter of absolute befuddlement. Which was good. Probably.

ARCH WAS HAVING HIS DOUBTS. Nothing was moving out here, other than the occasional dead, falling leaf, and the only sounds outside of human motion were his sword singing through the air as he kept it in front of him like his very own shield.

The sword glinted in the light, and he stared at it. Where had it come from? He still wasn't sure. Hendricks had gotten it for him, from somewhere – or someone, rather. Just another question the cowboy hadn't answered, another loose end he'd left open in Arch's demon education before he'd fled town a month ago without so much as a word of explanation.

Get your head out of your backside, he had said, *or get the hell out of town*.

Well, the cowboy had made his choice. He had always been a loner, ever since Arch had run across him on the square, killing that demon. What kind? Arch didn't even remember anymore. Funny name, turned to sulfur stink when you pincushioned it. Like so many others. Nearly all, in fact, except the greaters. Those took a bit more killing.

Arch didn't miss Hendricks, not exactly. He did miss the help. The counsel. The thought that he could call on the cowboy, ask him a question about demons, and be assured he'd get something close to an answer.

Nowadays all he had was Duncan and Guthrie. Maybe Nguyen, in a pinch, but the priest only knew a bit.

But when push came to shove, Hendricks had left town. And Starling with him, near as Arch could tell. Near as anyone could tell; Lucia had pulled up stakes at Madam Cherry's around the same time. Coincidence? Probably about as much as seeing the cowboy with stray red hairs on his collar the last couple weeks before he left.

"You smell something?" Erin asked from six feet beside him. Just enough space to give them a reasonable search line, not enough they couldn't close the gap quick if all hell broke loose. She was wrinkling her small nose.

Arch paused; he did smell something. And it smelled like...

Sulfur.

The wind rattled the bare tree limbs above and around him, they moved in the dark, lit by the rising and falling flashlight beams, making them look like skeletons dancing in the night. He swept his beam around, trying to find some hint of demon in the sea of motion, and settled it on something amidst the brown leaves and brown trunks and white-tinged beams...

Red. Red, in a sea of brown.

Arch stopped, and felt a pang of relief. For there among the rolling shadows and winter-dead trees was a petite, red-haired figure, her hair practically glowing in the night. He'd thought of her, and she'd appeared, just like that.

"Starling," Arch said.

"IS THAT LUCIA?" Melina Cherry's voice was sharp and pleased, the sound of a mother whose prodigal daughter had come home. Lauren stared at the redhead standing in the shadows beneath a big elm, her hair slightly aglow, as though tinged with real fire. She hadn't looked like that when Lauren had first met her in Red Cedar's ER all those months back, bearing the signs of abuse. Then she'd just been battered little Lucia. She hadn't looked that way when she lived at Miss Cherry's. Then she'd still been Lucia, just not so battered.

"Naw, that's Starling," Casey drawled. The whole line had stopped, and up and down it beams were glaring right at the redhead, picking her out in the dark. Her eyes were dusky, wide, and showed no sign of being affected by the spotlighting effect. She wore a long overcoat, and stood sideways, a leg showing where she had it resting, down to bare foot and toes, on a rock. It was almost like a model's pose; leaning slightly forward, hands at her sides, staring at the Watch's line of advance.

"Hello," Starling said, and to Lauren's surprise, it sounded like it was whispered right in her ear. A moment later, it continued, and removed any doubts: "Dr. Darlington."

"THE HELL IS GOING ON OUT THERE?" Gary muttered, trying to sit up in his wheelchair, to stretch and see what was going on. But the Watch was way too deep in the trees now; all he could see was flashlight beams dancing up and down between the trees.

"They ran into someone they didn't expect," a soft voice whispered at him. The little hairs on the back of Gary's neck stood right at attention, and he turned his head–

To find a tall, leggy redhead in a trench coat behind him, coat hanging open like a flasher, but her body covered just enough so he couldn't see the goods. She had a bare leg extending out and was leaning forward casually, like she'd posed for maximum hotness. It was a nice leg; smooth, creamy, and Gary wasn't too proud or too pussy-whipped by Marina not to give it a proper look.

"Who are you?" Gary asked when he got his damned wits back about him. "And who'd they run into?" He had a vague sense he knew this chick, but he couldn't quite place her. She was a little too pretty and a little too made up to be from around here, at least lately. Because Midian had gone through a rather immense cosmetics shortage of late, and even the women who'd stayed in the war zone that the town had become had higher priorities than prettying themselves up.

"Me," she whispered, and somehow, even though she was a solid five feet away, the words just tickled his ear, as though she'd leaned down and breathed them right in there, sweet honey-tinged winds curling around, sending a pleasantly warm breeze right, direct into the folds of his brain.

"Well, ain't they lucky," Gary muttered, because really, weren't they all?

"STARLING?" Erin asked, squinting in the dark. She hadn't cared much for the hooker/interloper/demon fighter in the past, but a lot of that might be fairly attributed to the redhead picking up her sloppy seconds. You never liked to see your exes happy once they'd parted ways with you, but you especially didn't care to see some angel hooker with – just, frankly, annoyingly – a better ass and bigger tits – take your man even if you were one hundred percent done with him.

And Erin wasn't sure she had been a hundred percent done with him. Which was why it particularly rankled that this specific redheaded, nice-titted, firm-assed angel hooker had swept in on her territory and got her filthy snatch all over him.

"Erin Harris," Starling said, and boy did it sound like she was talking right into Erin's ear. The redhead shifted; her long leg, extending out of her trench coat, seemed to begin to retract. The unnatural pose she had adopted had her leaning forward oddly, as though she were halfway into a lunge when she decided to just stand back up. Her toes seemed to snake their way across the leaf-lined ground. Erin imagined it was quite seductive – if you had a dick.

She didn't, but was still strangely entranced by the display. "What the hell are you doing here, Starling?" No one else was speaking, which...that was weird, right? You got ten members of the Watch together in a room, you had fifteen opinions and everybody was speaking them at the same time. But here in the woods, after the initial words of surprise about running into the redhead...silence?

Erin stared at Starling in bleary-eyed silence, waiting for the angel hooker to say something else. She didn't have to wait long.

"REMEMBER," Guthrie said menacingly, just to Duncan's side. Duncan could feel the OOC's eyes locked on him, boring into him in the dark, even though technically they weren't eyes and technically they didn't do anything in the demon's new shell. "Mouth. Shut."

Duncan did as he was instructed, though it took real effort. It was almost like there was a screaming voice somewhere deep inside him, hammering in waves at his inner essence, crying to get out. But after so many millennia of traveling down one particular road, it was a little too late, and he was a little too far gone, to turn around now.

Wasn't it?

BRAEDEN TARLEY STARED at the redhead who seemed to be whispering in his ear. The fact she appeared to be only wearing a trench coat was something. That she was doing a half-striptease was, well...something else. It had been long enough for Braeden that he had an impossible time prying his eyes off her, especially as she arched her back – visible in her bearing even though the trench coat hid nearly everything of interest.

"Braeden Tarley," she whispered again. "You have suffered so much. So much loss. So much pain. So much..."

"Yep," he said, voice almost contracting in the back of his

throat. Was it possible for vocal chords to retract? If so, they were definitely the only part of him that was retracting right now.

The woods were silent but for her whispering. A hush had fallen over the Watch, they had all gone quiet, which made it even more peculiar that this redheaded hottie was focusing all her attention on him, just the way his wife had back when...

Something about the bare memory of his wife caused a little chill to run through Braeden. The memory of her remained, frozen in time, commanding. Because only she could command him. Well...her and little Abi.

Something about the redhead lost its luster in that moment. If his memories of his wife were a dream, the redhead seemed like a strip club nightmare. Sure, she looked fine under the dim lights, but the moment they came on you saw the scars on her face from the meth habit, the dark circles under her eyes from being awake for days on end, the giant belly from...

...From pregnancy?

Braeden cocked his head, and it was like the lights had come on. There, beneath the trench coat, something was pressing. Something massive. Something like his wife had born when she was eight-nine months along and seemed to be smuggling a basketball under her maternity clothes. And when she slept next to him at night she needed one of those body pillows to cuddle up to in order the manage the giant belly.

Which was just the like the one the redhead bore.

A thousand whispering voices seemed to rise all around him, and Braeden looked left, then right.

The others were all talking to the air like the kind of crazy more commonly seen in an asylum, locked in a padded room, or wandering around downtown San Francisco jerking off violently in the middle of the street while maintaining intense levels of defiant eye contact with you.

"Oh, shit," Braeden whispered, realizing that he was the only one looking around...

...Except for the demons standing next to him, one of which – the pasty one – bore a look of surprising guilt, and the other of which – the black lady – was looking at him with narrowed eyes and a distinct hint of malicious, leering violence.

"LOOKS like somebody managed to slip the spell," Guthrie said, with distinct hints of malicious glee. Her baton's spring extended it with a loud *ka-chunk!* that didn't so much as stir the zombies standing all around them, talking to themselves. Duncan listened to it, to the voices, to all that was going on around them with a steadily rising concern welling in his essence. "What do you bet it was true love that did it?" Guthrie asked, jostling his arm as she moved toward Braeden Tarley. "I fucking hate love. What a pain in the ass." He glared sideways at Duncan. "Well? You gonna give me a hand here, or just stand there staring?"

"Since when do you need help knocking open some poor human's skull?" Duncan asked, looking at Braeden Tarley, who viewed them both with alarm. But Duncan deployed his baton nonetheless, though the *ka-chunk!* it made gave him no satisfaction. In fact, it seemed to ring out to the very corners of his essence like a tinkling bell, a warning of its own kind.

"WHAT ARE YOU DOING, STARLING?" Arch asked, once the initial surprise of seeing her had passed. He felt oddly feverish at the sight of her, something he ascribed mostly to the painkillers still dripping the last vestiges of their influence through his system. He tried not to pay attention to what she was doing with her leg, with her back, which all seemed designed to catch his attention and then titillate him in a distinctly unwholesome way. It made a hot blush rise in his face, and he looked about ten degrees off from the motion of her body, trying to keep his attention close enough she didn't take it as rude but far enough away that he wasn't caught up in whatever temptation game she was playing.

Mostly, it worked.

"Archibald Stan," she whispered, and it flowed through the woods like a rustling breeze, stirring leaves, stirring him. It felt like she was speaking right into his soul, and he found it uncomfortable, like when an acquaintance takes too much liberty putting their hands on you.

He jerked away, and the spell seemed to be broken. The voices of the members of the Watch sounded all around him, a cacophony:

"But how do I do that?"

"I do want it. I want it bad. More than anything."

"You've been gone so long, though. I missed you."

And somewhere down the way, a sharp cry. Arch turned to look, and saw Guthrie with her baton out, advancing on Braeden Tarley, who was shouting above everyone else: "Hey! Hey, y'all! Something's going on with the demons and that redhead!"

"They can't hear you, meatsack," Guthrie said, advancing in a slow, menacing way. "They're too busy having their tests tickled. So to speak."

"I can hear him just fine," Arch shouted, and it reverberated over the hills, bouncing off tree trunks and boughs, cracking like thunder over the darkened sky and flashlight beams.

Guthrie spun to face him, and a grin cracked her face. Insincere, wide, malignant. "Shoulda known. Fuckin' power of love.

God damn Huey Lewis." Duncan was beside her, but facing the opposite direction, still looking at Braeden Tarley.

"This where we're parting ways, Lerner?" Arch asked. He started pushing his way down the line in front of all the chattering members of the Watch.

He gave Erin a shove and she rocked back on her heels, jerking awake, as if out of a trance. "What the hell?" Her eyes went wide with panic, then narrowed as she focused in on him. "What was that?"

"Stop waking the dead," Guthrie said, striding toward them. She whipped her baton out and cracked Paul Wrightson squarely in the nose with it as she passed. Wrightson's head snapped back sickly; he fell to his knees as though all the bones in his body had been magically removed, then keeled over onto his face. Without even checking, Arch knew he was dead. "Okay. The soon-to-be dead." Another step, another swing, and Mary Wrightson joined her son, the old lady's nose exploding like an overripe tomato had been thrown in her face.

"Stop it!" Arch shouted, and charged, because he saw no other way.

But he did not get very far – maybe five steps – when everything changed around him.

Howling flames lit up the night as though a dozen gas mains had burst all around the woods. They billowed up, swallowing the trees whole, sliding across the fallen leaves as though tracing a path along an oil slick.

The woods burned. The light of the Watch's flash lights were instantly subsumed beneath the roaring ochre as demons howled all around them and set the woods afire.

And Arch watched it all begin, the flames surrounding the Watch within seconds, unsure what to do to save them – if they could be saved at all.

Three Weeks Ago

HENDRICKS GRUNTED as the doctor gave his chart a look-see. "I don't know exactly what you had, Mr. Hendricks," said the doctor, who was a gray-haired, slightly beyond middle-aged man with wire-rimmed glasses. "Some sort of infection, I suspect, based on the systemic organ failure. Whatever it is, it's gone now." He glanced up. "Blood work is normal. You've returned to ordinary kidney and heart function. Your liver is...well, it's a little worse than usual for a man of your age–"

"I was in the Marine Corps. In Iraq."

"That's as good an explanation as any," the doctor said. "Whatever sort of bug you picked up, you're out of the woods now. I'm discharging you."

"Cool," Hendricks said, and started to get up.

"Wait for the nurse to remove the IV, will you?" the doctor said, putting himself right in Hendricks's way by catching his arm.

"Nurse Ratched?" Hendricks scoffed. "After the way she removed my catheter, I'd rather have Michael J. Fox do it while on meth. At least he wouldn't be intentionally trying to hurt me."

The doctor chuckled. "All the same...best if you leave it to the professionals. For liability reasons."

"Well, then, against medical advice it is," Hendricks said, and promptly ripped off the tape and pulled the IV. He then put the tape back over the tiny pinprick of blood growing out of where the needle had been.

"Have it your way," the doctor said with a shrug, like he'd seen this movie before. Probably a few times.

Hendricks didn't care. His coat was waiting on the chair, along with his boots and hat. Not his shirt, though. Nor his pants. They must have cut those off when he was brought in. But it was fine; he could wander about like a flasher, keeping his coat tight around him.

"What are you doing out of bed?" The voice interrupted him about halfway through his dressing procedure. He'd decided to keep the hospital gown on until he could retrieve his sea bag. Which was, presumably, still parked in front of Gunny's house. The voice stopped him, though. It wasn't angry, wasn't that nurse with the eyes like a pissed-off howler monkey; it was soft, and questioning, and sounded sincerely worried.

"Ma'am," Hendricks said once he'd turned around and processed who was standing there.

It was Mrs. Gunny, of course. Sure, she'd said to call her Frieda after he'd married her daughter, but they weren't married anymore so that didn't really pertain, did it? "What are you doing out of bed?"

"They're kicking me loose," he said, buttoning up the drover coat. Honestly, the hospital gown beneath the coat kinda felt nice. Was that why the Scots wore kilts? He slipped on his boots wordlessly, picked up the plastic bag with his ID and keys in it – the shit from his pants pockets, just more proof his jeans were kaput – and started toward the door.

"So you're leaving?" Frieda Winthrop asked. Her tone was measured, calm. Kinda reminded him of Renee, and it made him miss a step. "Well...come on, then." And she turned to lead him out.

He was left standing there blinking for a few seconds. "You wanna give me a ride back to my car?"

She was framed in the doorway in silhouette, the weak, late December sunlight washing over her as she looked back at him very slowly, very quizzically – very Renee, usually just before she was about to scoff at him for doing something stupid. "You ain't leaving the hospital and then driving on out of town the same day. Where you think you're going, anyway?"

That caught Hendricks up real short. "Uh..."

"Mmhmm," she said, with the self-righteousness that only a black woman could seem to muster when she caught you doing something extra dumb. Or just dumb of the garden variety. "Come on, then." And she turned to walk away.

Hendricks remembered arguing with his wife. Pretty much any day, he'd have given just about everything he had to do it again, just one more time.

He didn't feel like arguing with her mother, though, especially when the ten steps he'd taken since he left the bed had already made him a little lightheaded. "Yes, ma'am," he said, and fell in behind Mrs. Gunny.

FOUR

KINGDOM COME

When Erin snapped out of her trance, it was like waking up after one of her brothers had poured cold water all over her. Jesse was always good for that bullshit.

Just a simple shove, and she caught herself before stumbling more than a step. But it was still like she'd been dropped in a dunk tank she hadn't even known she'd been sitting over. One second Starling was pouring warm, whispered honey in her ear, the next the world was cold again, and then...

Then it caught on fucking *fire*.

Starling was still standing at a distance, the trench coat billowing around her, and Erin saw some shit she couldn't really believe at first. Took a double take to convince her it was real.

No, not that Starling wasn't wearing a stitch other than the coat. She was a hooker, that was pretty normal, probably.

It was that her belly was swollen up to the point she looked like she was going to give birth to the biggest damned watermelon Erin had ever seen. And she'd lived in Tennessee all her life; she'd seem some fine, large watermelons in her life. Purple veins and angry stretch marks lined the thin redhead's belly.

Erin blinked at that, and the heat of the fire, and the shock of all this shit hitting at once. How long had it been since she'd seen Starling? Couldn't have been much more than a month. And to go from flat-stomached to 'fixin' to burst' in that span...

Well, that spoke of some bad things, man. Real bad.

And of course the one thought that could set her off the most clicked for her right then.

Because she *knew* who had been fucking Starling most recently. And something about it just absolutely lit her ass on fire.

"You fucking demon cunt," Erin said, watching Arch blanch at the language more than the flames, the pregnancy, the Watch all paralyzed or dying, and the OOCs down the line who were showing their true, ugly fucking faces. Not because those other things weren't important; this one just hit her a little harder viscerally. More immediate. More personal. Like a punch to the face instead of a punch to the side.

Because now she knew that in spite of all the last-minute saves, all the seemingly good deeds...

That Starling was a pure villain, through and through.

And she always had been.

WHAT THE HELL could Braeden do? He was staring down the pudgy-faced demon as he clutched his wrench, but the other one had turned her back, trusting her compatriot to watch it for her. All this while the woods were now on fire, all but a few of the Watch were in a damned coma of some kind, and Wrightsons were dropping like fucking flies. He didn't dare look at Paul or Mary; he knew they were dead as fucking pork chops sauced in gravy.

The pale-faced demon, Duncan, stared at him, then jutted

his chin forward. He held the baton in his hand, said nothing, just...angled his chin, like he was pointing it.

Braeden couldn't help but look; the heat from the flames was washing over him, and his lizard brain was screaming that shit was dire, but still, on his other side was Terri.

And Duncan was pointing at them. When Braeden looked back, the demon arched his eyebrows in one of the least natural expressions the mechanic had maybe ever seen. And he'd had regular dealings back in the day with Sunny Gresham, the most botoxed woman in all of Midian.

Braeden looked to Duncan, then to Terri Pritchard behind him. The meaning seemed clear, and so he reached out and gave her a hard shove.

"Don't touch my ass!" Terri said, jolting right out of that trance.

"Pass it on," Braeden said, not daring to look away from Duncan. Though he did catch a half-smile from the demon. And the pasty man did not come at him, not even a little bit. What the hell was that about?

ARCH DELIVERED a sharp back kick behind him, clipping Casey Meacham right in the ankle. The skinny man gave a quick, "Ow!" shouted to the fiery woods, then drew his breath in sharply to take in a smoky bit of air. "Oh. Shit."

"You wake the line up all the way down, Casey," Arch said, his eyes still firmly clawing at Guthrie. She grinned and struck out again with another lethal blow, this one killing Yuval Simon by opening up his skull like a smashed melon, and Arch found he had no more time to waste. He charged the OOC, who stood waiting, smile lit by the spreading flames.

"YOU SHOULD LEAVE, DOCTOR," Starling said quietly. "It isn't safe here. This isn't the home you grew up in. It's a house of fear." She rubbed a hand inside her own coat. She was somehow just in front of Lauren, so close she could smell a whiff of cheap perfume, and yet still far away.

"Doctor." A much more ragged voice cut through the dream-like whispers, and the smell of smoke cut into Lauren's nostrils, overcoming the perfume. The voice was familiar, was like Starling's, but rougher, less sure, less otherworldly. A girl's voice, and a scared one at that.

Instead of Starling's dark eyes, she saw terrified green ones. Where Starling had been perfectly shaped, Lucia's natural beauty turned up to eleven, this looked like Lucia at her worst, Lucia as Lauren had seen her in the ER all those months ago when they'd first met. Blood trickled from her lip, dark circles rimmed her young eyes...

...And an enormous belly hung there in front of her, just like Lauren's when she'd been eight or nine months pregnant with Molly.

"Doc," Lucia said, her voice raw, "you heard the truth...but you didn't think anything of it." Her dull eyes looked drugged, like morphine was kicking in. "Now there are monsters at the gate."

The fire died, Lucia was gone, and flawless Starling replaced her once more, the smell of smoke vanished and perfume returning. The voice was a sweet whisper, sultry in a way Lauren didn't go for, because women weren't her type. But something about Starling–

"Mom!" Molly collided with Lauren and the perfect vision of Starling evaporated again, pulled back like she'd gotten yanked on a string. Now she was fifty feet away, under a distant tree, and the curves of her trench coat were duller, more real, and more baggy.

Oh, and there was fire. Oh, so much fire. Every tree in front of her, half the ones behind, and a goodly segment of the forest floor around them was raging, and the heat was punching Lauren in the face. Dark, demonic faces were lit beyond the flames, hellhounds with faces aglow like in a candlelit procession.

Molly clawed at her arm, sending a spray of water uselessly at the nearest, out-of-control conflagration. "They got us, mom! They trapped us in dreamland somehow while they set this up and now we're – I don't know! Fucked or something!"

Lauren grabbed Molly by the arm, panic rising, clutching her in such a way that absolutely everything slammed home for her at once. This was a trap, the whole thing. Demons were beyond the flames. Starling was lurking beneath that tree in the distance, lit by the fires. And Duncan–

Duncan was standing, implacably, staring at Braeden Tarley, while behind him, Guthrie slammed her baton into Jerry Nathaniel's face, dropping him to the ground, leaving him plainly dead.

"Mom," Molly said, pleading, "what do we do?"

That was the last thing Lauren needed to hear. "We get the fuck out of here," she said, dragging her daughter back the way they'd come, back down the path of no resistance and least flame. "Let's get the fuck out of here!" she shouted, because why keep it a secret when the whole damned woods was going to burn down with them in it if they didn't move?

ERIN WAS in a fine fucking tizzy even before someone down the line called the retreat. Part of her had wanted to storm forward and slam her nail-covered baseball bat right in Starling's big, fat belly – that'd be a demon kill, right? – but the other part of her saw immediately how fucking futile and stupid that would be. Fire was every-damned-where, and spreading fast through the rotten leaves and desiccated trees. Midian hadn't seen a good rain since last spring, and boy was it showing in how quickly shit was torching up.

Thick black clouds were swirling up, up, and not nearly away, not nearly fast enough. They were hanging like a low ceiling on the proceedings, and getting lower all the time as more branches burned and more carbon tried to find its way into her lungs. Erin coughed, and suddenly Starling seemed twice as far away. She moved delicately, the little slut, not quite dancing, but definitely preening. Showing her belly, showing her huge pregnancy tits. It was obscene, that was what it was, and Erin was annoyed by it.

But not annoyed enough not to take the fucking cue for what it was. "Retreat!" she shouted, breaking to her right and shoulder-checking someone. Not hard enough to knock 'em over, but hard enough to jar them loose of whatever dream or nightmare was going on here. "Retreat!"

"THEY WANT TO RUN, GARY," the redhead whispered in his ear. She was practically straddling him now, and for the first time in years he could feel his legs, feel her weight on him – weight, and wetness, and more, God, so much more–

And boy did it feel good. So damned good.

"But you can't run, Gary," she whispered. Like a lick of his lobe, it sent a spark through him. "I like that about you. You'll stay with me, won't you?"

"I mean," Gary said, taking in those full, beautiful tits, not giving a thought to Marina, "how can I say no to that?"

He got jerked the fuck back to reality by getting t-boned hard by someone almost tripping over his goddamned wheelchair. They spun him half-around, and if he could have felt his legs, he was pretty sure they would have felt busted. In the dark – and it wasn't quite so dark as it had been a moment before – he could barely see the figure who'd run his ass over. He could hear 'em, though, all sniffling and crying like a little bitch, long, black hair falling around and obscuring this little pussy's face, but he'd recognize those sobs anywhere.

"Larry?" Gary asked, still trying to shake off that sexy-ass wet dream he'd been having. God, that had thrilled. He hadn't ever even had a thing for redheads before, not really, but he might have one now. "Get off my legs, I don't need you down there trying to suck my dick."

"Mom's dead," Larry said. He brushed back black hair from his face, his eyes, and his nose was snotty, his eyes were wet, and his damned cheeks also. "Paul, too. They got us, Gary. They fucked us good."

"The hell did you say?" Gary would have stood up right then – if he could have. Instead he pushed himself up in his chair as much as he could manage, which wasn't much. He could see the damned flames between the trees and piping up into the sky beyond. Any trace of a moon was gone now, black smoke curling up in huge wafts, blotting out whatever piddly stars you could have made out past the light pollution coming off Casey Meacham's bigass truck's high beams. He didn't believe it. Because he couldn't.

"EVERYBODY OUT! GET OUT OF HERE!" It was hard not to panic in the face of a rout, Arch figured, and the shouts sure didn't help. But he was too fixated on Guthrie and what she'd done to five or six members of the Watch to just walk away now, even if pretty much everybody else was turning tail.

Guthrie wasn't backing down, though, and neither was Arch. He had his sword in hand, he had righteousness on his side...

And he had the woods on fire around him and demons aplenty past that, eyes glinting in the darkness.

"See, holy man," Guthrie said, squaring off with him. All the others had run, and run smartly, Arch figured. He was the only one still standing around on this side of the field, anyway, other than Duncan, who seemed to be facing off with Braeden Tarley. "This is your future. You get it, yet?"

"No," Arch said, stealing only the barest glance at Starling, still standing beneath the tree to his right, her trench coat puddling at her feet, her belly on full, proud display, the first hints of some emotion beyond cold self-satisfaction showing in her eyes. "But you're about to, demon."

"I never hid what I was from you," Guthrie said, grinning. She started to circle so he'd have Starling at his back. Arch didn't much care for that, so he circled toward her, keeping his sword in front of him. Guthrie's grin faded as the blade got closer, and she dodged back, coming in the opposite direction.

"Yeah, you only hid your intentions," Arch said. "So, what was it? Fighting alongside us all this time for fun, only to betray us now, at the end?"

"It's not quite the end," Guthrie said. "But you can definitely see it from here." She swept an arm around to indicate the flames. "And smell it."

"Well at least you've got the demon excuse to be a Judas," Arch said, and nodded at Starling, still standing over his shoulder, just displaying herself. "What's her excuse?"

"Her? She's bad news," Guthrie said. "Worse than you can possibly imagine." She chuckled. "You thought she was helping you all this time? The only thing she was doing was keeping you alive so you could save the numbdick Marine at the appropriate moment so he could do...well...that...to her." Guthrie jerked a thumb over her shoulder. "It was all about timing. That and the appropriate sacrifices. A scared little boy without parents, lost in the woods. A very bad man, who killed your sheriff. A little blood from both of them, a little semen from your Marine friend, a swirl of other magics, and...whamm-o." Guthrie swung at him, and Arch blocked it with his sword, producing a clang that echoed, the force running through his arm making his teeth jar together. "All this right in front of your blind eyes."

"Lucia?" Miss Cherry had started across the gap toward Starling. Arch could see her over Guthrie's shoulder. "Lucia, what is wrong with you?" She had a strong accent, and her voice was even more scratchy than usual. The smoke, probably.

"That's not Lucia!" Erin shouted from somewhere behind him. Retreating? Just hanging back? Arch couldn't tell, and didn't dare take his attention off Guthrie to see for himself.

"Lucia," Miss Cherry said. She was all ahead full, hand extended, "I have known you so long, my dear. This is not you."

Starling stood there, looking down at her, forbidding, but saying nothing.

"What are you doing?" Miss Cherry asked. "Come back with me. I had no idea you were in a family way. I can help you." Her eyes glittered against the raging fires all around. "Come home with me."

Starling looked at her, silently, for just a moment...

...And then she moved, as quick as ever, bare flesh lit demonically in the firelight. She was suddenly beside Miss Cherry, and her hand was buried up to the elbow in the Madame. Out of Cherry's back something wriggled like an immense worm against the bounds of her blouse, a wine-colored stain spreading across its surface.

"I am home," Starling announced, and her arm moved–

Miss Cherry ripped in half; her legs toppled in one direction, and her upper body flew in the other.

A scream to Arch's right tore through the sounds of crackling flames; a glitter out of the corner of his eye made him look, though he tried to watch Guthrie, too, and didn't do so fine a job of it.

Casey Meacham was charging toward Starling across the field of battle, his tomahawk brandished in his hand. He flung it as he got closer, hurled it right at Starling's head–

But she was gone long before it got there; she was back under the tree, her dark eyes glimmering, her blood-coated hand shining in the fire light.

"Don't get sentimental," Guthrie's voice hissed in his ear. He'd gotten distracted, and she was behind him. Arch started to turn–

But she already had the baton on his windpipe, and his feet left the ground as she lifted him up. His toes dangled, his neck strained under the weight. It was a hanging, pure and simple, without rope or tree, but a hanging nonetheless. He could only struggle against the superior force being applied to his body, but not fight against it any more effectively than an infant could fight against a parent holding them tight in swaddling clothes.

"Arch!" Erin screamed from somewhere behind him. Far behind him, he figured, though he didn't have the oxygen or the mental security to think in such terms. His next breath was all he cared about; his sword was gone, dropped in the panic of being choked in such a way.

"This is the problem with you humans," Guthrie said. "I've pondered it quite often – why get so attached that you get blindsided when someone betrays you? You're all in competition – for food, shelter, money, mates, status – yet you seem surprised when those in competition with you choose the game over your feelings."

Arch was grunting. The baton was biting hard into his neck. Guthrie was shorter than him, but she had his feet off the ground like he weighed nothing.

"This is the meaning you've chosen for your lives. This is who you serve – your idols. Television, if you're bingeing the latest show on Netflix. Video games. Sports. Stanley cups," Guthrie said, chuckling. "Sexual satisfaction. And of course, money. This is what you worship, what you prostrate yourselves before. This is what you serve, you spend your time on."

Arch wanted to argue with that, but he couldn't manage the thought, couldn't get a word out around the lump of metal crushing his windpipe. Every second was an eternity, an agony with no air to breathe. Already he could feel his thoughts slowing, his ability to fight back dying off.

Not that he could fight back much. He was a drop of spit against this raging fire; thrashing wasn't doing a thing for him.

He was going to die right here and he couldn't even get his thoughts right to throw up a last prayer.

The fires seemed to dim, their glow fading. Starling was there, watching him, as she always did. Her fair skin was writhing, contracting, like a snake.

Something struck Guthrie like a train had jumped the tracks behind her, and she went sprawling. So did Arch, and the baton fell away from his neck.

He landed badly, but Guthrie tumbled over him and landed much worse, taking a dive and coming up rolling, on her feet and glaring back.

Arch didn't have time to worry about her. Air rushed into his lungs, blood came back to his brain, and suddenly the fire was brighter than ever, rampaging around him. The smoke came in with that first breath, and he coughed so hard he thought he might lose a lung. He had only the presence of mind to grasp for his sword and find the hilt with his fingertips, and look up to see who had saved him.

A pale white face looked at him, past him, almost sadly. A hand was offered, and he took it, and Duncan pulled him to his feet, keeping focused on Guthrie, who just glared at them both from where she stood between them and Starling, like a buffer, or a wall.

"You should go, Arch," Duncan said softly. He looked at the dead bodies to their left – Mary and Paul Wrightson, Miss Cherry in her divided parts. "There's nothing to be gained by staying except death."

"Stay," Guthrie said tauntingly, but she made no move toward them. "We'll have a party. Really set the woods on fire, like that old drunk cowboy used to sing."

"Arch," Erin shouted from behind him. Wisely, way behind him. "Come on!" Even Casey Meacham had chosen the better part of valor once his tomahawk had failed to find his target. Arch could see him now, glaring resentfully back from halfway between him and Erin.

"Yeah, go on, Arch," Guthrie called. "You go enjoy your last three days on earth." She cackled. "Because that's all you've got."

"Come on," Duncan said, and took hold of his shoulder. He pulled him as easily as Guthrie had, but away from the flames, away from the troubles. The black smoke filled the air, and Arch could see the darkness in Guthrie's eyes, and beyond that, Starling, as the flames rose around them and spread left, right, and forward...

...And the woods around Midian started to burn like a tinderbox, the glow and the smoke rising up to the sky in the night, like a sacrifice to some ancient divinity that would not be satiated by anything except death.

Which...was actually true.

FIVE

ALL HELL

"I don't want to go," Gary said, shaking his head. But he was already in the van, Marina, Larry, and Terry huddled around him. Ulysses was at the wheel, guiding them away from that absolute clusterfuck, the worst he could think of since the time he'd shit himself at the plumbing awards while laughing at the other nominees.

The flames were visible as an orange glow over everything; the smell of dry wood burning infused the clothes of the others, and himself, though lighter. Gary had his wheels locked in place. He wanted to cut himself loose, throw the door open, fling himself out and roll back to where it had happened–

To where he'd sat fucking impotently as his mother and brother were murdered by some redheaded demon bitch that had been busy sucking him off with some fakeass vision of the good life or something.

Gary fucking burned sitting in the back of the van. Marina, next to him, was quiet, her eyes downcast. "How many people did the others lose?" he asked. She didn't answer. Didn't even look up. There was a haunted-ass look in her eyes; whatever had happened back there, he didn't think it was related to his mother or brother. No, that demon bitch had got in her head.

"I saw Miss Cherry get ripped in half as I was leaving," Terry said softly. "I was trying to carry mom out, but...well..."

"What?" Gary asked.

"She had too much chocolate cake in her fucking life, that's what," Terry said, looking back at Gary with a fire in his eyes like the kind that had been full-on eating the woods when they'd driven away. "And I haven't done enough fucking deadlifts, okay? You happy now, Gary? I'm a lazy fat fuck and I enjoy sitting my ass on the couch at the end of a long day with a beer in my hand instead of going to a gym and moving plates of iron a few feet at a time. I don't see the fucking point, okay?" He looked away. "Or I didn't until tonight."

The temptation to bite back was strong – at first. But Gary let it pass, and with each second, it got easier not to. Was there a lesson in that somewhere? Probably, but fuck it.

"Where we going?" Ulysses called back to them. He was steering them toward Main Street.

"Sheriff's station," Gary said, without really thinking about it. It was where everyone would end up, surely.

THE SMOKE still clung to his clothes, and Arch could see the black clouds rising against the glow of the fires in the rearview as Erin squealed tires and they took off. Not the first to get out of there, but almost the last. Duncan had followed behind them at a trot, but other than him, no one remained in the woods but the demons and the dead.

"Aw, man," Casey said. They'd left his truck behind, headlamps still shining. The scrawny man didn't look like he could even drive. He had his head in his hands behind the protective metal grill that separated Arch and Erin from the back seat. "She killed Melina. Lucia just killed her."

"And our demon friends just split on us," Erin said, white-knuckling the wheel as she made a quick turn off Oak Street.

"At least one of them did," Arch agreed. He didn't know what to say about Duncan, who had gotten him to the car. No other demons had come after them; they'd remained in the burning woods, doing devil dances or eating the bodies of the fallen or something.

"Shit," Erin said, and slammed a palm against the wheel hard enough the tires squealed and the Explorer slewed a touch. She got control again – at least of the vehicle. By the look on her face, he didn't think she had control of her emotions. Not by a long shot.

"THE HELL DID I JUST SEE?" Terri Pritchard shouted in the back seat of Barney Jones's Buick. The reverend was at the wheel, staring straight ahead as he floored it down a side street. Braeden Tarley was behind him in the passenger seat, a few flecks of blood on his face from one of the dead Wrightsons, maybe. He couldn't remember the splatter, just knew it was there.

"If your vision was anything like mine," Pastor Jones said, "you watched a naked, slightly freckled, well-toned Irish lass try her best whispers in the wind seductive act."

"Uh, yeah, that's what happened," Terri said. "Look, I know there's talk around town about me that I've never bothered to dispel because I don't care if anyone thinks I'm a lesbian. But I've never harbored same-sex tendencies ever in my life. Ever. I like men. I just don't like any around here. Yet tonight that little red harlot got me about ready to sink to my knees in front of her and dive for muff. Can anyone explain that?" She slammed a hand against the back seat and it thumped. Apparently finding it satisfying, she did it again.

"What did you see, Braeden?" Pastor Jones asked patiently.

"Same as y'all," Braeden said. "Except reality kicked in for me, dragged me back to the woods, which were on fire."

"Someone hit you?" Terri asked through her gritted teeth. Seems she was still harboring a grudge.

"No," Braeden said, because he wasn't quite sure what had happened. "No one ever did, so far as I know."

"YOU SHOULD RUN, YOU KNOW?" Guthrie's voice reached Duncan over the crackle of the flames. She wasn't in sight of where Duncan was standing, at the curb, beside Casey Meacham's truck. He wasn't waiting for anything in particular. He was just uncertain of where he fit in now.

"Why?" Duncan asked. He didn't bother to turn around. The air was starting to get hazy, but not so hazy he couldn't have seen Guthrie if she was coming for him.

"So you can squeak a little more time on this miserable rock," Guthrie said, voice drawing a touch closer. "Not like you have much left, but you could...I dunno...hike out of here, go find yourself a Skee-ball game, and spend the last few days of your life putting balls in holes."

Duncan slowly turned to the partner he'd had for over a century. "What's the point?"

Guthrie was standing there in the field, a hellish backdrop

behind her. "Skee-ball is its own point. Its own reward. Or something."

"We still talking about Skee-ball?"

"Probably not," Guthrie said. "You know...you had a pretty good shot up until now. You might have leaned human-sympathetic, but you maybe could have explained that away."

"Where the world is going," Duncan said, "they don't tend to take explanations. They take souls, and just read the truth right off them like an old papyrus."

Guthrie nodded slowly. "Well, you've made your choice now. Better to leave." There was a sparkle in her eyes that Duncan didn't care for. Not at all. "You aren't going to want to see what happens next."

Duncan didn't answer that. Didn't need to. He just turned and walked away down the sidewalk. Didn't take the rental car, or Casey's truck. He just walked.

"ARE WE THE FIRST ONES BACK?" Molly Darlington asked, the holy water tank still sloshing around on her back as she thrust open the door of the sheriff's station.

"Why wouldn't we be?" Lauren asked. They had been the first to leave, after all. She shrugged out of her motorized squirt gun apparatus, dropping it with a careless clunk upon the stained white-tile floor. Then she helped her breathless daughter out of hers, and they lapsed into a silence as Lauren's head did what it usually did and kicked into overdrive. Or hyperdrive. Or Hyper-overdrive.

"Mom, did we just get hypnotized by Lucia?" Molly asked, looking at her very seriously.

"Yeah," Lauren said. "She put the whammy on us. For sure."

Molly's eyes widened. "How do we even counter that?"

"I don't know," Lauren said, feeling breathless. "Was it anything like...?" She didn't feel she needed to finish the thought.

"Having a demon at your steering wheel?" Molly took a big gulp. "No. That was...I could see everything, feel everything...I just wasn't in control. This was different. Lucia – Starling – whoever – they were whispering to me in a, uhm...I'm not sure of the right word to describe it..."

"A little Sapphic, maybe?" Lauren asked.

"Yeah, that's probably the word." Molly seized her collar and fanned it a few times as though to let out some heat. "It all reminded me of Mick. You know, the demon who–"

"I'm unlikely to forget the demon who nearly raped my daughter on a Ferris wheel. And nearly made me a dog grandmother. Of flaming demon canines."

"Starling's whole hustle, though," Molly said, "reminded me of Mick. The whole breathy, soft-voice, stirring, uhm, the, uhm, inner essence of your being–"

"What in the holy fucking fuck just happened there?" The door flew open and in rolled Gary Wrightson, in about his usual temper. "We got fires raging, demon hookers mentally seducing people, and–" He looked at Molly for a moment, up and down. "Damn, she got you, too? That's dirty play, going after an underage girl."

"Pretty sure a statch rape charge is the least worrying thing that redhead's got going at the moment," Terry Wrightson said, breezing in behind his brother with the Wrightson crew. They were short some people. Lauren didn't want to ask, because she'd seen bodies on the way out of the woods. The Eastern European woman, Marina, looked particularly shaken. Ulysses, though, looked steady, if a bit dazed.

And Gary...his cheeks were flaming red, his eyes furiously searching, but looking down, around the wood-paneled counters and walls as if for something to hit. Then he rolled right up to one of them and put a fist into it, over and over, until a piece of paneling about a foot long broke free. He caught it and then turned and threw it across the room into the plexiglas window beside the door, where it clattered and fell just as Arch and Erin came storming in, Casey sauntering behind them. "What the fuck happened back there?" Gary asked, and he seemed to be directing all his ire at Erin.

"We got bushwhacked," Erin said, very muted. And that was it.

Gary Wrightson changed about three shades in front of Lauren's very eyes. "Well, no shit. I just lost my mom and my least-disliked brother. You got bushwhacked? That's all you got to say about that?"

Erin just shrugged, looking very dead-eyed. The exhaustion seemed to weigh on her. She was, what? Twenty-one? And she had the look of a woman ten years older. Who had just given birth. To a ten-pound baby. Without an epidural. And after forty-six hours of labor. Lauren cringed inwardly for her.

The door banged open, and in came Braeden Tarley, with Barney Jones and Terri Pritchard trailing him. Terri's hair, never particularly well-styled, was a real mess now, with twigs and a stray leaf in it like she'd wiped out on her way out of the woods. Which she probably had. "That was a mess of a sort," Barney Jones said. The older preacher looked worn, too.

"I thought Starling was on our side," Braeden said.

"So did I," Arch said. The deputy looked withdrawn; but then he'd looked that way ever since Halloween.

"This changes some things, doesn't it?" Molly asked. The door opened again, quieter this time, and other Watch members came oozing in. "I mean, we haven't seen Starling in action since–"

"She hasn't lifted a damned finger since I been here," Gary said. One of his brothers was nodding behind him.

"She's been gone at least a month," Lauren said, because it seemed like not many people wanted to speak up. "Maybe two."

"Miss Cherry said she's been gone from the, uh, house–" Molly started.

"Whore house," Gary threw in.

"–since shortly after we left," Molly said, casting a pained look at Lauren. "Aw, man. Miss Cherry..." Lauren glanced around; Casey Meacham had found a bench and was sitting there head down in his hands like he was about to puke.

"Yuval Simon's entire crew got kacked," Braeden Tarley piped up.

"We got betrayed," Gary said, "by someone we thought was on our side." He glanced around, usual expression of intensity on his face. "So how long has she been playing y'all?"

"Since the beginning," Arch said, drawing every eye. "She showed up the first time, saving Hendricks and me from Hollywood and the cow demon."

"Y'all notice our other demon friends seem to have joined her?" Braeden Tarley asked.

"Or at least one of them," Lauren said quickly. "Guthrie went to the dark side quickly. Not sure about Duncan."

"They been stringing us along since when?" Gary asked. There seemed to be a dark, pointed suggestion behind his query, and Lauren felt it, even if she couldn't tell where this was going.

"Since shortly after the fatted calf," Arch said. "When Gideon showed up, trying to destroy the dam. They helped with that. Been helping since." He nodded at Erin. "Guthrie was known as Lerner until he went over the cliff with her. Cracked his shell, went back to hell." The big man made a face; he must have belatedly recognized the nursery rhyme quality of what he'd just said. "Didn't seem quite right since he came back."

"And now he's betrayed us," Gary said, positively seething. "Looks like all the shitbirds are returning to their roosts. Almost like you can't trust a demon. Any demon."

"Not Duncan," Barney Jones said. "He helped save our lives."

"Where is he now?" Gary asked. His crew nodded behind him like some Greek chorus of neck wobbling. Except that Marina. She looked like she'd withdrawn, like she might collapse into herself at any moment.

"He was scared to come with us," Casey Meacham said, voice scratchy. His eyes were real red, Lauren noted as he raised his head. "But he got us out of the woods at the last, and looked like he was about to take a baton from Guthrie to do it." The skinny man sniffed, pale as frost. "Duncan didn't do us wrong, I don't think. But you're right about the rest. Lucia – Starling. Guthrie. That means something real bad's about to happen, right?"

"Maybe," Arch said. "I heard the words, 'three days.'"

"What happens in three days?" Gary asked. His complexion was just getting redder and redder.

"Jesus returns," Barney Jones said dryly. "The gardener, not the savior. Your dry cleaning is ready for pickup. Or, just perhaps, and I'm speculating here – that's when Midian dies."

That caused an uncomfortable silence of approximately twelve seconds before Terry Wrightson piped up. "You think this is the end? The real end, not just another wave of bad demons coming through?"

"Look around you, man," Mike McInness said. The bartender was one of the squad leaders, and was bleeding from his hand. "How many people are even left in this town?" He was a middle-aged man with thinning hair and a lined face, despair wrought on every wrinkle. "I mean, I know we've been fighting the good fight, but...come on. It's over. We lost."

"Tell that to the folks still huddling in their homes," Arch said, fire clearly still in his belly. "The folks in St. Brigid's and the Methodist church. The ones counting on us to do what we said we were going to do – fix this problem."

"My momma didn't raise no quitter," Gary Wrightson said. "God rest her soul." Nods from behind him, too, along with his brother Larry crossing himself. Another precinct heard from.

"My momma raised someone who knew when to call a loss," Mike said. There was a lot of nodding for him, too. "I love this town. I've lived here my whole life. My family's been here since the 1800's." He shook his head slowly. "But there ain't a town here anymore. The woods out there on fire?" He pointed toward a random wall, at least to Lauren's eyes; it could have been the direction of Chattanooga, or Nashville, or even the damned moon, and she wouldn't have known. "That's gonna spread."

"What are you saying, Mike?" Chauncey Watson asked through his Coke-bottle glasses.

"We got just a handful of ways left out of town," Mike said. "That fire will close off two more by morning, I'd bet. These aren't big highways, y'all. They're two-lane roads. When a forest fire rips through, it fells trees. Trees block roads. And that's assuming you can even see to creep through the smoke." He shook his head. "I'm leaving tonight. Heading south, reckon I can be to Chattanooga in a couple hours. Who's with me?"

An uncomfortable number of hands started rising. Lauren watched, glum but not quite surprised. Besides, her head was on something else – what Lucia had told her in the moments it felt like Starling had receded.

GARY COULDN'T BELIEVE these fucking cowards. "Y'all just going to bail out?" he asked, watching the hands go up one by one. If courage was contagious, it must have spread slowly, like ebola, while cowardice went through the room like a flu.

"You just lost two family members, Gary," Mike said. "In a matter of seconds. Wasn't a thing anyone could do about it. How do you fight that? Some red-headed skank in your mind, taking away your will to fight, will to see."

"I think you mean she took away your balls," Gary said. "And here I thought your ex-wife got those in the divorce years ago."

"Oh, go fuck yourself, Gary," McInness said. "And I mean that sincerely."

"No, how about I fuck you! Right in your pussy little ass!" Gary rolled forward with a burst of speed, but Terry grabbed the handles of his wheelchair and held him back. "Let me fuckin' at him!"

"This is going really great," Arch Stan said with a big fat sigh.

"I ain't sticking around to argue," Mike said, holding his hands up like he wanted peace. Well, Gary would give him a piece – if Terry would let him go. He started to turn and smack his brother's hands, but thought the better of it. "Anyone wants to join me can. I say we convoy out in thirty minutes."

Barney Jones turned his eyes to Erin, and a few others followed. "Do you have anything to say about this?"

Erin was watching the whole thing, seemingly lost in her own yellow-gumball head. When she spoke, her voice was scratchy like she'd gotten a few lungfuls of air out of that smoky-ass fire. "You should stop by the churches. See if anyone else needs a ride." She was staring straight ahead. "We got a bunch of civilians still in town that can't fight or won't...and they really should leave."

"Erin, what are you saying?" Casey Meacham asked,

standing on those pitiful little stick legs of his. The man's dick was almost bigger than his legs. "We calling it quits?"

"Anyone who wants to should go," she said, not really addressing the meat of the question. "Anyone who can't fight should go, too. I don't know what this three days is about, but I can't imagine it's good." She ended by staring off into space. "Nothing around here's been good for a long time."

"What in the actual ass fuck?" Gary roared. "I thought you were the leader here! Now you gonna lead half or more of our people out of town?"

Her eyes were slow-moving, but they settled on him, and he saw a dead-doll look he didn't care for. She was either quitting or quiet quitting, and either way Gary couldn't abide it. "This has always been a volunteer army."

"Go Vols," Terry said under his breath.

"They want to leave...let 'em leave," Erin said with a shrug. "And some of the ones still in the churches, or huddling at home...they should have left a month ago." With that, she turned and walked toward the sheriff's office, leaving Gary steaming like a pipe that was about to reach max pressure. That meant he was about ready to blow.

ARCH WATCHED as Erin turned her back on everything, and everyone, in the Watch, and walked calmly to Sheriff Reeve's old office. It had been hers by acclamation for the last couple months, and he hadn't felt like challenging her for it – or leadership – because she'd done a fine job and he was hardly in the right frame of mind to take up this burden when he'd been busy fighting demons and outrunning his own problems.

But this? This whimper of surrender? This was more than he could easily take.

"You can't just quit," Arch said. A half dozen of them were already on their way to the door. Only a couple looked back. Quitting started in the heart, and they were already heartsick. "Does this town mean so little to you?"

"It meant everything once, Arch," Mike said. "But look around you, bud. There's less than five hundred people left. If I have it my way, four hundred of 'em are getting out of town tonight. I don't mean to leave you in the lurch, but anyone who don't get out this evening probably ain't getting out. That's my read of the situation."

"You can't read shit, you illiterate, pussy-ass bastard," Gary Wrightson said, to the surprise of absolutely no one.

Mike just looked at him. "Time was, Gary, I'd have fought you over your words. You know in spite of the fact I have a degree in Medieval French literature – I never backed down from throwing hands. Never feared a man's punch." He shook his head slowly, looking down. "But I reckon you're right, now. I finally found something scary enough it turned me yellow through and through. That ginger hooker, she got all in my head, and now I know – I'm a damned ant against the giants in this. Always was, maybe. Midian's gone. The town I loved, anyway. So yeah, I'm gonna leave. And yeah, I'm a coward. Because I can't fight this – whatever this is. I hope you realize you can't, either, before it's too late."

"I'll never realize it, because I'm not a gutless, dickless, little running weasel like you!" Gary shouted after him. "I still got a fire in my belly and no quit in my heart!"

"Gary, he's already gone," Terry Wrightson said. "You keep screaming at him, more people are liable to leave."

"I don't give a shit," Gary said, rattling the chair as he shifted his weight in it.

"Well, Gary," Ulysses said, "I wish I could say I'm glad to hear you feel that way...but I don't anymore."

Gary looked back at him, and maybe for the first time in Arch's history of knowing Gary Wrightson, the man looked like someone had hit him below the belt. Or maybe would have, if he could feel that sort of thing. *"Et tu,* Ulysses?"

"I don't mean it as a personal betrayal, Gary," Ulysses said, his bristling gray mustache stirring slightly. "But I don't see how me fighting to death while not being able to fight that thing is going to save Midian – or do much of anything other than bring a whole heap of heartbreak down on my wife. You can call me gutless, too, if you want–"

"You ain't gutless, Ulysses," Gary said in a hushed whisper. "I may have said a lot of unfavorable things about you over the years, but that isn't one I've found to be true. Not by a long shot. You just reached the end of your road with us, I guess." He stretched out a hand over his shoulder, and Ulysses shook it. "You take care of yourself."

"You too, Gary," Ulysses said, and headed for the door. "Maybe contemplate getting out yourself before it's too late."

"That's the one thing I can't contemplate," Gary said softly. Arch heard it anyway. So did everyone else.

THERE WAS CLEARLY a great parting underway at the sheriff's station when Duncan walked up. Cars were pulling out of the lot, heading down Old Jackson Highway in all directions. He was off the road a bit, creeping over the fields and behind the businesses that girdled the road, unwilling to put himself into a position to be run over by an eager Watch member who counted him as betrayer rather than betrayed.

And Duncan did feel more like the latter than the former. First time for everything, he supposed.

There were still a few cars left in the lot when he made it

onto the blacktop, his dress shoes scuffed, near-ruined. His clothing was tattered from his over-field journey. He hadn't dared to walk through the town like some brave man. He'd slinked through, like a serpent in a garden.

Now he stood outside the door and peered in. No one was going for it; all the leavers had left. Predictable, really, given the turn events had taken.

Duncan was torn; he recognized pretty much every face still in there, and there were few. He thought of them in associated clumps: Arch, the Wrightsons, Lauren and Molly, Barney and Braeden, Terri Pritchard, Chauncey Watson, and maybe Erin, if she was behind the closed door to the sheriff's office. Which was a weird place for her to be right now, but not improbable given the shellacking the Watch had just taken.

Hovering outside the door was a coward's place, Duncan thought. In spite of the constipation that seemed to fill Midian's air these days, he could at least pick up on the mood of the humans within. It was a sauce thick with despair, hopelessness – oh, and a simmering anger lurking beneath it all.

Three days. That wasn't a lot of time before things went to hell. And they were going to hell.

Without even the option to take a cleansing breath and steady himself, Duncan reached for the door handle, felt the cool metal grip against his shell, and pulled open the door, bracing himself for a hot reception. Given the choice between this and hell...well, it was going to be hell either way, so might as well at least try and seize the thinnest thread of possibility that might keep him from having to go back there.

"YOU GOT SOME STONES, showing your pudgy pale face around here after what your kind just did." Larry Wrightson was the one who said it, and Braeden felt an eyebrow raise as he did. Not overly concerned with broad-brush painting, that's almost exactly how he would have described the Wrightsons. Possibly willing to use a nuclear weapon to resolve an argument with a neighbor – that was another.

"Hang on, little brother," Gary said, seizing Larry by the arm. "Weren't we just decrying the lack of balls around this place?" He was quiet, a rare thing for him, at least in Braeden's experience. "What brings you back to our door, OOC? You have to know you'd be at least a mite unwelcome here."

"I know," Duncan said. The demon was hard to read, all right, though Braeden felt like he was giving off waves of worry and contrition, like a parent who'd lost a kid. Braeden could empathize. "And I don't blame anyone for wanting to give me a crack."

"Okay," Larry Wrightson said, and raised a pipe.

Marina snatched it out of his hand at the highest point of its arc. "Listen to demon man first," she said, waggling the end in his face threateningly. "Then, if you not like what he say, crack him. Hm?" She was still very pale in the face.

"You all heard the 'three days' thing?" Duncan asked. He looked like he was holding his breath, and other than the words, he was completely still and didn't make a sound.

"Heard it," Arch said. He looked cautious. Well, fools rushed in, and Braeden didn't see Arch Stan as much of a fool. "Weren't sure what to do about it. Or its truthfulness."

Duncan stared straight ahead for a moment. "It's true. Three days, that's all you've got. Then Midian is over, and with it – the world."

ERIN HEARD the muffled sound of Duncan's words through the door. She'd been listening, her back plastered to the wood paneling from the moment she shut it, just listening, racking her brain, flogging herself for being such a fool. How could she have believed that she – underage, underexperienced – could lead the defense of this town?

Idiocy. That was the conclusion she came to. With a touch of sleep deprivation on the side.

The smell of smoke still wafted strongly off her uniform as she listened to Duncan drop his bomb. She couldn't even help herself; she flung the door wide. "How?" she asked. Because no one else had yet.

ERIN RE-ENTERED the chat and nobody batted an eye – except Gary. He felt a twitch at the corner of his eye beginning anew. But he'd deal with that later. Right now, he had a bigger fish to fry.

"The world ends in three days?" Gary asked, taking what she'd said and expanding it out for the general audiences all around them. God bless 'em because they were what he had to work with, but most of them weren't that smart. "I'm gonna echo her here and say, 'How?' But, you know, with more threat and less credulity."

Duncan searched around until his eyes landed on the doctor. "You know how." Then, he shot a glance at Erin. "You, too. Just maybe you didn't know you knew."

LAUREN FELT like someone had whirled a stethoscope around like a sling and whacked her in the face with it, minus the physics – a little bit. Gobsmacked might have been the right word. But without any actual gob.

"You're talking about what Lucia said, right?" Lauren asked, widening a few eyes pointing at her as she did so. "What the guy – the dead guy, the one in the cell – said to me and Erin?"

"I'm going to need a translation on that." Molly had her hand in the air.

"The guy from Halloween," Erin said. "The receptacle for the legion of demons. The one that had a feeding tube in. The one that died a couple weeks ago. He told us that hell was going to eat us up. That gates to hell and heaven were here, in Midian." The guy had died not two weeks back after months of lingering, speaking only occasionally. He'd just wasted away after a lifetime of demon servitude. She hadn't much mourned his loss.

"Yeah, that," Duncan said. "It's the reason why everything's happening in Midian." He looked around. "It's all demon mythology, see. There are paths between what you'd call heaven and hell."

"What do you call it?" Gary asked suspiciously.

"Unpronounceable, at least with your tongues," Duncan said. "But you understand the concepts."

"One has God in it," Arch said, and there seemed to be a glow in that holy roller's eyes, of course. "And all his angels. And the other – fire, torment, and, if the worst myths are to be believed – a devil."

"You got the torment part A-1 right," Duncan said. "The rest is good enough for discussion purposes. Human reality and demon reality are different animals, it's like comparing apples to poltergeists. You couldn't understand it if you tried, so let's just get to the point – demons want to leave hell and get into heaven."

"Because they were cast out?" Casey Meacham asked in a very, very small voice.

"We don't really talk about it," Duncan said, and then held up a hand because Gary Wrightson looked about to erupt. "If I thought it had any bearing on what is going on and would help you, I'd try and explain. But communicating with humans – I'm sorry, I know I sound like Lerner – it's like trying to talk to dogs. They get the gist, maybe. But it's really not understandable except in the vaguest terms. There are rivalries both subtle and terrifying, powers and principalities that could easily leave your world a smoking cinder with minimal effort. So let's keep it simple, for both you and me: Demons want to leave hell. They want to go to heaven. Invade it, really."

"And the passage to do so is here, in Midian," Lauren said, because now, maybe, it was starting to make sense. Or at least the kind of basic sense that a piddly human could understand. Not that she was reeling from the insult of all that. A doctorate, but she couldn't possibly comprehend some sort of spiritual plane beef between these entities? Sure, Jan. These demons certainly didn't suffer from a lack of sneering confidence.

Except...Duncan did. Well, usually.

"Somewhere here, yes," Duncan said. "Not sure exactly where, but in the vicinity of Midian. It's what caused the hotspot. It's what's drawing everything here now. All the armies of hell on earth have heard the call, and are coming." He didn't so much as blink as he delivered this news. "If you don't leave tonight, you will probably die. And if no one stops them from finding that gate, opening it, and flooding into heaven...the world ends in three days, and earth becomes a new hell."

"THE DAY of judgment is at hand," Arch whispered. He'd read the Book of Revelation. More than once, in fact. It was…confusing. It seemed like it might be written to be confusing. But that's how prophecy was, he supposed: a tale told by someone in the past, describing events they were inadequate to describing. Trying to imagine a man from 50 AD talking about a modern American city scene with cars driving, horns honking, trains rattling by, and metal skyscrapers blotting out the sun…well, how could the ancient mind comprehend such things?

They comprehended them as best they could. And as a result you got tales of riders on pale horses and such.

Duncan was looking right at him. "Well…you're not completely wrong. But you're not completely right, either. They find the gate to heaven, it's not going to be the kind of judgment you will enjoy. No one will be spared. A balance – a very precarious balance – will tip. The results will be…" Duncan shuddered, a very disquieting motion from the demon. "Ungodly, for lack of a better word."

"How do we stop it?" This from Dr. Darlington, whose daughter was huddled close to her, and whose voice was hushed like death.

Duncan shrugged, another unnatural motion. "I don't know. I don't know if it can be stopped. Every demon with even a smidgen of ill intent on this planet…they're coming here. The fire that was set tonight? It's not a normal blaze."

"It was hell fire," Barney Jones said.

Duncan snapped fingers and pointed and Jones. "Correct. It's like a beacon to call us all in. Some will ignore it. The more peaceable among demonkind, the ones most settled, the ones that like living here on earth. But the ones with even a touch of the darkness, the ones who feel even the lightest, unsettling stir within…they're going to hear it, vibrating in their essences like a tuning fork held up to your ear...and some of them – some very large number of them – are going to answer the call."

"There's like a dozen of us left," Terry Wrightson said. "Who knows how many more scattered through the town. We're supposed to face down whatever demon hordes are coming? And we don't even know where in town this gate is?"

"You're damned right we are," Gary said with solemn resolution. "If it's that or the world dies, and we all go to hell?" He looked up at his younger brother, who'd at some point stopped clutching handles and holding him back. "Why not go down fighting?"

"Gary," Terry said, "you've never needed a reason to fight. Ever. But this one might get you killed. Might get us all killed."

"Didn't you hear the demon?" Gary asked. "We're all going to die anyway, they get to that gate. And furthermore, we're going to hell. Do you know what hell's going to be like for you, shitstain? Because I have a suspicion it's you getting Eiffel Towered between two demons with fifteen-inch spiked dicks for all eternity while your flesh constantly heals and regrows so you can feel the pain anew in every moment. Oh, and you're basting in an oven the whole time."

"Jesus." Terry's eyes widened in horror, and he looked to Duncan. "Is that really what hell's going to be like?"

Duncan shrugged. "That's as workable an explanation as any."

"Ohmigod," Molly Darlington said. "I don't want to be Eiffel Towered by demons for all eternity, whether it's in a sauna or not!"

"Sweetie, no one does," Lauren said, patting her daughter on the shoulder. "Except maybe Casey."

"That is a blatant–" Casey rose up. "Truth, now that I think about it."

"What are we going to do, Erin?" Braeden Tarley asked. He looked right at her, in the still hum that came after the question.

Erin just stood there. "Hell if I know," she said, at last, and moved toward the door. Not the one to Reeve's old office, but the exit. She left, walking out into the cold night, and the sound of the Explorer's engine starting came to them shortly thereafter, followed by it pulling out of the parking lot.

Three Weeks Ago

HENDRICKS STOOD at the bottom of the porch stairs of the Winthrop house, trying to decide whether to take that step up or not. He was still feeling weak and weary, and a steady drizzle of the gray skies upon him made him wonder if hitting the road, trying to find a visible sun and clearer skies was the better plan.

Except...he kinda knew where his next destination was, and it seemed unlikely New York City would have clearer skies. Not in December.

"Well?" Mrs. Winthrop asked. "You coming in? Or you just going to stand there? Or you going to come in?"

"I get the sense," Hendricks said, with a wry smile, "that Gunny might be more pleased if I were to just move on, ma'am. And I have this little rule, see: I don't go where I'm not wanted."

"You must not go much of anywhere, then." Gunny's voice, hard and strong, struck Hendricks from behind. The big man came marching around the corner of the house from the garage side, wearing a rain slicker that was wet.

"Oh, I go all sorts of places," Hendricks said. "Places where my cash spends just fine, see. My money's wanted, so I'm wanted. It's a simple life."

"'Simple' is a word I've used to describe you more than once,"

Gunny said, bumping past him without bothering not to. Plenty of room, but Hendricks still got a light shoulder check.

"You want to just send the boy on his way, Micah?" Mrs. Winthrop asked. She was stiff, distinctly so. Renee got the same way on occasion. And on those occasions, Hendricks knew he was not going to be getting laid for quite some time if he didn't come around to her way of thinking.

Gunny had been married a long time. If Hendricks could pick up on that, no doubt Gunny did. He stiffened on the porch steps. After a moment's pause, he turned to Hendricks, rain drops coursing down his slicker. "What are you here for, boy?"

Hendricks hesitated. Did he really want to open this can of worms and chew through it here on the porch? That only took a moment's thought: there was no time like the present. "I found her."

Gunny stared at him like he was simple. "Found who?"

"That night in New Orleans," Hendricks said, "those goons that...I heard 'em talking after they did what they did. They mentioned a name. 'Kitty' Elizabeth." His voice cracked. It was hard to say it, even. "Katlin Elizabeth. She's a, uh...gangster, let's say. The guys who killed Renee, they worked for her."

"I thought you said it was demons," Gunny said.

"Turns out demons organize themselves, too," Hendricks said. "You want to know what my next stop is? It ain't here. You want to be my waystation for a minute? I'm fine with that. God knows I could use a minute to recover my strength. But she's in New York, and once I'm back to feeling my best, I'm going to settle all my accounts with her."

"How many accounts you got with her?" Mrs. Winthrop asked.

"I picked up another one recently," Hendricks said. "When I met her for the first time. But we don't need to talk about that."

He squeezed his hand so tight his fingernails – not that long – bit into his palm.

"What'd she do to you?" Gunny asked.

He got a slap on the arm from his wife. "Hush up, Micah."

A long moment's pause had Gunny looking him over while Hendricks just stared down the street into the drizzling rain. Was Midian getting this rain? He found his thoughts drifting there in spite of what he'd just been talking about, dwelling on, really. Should he have been thinking of Starling? He wasn't, really. But he was thinking about–

"Stay," Gunny said, his face like stone. "A few days, maybe. Get your strength back. Then take your circus back on the road."

Hendricks blinked in surprise. "Okay," he said, catching the very self-satisfied smile Mrs. Gunny was wearing behind her husband. "I'll stay. Just for a few days."

SIX

THE CHOICES WE MAKE, THE CHOICES THAT MAKE US

No one stayed long at the sheriff's station once Erin left. Arch didn't take much notice; they just split and broke away, a little group at a time, while he was deep in his own head. Verses from Revelation were coming to him unbidden now, in the silence of the sheriff's station. Benny Binion had left at some point; either before they got back or after, but he'd done so silently, so that for the first time in months even the radio dispatch console lacked someone. The bullpen here was quiet in a way it hadn't been since the demon invasion had begun.

Except for one remaining. One last soul, still hanging around quietly, watching him, waiting.

"Duncan," Arch said.

The OOC nodded at him. Maybe he didn't know what to say. Maybe he just didn't want to be alone. Then he went and broke the silence. "I hope I didn't mess with your conception of this world and the next."

"Nothing you could say would do that," Arch said.

One of Duncan's rare part-smiles showed itself then. "Don't know whether that's good or bad, but it's definitely you."

Arch nodded slowly. "You going to pay the price for going against Guthrie and Starling?"

Duncan's face fell, visibly. It was one of the bigger reactions he'd ever gotten out of the OOC. "Yes. We make our choices, then we pay the consequences. It's just the way things go."

Arch cocked his head at Duncan. "And you decided to go against them...why?"

A flicker of extreme discomfort ran across Duncan's face. "See, the answer to that question is uncomfortable."

"Why?"

Now he almost smiled again. "Because there's no way to tell you without you reading into it what you want to hear."

"The only thing I want to hear at this point," Arch said, "is that we've won, and no one else has to die. Any chance you're going to be delivering that message?"

"No," Duncan said. "And touche. What I was going to say is...in my past...way back...I made a terrible choice, one absolutely pregnant with awful repercussions."

Arch just looked at him, filled with a smoky sense of amusement bordering on self-satisfaction. "Would you call this choice...a betrayal?"

Duncan looked pained. "In your limited terms...yes. And this is why I didn't want to tell you. You think you know what happened, but you don't. You have in your head stories of hubristic creations gone astray from their creator. Don't you?"

Arch shrugged. "If my tiny baby caveman mind couldn't possibly understand your complex existence, then what does it matter what impression I'm left with?"

Duncan ran a hand through his thin hair. "Because I don't want to deceive you, Arch. I've done enough of that for one eternity. I've had my fill."

"How long have you known Starling was pregnant?" Arch asked quietly.

"That I just found out tonight," Duncan said. "Though I suppose we shouldn't be surprised, given how much Hendricks was banging away at her."

"And the gate?"

"For a little while," Duncan said. "Order came through Guthrie, from home office, to keep it quiet. Listen – everyone knew there was a gate on earth. Everyone. It's the location that's the new data, okay? Hotspots have cropped up throughout history, nothing new there. Some have been worse, even, than what you've seen here–"

"It's the gate that makes this special," Arch said. "It's the gate that turns it from the end of a town to the end of the world."

"Yes."

"Which begs a certain question," someone said, the door to the sheriff's station opening in a rush of wind, a clink of metal as the door left the frame. Arch stared at the new entrant, certain he had never before laid eyes upon them. His hand fell to his sword's hilt, resting upon his belt, but Duncan caught it. He looked at the OOC, whose face was intense with concentration. His touch was not light, but not painful, either, as if he just meant to stay Arch's hand. A moment more and he let go; long enough for the asker to enter, to be viewed, to allow a pause and the still quiet to settle back over the room. "Are you to be a steadfast defender of heaven, Archibald Stan? Or will you run like the others before you?"

It was a girl, no more than twelve, with a dark complexion and features that suggested to him India, perhaps, or Pakistan. Her voice bore an unmistakable, crisp British accent, and she looked up at him with dark eyes that twinkled with a hint of intelligence far beyond what he'd normally have expected from a preteen girl. "Who are you?" Arch managed to get out, hand still on his sword's hilt, though she made no move, menacing or otherwise. She wore a backpack that was large enough that it should have toppled over her slight, skinny figure.

"If I'm not much mistaken," Duncan said, "that right there...is who's been giving Hendricks his stage direction this whole time."

DARLA PIKE COULD SMELL the smoke. It was in the air, in the darkness, flooding her senses as she sipped her coffee and stared out the kitchen window at the orange glow on the horizon. "Hmmm," she said. Was it for good? For ill? Who could tell these days?

"Would madam like breakfast?" her servant asked.

She glanced at the speaker; pale, he blended against the tones of the kitchen with its white cabinets and white-black granite countertops. "The coffee will do for now, Rousseau."

"As you say, madam." He hadn't come with the house; he'd come with a marker that Darla had traded in. For Rousseau was very dead – or had been. Good help was hard to find in Midian, after all, especially now. That she'd had to revivify and zombify a servant in order to get someone to make her coffee, clean her baseboards, etc, while here...well, that was just the beginning of the state of things. A new abnormal, if you will. "Will you be returning to bed?"

"Perhaps," Darla said lazily. There were certain books she could read, either for power or pleasure. Deals she could strike that might increase her position. She felt fairly assured, but fairly was not completely. Still, her waking eyes stared at the glow over the distant trees and thought...yes, this was probably the beginning. Or maybe a middle.

"Or maybe the end," came a quiet voice from behind her.

Darla turned...

...and dropped her coffee cup, letting it shatter into a million pieces on the clean, white tile floor.

"WHAT ARE WE GONNA DO, GARY?" Larry's question hit like a plumbing snake up the ass, making Gary jar in his wheelchair, which was rattling with every damned bump the van encountered. Larry was driving, Terry was behind him, and Marina...well, she hadn't said much since everything went to shit.

"Then there were four," Terry said ominously.

"You can shelve that bullshit right now," Gary said, with all the patience of...well, Gary. "Listen to me well, brother. I am sick to fucking death of the losing spirit in this town. I ain't seen us so defeated since that season we got beat by Cleveland, Ooltewah, and Benton, all in turn."

"That was a gangbang of a season," Terry said.

"But did we give up?" Gary asked.

"Hell yeah we did," Terry said. "We went 0-10 that season. If that ain't quitting, I don't know what is."

"No," Gary said, "we fired the head coach, and the next season we came back and went 8 and 2."

"Aren't you the head coach, Gary?" Larry asked.

"No," Gary said fiercely. "If I was the head coach, you'd know it because we'd be winning, and because ninety percent of our team wouldn't have just walked out on us going into the championships."

"Yeah, it'd be ninety-nine point nine," Terry said dryly.

"Fuck you, shitweasel," Gary said, throwing a pointed finger up at his brother. "Our mom just died out there tonight. We lost a brother."

"I know," Terry said. "I was there."

"Question for you, Gary," Larry said. He was huddled over, rubbing the web of skin between his finger and thumb. He looked up, his black hair flowing over his shoulders. "You really think what that demon said was true? The end of the world's coming in three days? And we die if we don't stop it?"

"And maybe we still die if we do," Marina said softly, almost inaudibly.

"Hell if I know," Gary said roughly. He had a bee in his bonnet something fierce. "All I know is we gotta...we gotta keep fighting. Until we win!" His voice cracked and broke, though, as he raised it, and suddenly he wondered if he even believed that anymore.

THE HOUSE WAS silent when Lauren returned to it, Molly in tow. It was a rough, exhausted sort of silence, the kind that follows a fight with your lover, the kind where all the names are called, and all the salt is rubbed in all the old wounds. She listened to Molly move about the house, lighting a couple candles, and watching the flickering glow of orange on the walls. It reminded her of the sky outside.

"You really think the world is going to end in three days?" Molly asked, shuffling toward her with a candle in hand. It was in a jar so she didn't have to worry about burning her hands, dropping it, screaming as the searing wax left a mark.

"Hm?" Lauren had been lost in thought, but her brain caught the remark. It just took a little extra long to translate it into a concept her mind could understand. "Oh. Maybe, yeah. It's possible, I guess."

"Because it jibes with what you heard from the demon colony guy?" Molly sat on the couch, her face in the glow showing the last hints of girlhood. It reminded Lauren of the doughy little baby face she'd stared into sixteen years ago, a little face that dragged itself across this very carpet. All her memories of Molly were here – her dad's homemade peach ice cream eaten on the steps outside on summer days, and later, watching her cavort across the lawn. All while Lauren buried her face in medical textbooks and study guides. First steps, first words, first everythings – all here.

Lauren reached for her walkie-talkie and thumbed the talk button. "McInness, you there? It's Lauren, come back."

There was a moment's pause, Molly frowning at her in the dark. "I'm here – for a few more minutes, anyway. Come back, Lauren."

"Can you come by and pick up my daughter on your way out of town?" Lauren asked, watching Molly's face dissolve into shock.

"What the fuck, mom?" Molly stood, causing the ceiling to glow brighter.

"Yeah, I can be there in a few," McInness said. "We're heading out right after. You not coming with us?"

"Not me," Lauren said. "But she'll be ready." And she looked up at her daughter expectantly. "You need to pack. Just what you need. What you can't live without. Clothes for–"

"Three days?" Molly said, shooting at her, like a bullet.

"At least," Lauren said, not letting it get her down. She had a decision, she had a plan, and she would not be deterred. Once that was said, she stared up at Molly. "Well? Get to it."

"How about no," Molly said. Not a question. "I'm not leaving, mom. This is our home."

"Oh, I am keenly aware," Lauren said. "I'm having visions here of all your firsts. Remembering the winter days when you would run outside to play in just the tiniest dusting of snow. Watching the flakes fall by the window with that look in your eyes that you probably only reserve now for when a new Taylor Swift CD drops–"

"It's 'album,' mom. CDs are from your generation."

"I saw your life begin in this town, kiddo," Lauren said, catching her with one hand on each shoulder. She still had just enough height on Molly – maybe a couple inches – to look down at her. "And I'm fine with it ending here someday. When you're an adult. When you've lived a life. Not when you're sixteen."

"Sixteen-year-olds have been the tip of the spear for the entire history of warfare up until very recently," Molly said.

"Sixteen-year-old *boys*."

"What was that sound? Was it the lighting of your feminist street cred on fire?"

"I'm a woman, a single mother, and a doctor," Lauren said. "I think my feminist street cred is pretty secure at this point." She tightened her grip on her daughter's shoulders. "No one wants war for their kids, sweetie. That's the joy of the modern world, we've left a lot of that bloodlust behind in favor of marginally less lethal pursuits than world conquest. Like MMA fighting."

"And NASCAR."

"And Stanley cup collecting, yes." Lauren looked her daughter in the eye, and could see, like a split image, her as a baby, and her now, on the cusp of womanhood. "You want to think about this like a war, fine – I can't fight while you're here. I worry about you."

"Get over it," Molly said, and tried to shrug off her grip.

"No," Lauren said, shaking her head, hanging on with all she had left. "You're sixteen, not eighteen."

"It's an arbitrary number."

"It's the way we do things now," Lauren said. "I'd keep you safe until you're seventy if it were up to me, but it's not. And I'm not commanding this, by the way–"

"Great, then I'm staying."

"–But I can't have you here if you expect me to actually figure this thing out," Lauren said. "I can't try and find this gate with the others, can't give it whatever I've got left if I'm worrying about you being in immediate peril as well as the inevitable world-ending variety, too." She sighed out a long breath.

"You can't ask me to just leave," Molly said, first signs of tears in her eyes, though it was clear she was holding them back hard. "This is my home."

"And I want it to be here when you get back," Lauren said. "I want there to still be a world for you to grow up in, because the planet's kind of your home, too. And if someone doesn't save it, all my measly worries about this town? Pointless. With the others leaving, we're going to have to dig real deep here–"

"Then you could use my help!"

"–But how much clear thinking do you believe I'm going to be capable of with you stuck here in this rapidly post-apocalyptic war zone?" Lauren asked. Her daughter looked away; Lauren had scored a direct hit. "How useful do you think I'm going to be if I'm worrying about you every few seconds? Seconds, not minutes, because that's how often you're on my mind. Kid, you never leave it, because you're all I've got left–"

"You're all I've got left, too." Molly shrugged out of her grip and slammed into her, wrapping her arms around Lauren and hugging her tight. "What am I supposed to do if you die here in Midian while I'm off wherever? Atlanta?"

"First of all, leave Atlanta, because life is too short to deal with that traffic for twenty hours out of every day."

Molly snorted, breathing out a bit of watery snot.

"And then," Lauren said, putting a cool hand on her daughter's red-dappled cheek, "be grateful you've still got your whole life ahead of you. Because we know a lot of people who don't after this last few months. Hell, even after tonight. You've been pretty close to grown up for a while, and you've gotten wickedly hard to shop for. The only gift I've got left for you is this, Molly: your life." She lowered her voice. "Please don't waste it."

"Okay," Molly said, sniffling quietly. "I'll go. But you better not die on me. I need – no, I deserve – the right to put you in a nursing home when you get senile in repayment for this."

Lauren chuckled through her own tears. "I promise I will do everything in my power to save the world and survive." But there was a real twinge in her gut as she said it, because it wasn't really a promise that was in her power to keep.

ERIN SAT in the dark on the bank of the Caledonia River. The once-mighty Caledonia, hundreds of feet across, was dry and barely a trickle at this point. Part of her idly wondered what the story was downriver, where people might notice a suddenly dry tributary. Probably blaming the earthquake. She found it funny that she could generate a bullshit PR story that quickly.

Then she took another slug of whiskey.

It wasn't the good stuff, but then, she'd never needed the good stuff to have a good time. How many nights had she spent in the bar, drinking this shit, piping down beers? Enough to put on half the freshman fifteen – even though she'd never been a freshman other than in high school.

What a fucking weird course. Like the river, she'd really made some bends, hadn't she? Joined the sheriff's department almost right out of high school, been a dispatcher and office assistant. Done that while pissing her nights away in the bars, just having fun, raising hell, enjoying the company of whatever man caught her eye. Nothing serious, because what would she seriously want out of this town?

Then came Hendricks. And then Hendricks came.

God, he'd rocked her world, hadn't he? Upended the applecart by being handsome first, a good lay second, a damned hero warrior right out of some fucking storybook, complete with sword.

But he hadn't been *right*. Not in the head. Nor in the heart.

And she'd gone over a cliff after getting drawn into this demon war. Literal, figurative...it all fit. Crashed down, nearly died, lived only because Arch had smuggled in that serum from that whackjob demon Spellman.

So she'd gone back to how things were before. Total regression, head in the sand, eyes closed. She'd slept with the same crappy guys. Pretended demons didn't exist. Drank like a fish.

And all the while, the apocalypse clock was creeping closer to midnight.

What had been the point of any of it? All those barflies she fucked, all those shots and beers she'd drunk, all of it had been pissed away now. Was that all life was, in the final analysis? Piss running down the gutter on a street?

Erin stood and dropped trow. The world was swaying around her, so she kicked fully out of her pants, and lurched down to the river bank. She didn't even bother to squat, she wide-legged it and let it just dampen the dried-out clay. Listening to the droplets fall on ground that hadn't touched wetness in months, she deemed it a strangely satisfying noise. She tried to shake afterward like a man would, but it didn't really work, so she swayed her way back to the dead, dried-out grass and just plopped down, let it tickle her, because that was as close as she was going to get to a good time tonight. And closer than she'd been in...hell, many months now. Since the last barfly. Since sobriety came crashing in.

But if she was honest...the last time it was good was with Hendricks.

There was a river of fuckups between them now, though. And not a dried-out one, like the Caledonia. A free-flowing, lava and fire river. The dickbag had shot and stabbed Jason Pike to death and thought they wouldn't notice in the chaos. Left his wife a widow, his kids without a father. Accused the man of collaborating with demons, with killing Sheriff Reeve. He'd been a loose fucking cannon rolling around her deck, and she'd told him to bend the fucking knee or get the fuck out.

If she hadn't learned the lesson about ultimatums with her first boyfriend, she'd recognized the truth of them now. They worked, at least for getting a man out of your life in a hurry, provided he had even a small helping of a spine. Having a spine was never Hendricks's problem, though. The man roamed from town to town fighting demons; balls wasn't his issue.

What was his issue? Maybe himself. Maybe her. Who the fuck knew anymore?

"Maybe I've always been the problem," Erin muttered to herself. In the distance, that warm, orange glow lit the horizon.

"DOC IS SENDING HER DAUGHTER AWAY," Braeden said, listening to Doctor Darlington's call on the radio, signaling for pickup for Molly. He nodded his approval. For sure, if Abi had still been with them, he'd have sent her away. Probably gone with her, too, months ago, since he was a single dad and couldn't imagine leaving her without a dad just to save Midian.

But the world coming to an end? That sure changed things, didn't it?

Barney Jones's Buick bumped as it rattled into the preacher's driveway. Terri Pritchard was sitting beside the reverend in the front seat, lapsed into silence as she stared off into the middle distance. The Buick's beams were spotlighting the front of the old house, casting it in a pale shade of yellow.

"Maybe I should have left, too," Terri muttered. "I just can't see ducking out in the middle of this fight, though."

"Especially with nowhere to run," Braeden said. "And no one to protect anymore. 'Least in my case." He turned his face away, staring out into the night. The smell of wood smoke was strong, and getting stronger with each passing hour. How long did it take fire to double in size? Six minutes? Braeden thought he remembered that. "The doc's making a smart move, though – get her daughter out so she can–"

"Die with the rest of us?" Terri asked. There was a bitter twinge.

"You really think we're all going to die?" Barney Jones asked. He had that half-smile twisting the corner of his mouth, one that Braeden had come to recognize. It always showed up just before the preacher turned your world around in the best possible way.

"Sure looks like it," Terri said. She sounded dead inside. Maybe outside, too. "You see a way out?"

"No," Jones said, very matter-of-fact. "But that doesn't mean there isn't one. Just means we haven't see it yet."

"And if we don't see it?" Terri asked. "Before it ends?"

Jones looked at Braeden. "Then it ends – here, at least. Doesn't mean it's over forever, though."

"Duncan said if those things break through," Terri said, "they're going for heaven. You think you'll have a heaven to go to if they do? Because it sounds to me like everything goes into ruins. Like some kind of balance flips, and everything tilts toward hell."

"Every action you take has the possibility of tipping the world toward hell," Jones said. "Every server you're rude to. Every child you don't encourage. Every time you make a choice to keep your light to yourself rather than share with others, the world tips toward hell." He shrugged. "Not much; just a hair.

But across eight billion people, a hair's breadth difference per day is quite a bit."

"I've already touched hell," Braeden said. "I don't think I care to spend any more time there." He nodded. "I'm gonna fight to the end, and when I go..." He stared out at that glowing horizon, "...well, I just hope I get to see Abi again."

Terri grunted, like she accepted what they were saying without accepting it. That was all right, though; Braeden hadn't been ready to accept much of anything when he'd first been picked up by Barney Jones, like Terri just had. Another stray, and the preacher collected them.

But all was going to be fine, because the mere thought of seeing Abi again – and soon – did more for Braeden's heart than anything else had since that awful Halloween afternoon.

LAUREN SPENT a few minutes curled up with her daughter. They were the last few minutes they might share together, so she took advantage of it. It had been a long time ago that her daughter had decided she was too grown up to be hugging, and, frankly, Lauren missed it. Not that she'd ever been much of the hugging type, but for Molly she'd made an exception.

All curled up there on the couch, her shit packed, almost ready to go, her daughter lifted her head and asked the one fucking question – the fucking one – she'd known was coming, and yet could not quite escape the dread of:

"Mom...since I'm leaving, and this might be the last time we see each other...can you tell me who my dad is?"

DARLA'S COFFEE cup lay shattered in a million pieces on the floor, warm liquid tickling at her toes like drained-out piss, and there she stood, staring at–

That fucking redheaded hooker. Except...not.

"Wow," Darla said, trying to still the loud thudding of her heart. "Is that really you, hiding behind a prostitute's facade?"

"You recognize me?" the redhead asked, but she had a cool certainty to her tone. "Even in spite of the outside decorations. Interesting."

"When you've spent as much time in demon company as I have," Darla said, trying to steady her pulse through extremely slow, careful breathing, "you learn to see things others don't." Behind her, Rousseau wasn't breathing at all. Because he was dead. "But to have you come and visit me...what an honor?"

"You choke on your words," the redhead said, with those dark eyes, not a fleck of emotion on her face. "Like a dick that's too much for you to swallow."

"Have you been watching replays of my greatest fails down there in hell?" Darla took a couple steps to the side and grimaced; she'd been trying to avoid stepping on shards of coffee mug, to get her feet out of the wetness, but here she'd properly failed.

"I can feel your pain," the redhead said.

"Can I ask–" Darla started to say.

"Don't dare say my name." The redhead was beside her in an instant. "You haven't earned the right." She leaned over, pregnant belly interfering with her bend, but managed to latch a hand onto Darla's thigh nonetheless. She clapped it once, as if to say up, and Darla obliged, lifting her foot up onto the kitchen island with a grimace. She wasn't as flexible as she used to be, having not had cause in the last month or two to get her legs up in the air. "You call me Starling, if you call me anything at all." She slid a hand around Darla's heel, and raised her foot higher.

Darla almost toppled over, but Starling caught her. She was stretching Darla's calf like some ballet move, bringing Darla's blood-dripping toes up to her crimson lips. The bleed was on her big right toe, and Starling placed it in her mouth. Darla felt an electricity between them, a warmth from the touch that she had not felt since Jason died.

And...maybe a little something more.

Starling sucked her toe. Not violently, but not sensually, either. It had the mark of something else – a leech upon her skin, maybe, like her very life force was being drained. Those dark eyes met hers and wouldn't let go. They fixed in place and held there, as if daring her to pull her foot away.

She wouldn't, though. It didn't hurt as much now, and the redhead's tongue probed the edges of the wound, and suddenly Darla felt a searing pain that lasted but a second.

Then her toes were out of Starling's mouth, and where the blood had been coursing only a moment before, a little black mark remained. Darla felt a bit light-headed for a moment, and Starling let drip a glob of blood-soaked spit onto her bare belly, shirt pulled up to expose it. Rubbing it onto the stretched yet flawless white skin, she kept that uncomfortable eye contact with Darla.

Or it should have been uncomfortable. It was only mildly so, she found, just a touch awkward, like when one of her college dalliances was still in her bed the next morning after she'd considered them finished.

"What do you want from me?" Darla said, because of course there was an ask.

Starling slowly lowered her foot, letting it rest on that big belly. Something moved within, and Darla felt it. Something slithered inside, and Starling did not react at all save to watch her, like a queen searching for some sign of disloyalty from a subject. "The time draws near."

"The time...?" Darla asked, brushing stray, wild blond hairs out of her face. She didn't have her glasses on.

"The time of your ascent – and mine," Starling said. "The time of this world's end. Play coy all you like – you know it comes, and that right soon."

"Didn't know the timetable," Darla said, letting her toes probe back even as the belly probed her. She had to be eight, nine months along – except she wasn't. Couldn't be, in fact. Because this very belly, flat, muscular, without any sign of bowing, had been beneath her only a very few months ago when she and Jason had brought the girl over to their house for a three-way. She'd rested hands on that belly. She'd watched Jason squirt dollops of cum on that belly. It hadn't been bowed in the slightest then. It had been perfectly flat, semen glistening on it in the dim light like rain on nighttime roads.

Which suggested something...unnatural was growing within.

Did that bother Darla? Not so much.

"Three days," Starling said. "Then..." She touched her belly.

"Speaking from experience," Darla said, kneading into the tummy with her toes, "you can speed that up sometimes. Home brew tonics. Orgasms. Et cetera." She leaned forward, batting her eyelashes at an entity more ancient than the world hidden behind the face of a barely-legal hooker. "That is an offer, in case you're wondering."

"I have other needs for you," Starling said. "If you're willing to serve."

"If I am," Darla said, thinking very carefully about what was coming next, "are you willing to uphold the agreements I've already entered into?"

Starling leaned forward slightly, and the pressure against her foot from the belly increased. "And more, if you help me. You would have my...gratitude."

"When you put it that way," Darla said, "how can I possibly refuse?"

A QUIET FELL over the sheriff's station, and Arch was left staring at the skinny little girl with brown skin and big eyes watching him. She shrugged off her backpack and it thumped hard against the floor, hard enough to reverberate through the scuffed tile and maybe even the concrete beneath. She was staring right back, alternating her big eyes between him and Duncan, not saying a word, like the world's best poker face.

"Her?" Arch managed to spit out to Duncan's observation that this – this skinny little teen – was somehow the sponsor behind Lafayette Hendricks. The one who'd sent him his sword, the one who'd told Hendricks where to go. Hendricks, a full-grown man, taking instruction from this – this *child*.

"Yep," Duncan said.

"Yes," the girl said. "My name is Rhea Sharma."

She glanced at Duncan for but a moment. "In you, oh secret-named one, I see long-suffering consequences come home at last."

"Nothing surprising there," Duncan said. "That's been going on literally forever. At least to your insect minds."

"What are you here for, then?" Arch asked. "And how does a little girl like you get to bossing around Hendricks?"

"He listened to me because I *knew*," she said.

"Wait," Arch said, getting that sinking feeling. "Are you a demon, too? Is that what's going on here?"

"She's human," Duncan said. "Mostly, anyway."

"I am gifted with knowledge," she said. "Do not let my appearance fool you. Hendricks listened to me because I proved

I could be of assistance. Not with the fighting – obviously – but with wisdom and knowledge."

"Yeah," Arch said, "that's what I always think first when I run into a problem. What does a little girl think I should do in this situation?"

"You make light, but I tell you true – I know things," she said.

"Such as...?" Arch asked.

"Such as that Erin Harris is about to walk through that door and inform you of her decision made this eve," Rhea said, and sure enough, the rumble of the Explorer's engine came to a halt outside in the parking lot and died. Erin came swaying in a moment later, the hard stench of alcohol preceding her, and she didn't even take notice of the new arrival, just announced to him and Duncan, "I'm fucking done."

SEVEN

I FEEL THE EARTH MOVE

"This it, then?" Arch asked, the smell of smoke thick in the air of the sheriff's station, making his eyes water from that – or something else. "You packing it up and leaving town?"

Erin stared at him blankly, her face smudged and blackened in a couple spots by a light covering of soot. "What? No. Why would you say that?"

"Because you just quit," Arch said, feeling his blood pressure rise.

"I mean I'm quitting leading, Arch," Erin said, like she was explaining basic math to a moron. "I'm not leaving the Watch high and dry. I just can't do the leading thing anymore. I've done nothing but fuck it up." She looked to the side, for the first time seeing Rhea. "What's up with the kid?"

"Long story," Arch said.

"This is Hendricks's source for demon knowledge," Duncan said.

"Okay, I guess it wasn't that long," Arch said.

"But it is," Erin said, blinking and making a face like she'd just taken a long drink of unsweetened tea. "And full of unanswered questions, the preeminent of which is: what the fuck?"

"Language," Arch said.

"You really think this girl hasn't heard worse, talking to Hendricks?" Duncan asked.

"Doesn't mean she has to hear it from us," Arch said.

"I don't think it's escaped your notice, Arch," Erin said, "but shit's gone real wrong with me at the helm. I'm not quitting the Watch, but I ain't leading the parade anymore, either." She burped and the smell of alcohol got more distinct: whiskey, Arch realized. A familiar aroma. "I'll march in it with the rest of y'all, but me being up front doesn't make sense considering how bad I've fucked shit up." She glanced at Rhea. "Sorry."

"I have heard worse," Rhea said. "And said worse, frankly. I'm fourteen, okay?"

"They grow up so fast," Erin deadpanned, looking right at Arch. "I'm gonna go crash." She lifted her radio and wagged it at him. "Call me if shit goes sideways." And she stumbled back out into the night, unable to walk straight.

"You gonna go write her DUI ticket?" Duncan asked. Very serious.

"She will make it to her destination unharmed," Rhea announced.

"But will everyone else be all right?" Arch asked.

"Except for one lone possum, yes," Rhea said, staring off into the distance. "But he can live without the tip of his tail." She broke into a goofy grin. "Kidding. He's going to die. I'm going to set up in the office she just vacated." She waved at Reeve's office. "No one else is going to be using it." And she retreated while Duncan and Arch watched, and closed the door on their unblinking eyes.

"Things are really starting to come apart now," Arch said, very quietly, because...heck, they were.

"You ain't seen nothing yet," Duncan said. And Arch had a bad feeling about that pronouncement.

LAUREN WOKE JUST BEFORE DAWN, feeling oddly refreshed in spite of the short night of sleep. She'd seen Molly off into the hands of Mike McInness, then curled up with her pillow, feeling the tears come hard until she'd simply passed out, smell of her mother's faded detergent mingling with the growing aroma of smoke that wafted through the entire town.

When she got up to the empty house, she felt freer than she had in years. Because she was alone, in her parents' house – now hers – without anyone around.

In its way, it was terrifying.

She was so used to Molly's presence that being in the house alone unnerved her. She went to fix coffee before realizing – it was all gone. The consolation prize was a cup of Earl Grey left behind by her mother. She skipped breakfast like always, and, her plan already predetermined, packed up her shit, including squirt gun, and her daddy's old snub-nosed .38 with a few rounds of blessed bullets, and got in the car a little after seven.

The air was brown, a smell of perpetual wood smoke casting a sick pall over the town. It was strong in her house, but absolutely relentless out of doors, only a hint of the sun as a faintly glowing disc on the far horizon. The street lights were dead, had been since the earthquake, but if they hadn't been, they'd have surely been on.

She pulled in next to city hall. Not a soul had been visible, human or demon, on her entire five-minute drive. Hardly a representative sample, but it gave her hope that perhaps the daylight was a small respite from the coming apocalypse.

Lauren tried the door to the city archives and found them

unlocked. Not that surprising, really. Who was going to waste time in an apocalypse rummaging through musty old books and the minutes of town meetings long past?

Her, that was who.

The archives were down in the basement beneath city hall, and she descended a quiet staircase, taking particular care to listen for trouble of any kind. She didn't hear any, she didn't smell any – over the burning smell that infused everything – but that didn't mean it wasn't about, waiting to tear her into tiny pieces of chum. Or worse.

A medium-sized basement room, the archives consisted of a couple of battered desks that could have been purchased in the wake of the Revolutionary War, with chairs to match. She set her backpack down on one of them, resting the tea beside it, and took out a pen and yellow legal pad. This was just like studying during med school, she told herself.

She'd barely started sifting the archives, still unused to the strange weight of the .38 on her hip, when she heard something.

It was soft, it was subtle. It was like the squeak of a shoe.

Demons wore shoes. And she couldn't imagine any other member of the Watch deciding to take up this task as their own. Not with their limited manpower.

Soft shoes on the stairs coming down into the archive drew Lauren's eyes to the door. It remained cracked, enough to let sound and smoke come through into the musty, paper-laden room. If anything in town was to burn, this would surely go up first and longest.

Lauren drew her pistol after a ten-second freeze, coming back to herself and a heart that pounded out a staccato rhythm in her ears. Blood rushed in her head, too, adding to the soundtrack of terror.

She didn't dare call out for fear it would only draw whatever evil was coming to her. The curved frame of the pistol felt unnatural in her hands. Not that she'd never used one, she just didn't love them the way some folks around here did. And she'd worked on enough gunshot wounds at her job that causing one to a human held a particular revulsion for her.

But this wasn't a time of humans. It was a time of demons, and demons seemed to recognize that it was their time, and that Midian was their place.

Lauren took a long breath, finger coiled tight on the trigger, afraid to pull it before she knew what was coming was a demon, afraid if she waited too long it would be too late, that whatever was coming would be here, thrashing wildly around and trying to eat her.

So it came as almost a relief when a polite, cultured, British accent that sounded very girlish called out to her, "Doctor? I'm not a demon. Do you mind if I come down so we can speak?"

Lauren just about passed out.

"THIS IS GOING to be the last load, Arch," Addison Longholt said, looking up from the clipboard. She was leaning over the counter at the sheriff's station, eyes as weary as anyone else's around here. She'd weathered the death of her daughter, Alison, and her husband, Bill, within days of each other, and yet the woman still stood here, unbroken if not unbowed. "Paul says the woods were on fire this morning, he wanted to get his truck out before they got impassable. He's going to get unloaded, and then he's gone."

"Mmhm." Arch rubbed his eyes. He'd slept in the back room, as usual, for too short a time, also as usual. "Can't blame the man for that." Paul Cummings had been trucking in supplies for them in his eighteen-wheeler for months now, sometimes multiple trips per day. He'd had demons attack his rig multiple times, had to haul over increasingly dangerous roads, and now it seemed like he was down to a half dozen options to get in and out, none of which was particularly good or navigable. "Should be fine. We only need enough for three days, one way or another."

"Well, we've got that," Addie said. "Especially since our numbers are reduced." She hesitated. "You been by the church?"

"Which one?"

"Only one left open now," Addie said. "St. Brigid's. Barney Jones decided to throw in with Nguyen, sent Olivia on with the others last night. I even saw Casey there this morning. Looked pretty rough, even for him, that little scrub."

Arch frowned, making a mental note of that. Casey had his own place, a little out of town, but still. What had possessed him to seek shelter at St. Brigid's?

Probably the death of Miss Cherry. Upon reflection, that seemed the obvious answer, even to a man who couldn't understand the appeal of visiting a harlot. "Reckon he lost something," Arch said. "Something that mattered to him."

"Familiar feeling, huh?" Addie set her clipboard down, and he had a feeling she wouldn't pick it up again. Why bother?

"All too much," Arch said. "Addie...have you thought about leaving town, too? You could catch a ride out with Paul."

"I thought about it," she said, studying the age spots on the back of her hands. "Decided against."

"Why?"

"Let's not go mincing words, Arch," Addie said. "Alison was my chance at grandchildren. Brian...well, he's Brian. He'll live and die up his own ass, philosophizing and caring about himself alone. He don't need me. And he's not likely to attract a woman who wants to be a mother, so...my family ends with him. Really, it ended with your wife. My past and future is buried here in Midian." She held her chin high. "Reckon I ought to be, too."

Arch felt some concerns bubbling up; words for his mother-in-law that might dissuade her from this decision. They came…

…and they went, unspoken. "I can't say as I blame you for that." When hope was lost, what was the point of striving? She had a good idea of things; Brian was alive, in New York City, but a dead end, only ever caring about himself, really. Alison had been the future for Addie's family. All she had now was a past. What was there to go on for outside of Midian?

There was a subtle rumble that caused Arch's legs to quiver, making him wonder if he was just tired. But, no, Addie had a look on her face, like she'd felt it, too. "What was that?" she asked. Because neither of them had the faintest idea.

BRAEDEN WOKE out of a light sleep to hear the plates in the dining room hutch rattling together. "What the hell," Terri Pritchard asked, loud enough it could be heard through his closed door, "is that?"

GARY WAS STARING at the ceiling, pale light shining in as if through a blanket of smog. He had a choking feeling of self-pity that was strong enough in the back of his throat to gag him. "No time to indulge sucking on my own sad dingus," he said. Marina was not beside him, and that was probably for the better. She didn't need to see him like this. He hadn't made a sound, but his cheeks were wet with fresh tears.

It wasn't as if Gary hadn't suffered some loss in his life. His dad had died, after all. He'd lost friends over the years, mostly to being an asshole, but also a couple good ones to death. He knew they were good because they stuck by him, unlike the rest of those peckerwoods.

But the proper remedy for loss and pain was to suck it up and keep moving toward your goals. Sitting there in not-his-bed and deep throating a self-pity cock wasn't going to make him happy. It was going to make him feel like shit, guaranteed. Some people seemed to want to feel that way, to just swallow that nastiness, really glorying in the awful flavor.

Not Gary. Gary listened to people talk about "trauma" when it came to the least little thing. You stubbed your toe? Trauma. Someone called you a pussy-ass bitch? Trauma, clearly, and you'd be holding on to it for life, *plus* passing it on to any kids you had. Because of that bullshit pseudoscience they called epigenetics.

Gary thought it was all bullshit, a product of a generation of navel-gazing pussies who didn't have the wherewithal to survive so much as a speedbump in the road without falling to pieces sobbing like little bitches. In the past, people had gone to war, torn their fellow man to pieces, watched their cities destroyed, seen their relations raped and murdered before their eyes, and somehow fought on through all that to build lives for themselves.

Yet now the most coddled-ass generation, who couldn't sleep a single night out in the wilds without shitting their pants at the sound of a cricket in the middle distance, could barely function if the least little thing went wrong. Gary hadn't wept this much when he'd gotten his spine crushed. But this was the real shit, the stuff you had to process and take on board, and he wouldn't let it reduce him to tears like some twenty-year-old pussy named Kaden who went to USC and just couldn't even, man, because of his trauma and PTSD from having once walked in on his mom getting railed in the ass by the pool boy while his dad watched, jerking off, while crying softly into the same tissue he then ejaculated into.

It was a world of cucks, that was what Gary thought. And he hadn't seen much evidence to prove him wrong. Not that he'd gotten out of Midian much. Some trips to Reno to visit the brothels, a few other places, but that was about it.

Now as he lay in his bed in the smoky malaise that had descended over Midian, outside the window he could see a deep brown tinge, the air shit-colored. As though his brother Larry – that flatulent fuck – had let the world's greatest shart, and it had discolored the whole damned atmosphere around them.

"No time for pity," Gary said to the empty room. "I'm gonna get moving and after it again in 5...4...3..."

He didn't even make it to two before a rumble in the distance made him lift his head up. The whole house shook, windows rattling in their frames, cupboards thumping closed after a brief open. Gary threw himself into motion, because damned if he didn't know that surely meant some shit was coming this way.

ERIN WAS STARING at a wall in the narthex of St. Brigid's when the whole building shook lightly, like someone had lit off a couple cherry bombs in the basement, or some blasting with dynamite had occurred down the street. She was already nursing a five-alarm hangover, treating her head gingerly but still trying to be of some sort of fucking use beyond being a whiskey disposal unit, so she was here, and had been carrying boxes out of the last truck come to Midian to drop off supplies. It had *Rogerson's* painted on the side, as it was once distribution for the Longholt family's grocery store.

She blanched, trying to not let the pains get her down. Not the aches in her arms and shoulders from humping all those canned goods, nor the much deeper-seated one in her fucking skull, sitting behind her eyes like an angry, oversized troll, swinging his craggy arms and ripping up her brain. The only thing that mattered just now was that something really had rocked the building, and she wasn't just experiencing a post-workout, post-drunken quiver.

"Did you feel something?" Father Nguyen asked, his youthful face always making her think he was more of a brother than a father. His almond eyes were squinting in concentration, and he'd foregone his clerical collar and shirt for jeans and a t-shirt to help carry shit in. There were only a few other souls scattered around the church, sleeping on the pews, a far cry from the fifty or so they'd had in here about a month ago.

"Unless someone just rocked my world without me realizing it, yes," Erin said, doing a little frowning in concentration herself. She immediately cringed; she shouldn't have said that shit in front of a fucking priest, and she regretted it now even though she wasn't Catholic. "Aftershock?"

"Felt like it was in the distance," Casey Meacham said, sitting up in his pew a few rows up. "Maybe east, toward the town square?"

"Maybe," Erin said, though she was uncertain. But just as she was ready to write it off as some aberration, she felt it again – and stronger, this time.

"WHO ARE YOU?" Lauren asked, staring at the small girl in the entryway of the archives.

"My name is Rhea," she said, brushing back stray strands of raven-black hair behind slightly out-jutting ears. She couldn't have been more than twelve – small of frame, knock-knees sticking out of jean shorts. Molly's shorts would have been like full jeans on this girl. "I've come to town to give the Watch a hand."

"Just a concerned citizen?" Lauren asked, feeling her pulse pound in her ears. "Albeit a really young one?"

"I'm hardly a citizen, of America or this town," she said. "But I am concerned. Deeply, because this place is the hinge point on which this world turns, you see." She put a hand up, palm flat to the floor. "If you view the world as a scale, the balance is tipping at present toward...well, the side you'd probably prefer not to win. If they find that gate–"

"Yeah, I got the basics of how it works," Lauren said, trying to keep the gun from shaking. "Unless you have something new to tell me, I don't see how you can be of assistance."

"I've long been of assistance to those who didn't even know they needed it," she said. "For example, on a rainy night in New Orleans a few years back, I found myself at the side of a Marine who had suffered an incredible loss, followed by his own near-drowning. The information I provided to him started him down a path that led him here, where he was able to awaken others, including you, to the threat that is coming."

"Now here we are," Lauren said. The slow drag of suspicion might not be a wildfire like the one that burned across town, but it was sure as shit not mere embers, either. She had more than a healthy suspicion that this kid – demon, more likely – was telling her exactly what it wanted her to hear, what it thought would move her in the direction it wanted. What aims might it have? Who knew. Doubtless they were unsavory. "Brought together by destiny, fate, or the Rube Goldberg machine that is life. So...what do you want from me?"

"I want to help you find what you're looking for," she said.

Lauren stared at her, then laughed. "And how do you propose to do that?"

The windows rattled in their panes, and Lauren felt her legs grow unsteady – again – under the quaking of whatever the hell just did that. It felt like a long-delayed aftershock to last month's earthquake, except it was so *powerful*. Maybe it was a new quake?

Rhea shook her head. "It's not another earthquake. This is why I've come to you now." The rumble began low, and became continuous, dust motes flying off the shelves like fighters joining a bench-clearing brawl in baseball. "That," she said, "is a Glugh-teh-vah. And we should really get out of here...because it's headed this way."

"ANYONE ELSE FEELING like it's a Carole King song out here?" Gary Wrightson's voice spat forth out of Arch's radio as he drove, Duncan beside him, down Old Jackson Highway toward Midian proper. The fire on the horizon glowed, billowing clouds of black smoke that seemed to rise purest ebony but then fall back a deep brown in every other direction, turning the air into a hazy soup. He'd left Addie back at the station, and Duncan had emerged from the jail section of the building, where apparently he'd camped for the night in one of the cells.

"Is it another earthquake?" Casey Meacham's voice cut into the transmission.

"There's something out there," Duncan said, pointing a pasty finger at the horizon; not the burning, hellish-orange part, but over the town itself. Clouds of brown were there, sure, like the smoke wreathing everything, decreasing the visibility. But something else seemed to be rising, moving.

Arch squinted. It didn't help him see, but maybe it helped him concentrate. Like turning down the radio to free up his brain space from whatever song was playing so he could think more clearly. "It looks like...like..." He cocked his head. That didn't help either, not really. "...Like a tornado, maybe?"

"But without the funnel coming down out of the clouds," Duncan said.

"GARY, that shit is deeply concerning right there," Larry announced, like it wasn't fucking obvious to everyone in the van. They were all staring forward, rolling down Elm Street, watching fragments of a house two streets ahead fly up into the air like a bomb had gone off somewhere beneath the roof lines between them.

"Anyone remember that night when that big demon came tearing through town like a damned wrecking ball?" Terry asked, his cheeks puffing out even more like a squirrel than usual.

"I remember seeing the big-ass scars and craters where it came through the next day," Gary said tightly, clinging to the driver's seat, where Marina was at the wheel. "And yeah. This feels kinda like that, part deux."

"Fancy French words don't distract from the terrifying nature of this shit," Larry said. He had red eyes, the pussy, the sclera all scarlet and veiny. Little bro never had been very good at controlling his feelings. Or his impulses, which was why he seemed to be constantly banging the worst chicks in town. "What the hell are we supposed to do here, Gary?"

"Duh, dumbass," Gary said, pointing his hand forward like he was calling for an artillery barrage. "We get right the fuck after it – whatever it is."

LAUREN HEARD Gary's words faintly, over the radio, cocking her head as she ran up the stairs out of the archive, following the little Indian girl. Who had decided to really pour it on and remind Lauren that cardio had not been a fixture in her life lately. As if she couldn't tell that by the cottage cheese developing on her thighs.

"The hell is a...what did you call it?" Lauren asked, doing a little huffing, little puffing, not blowing any houses down – or anything else.

"It's large," Rhea said, no huffing, no puffing. The little bitch. And that was it. No further explanation.

They burst out of the stairwell and into the smoky town, under a sky of shit brown. Lauren stumbled as the earth shook particularly hard. "Guys," she said into the radio, "we've got a, uhh...vog-wog-wog? Which I am assured is big. Over. No eyes on it yet in downt – oh, *fuck.*"

"That you, Lauren?" Casey's voice came over the radio, sounding real thick. She might not have noticed, but it was a little detail in a moment that her brain was trying to grapple with a much, much – much, much, much, much – bigger one.

About ten stories long and three stories high. That's how big a detail she was grappling with.

It looked like a nightmare crossed with a sandworm out of one of those sci-fi movies she never liked but always seemed to get dragged to on dates. It was rolling through the east side of town, cruising as though propelled by a motor, driven along doing forty or fifty as it tore through the town, pieces of houses and rooftops and fire hydrants, trees, and all manner of other detritus flying up around its sides as it ran right the fuck through everything.

Also...it looked like a dick. Not an appealing one, either. One of the ones that bent at a funny angle, that had a misshapen head, that looked like it hadn't been properly washed in a few days, that had her wondering, could she get away with a half-hearted hand-job? Or would she have to take matters into her mouth, or her vagina? And how the fuck had she ended up in this situation with a guy who had seemed so charming he made her feel lightheaded? But suddenly all that tingling had ended, migrating and settling in her stomach in a pit of disgust and despair from which she could see no escape save for one(ish)?

Yeah...it kinda looked like one of those dicks.

"We are in a great deal of danger right now," Rhea said with a shocking amount of calm as a twisted hunk of metal crashed down on the sidewalk twenty feet from them. Lauren recognized it as a jungle gym from the playground on Chester Street. Rhea grabbed her hand, dragging her down the street, away from the archive, and away from the gliding, stubby, dick-shaped worm that seemed to be circling its way around the town in a slow arc toward them. "Focus now."

"I was definitely one hundred percent focused on that...thing," Lauren ran, still huffing, still puffing. Now she couldn't get the dicks off her mind as she ran, and a look back revealed that yes, the dick-shaped worm was after her like an angry tornado. And all she could do was run, and think about the dicks she regretted, cheeks burning all the while.

DUNCAN KNEW what this demon was, but he'd never seen one in the flesh. Or shell. Carapace? Honestly, demonology wasn't an exact science, even for him. But no science was, really.

He was riding along in the passenger seat of the Crown Vic that had a busted windshield, Arch at the wheel. They were almost at the edge of Midian, where the countryside with its woods and pasturage gave way to clapboard houses of various shades, and the spaces between buildings grew smallish, city lots designed to accommodate tighter densities taking over.

Well...tighter densities for Midian. It wasn't exactly Chicago up in this place, except for the path of destruction straight ahead.

And it was a path of destruction. Wider than the swath of a tornado, the demon had emerged from the earth's crust and kissed the sky, belly-flopping into a row of houses at the outskirts. Why there?

Well...why the hell not? The damned thing was a hundred feet long and thirty feet in circumference, tapering to a near-point where a smaller mouth waited to eat anything person-sized or slightly larger. It could probably take a horse or cow, though it might require a couple bites and some chewing between. It wasn't a wide-mawed, unstoppable thing. Or rather...it was unstoppable, at least to these skin-bags.

"This is gonna be a large lift, people," Duncan said, picking up Arch's radio. "Ordinary weapons are not going to make a dent in this thing's shell."

"I got it covered!" Casey shouted over the radio, and Duncan had about three seconds to wonder what the hell he meant by that before he saw.

ERIN WAS a couple lengths behind Casey, revving her engine as he revved his own. They'd made two quick stops – one to get Casey's truck from the scorched lot at the edge of town, blessedly not burned.

And the other to pick up Erin's monster truck, with its holy cowcatcher.

They'd faced trouble like this before, albeit on a smaller scale. The shadowcat demons, which they'd run into the quarry and then proceeded to pop like a collective of zits on an acneated teenager's face. And then the troll thing a couple months back, which had been a hell of a trip.

This wasn't their first rodeo in Midian, that much was sure. And as Erin steered her oversized vehicle through the debris-ridden trail that the worm was leaving behind, pedal to the fucking metal, she had one thought in mind–

Don't fucking fail this time.

She wasn't in charge, after all. She was just doing the thing, steering the car, ready to smash it into that big-ass worm, whose tail she could see up ahead, making a slow-ish turn. Instead of a slime trail, though, it was leaving a cleared path of wreckage, everything left in the debris trail smashed to splinters or pushed to the side as though the world's biggest bulldozer had just plowed its way through. Houses were cut in half, interiors open to view. There was a kitchen. There was a bedroom with fluffy, frilly doilies and pink paint. There was a dominatrix's dungeon, with a fuck swing hanging from the ceiling and riding crops hanging from the walls next to a gimp suit.

Erin did a double take at that one. Even for Midian in the apocalypse, that was fucking weird. Was that Zack Shannon's house?

Never mind that. She didn't really want to know; Zack Shannon was almost fifty, and obese, and married to a woman who was bigger than he was and whose face looked like the ass of a duck.

Ahead: the worm. It didn't seem to slither side-to-side, like a snake, or up-and-down, even.

So how the fuck was it moving?

"Uhm," Lauren's voice came over the radio. "Help. Help, please – it's curving to come down Main Street, and that's where I am."

"Hang on, doc!" Casey shouted as they slewed around the debris path's slow curve. Man, it really did look like an uncircumcised dick, a little, albeit pointier. Erin didn't have much experience with those – at least not while sober, that she could remember – but it kinda looked like what she recalled of them. She half-expected it to be spitting or foaming at the mouth or some such gross shit. Because demons were like that, she realized, always going in the fucked-up directions, like ejaculating acid, or impregnating entire towns, or forcing a man to go down on your sulfuric snatch while digging a knife into his scalp–

Aw, fuck. She was thinking of Hendricks again.

The worm's tail was writhing ahead, barely moving left and right or up and down at all. It seemed to be crawling along like it had little legs hidden under its massive bulk. That was all she could come up with for how it motored along at the speed of a small car, tearing up the town way worse than that fucking Rog'tausch. That goddamned thing was a piker compared to this; the difference between a dog and an elephant, almost.

"I'm going in, Erin!" Casey shouted over the radio, gunning his engine now that they were on a straightaway. The tires bumped and thudded, finding stray pieces of shattered pavement, strewn boards, and lined up with the worm. "This motherfucker is going to feel the pump of revenge!" He guffawed; even death couldn't keep Casey's mind out of the gutter for long. "This is for Miss Cherry – and she'd damn sure appreciate that revenge enters through the ass."

Erin cringed; she'd seen Casey's member, and not because she'd ever wanted to, or done anything with it. Just the dumbass showed it off like a museum piece he was especially proud of. She would not want that thing anywhere near her ass; she felt her anus pucker at the mere thought as Casey's engine roared loud enough for her to hear it even over the crashing sounds of the worm wrecking the town, and her own not insubstantial engine racket. He accelerated to twice the worm's speed, aimed for its ass.

Casey slammed into the back of it, and the effect was immediate. She expected a *pop!* maybe a *kaboom!* and then that sulfur blast clouding her vision and blotting out the brown-colored, smoke-filled sky.

That wasn't what happened, though.

Casey's truck hit it–

–And bounced right off like a goddamned giant had kicked it, suddenly racing backward with no front lights, no hood, and a busted windshield. It landed in the wreckage of a two-story brick building that had been there since the early 1900's but was now completely missing a facade. Along with half the rest of the fucking building.

"Fucking shit," Erin said, stomping the brake and letting the worm slither ahead. "Casey's truck did nothing – repeat, nothing – when he ran into it!"

"You sure he didn't fuck it up?" Gary Wrightson's voice broke in. "He does have a tendency to fuck it up, you know."

Erin felt a flash of irritation. "He ran his truck into the demon. No, he did not fuck that up. The thing didn't pop! Over."

There was a pause, and then Duncan spoke. "Yeah. I was kind of afraid of that." She waited for him to elaborate, watching the worm start to turn.

He did not elaborate.

"HEAD FOR THE CHURCH," Rhea said, with a surprising amount of calm considering a thirty-foot-tall worm with a pointy dick head was coming hard after them. It was only a football field away now, and Lauren was tiring. Okay, she was tired – of this town, of the giant dick worm, of the sound of buildings falling down behind them, and more than a little worried by the screech of Casey's truck having no effect when it rammed the worm's ass.

At least she'd gotten Molly out of here. Now all she had to worry about was herself...and a slightly-younger-than-her-daughter Indian girl who'd shown up out of nowhere. "Will that help?" Lauren asked, gasping and gulping from the run and the awful smoke pervading her lungs and threatening to choke her out. It was like putting your lips on a car tailpipe and taking a deep breath around here.

"...Maybe," Rhea said, in a very small, thoughtful voice. Still, small assurance was better than no assurance, so Lauren hoofed it for St. Brigid's, the worm closing fast behind.

"WHAT DO WE DO, DUNCAN?" Arch asked. The OOC was sitting next to him in the passenger seat, staring straight ahead at the storm of debris rising up over town, another cloud in a town that was already covered over in a brown overhang that made the air seem murky.

"If I were you," Duncan said, "I'd start praying."

GARY LOOKED out the window of the van as they followed in that bigass worm's wake. Casey Meacham was pulling himself out of his truck, the hood all fucked up, walking like he'd just experienced his boy Gus Terkel during one of his bouts of getting shut out by the wife. It pissed Gary off that he knew that detail about Meacham and Terkel, but he did, and there was no brain bleach to clean that fucking fact out of his brain, so he just growled and watched the skinny bastard face-plant. He was bleeding from the scalp, but it didn't look too serious.

Not that he would have told Marina to stop to help. They were on a mission, after all, and only losers got distracted by bullshit. The rest of this town may have been filled with losers who couldn't get shit done, but Gary wasn't going to fall into that trap. He was going to make this shit *happen*.

"What the hell do we do, Gary?" Larry asked, munching his fucking fingernails like a pussy. Which meant he was acting about like normal. "Look what that thing did to Casey's truck. And it was consecrated!"

"I fucking know that," Gary said.

"Then you know if a consecrated truck at high speed didn't punch through it," Terry chimed in as the van made a slow turn to follow the path of destruction. As they came out of the turn, the ass end of the worm was visible ahead, taking a right toward the end of Main Street, still chasing the doctor's sweet ass, probably. "We ain't got much of a shot with guns and this rig."

"You don't know shit," Gary said, and turned his furious gaze right to Larry. "You. Get me...the hammer."

Larry's face fell. "Shit, Gary, you cannot be serious." His voice fell, too, like he feared to speak aloud of this thing. "You're really gonna try and use it?"

"Bitchass motherfuckers try," Gary said, watching the worm turn that corner and knowing Marina would follow. They were closing on it, and would catch it soon. "I'm going to fucking do it."

ARCH FELT a certain rising frustration from being locked into a course. The worm's path through Midian had done a number on what was left of the town. He'd thought things had gotten properly messed up after the Rog'tausch had torn through.

Well, that was nothing compared to what had happened here. Roads were blocked off now where it had slid through, destroying houses and strewing their wreckage across intersections, making them impassable. Arch managed to jump the debris wake, but now he was locked in to following it, with few opportunities to escape the trail of ruin, and even less clue what to do if he managed to escape it. Navigating the town was nigh impossible now because of the crisscross nature of the demon's pattern. It had ruined nearly every thoroughfare at the center of Midian, cutting off every cross street and leaving a FEMA-scale disaster area that one might be able to climb over on foot, but that was not traversable for a ground-hugging Crown Vic.

Ahead, around a curve, Arch watched the Wrightson plumbing van take a hard corner and disappear behind a berm of rubble, clapboard, and interior walls of what had once been someone's house. Ahead of that, somewhere, was Erin, and the thing itself, though he now could no longer see it thanks to the wall of destruction. It was as though a meteor had landed here, and then rolled forward unstoppably, creating a sliding crater all through town.

A look back in his rearview revealed a flash of motion; Barney Jones's Buick was behind him. For whatever good that would do. Probably had at least Braeden Tarley with him. For whatever good that would do, too.

"FEELS like I should be driving a consecrated garbage truck," Braeden Tarley said, peering out the front windshield as Barney Jones drove them along, a few hundred feet behind Arch's Crown Vic and losing ground. Because Barney wasn't insane out of his mind. Braeden applauded that thinking; what were they supposed to do if they caught the damned worm? Ramming it clearly wouldn't have much effect, though the reverend had blessed his own car. But if Casey's massive truck hadn't had any effect, this vehicle surely wouldn't do much.

Reverend Jones had an uncertain look on his face, but he did nod. "The bigger, the better."

"I feel like we're totally fucked," Terri Pritchard said from the back seat. She was leaning up, too, straining the bounds of her seatbelt. Braeden glanced back at her and noted – not for the first time this morning – that she was wearing a spaghetti-strapped tank top and no bra – and she was *stacked*. She caught him looking and grinned, made him blush, and he turned his head away in a hurry. Hell of a time to be thinking about that, when they were facing a demon that was ripping through the town, and the end of the world in just three days or less.

"SHIT shit shit shit shit shit shit," Lauren said, a stabbing pain in her side affecting her gait, her pace, and her entire future. It was hard to believe at this moment, running from a giant demon worm, that she'd once prided herself on her speed, on her endurance. On her tight ass in yoga pants.

Gone was all that – except her ass still looked decent in yoga pants, if not quite as nice as it had been when she actually had a chance to run – and what replaced it was a desperate desire to live. Stitch in her side? Fuck it; pain was temporary, death was permanent.

But St. Brigid's was ahead, only a hundred yards, and the demon worm had skidded on the turn, wiping out the old insurance brokerage/home residence of Hank Starky, once Midian's most annoying salesperson, now nothing more than a memory because he'd been eaten by a bed of demon clams a few months back when he'd stumbled into their nest next to the Caledonia while out for a jog.

So maybe Lauren's skipped runs had saved her life – at least up until now. As she looked back and saw the demon writhing its way through Hank's old house/office, though, she reflected that it was not going to be a winning strategy for her this day.

"Eyes...on the prize," Lauren huffed, because huffing was all she had. She was too tired even to puff, and her legs were screaming. When was the last time she'd had a proper run, anyway?

Oh, right. Probably all those months ago near the summit of Mount Horeb, when she'd almost been run down by demon bicyclists, and discovered the Watch.

"Come on, keep going," Rhea said, sounding only lightly strained, like she was running a 5k when she'd been trained for a marathon. "We're almost there. We can reach it before it catches us."

"What the fuck...kind of race...are you watching...?" Lauren's breath left her, the stabbing pain in her side joined by one in her shins, like she'd nailed the coffee table in the middle of the night on her way to the bathroom.

The worm was only a hundred feet away now – then fifty, then thirty.

But St. Brigid's was so close, the portico was thirty feet from them, the steeple and spire looming above, no shadows on this day with the brown sky. She was going to die to this dick worm, it was going to be the last dick she was going to get, and it was going to be less satisfying than any she'd previously had – with the possible exception of that one tech bro in Chattanooga who couldn't stop talking about his portfolio *in flagrante delicto*, like she gave a fuck about that while she was trying to get off.

Father Nguyen was there in front of her, standing in the doors, staring up in open-mouthed horror at what was coming his way. With a sinking feeling in her gut that was, somehow, worse than the shin splints and the side-stitch, Lauren realized...

...They'd just led this thing right to the church. Which was the last refuge in Midian.

And the fucking thing was going to plow right through St. Brigid's.

GARY'S VAN wheeled around the corner and hit pavement where the stupid worm hadn't turned quite fast enough. Erin Harris was just ahead now, blocking Marina from driving faster, but that didn't matter. The worm's tail was right there, too, working its way around in a slow turn, because it moved fast on straightaways but blew big goat cock on cornering. If Gary had been in front of it rather than chasing its tail, he knew what he would have done: zigzagged like a motherfucker, because it cornered like a semi with a drunk driver at the wheel.

"The doctor's making a real Rickon Stark mistake here," Larry observed as Marina floored it, trying to pass Erin in the narrow slot of the debris path. She was still looking mighty pale, but her face was set, determined. She'd had nerve, and Gary gave points for that. "She should be weaving and wobbling, y'know?"

"It's got little legs on the side," Terry said, anchored to the window like a Garfield cat. "That's how it's moving." He turned back inside to look at them, and the van lurched, but he caught himself on the arm rest. "I bet if you ran along the side and took out the legs, it'd spin round and round without being able to do much of shit."

"I don't want it to spin in circles," Gary said, looking at the long-ish crate draped across his lap. He had a pry bar and was trying – delicately – to open the damned thing without impaling himself as the van jerked. "I want to send it back to *hell*."

ERIN SAW her opportunity and she took it. The dumb fucking Wrightsons were trying to pass her in the wreckage-lined street, and she was inclined to let them because she had zero plan for how to deal with the giant worm that had already shrugged off one consecrated car in the ass like its cheeks were made of steel and were trying to be clapped by a limp-dicked mosquito.

So she honked her horn, because ahead was Dr. Darlington and that little Indian girl, hurrying as fast as they could toward the church, and there was nothing but open street and jack shit between them and that pissed-off worm. She really laid on it, too, like she was in Chattanooga traffic and there was nothing but dumbfucks all around her. Which was basically just normal Chattanooga traffic. She didn't bother flipping the bird, though. She saved that for Atlanta traffic.

It didn't do much of anything except make the worm turn slightly in her direction. Maybe caused it to miss a half-step or two. But it didn't waver long, then it was back to trying to catch Dr. Darlington and the girl. And Erin was back to trying to figure out a way to keep the doctor from being turned to mush, because that was only about ten feet from happening.

"FUCKETY-GOOSH," Terri said as they came hard around the corner, riding tight behind Arch's Crown Vic. The Wrightson plumbing van was already skidding to a halt because St. Brigid's was right there, and the demon worm was plunging straight for it. Braeden grimaced; there were a number of decent people still in there. This wasn't going to end well.

ARCH WATCHED the demon surge forward toward the good doctor, who looked as if she was about to be either eaten or run down, depending on what the demon felt like. It was hard to tell whether it was focused on catching her to eat, or catching her to splat her, and either way, Arch hated it. He'd never quite gotten along with Lauren Darlington, not in their ordinary lives in Midian, but he bore her no ill will, in spite of whatever angry feelings she'd harbored about him with her list and whatnot. Seeing her turned to mush by a demon, especially after they'd made their peace these last few months...well, that was a special brand of awful he was starting to accustom himself to. And hate.

But there wasn't much of anything for it, so he just braced himself and hammered the accelerator. Beside him, Duncan understood and buckled up, knowing what was coming – a crash, the only thing that might save the doctor. But probably wouldn't.

But at this point...what did it really hurt to try?

LAUREN HEARD THE HORN BLARE, but ignored it, trying to compel herself to go the last mile – or the last thirty feet. It wasn't going to work, wasn't going to happen, she was going to end her life in Midian as a smear on the belly of an uncircumcised dick-worm, which was really embarrassing if she'd had time to think about it.

This was it, and the only relief she had was that Molly was going to live a couple days more than she was. Maybe more if the Watch somehow got its collective shit together and figured out the thing she'd been trying to figure out.

Fuck. They were doomed without her, this bunch of lovable misfits and hillbillies and weirdos. They weren't stupid or anything, but goddamn, would it kill them to just put aside the fuckery and think for a while about what needed to happen? Of where this trouble was coming from? About this ancient gate, and where it could be hiding in the topography of Midian?

A thought occurred to her, a hiding place for the ages: the Tallakeet Dam. Federal construction project, lots of digging, and who the hell knew what was beneath the ground on either side? Or in the reservoir, for that matter? Hadn't a piece of the Rog'-tausch been buried in the flooded section of the reservoir? And God knew, the federal government had tried to fuck the people of Midian over, and hard, too.

Fuck! To have that insight about the hiding place of the gate, and then get flattened before she could say anything. She started to shout it out, hoping someone – Father Nguyen, maybe – would hear her and survive, but she couldn't even get the breath together to say it.

She almost didn't dare look back, but since there was no hope, and her legs were turned to jelly, and she was about to collapse anyway, why not? She glanced over her shoulder, intending to look her death in the face, maybe piss herself on the way out, because why carry an uncomfortable, full bladder into death when it was just going to spray everywhere along with all her blood when the worm ran her over like a bum under a speeding train? Which she'd seen once, in the ER in Chattanooga. It hadn't been pretty; there had been a collection of pieces more than a cohesive human body, and she wondered what the idiots who brought what was left of him in had been thinking.

Lauren looked back...

...And then she froze.

Because the worm wasn't coming to kill her anymore.

The damned thing had stopped, and was rearing back like it was rising toward the sky like a spooked horse, or an orgasming penis. It seemed to be controlled, like a giant, invisible hand had grabbed hold of it (fucking dick again!) (but at least it wasn't her hand grabbing the ugly fucking thing).

Her breath caught in her throat, anticipating it releasing, crashing down on her as it laid itself out lengthwise, fucking spent, because it sprayed spittle that made her jerk in fear. But it didn't burn, and didn't hurt; it just smelled faintly of ammonia as it wiggled back and forth, now fifty or sixty feet above her and writhing like that invisible hand was either choking the shit out of it or – no, that was it. Choking the shit out of the demon dick worm. And it was spraying on her.

Fucking dick again. But she was done chiding herself over it.

"Why did it stop?" Lauren whispered to herself.

A small hand slipped into hers, like when Molly was a kid and would grab her hand, usually as a prelude to going boneless and dropping like a stone with all her tiny weight, yanking Lauren over. That didn't quite happen this time, though; instead she was pulled forward.

"Because the church is consecrated ground," Rhea said, pulling her forward, again, toward the open door, where Father Nguyen stood, staring up at the foaming-at-the-tip immense demon dick. "If it crosses the property line it will burn. Come!"

"I think that's what he's doing," Lauren said, letting herself be led as another wave of ammonia-laced spittle fell over her from the demon worm. God, it smelled funny. But at least it wasn't acid. Or semen.

"THE HELL IS THAT THING DOING?" Larry asked as Gary launched himself out of the van's open door.

"Jerking itself off, looks like," Gary managed to quip before landing with a grunt. He held tight to the tube sitting across his lap as his wheels skidded on the debris field left in the demon's path. It was so damned heavy it even tore up the road, leaving chunks every which way, like someone had come along with a great big damned hammer and smashed up the blacktop. If Gary weighed that goddamned much, he'd go on a fucking diet. But he was a fucking achiever, and this worm was a disembodied giant dick, just crawling its way across his hometown, fucking everything up.

And he was going to put a stop to that shit *right now*.

Yanking the tube off his lap, he didn't even quite get his ass situated, or do something prudent like apply the brakes on his wheelchair. He was on a time crunch, after all; this uncircumcised demon dick was about to crush St. Brigid's, the last refuge of the non-fighters in this town, and he could not abide to see even a bunch of cowardly pussies getting smashed to pieces. Not on his watch, by God.

He lifted the tube over his shoulder, felt the hard end of it thump on him as he raised the shitty manual sight to his eye and lined it up with the giant, rocking worm spraying saliva forth. Looked pretty gross to Gary.

But, if he had his way, it was about to get a whole lot grosser.

Hanging over his shoulder was an RPG-7, a Soviet-made rocket launcher designed for putting holes in tanks and fucking up the crews inside, if not killing them. It worked on just about anything, though, like a hammer on the human body. It had a rocket at the tip that looked like an overly angular football, and as he pulled the trigger it shot off, streaking into the sky like a fucking firework, launched by the chemical propellant housed within.

"The fuck are you doing?" Erin Harris screamed at him. Because she was out of her car, and here, so of course she'd be screaming like a hysterical bitch.

"Solving this town's problems," he said, his wheelchair sliding backward because fuck, he'd skipped locking the brakes and the recoil from the launch was not insignificant. "One bitchass demon at a time."

She stared at him, then the worm demon as the rocket struck home. Burying itself in the demon's side, it did not explode on impact, surprisingly.

It exploded about a quarter-second after, once it had a chance to slip through the worm's pink, baggy skin.

The boom wasn't too loud, as these things went; like a firecracker, really, like the one Gary had lit when he was ten, a bit too far down the fuse. It had gone off about two feet from his hand, and, more importantly, about three feet from his ear, leaving his head ringing for some time.

This explosion was like that one, channeled through the body of the worm demon. A little bit of gore exploded from the site of the entry wound, a geyser of sludge in the shade of white pus coming out the side like he'd just popped an enormous zit.

But that wasn't the whole of it. Oh, hell no, not by a long shot.

The beast jerked and writhed in the air, reaching a new height and twisting sideways, as if trying to figure out how to learn to fly. A ripple went out across its body from the site of impact–

And then the sonofabitch went stiff as a board, hung there frozen in the air for a good second–

Then it spurted white gore from its mouth that was clearly its version of blood, like a fucking geyser. It blew out the end in a wave, spraying into the sky like the demon was an oil well and they'd just struck albino fucking gold instead of the black variety. Gary dodged it himself, because it didn't spray in his direction, but it came down on the church like the wettest snow you'd ever seen, or like the Stay Puft marshmallow man exploding at the end of *Ghostbusters* and drenching that ball-busting fuck from the EPA in white wash.

Dr. Darlington got absolutely drowned in that shit, unable to escape the wave of white blast. She disappeared under the flood, and so did the church, at least for a moment as the spray came down, down, down in a rain of white.

"Fucking squashed that bug!" Larry shouted, pumping his arm. He grabbed one of the handles of Gary's wheelchair and straightened him out. "Hey, bro, you might want to toss that tube. Think your shoulder's about to catch fire."

Gary looked down; sure enough, his shirt was smoking between the flannel stripes; he'd dipped the RPG launcher's tip a bit too close. He threw it and it landed with a clang a few feet from Harris, who looked at him. "The hell did you do?"

"Hit it with a consecrated RPG round," Gary said, because, duh, wasn't it fucking obvious?

"But the consecrated truck didn't work," she said, staring blankly at him. "Casey tried that."

Gary just rolled his eyes. He almost felt bad doing it, because that was supposed to be the province of teenage girls. "Listen," he said, "I don't know if you've noticed, but Casey Meacham is a fuckup. Good taxidermist, bad at everything else." He shook his head. "It's okay. People are like that. But I wasn't going to trust that this thing was immune to holy objects without testing the assumption for myself."

She stared in awe as the worm came crashing down – sideways, thankfully, and not onto the church. It took out three houses on Crosser Street, and the crunch was like a demolition crew had just come in. "Man. It really did look like–"

"Yeah," Larry crowed, "Gary just cleaned out that demon's pipes for him. Blew out the main vein." He cackled.

Gary clapped his brother in the kidney as he spun the wheelchair around, making Larry bend over double in pain. "Grow up, you pissant. And why don'tcha go check on the doctor? Make sure she's okay under all that demon spunk."

"Why don't you?" Larry asked, clutching his back. Gary had not restrained himself much when delivering the hit. To pull his punch would have been pussy-ass shit, and Wrightsons didn't truck with that.

Gary sighed, already halfway back to the van, where Marina was staring at the fallen worm in disgust, and Terry was nodding in admiration. "Because I can't roll through that mess," Gary said, waving a hand at the field of destroyed pavement and building debris. "You dumb shit."

"YOU GOT any theories about what happened there just now?" Arch asked. He and Duncan were out of the car, standing with the doors open, leaning on them as they watched the giant, phallic demon take its final bow and crash down on Crosser Street. "Why that worked when the holy truck didn't?"

Duncan was almost inscrutable. Almost. "Maybe," he said, squinting just a hair at the fallen demon. "An idea, at least." He started to slide back into the car. "Come on. Let's go check on Casey, see if I'm right."

LAUREN WAS FUCKING BURIED in jizz from that enormous demon dick...

And it was not everything she'd been hoping for.

The white expulsion bore the same sickly ammonia smell that the earlier spray had, but much stronger, enough to take Lauren's breath away – if she hadn't been holding it. The moment that first wave of white had erupted from the mouth of the dick demon, she'd held her breath, knowing it was coming. So to speak.

And she hadn't been disappointed – at least in this way. It sprayed all over her like a bukkake scene, and she kept her eyes squinted tightly shut, lips pressed together for dear life, and nose huffing out, only as it washed over her like some great wave falling upon a beach. Key rule when dealing with a dick – don't inhale at the wrong time, and don't swallow. That's where she was at. Rules for life.

The high water (jizz?) mark faded moments after the first wave crashed over her, only threatening her balance with the ferocity of its landing. She managed to keep her balance, keep to her aching feet and screaming shin and furious thighs, wobbling as it rinsed away, white ichor washing off in search of the paths of least resistance. It found them, presumably, because mere seconds after the wave of awful-smelling demon ichor (jism, fucking *jism!*) hit her, it subsided, and light streamed in through her tightly-closed lids, and air touched her skin where the stuff was falling away. It still clung to her skin like a fucking cream, though, and she didn't dare open her eyes.

She did open her mouth, just slightly enough to squeeze a few words out the side of her lips. "Can someone," she said, trying to exhale so none of the vileness would enter her mouth, "get me a towel?"

BRAEDEN WAS LEFT WATCHING the mighty worm fall, and felt it rattle through his legs, up his body, into his teeth as it landed. A debris cloud formed over Crosser Street where it crashed into the houses on the west side of the road, and sent shit flying mostly in that direction, but a little everywhere. He felt a few spatters of the geyser effect like a warm rain on his skin, droplets the size of pinpricks and eraser tips. It didn't burn, but he hastily wiped it off anyway and glanced at the hood of Barney Jones's car. It was properly spattered.

"Well," Pastor Jones said, unable to hide a look of wry amusement, "I ain't gonna say it, because it ain't proper, but I am going to think it, because we all know what that looked like."

"Yeah," Terri said from behind, sounding distinctly unamused, and Braeden turned to look at her.

She'd been sprayed in the face and her tank top was dripping, too. She mopped a long string of white goo from her brow and slung it against the ground. "God, I hope this shit's nontoxic."

"If it's not burning, it's probably fine," Duncan said, climbing back into Arch's car. They did a delicate turn to avoid Jones's car, then burned out past them, heading back the way they'd come along the trail of destruction.

Braeden regarded Terri, cringing a little. Her blond hair was wet and slick, and she looked a little like Cameron Diaz in *There's Something About Mary* during that one scene. As a diesel mechanic, he'd had oil in places. Lots of places. But he'd never had demon gunk that looked like cum sprayed in his face, and he felt his life was all the richer for it.

"I got a pack of spare water bottles in the trunk," Jones said, hustling around the car. "We'll get you washed up in no time."

Braeden just stood there, cringing on Terri's behalf. She squeegee'd some of the slop off her face with her fingers and flung it right into Braeden's chest. He accepted it with equanimity, knowing he definitely got the better end of the deal. "Bet you think this is pretty funny, huh?" she asked, leaning over and wringing out her hair. He didn't mean to, but he got a real good view down her tank top as she did so, and he didn't quite avert his eyes in a gentlemanly manner quick enough to avoid a beautiful view. But he did look away. Eventually. Long before she got her head back up. "The hell are you doing?" she asked when she did come back up.

"Being a gentleman or some such shit," he said, admiring the low-hanging brown smog that had settled over the town. He made a vague gesture toward her chest, and received another splop of demon gunk as his reward. He flashed her a slightly annoyed look. "Well, what would you like me to do?"

She was wearing a grin as she took a water bottle from Barney and cracked the lid, dumping it over her head and soaking herself. "Nothing," she said, as it streamed down her face and yes, onto her t-shirt, which – damn, wasn't it already wet enough? "Just didn't seem fair I was having to deal with this alone." And she kept going, trying to get that crap off her, while he stood there, kind of afraid to walk away like Barney had, and not really wanting to anyway.

"YOU WERE lucky to make it out of that one alive." Arch stared at the wreck of Casey's truck, the hood pinched off. Well...not quite. It had been smashed back into the passenger cabin, at least in part. The rest had been flattened, but the net result was the same.

"Tell me about it," Casey said, holding onto his knee, which was bleeding. "Gave me a hell of a ding. Almost lost my pecker, I thought." He grabbed his crotch, because of course he did. Then he rubbed his chest, raising his t-shirt to reveal an array of bruises in a half-moon wide across his chest. "Hurt like a motherfucker, too, when the wheel gave me a kiss."

"Uh huh," Duncan said, standing next to the ruin of the truck. He was giving it a once over, for whatever that was worth. The OOC wasn't a mechanic, after all – or was he? Man of mystery, that one. Except he wasn't a man at all, not really. He started to lean forward to touch the remains of the bumper, and Arch cried out–

Except Duncan touched it and...nothing happened.

"What...?" Arch asked.

"Huh," Casey said.

"This vehicle isn't consecrated anymore," Duncan said.

"How does that work?" Arch asked, frowning.

"Pretty simple," Duncan said with a shrug. "Your preacher consecrates it to make it holy. Something else deconsecrates it by doing something...well...unholy."

"So, for instance," Arch said, crossing his arms over his broad chest, "if an unmarried man were to have premarital sex–"

"I prefer the word 'fornication,'" Casey said. "It's a term of art."

Duncan came close to making a facial expression before shaking his head. "It takes real work to break a holy blessing. Fucking around in the cab with almost anyone, even a, uhm, madam, or a guy, for instance, shouldn't do it." He pressed his lips into a tight line. "You'd have to do some pretty...abnormal things to deconsecrate the vehicle."

Casey's skinny chest puffed out. "What you call abnormal, I call a Tuesday night."

"Not sure that's what I'd be proud of, but okay," Duncan said with another shrug. "Point is – don't do it in any holy vehicle next time?"

"That was half the fun," Casey said, grumbling a bit. But he took the point. Probably.

"THANKS," Lauren said, using holy water right out of the baptismal font to clean herself off. It wasn't a small font, and there weren't many baptisms happening presently, so she didn't stress about it as she poured it over herself. Rhea was already done, wiping off with a towel.

"I'm not sure if my heart can handle three more days of this," Father Nguyen said, offering Lauren a towel of her own once she was done.

"Let's hope someone doesn't cut it short on us, Father," Lauren said, turning her head to try and get out the sensation of water in her ear. "Because personally I'd like as much time to work with as possible, especially if we're going to be constantly interrupted by giant dick demons that spray everywhere."

Father Nguyen coughed, then inclined his head toward Rhea.

"Look at that," Gary Wrightson said in that loud, blaring voice of his. "A priest trying to protect a youth. Never thought I'd see it."

"I'll pray for you, Gary," Father Nguyen said.

"I won't turn it down," Gary said, rolling on in. He skidded his wheels to a stop next to Lauren. "You all right, Doc?"

"What do you think?" Lauren said, pausing in rubbing the towel over her hair.

"I think that thing about turned you into roadkill," Gary said, wheeling forward again, and showing her his back. Why did that matter? Lauren wasn't sure; she wasn't the queen, after all. Though in her heart some days she wished she was. Being the queen probably meant you didn't get demon guts that looked like jizz sprayed all over you. Probably. And the wardrobe was certainly better, if perhaps a bit more formal than she preferred day to day.

"And yet you still managed to get me doused with this stuff," Lauren said, slinging the glop that had been clinging to her sleeve down at his feet.

Gary regarded it with near-indifference. "On the plus side, that demon's refractory period just got pushed into infinity. So count your blessings, since now you don't have to worry about getting spurted on again."

Lauren's face scrunched in disgust. "Jesus."

"Nah," Gary said. "He's going to come again."

"You've been an asshole almost your entire life," she said, "haven't you?"

He paused, turning about in his wheelchair. "...And?"

She just shook her head.

"'Thanks for killing that thing right before it annihilated me, Gary,'" Wrightson said in a high and mocking tone, as if imitating her voice. "'I was real worried there for a second that it was gonna get me, and I was never gonna be able to go to a yoga class and hit the wine afterwards ever again.'"

"I'm not a yoga fan, though I like the pants," Lauren said. "But yes, thank you. Much appreciated." And she slopped more of the white stuff at him that had been hanging on her shoulder. Probably from her hair. This shit was impossible to get out. "Say, shouldn't you be mourning?"

Gary's face changed a couple shades to paler, and so did his brother's, before shifting to a bright red. "We all mourn in our own way," Gary said. "My way is to kill the shit out of demons." And he rolled past her, conversation apparently over.

Rhea watched him go, taking his entourage with him. "What a unique fellow."

"That's one way to describe him," Father Nguyen said. "Not the one I'd pick, but it is one way to describe him."

"SHUT THE FUCK UP," Duncan said, mostly to himself, mostly in irritation at the self-recrimination running through him. Then he realized he'd spoken aloud.

Erin Harris blinked slowly, and coolly, at him, then sort of shrugged and said, "Not the way I'd have put it, but he's right, Casey. No one cares about your truck's hanging balls tow hitch decoration."

"But they were right there," Casey said, gesturing to the back of the smashed-up truck. "I saw 'em on it when I started, and they're just gone."

"You ran your truck into a building-high demon worm," Arch said, his arms still folded across his broad chest. "I'm not searching this mess looking for your crude profane accessory. And I wouldn't suggest you do it, either, given what just came through town. It's not safe."

"We should get back to the station," Erin said, then froze, like she'd just flashed them her ass or something. "Just a suggestion," she said, then turned and quickly strode back to her car.

"She's trying real hard not to lead," Arch said as she started it up and threw it in reverse.

"Who can blame her?" Casey asked, peering around, clearly looking for his ball hanger. "It's a shit gig. Brings you nothing but misery." He made a low, whining noise. "My balls."

ERIN PULLED into the parking lot of the sheriff's station and let go a heavy sigh. It had been stressful finding her way out of the ruined labyrinth of the town, the giant dick demon having turned it into a nearly non-navigable warren. If she'd thought the Rog'tausch had been bad, he'd been nothing, a fucking prairie dog to this thing's T-Rex. But back when the T-Rex was impressive and scary, like in *Jurassic Park*, rather than the new research that seemed like they were doing the same shit to him that they'd done to Pluto when she was a kid. "It was a fucking planet," she muttered to herself, looking at the half-drunk bottle of whiskey in the floorboard of the passenger side. "Now what the hell is it, even? An asteroid? Talk about a demotion. Like going from a man's girlfriend to his maid, cook, and hand jobber. For no pay."

She thought real hard about picking up the bottle. And she stopped herself – but only just.

Three fucking days. She wasn't sure she believed it, still. The only thing she did believe?

That there wasn't so much as a jizz squirt of hope if she was in charge. She frowned, wrinkling her brow. Was she thinking of jizz squirts because of what she'd just seen downtown? Or was it because of...

"Fucking Hendricks," she said, loud, then noticed Arch pull up beside her in the lot. She forgot about the bottle, forgot about taking a drink, and climbed out of her car, leaving it behind – for now.

"I notice we're still running without a plan," Arch said, coming alongside her.

"Yeah," Erin said. "Someone should get on that."

He gave her a sidelong look that she didn't have to guess at the meaning of. Apparently he didn't have any good ideas, either.

Arch hustled forth to open the door for her, like a proper fucking gentleman, and she rolled her eyes where he couldn't see it, and helped herself to the interior door. Barely had she reached it when a wail of despair hit her.

It was a woman – blond, hair all a mess, eyes red from crying, cheeks about the same. It took a minute to recognize her, but recognize her she did as the woman, seemingly drained of life, energy, and all else, practically threw herself at Erin. She caught the blond – barely – with a quick assist from Arch. "Please," the woman said, voice scratchy and raw, "they took my children. Please. I need help. I don't know who else to turn to."

She shared a short look with Arch. "Who took your children, ma'am?" Arch asked, trying to get her back on her feet and off hanging on Erin. She was about to take her down, Erin thought, feeling her legs wobble from the woman's weight. And that'd be a fine fucking experience, ending up on her back with a sobbing middle-aged mother on top of her.

"Yeah," Erin said, once she was safely assured she'd remain upright. She looked down into those red features, could see the anguish on the woman's face. It was no lie, the horror of a mother who'd lost it all. "Who took your children...Mrs. Pike?"

Two Weeks Ago

HENDRICKS WAS DOING pullups in Gunny's garage when the old man himself came in. He didn't say anything, just let Hendricks keep sweating. It was coming off him in beads, right in the middle of his ten-pullup set. He was on number eight, then would drop, take a break, and come back at it in two minutes. Repeat until his arms were numb; and that was his plan.

"Renee sure did like watching you do that shit, didn't she?" Micah asked when he dropped. He caught himself on the balls of his bare feet, feeling the shock of the cold, concrete floor come through his ankles, his knees. Was this what being an old man felt like? He had aches he hadn't had a few years ago, all inflicted by doing dumb shit at various hotspots. Some of it he even regretted.

"She did," Hendricks said, feeling a little like he was stepping foot-first into a bear trap. But the old man didn't look spiteful. Gunny wasn't the backbiting type; you always knew where you stood with him. "We didn't have enough time together for it to get old."

Winthrop made a noise deep in his throat. "There are two

kinds of Marine marriages. Those that stick – and those that don't. When you get married ten minutes after meeting the girl, it tends to be the latter." He lowered his voice a little, and it almost broke. "But I was hoping it wouldn't be like that for my little girl."

"I hope you know," Hendricks said, feeling a real lump in his throat, "I never did get over her. Everything I do, it's–"

"Shut your flapping, white boy mouth, Wisconsin," Winthrop said. "Revenge is not for the person who died, son. It's for the person who lives." He shifted on his trunk-like legs. "And my daughter would be mad as hell at you pissing your life away."

Hendricks felt the sweat drip down himself; a bead slid down his shoulders to the small of his back. "Yeah," he said. Nothing else.

"But you're gonna do it anyway?" Gunny asked, staring at him hard, not an ounce of yield in his dark, penetrating eyes.

"I can't let it go," Hendricks said, and it felt like a confession to a crime he'd committed long ago, making its escape from his lips the way he'd always wanted it to. It felt good to say it, good to know it. "She's done me so wrong, Kitty Elizabeth. I can't let it go for Renee." He looked up, and felt a burn of his own behind his eyes. "And not for me."

"Fucking idiot," Gunny Winthrop said under his breath, and shifted on those big legs. He had free weights in the corner of the garage, a full power rack, and Hendricks felt sure the old man still loaded them up and did squats and deadlifts at least once or twice a week. He was just built like a fucking freight train. "Where is this Duchess bitch at?"

"New York City," Hendricks said. Felt good to let go of that, too. "Central Park West."

Winthrop whistled low. "Nice neighborhood."

"Too nice for riffraff like me."

Winthrop nodded, seemingly deep in consideration. "Gonna need to get in and out quick, then."

"Yep."

"You thought about a wheelman? Someone who knows the streets?"

"I have an idea of one that might be available," Hendricks said. "But...she's a fucking handful, Gunny."

"Then you need an extra hand," Winthrop said. And he seemed to have made a decision. "Don't look so surprised, shitheel. She was my daughter, after all." He raised a single large finger and pointed it right at Hendricks. "But you better be right about this. About her being responsible. I'm not going to New fucking York to settle anyone else's hash, you hear me?"

"Oh, I guarantee you that not only is she responsible," Hendricks said, "she's the baddest bitch around." And that thought sent a little quiver through him that had nothing to do with all the pullups he'd just exerted himself doing. This one was deeper, and started in the guts. A thought of Erin Harris bobbed into his mind. Just a thought of her, angry, like Winthrop had been, for him being a moron. An evergreen concern, really, and the vision of her with mottled cheeks and flashing eyes stayed in front of him as he walked Gunny through his plan. Always there, just beyond the margins of his thought and consciousness, ever present.

And for some reason, he couldn't let that go, either.

EIGHT

WITH KINGS AND COUNSELORS

"Where we going, Gary?"

The questions started the second he wheeled his fucking chair out the front door of St. Brigid's, because of course they did. Some led and some followed, and naturally his moron younger brothers had developed a dependence on him that he found annoying. A flash of cloying anger bubbled up within him, but his teakettle was already boiling, and he managed to keep his tongue civil to avoid nuking 'em with his first shot. "Back to the house, stupid," he said. Well, if not civil, at least it wasn't a verbal nuke. "Where else would we go?"

"We could drive over there to be sure," Terry said, rubbing fingers over the stubble on his puffy, baby-like cheeks, "but I think the worm might have trashed the house we were staying in."

Larry nodded along. "Yeah, it tore up Worth Street pretty good. Even if it didn't wreck the place, we ain't gonna be able to get the van over there."

Gary stopped rolling and let momentum carry him the last ten feet to where the van was parked, wheelchair lift already down and waiting for him. He stared out over the town; the worm had just completely altered the whole landscape. It had gone from somewhat wheelchair accessible to a series of artificial trenches where the wreckage from the worm's slog created a ten to fifteen foot wall of debris on either side of its crawl path. He couldn't even effectively roll down the center of it, because wherever it had crawled over pavement, it had shattered it into a billion pieces.

"Fuck," Gary said. "Goddamn."

"I think he just said we're right," Larry exchanged a grin with Terry. "In his own, special sort of way."

"Let me give you a piece of advice, you cucked-out, tucked under, limpdick," Gary said, pushing onto the lift and savagely hitting the button so it began to carry him upward. Slowly. Always fucking slowly, annoyingly so, like everything. "Why don't you act like you should when you eventually lose your virginity, and pretend you've been there before? That's called being manly, and I know you're new to the idea, but you should waddle your way on over to the concept and give it a gentle embrace. It might eventually allow you to achieve an erection without thinking of Henry Cavill in the bathtub while you stroke your baby-oiled pecker."

"Goddamn it, Gary," Larry said, his face turning crimson, "it was one time, and I told you that in confidence!"

"You told me when you were three sheets to the wind," Gary said. "All's fair in drinking and war. Now shut the fuck up, I got to think through where we're going to hang our hats next." He swore again, under his breath, catching Marina looking at him from the front seat. "Y'all are going to have to go to the house and see if you can salvage any of our shit."

"And you?" Larry said nastily. "Just gonna cool your wheels while we climb over the ruin of the town?"

"Yeah, so I'd appreciate it if you didn't stop and fap one off to

Timothy Chalamet while I'm waiting," Gary shot back. The ramp was only halfway up.

"But he's got such delicate features," Terry said, with a clear taunting voice aimed right at Larry.

"Fuck you guys," Larry said. Was a tear streaking its way down his cheek? Probably. Gary figured he'd take the high road on that one; no point in making his brother cry after mom and Paul had both died.

"So what do we do now, Gary?" Terry asked. "After we get our shit from the house. If we can, I mean."

The ramp made a metal clunking noise as it reached its apex, and Gary rolled backward into the van. "We find somewhere else to stay, and then we figure where to attack next, and then next after that, until we win this fucking thing," he said, and then, not bothering to mutter it. "Dumbass."

"Okay," Terry said, but the skepticism bled through. "If you say so."

"I say so," Gary said, locking down the wheels and reaching for the straps to lock the wheelchair in place during the ride. Fucking annoying, but better than rolling every which way. He lowered his voice as the engine started and his brothers climbed in. "I fucking say so," he whispered. And he didn't know why.

"YOU LOOK like you still need a shower," Father Nguyen said, kind of grimacing at Lauren. "Sorry to say we don't really have the water for that on hand–"

"I don't *need* a shower," Lauren said. Her hair was still a little goopy, a little clingy, getting to be a little stiff, even though she'd rinsed the worst of the demon foulness out of it. "I *want* a shower. But I also want Midian to have power and water again, so..." She shrugged, her clothing also vaguely stiff, like she'd soaked it in a swimming pool and then left it to dry in the sun for too long. "I guess I'll just have to deal with smelling like..." She plucked the corner of her shirt up and to her nose, giving it a sniff. "...Apple cider vinegar?" She made a face, then shrugged. "Well, it could be worse."

"And so say all of us," Nguyen said, treading his way through the central aisle of the church. She followed – for some reason. Rhea remained at the entry, looking around and wringing her hair out. Nguyen gave her a stray look. "What's up with the kid?"

"I don't know, she's...weird," Lauren said, reaching for her bag before realizing she'd left it behind at the archive. Shit. She had hair binders in there, among other important things. Had the archive been destroyed by the demon dickworm? Or had she successfully led it away in time to keep the archive from being destroyed? There was no telling without going to look, and now that she had a working thesis to check out – the Tallakeet Dam – she wasn't excited about venturing out into the ruin of town to chase that hare.

The town was a ruin. That much she was sure of. The swath of destruction that thing had left before disgorging its contents onto her had done more damage in five minutes than a plague of demons had brought down in the months leading up to this. Impressive, really, when one considered it. Getting home later might not even be a possibility, by car or by foot. And who the hell wanted to spend the night in isolation while demons prowled everywhere? Not her; that sounded like a formula for getting her ass picked off like a blond in a sexy horror movie who'd just given it up to her quarterback boyfriend.

"What isn't weird around here lately?" Nguyen said, stopping next to a pew that had Addie Longholt sitting on it. She stared up at the giant crucifix on the far wall, behind the pulpit. "Addie? I think Paul is going to try and leave now."

"Yes, I think he would have left before if a giant worm demon hadn't been tearing through the town," Addie said dryly, looking up with a sparkle of amusement in her eye. "Still, better he go now before the next Midian surprise gets sprung. I'll go tell him – provided you know the big demon is dead."

"I can confirm it," Lauren said, catching the older woman's eye. "I think I've got its heart's own blood all over me."

"Is that what that is?" Her smile turned wry. "I suppose, as a doctor, you would know. To a laywoman like me, it looks like a very different bodily fluid."

Lauren felt her lips twist into a sour expression. "Great. So the world is ending, and I now physically resemble what everyone thought I was as a pregnant teenager: a whore."

"Oh, honey," Addie said, putting a delicate, age-spotted hand on her arm. "When you get pregnant by Jesse Harris while he's got a long-term girlfriend that's aiming to become his wife, can you really expect anything more?"

Lauren felt her eyes widen, kind of dramatically, really. She'd never told anyone – not her parents, not her friends (such as they were), not even Molly – who her father was. Because their whole goddamned romance was a secret, and it was secret for a *damned good fucking reason.* That reason being that Jesse had a girlfriend at the time, who was now his wife and the mother of his – according to Facebook, presently – three children. Who definitely did not know that Jesse had a teenage love child back in the hometown they'd beat feet to get out of the moment they graduated high school.

But come to find out...of fucking course...someone knew. Maybe more than one someone, because this was Midian, Small Town USA, and the fucking gossips here were legendary in their capability and whatnot.

Lauren knew she'd been had a second after she let her eyes flare in surprise; Addison Longholt was no fool. She'd guessed.

A damned good guess, but a guess nonetheless, and at a moment Lauren hadn't expected this to come up. Here at the end of the fucking world, and something she really thought was buried deep came flying out and smacked her square in the face.

"I'm sorry, did you ladies say something?" Father Nguyen seemed to appear back in her vision. She didn't even realize he'd stepped away, moving off to look at a crate of supplies that Paul Cummings had brought.

"Not a thing of substance," Addison Longholt said with a smile. Lauren matched it, as a southern lady should. But inside she burned at being, well...burned.

"PLEASE," Darla Pike said, holding onto Erin's jacket, practically hanging on it, "you have to help me. My children–"

"What happened and where?" Arch asked, brusque, business-like.

"We were trying to get out of the county," she said, looking like she was trying to keep from sobbing. The occasional one was leaking out, though. As was proper for the situation. "We were coming north, you know, out of Culver, where we lived? I just wanted to get us out before anything else went wrong. And as we were coming up Mill Road – they came out of the woods." She sniffed. "I swerved, crashed. When I woke up I saw them dragging my kids, screaming, into the woods toward the mill. I tried to follow," her eyes were wide, wild, "but something lurched out at me." She lowered her head. "I ran. I ran, and I couldn't hear them anymore and–"

"That's bad," Duncan said, a little blandly. He was frowning, or as close as he ever got to frowning. She cocked her head, waiting to see what he said, if he was picking up something she wasn't. He offered nothing but a shrug after a few seconds, and that settled that.

"Shit, let's get the crew moving," Casey said. She'd forgotten he was here. "We can't let kids die."

"Which way were they heading?" Arch asked. "The demons you saw?"

"Demons?" Darla Pike seemed to gasp, as if trying to acclimate herself to this new news. "Well...whatever they were, they were heading toward the mill, like I said."

Erin pursed her lips, feeling Darla Pike's grip hard on her arm. "That'd be a good place for them to go, yep," she said.

The mill had been the lifeblood of Midian. The number one employer. Producer of several hundred thousand metric tons of newsprint and specialty paper per year.

All that had come to an end the moment Interstate 75's bridges came crashing down from the earthquake. Whether it was because the parent company knew what was going on in the town, or they'd just seen the winding roads into Midian and their hours-long detours required to use the mill, they'd made the announcement a mere two days after the closure: the mill was shutting down, idling until the situation improved. No reopen date announced, just a vast limbo.

And that was it; Midian was dead. The citizens could read the tea leaves: no jobs, no money, lots of demons – better to move on. That had kickstarted the exodus. Now they were down to the last...how many were still here? Fifty, maybe? Probably less. And it wasn't just Midian; people were fleeing all the way out in Culver, which was forty minutes away on the other end of the county.

"We were trying to get to Chicago," Darla Pike said, biting her lower lip. "To my mother-in-law's. I just..." The tears were flowing now. "...I just wanted to get out of here before anything else bad could happen."

Boy, did Erin ever understand that sentiment, especially today. "Okay, ma'am, we'll see what we can do."

"Please," Darla said, clutching at her. "Please." Her eyes were watery, distorted, but Erin could see the blue in them.

She guided the overwrought woman to a chair behind the counter. Arch was already calling out on the radio. Casey had disappeared into the back somewhere – probably to the armory, because this was going to be a time for gunplay, no doubt. "Just wait here, okay?" And she sidled over to Arch, waiting for him to finish on the radio.

"...We should rendezvous at..." he glanced at Erin. "What do you think?"

She stood there, staring blankly for a minute. "Mill road, maybe?" Why was he asking her? She'd been clear that she was out, hadn't she?

"Mill road," Arch said. "Meet in twenty. Over." He looked past Erin, lowered his voice, and said, "Those kids will be dead by then, won't they?"

"Maybe," Erin said, not really sure of the answer. "You think we should pass on this?"

Arch shook his head. Noble as always. "There was a thin chance of success when I chased that cannibal demon into the tunnels with those kids, too. Wasn't about to let him get away without making an effort then, and I can't see not doing the same now. Hopefully we'll catch them in prep."

Erin cringed. "Meaning you're hoping they're gonna eat the kids fresh rather than–"

Arch leaned in a bit. "I don't want to dwell on that. I'm hoping we find them alive, and in good condition." He nodded to Darla Pike. "Shame she's got to deal with this. You know, what with already losing her husband."

Erin felt a tightness within, right in her gut, like someone had stuck a crank through her middle and given it a few good twists. "You mean because Hendricks murdered him?"

Arch stiffened like a cat that had just sensed a more apex predator taking interest in it. "Yes." He did not elaborate. Not a man of expressive feelings, that Arch Stan. She wondered, just for a beat, if Alison had gotten more out of him than this, or if he'd been this quietly stoic even for her. Surely not...but it was hardly impossible.

He didn't stay quiet for long, though. "We need to get moving." He looked over her shoulder. "And she should stay here. For safety."

Erin felt a mild prickle at that...shouldn't the mother do anything to save her babies? But no, Arch was right. After all, she remembered all too well that kid who'd lost his father to a demon while deer hunting, then his mother to an ambush by the cannibal, and then himself in the woods after, presumably to demons, since he'd never shown up again. There was no such thing as a non-combatant in Midian these days. Though with a stolen glance over her shoulder, Erin had to admit that Darla Pike, red-eyed and crying, seemed the very definition of one.

DARLA WAS WATCHING the quiet discussion between Erin Harris and Arch Stan out of the corner of her eyes only. She pretended to be a traumatized mother who'd lost her children...which was true, if it left a few important points out.

Like the blood, the slaughter, the wheeling, the dealing, the demon sex–

Well, that last one wasn't immediately applicable to the blood and the slaughter, but it had happened. After. She had suitors, impressed by her willingness to do things. Wanting to taste darkness, to make deals.

Well, she had plenty of darkness for them to taste, especially if they started below her belt.

But Darla Pike had oodles of experience holding these sorts of thoughts back. She'd learned early to construct a facade behind which she held all her truest thoughts and beliefs, the ones that got you in trouble if you said them out loud, or others found out. She'd lived almost her whole life hiding behind that facade; it was second nature to her, or first, in the moments when the line blurred and she almost felt herself become that person that was the facade. A doting mother, a loving housewife who smiled at every gun-toting, slack-jawed fucking yokel who might be able to exercise even a whit of say over her husband's career. Of course she had a hot dinner waiting on the table every night when he got home, she said to these traditionalist cunts who'd never read Foucault at all, let alone in the original French, and whose whole life revolved around a meal served to their smelly, mill-working husbands, and probably sucking their dicks afterward with no reciprocity. Of course she breast-fed her babies, she lied through her fucking teeth to these country hippy-harpies, thinking of the moments when she shoved a formula-laden bottle into their screaming little yaps to shut them the fuck up. Of course she was raised Episcopalian but believed now Presbyterianism/Methodism/Baptist doctrine was correct, she said to the pastors, while remembering the time she'd gotten triple penetrated by a triad of qual'en'thoth demons on a the bloodied corpse of a nun who'd been raped to death and covered in demon piss after being strapped to a deconsecrated cross. That one had veered between alarming and arousing from moment to moment, and she hadn't gotten off, but that was mostly down to the awkwardness of the whole experience. The positioning and whatnot; qual'en'thoth were not shaped quite like humans, so they were able to make it work, but at some minor expense to her back and thighs. They made it fucking happen, though, or made the fucking happen, in that case. Degrading, debasing, unholy – another pact sealed, her pleasure be damned in favor of the job at hand.

Besides, she'd taken care of it herself later, a skill that had come in handy throughout her marriage. At least on the occasions when Jason had been too tired from fucking his latest mistress.

All this was behind the facade, under a perfect wall of control and discipline. She could see them talking just fine, but out of her peripheral vision. She concentrated on rocking back and forth very slightly, on mumbling under her breath to herself, just the names of her children: "Jason. Mera." Over and over, like the fucking basket case she was pretending to be.

It wasn't hard. She just pretended she was one of the piggy little porker housewives around here who thought of nothing but their little piggy children and their fat piggy husbands with their big trucks and micro-dicks. The only thing smaller was their brains.

This all came down to how willing Darla was to play games to get what she wanted. And the answer was: infinitely willing. It was why she'd become Jason Pike's wife instead of marrying herself to someone with the potential to be president, or some king somewhere. That hadn't been out of her reach, outside her capability. She could have done it, if necessary, worming her way into the confidence of some man of supreme power somewhere. Or just climbed the ladder herself; it was certainly possible in these days.

But that would only last a lifetime. And Darla thought far, far beyond those conventional timeframes.

Erin Harris broke away from their small huddle. Funny; Darla couldn't have predicted this little cunt would have picked up the mantle after she shot Sheriff Nicholas Reeve in the back of the head and watched his brains explode all over her husband's surprised face. She didn't look so formidable now as she sashayed her non-childbearing hips over. Pop out a couple of kids, she wouldn't look so hot anymore. Things would sag, like they did on Darla. That bitch.

"Mrs. Pike," Harris said, leaning close, talking low. Like she was a wild horse Harris was trying to calm. L-O-Fucking-L. "You should stay here while we go look for your children."

"What?" Darla pretended to shake herself out of her rocking and humming fugue state. "Why?"

"It's dangerous out there," Harris said with the tight-lipped smile of a country cocksucker. She just dripped compassion, and it made Darla sick behind the facade. "We don't want you to get hurt while we're trying to save your children."

"But you're going to get them?" She put a desperate, claw-like hand on Harris's arm. "You're going bring them back to me?"

A pained look crossed the little deputy's face. God, Darla could beat her ass in a fight. Split those cock-sucking lips, break that pert little nose, blacken both her eyes, watch her drown in her own blood. She wanted to shove her stretch-marked belly right into Harris's mouth, make her choke on it. "We're going to try," Harris said.

What more could she ask than that? It was certainly all that had been asked of her, Darla reflected. But she didn't want to sound too eager. Shell-shocked. That was what she'd go for. "Okay. Okay. I'll wait here and you'll bring them back," she said, staring straight ahead at the shitty wood-paneling that had fallen out of vogue in the rest of America in the 1970's, but still reigned here. "You'll bring them back to me." And she lifted her knees up and curled into the fetal sitting position, still rocking back and forth.

"Is she going to be all right here?" the plain-faced OOC asked. That fucking dick; she'd been warned about him.

"Safer here than anywhere else," Harris said with a shrug.

Darla could have tackled her flat, skinny ass and broken her into about twelve pieces in the process. She looked exactly the type Jason used to like to make his playthings. Inevitably, Darla was able to convert at least half of them into her playthings, too, which was always fun.

Not so with Harris. She needed to suffer and die, and maybe not in that order. Because her own orders were clear, and what was even clearer – in spite of being relatively unspoken – was exactly what was on the line if she failed.

GARY WAS SITTING. Just sitting, under a shit-brown sky, wheelchair on the ripped-up ground while his team climbed their way over the mountain of debris that obscured the site of the house where they'd been squatting (sitting, in Gary's case, he thought with a wry chuckle, no squatting for him, since it wasn't physically possible). Watching those fuckers labor did his heart good, Larry losing a foothold, crying out, and almost coming back down as they picked their way over the berm was a hoot. But it left Gary cooling his wheels out here, one hand on the smoothed-out handle of a sawed-off pump shotgun with blessed shells while those numbnuts (and Marina) retrieved their shit.

The air was surprisingly cool given the hellish fires going only a few miles away. Not surprising for January, he guessed, but everything felt so different. The world had a different color now; not slate gray, it instead had the aura of brown, as if to reflect how shitty everything had become.

Gary cleared his throat for about the thousandth time today; felt like wood ash was settling in the back of it, and his nose was definitely doing a slow drip in the back from all the shit accumulating in his sinuses. Gave him a little tickle in the back of his throat. Fucking demons set the woods on fire during a drought. What a bunch of dickbags.

He brushed a little wad of ash off his skin that he hadn't even noticed landed there. It wasn't hot, wasn't an ember, just a stray piece streaming down out of the shit-brown sky. He'd seen the footage from California wildfires. The skies didn't look shit brown. Of course, a lot of the footage had been from night. "Because the fires look scarier at night," Gary muttered. Fucking cable news. Always trying to scare you or piss you off. They couldn't exist without keeping your eyeballs attached to their shows with fucking high-power suction. Lie, inflame, push the damned outrage button in your brain full force, whatever they had to do to keep you watching that shit – and the commercials that came with it. Bunch of pig fuckers and donkey dick suckers. Well, up theirs. Gary didn't need any help being outraged, and he didn't need a whit of assistance choosing a target for said outrage once his dander was up.

"You missed the point, you know."

Gary jumped in his fucking chair. Or at least as much as one could jump without the use of any-damned-thing beneath his tits. He had the sawed-off pump up and around in about a quarter-second as he spun the wheel with one hand and aimed with the other. If he had to fire one-handed, he'd regret it.

But not as much as being eaten by fucking demons.

Turned out, he didn't have to fire. "What the dry-asshole fuck?" Gary asked, moving the shotgun off target. Slightly.

It was that little Indian girl. Dots, not feathers, as they said. Skin like a proper cherrywood, big eyes looking at him with a scary amount of innocence considering the shit he'd just unthinkingly said in front of her. She had such raven-black hair that her upper lip bore just the trace shadow of a very light mustache because of it.

"The fuck are you doing here, Slumdog Princess?" Gary

asked, keeping his finger proximal to the trigger, and the shotgun only a few degrees off in case she was actually a demon. Gary didn't trust kids overly much, but he certainly didn't trust them when they showed up in an apocalypse. "Don't you know there are dangerous demons walking these streets? And other dangerous humans rolling 'em?"

"That'd be you, then?" she asked, barely glancing at his shotgun.

"Among others," he said. "All quick on the trigger, and not counting on a half-pint like you to come sneaking up on us. We hesitate, we're liable to get demon fangs buried in our necks – or our asses." He waved a hand at her dismissively. "You get on back to that church, and catch a ride out of town with Paul, that shaved-assed mother...trucker," he finished, finally realizing he shouldn't curse in front of a child, even a near-teenager like this. What'd they call them now? Tween-agers?

"I can't leave," she said, holding onto her backpack straps as she shuffled on over to him. Her shoes had seen some mileage, and she was wearing denim overalls, like she was aiming for farmer chic. "The world's going to end if someone isn't here to set things right at the appropriate time."

"You see that on Tiktok or something...?"

"I see it, yes," she said, placing two skinny fingers right against her temple. "That's my burden in all this. I receive cloudy prophecies that give me enough clarity to guide certain willing parties to be of assistance in these events, but not enough to, say, give you the lottery numbers for Saturday night."

"And I was just about to propose a split that would make us both very rich." Gary shifted his in his chair. "You got some kind of super powers that make you able to survive demon acid? Or being squashed? Because it looked to me like before I launched that rocket, you were about to get pulped just like the good doctor. And it sure did feel awkward when that stuff rained down on you." He cringed. "It was not proper. And that's this whole damned place nowadays, not proper for children or any living thing, really. Which is why you should leave."

"If I leave, the world ends," she said, raising one hand, as if balancing it like a scale, with real weight on it. "But if I stay, I could die with the rest of you – and the world follows shortly thereafter. So...why leave?"

"I guess maybe because I don't necessarily believe the world is going to end," Gary said, really getting to the truth of his feelings on the matter. And he fucking hated it, because touching his feelings was worse than touching raw sewage. And he knew, because by God, he was a plumber and that shit happened sometimes.

"What do you believe?" she asked, and God her accent was thick. Like she'd just caught the plane from Calcutta, or Kolkata, or whatever they were calling it these days.

"That we're up to our necks in it here. But ending the world?" He shook his head. "Guess I just don't see it. I still think the end of this is me killing every last demon in the place and saying bye-bye, yo."

"Gary, you talking to yourself again?" Larry shouted over the wreckage of at least two houses.

"Have to, to have an intelligent conversation around here," Gary piped up. "Get done so we can go, will ya?"

"But where we going, Gary?"

"Why don't you stop worrying your pretty little head about that and get the damned job done?" Gary shouted back. Lowering his voice, he added, "That's one of my idiot brothers. The smart one died, unfortunately. Now, little lady, you should get back to the church, at least. Wandering around town in the wake of that big di – err, demon – attack is a dumb idea that stands out in a sea of them."

"The town is relatively safe for now," She said, holding tight to her backpack straps. "It will become more dangerous after nightfall."

Gary frowned. "Why? Is it the darkness?" Wait. Was he taking this pint-sized broad's pronouncements seriously?

"No," she said, a slight frown coming over her small features. "I think *she* is holding them back. Though I'm not certain why."

"One of the blind spots in your gift of prophecy, huh?" Ah, there was his natural skepticism. Just in time, too, because the story was turning to bullshit.

"I don't think so," she said, as if concentrating on something, thinking hard about it. "If so, it's an unnatural one, caused by her attempts to shroud her workings in mystery. It's as though I'm trying to shine a light on something that absorbs every lumen of it. Like a black hole."

"Oh, you're an astrophysics major in addition to being a prophet?"

"No, I just watch documentaries sometimes," she said. "But Gary–"

"Who told you my name?" Gary asked, and boy that suspicion was flaring back up again.

"God himself," she said, and he couldn't tell if she was jesting or not. "Before the end, you will see that you were wrong. You will be left with nothing but yourself. And you will have to make do with that."

Gary just stared at her. "Well, yeah. That's how it always is. What the hell kind of fortune cookie wisdom is that?"

"We don't have fortune cookies in India. We have samosas. Have you ever tried one?"

"Is that the thing with the fried outside and spiced meat inside?" Gary rubbed at his chin, where months of stubble had turned into a beard. "Because if so, yes, those are pretty great. Better than a fortune cookie, at least for a carnivore like me."

"You'll see what I mean," she said. "Before the end."

"Yeah, well, hopefully we'll have a bit of time on that," he said, humoring her, because what was the fucking point of arguing with a tweenager? A clunk of a foot on wood made him spin, only to find Terry climbing over the debris wall, shit hanging from his back like it was going to pull him back down. The whole pile shifted, and he paused as it settled two feet lower, just about pitching him down Gary's side of the ridge o' crap. "Watch yourself, dumbass, or you're going to end up worshipping at my feet literally as well as figuratively."

"We got a call from the Watch," Terry said. Larry's dark-headed self popped up just behind, and Marina's came up after. "Some kids got snatched out by the mill. Demons looking for a tasty treat, I guess."

"We're heading out, then," Gary said, and turned to look back at the little girl, but she was already walking away. "Where you going?"

"Back to the church," she called over her shoulder. "I can't see what you're going to encounter at the mill, and that usually means it's not for my eyes."

"That's smart," Gary said, nodding as he watched her go. "Smarter than any of us," he added, muttering under his breath. By the wave she gave him, she might have heard him anyway.

THERE WASN'T a lot of question in Arch's mind what needed to happen now. The call had already gone out, the Watch was moving, and the assembly point was Mill Road. He had a department AR-15 strapped to his body with a few extra magazines, and every last one of the bullets had been prayed over by Barney Jones, making them implements of God's will. Not too terribly long ago, Arch might have struggled with that idea – a bullet as a vessel of God's will.

But that was before demons, and now he was thankful for them every time he fired a round and watched a demon dissolve into a black sulfur cloud, sparing the life of someone in this town. Or his own, maybe.

"How are you feeling about this, Duncan?" Erin asked. They were almost to the cars; funny time to bring that up. But then, they'd been watched inside. He cast a look over his shoulder, but the Pike woman wasn't visible. He couldn't blame her much. Not after all she'd been through.

"I can't read anything anymore," Duncan said. "But she seems sincere. She did have children, I assume?"

"Two, I think?" Erin supplied the answer.

Duncan greeted this with another shrug. "Mother losing her kids trying to get out of town? I doubt that's the first time that story's happened in this town. More commonly the mother gets lost too, if you know what I mean." He paused a beat. "I mean eaten."

"Yeah," Erin said. "I think we picked that up. By context."

"And experience," Arch added, opening the Crown Vic's door and securing the AR in the holder right in the center of the car. It wouldn't pay to not be ready here. Not given what the stakes were. Especially for what they were marching into.

"See you boys there?" Erin asked, getting in her Explorer.

"I'll ride with you, if it's okay," Duncan said. He only offered a passing glance to Arch, then yet another shrug. Was the OOC certain of anything anymore? His body language didn't suggest he was. "You have a windshield."

Arch found he didn't much care, and off they went. He led, getting the Vic out of the parking lot before Erin. He was usually the one that was more reserved on the accelerator, but today he found himself really putting the pedal down. Something about...

Kids? In danger?

Yeah. That was it. But what about it tickled him as so wrong?

Kids are our future, the answer came to him. The voice was light and dancing, just in the back of his head, so familiar.

"Except we don't have a future anymore," he found himself saying. "Alison."

Dang. That struck him, hard and cold, right in the space around the heart. Talking to his dead wife? That was the mark of a crazy man. He didn't allow himself that much lead, so he shut up and drove, let himself fall into silence, rather than continue a conversation that wasn't happening anywhere but in his head.

One Week Ago

IT WAS the morning rush in a little coffee house in the Upper West Side of Manhattan, and Brian Longholt was dealing with it as best he could. It did occasionally burn him that he'd spent all that time, energy, and money getting a philosophy degree from Brown University only so he could end up–

"Um, excuse me," a girl said with strong vocal fry, SoCal inflection, "my triple soy macchiato, like, totally has dairy in it." She looked like she'd come in from the West Coast just last night, in fact, wearing long PJs with teddy bears on them, the hood pulled up to hide her tangled hair, as though she'd rolled out of the hotel bed shortly after sunrise and just shown up here to get caffeinated. She was looking at him with the greatest disdain, like he was a bug she'd squished on the bottom of her shoe. "I've been a vegan for, like, two months. You just ruined that for me. You ruined *me*."

"Pretty sure your parents' upbringing did that, actually," Brian said, holding a damp rag in one hand, and a series of dishes stacked atop a tray in the other. Balance was important for a busboy. And that's what he was.

Just weeks ago he'd been a son, a brother, and a demon fighter...and now he was barely one of those, because his father and his sister had both died, the former after Brian had gotten possessed by a demon and shot him in the head. He'd watched the whole thing through his own eyes, done by his own hand...

...And been able to do nothing about it. Watching his father linger on the edge of a coma, then permanent brain injury before finally sliding into death? And all after Alison had died on the square, helping deliver the coup de grace to the big bad that had done such evil to him?

He'd left. What else could he do? His philosophy degree had a lot to say on matters of good versus evil; none of it was much consolation when you watched two out of four members of your immediate family die within days of each other. His mother was surely next, for she hadn't left Midian with him, and now...

...Well, he hadn't heard from her in a long while. And it was starting to work his nerves just a bit.

"What did you just say to me?" The vegan Valley girl asked, shock parting her overly-filler'd lips.

Brian paused. He hadn't meant to say what he had; it wasn't a proper thing for a busboy in a small cafe on the Upper West Side to say to a paying customer. He was supposed to be *nice*. He was supposed to say, "Yes, ma'am, I'll see you get a new coffee with triple soy and not an ounce of animal product. Whatever you say, ma'am, and please, if you could leave a single penny in the tip jar over there in remembrance of what I've done for you here today, I'd be grateful." That was how a refugee from the demon wars ought to handle things; how a busboy grateful to have his measly job should conduct himself, how Brian, sleeping on his friend's couch and without a job prospect in the world, should have done it.

Instead:

"Listen, you plastic-faced Bratz doll," Brian said, dropping the collection of dishes he'd accumulated from bussing other tables onto the one he'd been working on, "if you ordered a soy macchiato, you got a soy macchiato. Our baristas," and here he swept an arm around to regard the mother-daughter team working behind the counter, both of whom had stopped and were now watching him, because he wasn't quiet, "are extremely sensitive to customer needs and allergies. We would not feed you animal product if you ordered it soy. The fact you think we would tells us more about you than anything else, because if you think we'd do it – well, that's the type of shitty person you are. Which does not come as a terrible surprise, since you're – what, twenty-five?"

"Twenty-four," she said, meekly, all the expression drained out of her face under the violence of his reply.

"And you've already got the markings of being Botoxed out of consciousness multiple times," he said, waving a finger in front of her partially-paralyzed face. "Who told you this was a good idea? Was it Instagram? Because they lied to you. They lied to you about that, and they lied to you about veganism being healthy, and they lied to you about any of this," and he waved at her pajama-clad self, "being a good look. Maybe this is how you conduct yourself in California. I don't know. I don't care. But if you come to this cafe, *by God*, put on some decent clothes and run a comb through your hair first. This is not the Tenderloin district of San Fran-fucking-cisco, and we don't serve customers that are on tranq or fentanyl. Get your shit together and get a job."

He started to turn away and collect his discarded tray and dishes, wondering exactly where the hell that had come from when a scattering of spontaneous applause broke out around the cafe. It was led by the ladies behind the counter, but was not limited to them, and he managed to keep his head down and mumble only a few thank yous as he made his way back there and gently placed the dishes beside the sink, intent on keeping his head down and doing his job. Yet the applause continued.

"What was that all about?" Shirley asked. She had to be getting close to seventy, and she was peering at her daughter.

Heidi stepped closer to her mom. "Don't freak out, but that girl in the fuzzy pajamas accused you of putting cream in her soy latte."

"That little skank over there?" Shirley asked, pointing right at the girl. Brian cringed inwardly; Heidi did it outwardly. Shirley maintained her point for a good few seconds, then, low enough that no one but Brian and Heidi could hear her, said, "Well, she's right. I did."

Heidi's face fell; aghast. "Why would you do that, mom?"

"Why?" Shirley asked, utterly unfazed. "Because fuck her, that's why. Also, we're out of soy milk, and I ain't paying bodega prices for a refill when I can buy another two tubs of that shit tonight at Walmart for a fraction of it."

Brian kind of felt like he wanted to die of mortification. But he couldn't because there was still a trailing amount of applause filling the place. The vegan girl had already gathered her things and was leaving, which made him feel...something. Not good. Not bad. But something.

"I think they want an encore." Heidi Schweizer, the younger of the mother-daughter duo that ran the place, sidled up to him, a half-made cappuccino in hand. He gave a her look; she was dark-haired and middle-aged, but with a puckish sort of cast to her face most of the time, like she had caught a joke that most around her had missed, and it gave her real power. "Where'd that come from, anyway?"

Brian had an answer, but he didn't really like it. "I just opened my mouth and my father came out."

"That happens," Heidi said, giving him a pat on the arm. "And let me tell you something else: it gets worse as you get older." She said it all loud enough her mother, only a few steps away, could clearly hear her.

"Yes, you're now halfway to brilliance," Shirley Schweizer said. Steel-haired, steel-countenanced, she was a good boss – but not someone he'd want to cross. "I estimate that by you time you reach my age, you'll be steeped to perfection. Speaking of," and Shirley raised her head from the drink she'd been working on, "Chai tea! for..." She stared down at the customer ticket. "Hendricks. Oh. You. Cowboy hat guy."

Brian spun, making a mess of things as a wave of water came out of the sink where he'd been washing the dishes. Hendricks? Cowboy hat? Here?

And sure enough, leering at him with a cup of tea in hand, looking a little leaner, a little rangier than when last he'd laid eyes on the cowboy, was Hendricks, that big hat hanging over his head like a beacon that said, "I don't belong in New York."

"WHAT THE FUCK are you doing in New York City?" Brian Longholt asked Hendricks, miserably, sitting across from him at one of the little coffeehouse's tables.

This was Hendricks's first time in New York City, and he was not, thus far, loving it. Everything was so fucking small. Take this booth, for instance: it was a tiny table, a two-seater, the only open one in the place, and it was a foot, max, from the next table just like it. He felt like he was practically sitting on top of the glasses-wearing dweeb pecking away at his keyboard.

"I'm here to play Sulla," Hendricks said, brushing the little granules of sugar off his palms where they'd collected when he'd put them, slightly moist, upon the surface of the table. "You know what I mean when I say that, college boy?"

Brian just stared at him blankly. "You're going to invade Rome and issue proscriptions for people you want to steal from?"

Hendricks felt an exceedingly steely calm. Maybe it was because Micah was standing over his shoulder like the Wrath of God ready to descend. Maybe it was the knowledge that Katlin "Kitty" Elizabeth was not long for this earth. Maybe it was that he half-expected something snide and shitty from Brian, so receiving instead an earnest attempt to decipher Hendricks's cryptic statement was a welcome pleasure, like waking up to a surprise blowjob from your wife. God, he missed those.

"'No friend ever served me, and no enemy ever wronged me, whom I have not repaid in full,'" Hendricks said. "You know what that means? In this context?"

Brian looked up at him, a little extra misery poured over him, and nodded. "Kitty."

Hendricks looked up at Micah. Hell, he'd offered him the seat, but Gunny wanted to stand. "Smart boy," Micah said, standing there like an oak. He was casting a look around the place, as if expecting demons to come busting in at any time. Not that Gunny even believed in demons – yet. Though they were about to fix that.

"Well, he did spend his parents' fortune trying to disprove it by getting a degree in philosophy from Brown," Hendricks said. "But yeah, he's not totally stupid. And yes – I'm taking her off the board tonight. Could really use a hand."

"I'm out of that business, man," Brian said, keeping his eyes squarely on the table in front of him. "You know that."

"No," Hendricks said. "I know you left. I don't think you're done, though. Because a man who's been through what you've been through? He's bound to have some real regrets, the kinds of things that keep him from getting a full night's sleep." He lowered his head, trying to invade Brian's field of vision; he'd already knocked the implacable look from the kid's face. Now he was grimacing, and it was doubtful he even knew he was. "A man who's been through what you have who runs? He's going to be running the rest of his life. And that's some heinous shit to always have over your shoulder."

"What do you want from me?" Brian asked, finally looking up at him. And boy, did the despair just drip out of him. "I already showed you what kind of person I am – I ran. I'm a coward."

"You fought before," Hendricks said. "I've seen cowards. They're cowards all the time. They don't get a semi truck and crash it at high speed into a nigh indestructible demon. They run."

"But I ran," Brian said softly.

Gunny came down on the table and hit it, rocking Hendricks's tea. "And the question in front of your candy ass now is – are you going to keep running for the rest of your life? Or are you going to turn and make a stand?"

Hendricks picked up his tea. He'd just driven umpteen hours to get from Nashville to NYC, and needed this as a soothing balm before he'd – hopefully – get a little shut eye before the operation tonight. Fancy way of saying they were going into Kitty Elizabeth's penthouse to conduct business. "Gunny here, he's the best. He trained me. See, I don't necessarily believe in cowards. I think there's trained and untrained people. Maybe you hit your limit. Maybe your got in over your head. Whatever happened to you, it seems obvious you have at least a little glass still in your gullet. So my question to you, Brian Longholt," and here Hendricks leaned in, conspiratorially, "you want to think yourself a coward unto the end of your days? Or do you want to take one last chance to prove to the man in the mirror that you have some fight left in you?"

Brian stared at him, just for a moment, and then his eyes fluttered closed. "What do you want me to do?"

"To be a man, goddamn you," Gunny said. Which seemed over the top, because Hendricks knew they already had him.

"We need you to watch our backs," Hendricks said. "And also...to drive. Because this town?" He waved a hand around him. "This place is nuts."

Brian seemed to think about it for a moment. "All right." And that was it. They had one more.

NINE

DESOLATE PLACES

Erin stared out the window at the shit-brown sky. She'd seen a lot of colors of sky in her time. Blue, of course. Black. Sun so bright it turned it yellowish. Even, naturally, purple, navy, and all the shades between blue and black.

But brown? That was a new one on her.

"I saw the truck leaving as we pulled away," Duncan said, almost wistfully – or was she imagining that? "Last cord with the outside world, cut." He made a light chopping motion with his hand, as though he were planning to cut off his own arm with his hand. Could he do that? Maybe. He was a demon, and those shells were weirdly firm and unyielding.

"We don't figure our shit out," Erin said, through the faint stirrings of a whiskey headache (she did not wish to say hangover), "there's not gonna be an outside world." She let a blistering string of curses escape her lips as she contemplated the past, the future, and all points between.

"That was for Hendricks, right?" Duncan asked with a faintly self-satisfied smile.

"What?" It came out much more snappish than she anticipated, like he'd snuck a punch under her defenses and got her right where it counted. "I wasn't even thinking of that dickweed."

"Until I said something? I doubt that."

"Well, I wasn't," she said, putting a growl in it. She'd been having a perfectly reasonable pre-apocalyptic day until he'd said that. Why the hell had he needed to go and mention the cowboy? Talk about a sore spot. Or a soft spot. Or both. Though Hendricks himself was more of a hard spot, one that fit nicely between her legs–

"Fucker," she said under her breath.

"I do miss reading," Duncan said, looking out the window.

"What?" she asked, whole face scrunched up. "Do you mean miss reading? Or you misread people?"

Duncan cocked his head slightly, in the manner of a dog contemplating an extreme pronouncement from its master. "Well, I have lost the ability to read people. And I miss that. That's the point I was trying to express. Never been much of a book reader. Though I did try to get into it at one point, right in the middle of the *Twilight* craze."

Erin felt like he might be pulling her leg, but she was game. "...And?"

He shrugged. "They were fine. I don't think reading's for me, at least not that kind."

"Not sure small talk is a strength of yours either, buddy boy."

"Very true," Duncan said. "Lerner was always the talker. Could not get him to shut up, even when I wanted him to."

"That betrayal come as a surprise to you?" Erin asked, watching him out of the corner of her eye.

"'The betrayal?'" Duncan asked, face now its normal blank. "Do you mean the most recent one, by me, against the Pact? Or the original one, all those millennia ago?"

"Well, I was talking about the freshest in mind. Since I wasn't alive for the other one."

"You're right, you weren't – unless you're hiding some deep secret I don't know about."

She bit her lip a little. "Only secret I think I'm hiding is that I might have been a little in love with Hendricks."

He didn't react much to that. Not that he did to anything. Except to say, "Sweetie, that's not a secret to anyone except maybe – maybe – Hendricks himself. The lunkhead."

"Yeah," she whispered. "I messed up, Duncan. Did you mess with Lerner like that?"

"Our relationship was never sexual, but no," Duncan said. "We just grew apart. He wanted things to go along the same path, and I...didn't. Rather suddenly. Which is funny, because, before he went back, he was on much more of a path to change than I was. Way more into people and emotions than I was. You probably don't remember when his shell cracked–"

"I was a little busy being in a coma at the time."

"–but his last words, his last memory, were about a woman we watched die years and years ago. And he was picturing himself in that moment with her, actually identifying with her, seeing himself in her shoes." Duncan paused, staring out the window at the shit-brown sky, the skidmarked sky, the sharted sky. "When he came back, everything was different."

"Why do you think that is?"

Duncan bestirred himself to look at her. "My guess? Based on what he said? He went back after a hundred-plus years of exposure to human culture and got a blast-dose of the old war propaganda. Demon boots on the march, songs of conquest and victory, like going to a rally after being in solitary confinement for a long stretch. You know at a concert there's an energy in the air?"

"Sure. If the band doesn't suck."

"People feed off each other in crowds," Duncan said. "Demons are like that, too – or we can be, if you get enough of us together. You see it from humans when riots break out these days, especially all the negative emotion just bleeding off you. You could see it, too, in societies before war, like the Nazis before they jumped off into all those various countries they invaded. Not that I was there for all of it, but I saw enough–"

Erin found herself doing the dumb-dog head-cock. "You were in Germany 'round World War II?"

"Just before," Duncan said. "You surprised that demon activity rose around the Third Reich?"

"I guess I shouldn't be," Erin said. "What they did was demonic."

"Oh, I'm sorry," Duncan said. "I didn't mean to mislead – very little of what the Nazis did – maybe none of it, even – was caused or steered by demons. That was all you." He flashed her a sad smile. "Some of our kind did opportunistically take advantage of the cover it provided, though. That's why I was there. To limit the exploitation. Anyway – point is, crowds. They go mad, because humans in groups transmit emotional energy. Demons are the same. It's really hard to be that one guy in the Nazi photograph who's not saluting, because 99 out of a 100 of you are go-with-the-flow types, and whenever you get that many people together, the flow is powerful. Like a raging river overrunning its banks."

"Huh."

"Imagine that, times a million, times more. That's what Lerner got a dose of when he went back." Duncan stared out the window again; Erin was bringing the car to a coasting stop along Mill Road's green edge. "It washed away whatever changes he was going through. All that's left now is what was there to begin with – a bitter, angry soul that's been cut off from the possibility of anything but damnation. And we are about to see the damnation in full force, on the march."

"We're here," Erin said, almost sorry to have to break the spell he'd been casting. Behind her, she could see Arch pull in, and behind that, the Wrightson plumbing van and Barney Jones's Buick.

"Let's go save these kids, huh?" Duncan said, throwing his door open. His feet crunched against the dry grass.

"Yeah," Erin said. And she got out in spite of that nervous tingle in her stomach that seemed to eat at the lining like strong coffee with no breakfast to dilute it down.

ARCH CHOKED on the increasingly strong smell of green wood being burnt all around them. The fires had spread into the older, deeper woods, and the scent was terrible. Most people were used to smelling wood smoke of the variety that had been properly seasoned, left to dry for a spell, given a chance to get all that fresh, wet sap out before it was thrown on the fire. The result was a pleasant aroma.

None of that here. This was rank, and in such volume that Arch felt tying a wet bandana to his face might be an appropriate option if any more acreage went up. No time for that now, though. He popped the trunk and snagged his rifle. "Gonna need to go in fast and loud here," he said, to no one in particular and yet everyone all at once.

"Fast and nasty is the only way our family does things, deputy," Larry Wrightson said. He cackled as he wandered away, carrying an AK-47.

"That is the least surprising bit of news I've maybe ever heard," Erin said, appearing in front of him with her own rifle.

She glanced over her shoulder. "We're gonna need to be a little careful letting loose with Duncan hanging around."

Arch raised an eyebrow. "Those bullets will kill us just as sure as him."

"Right," Erin said, shaking her head. She had a green-at-the-gills look about her, like she'd been sick today. Which she probably had, judging by the scent of whiskey coming off her.

"Take it easy with the gunfire in there, folks," Arch said, raising his voice. Everyone had one now, mostly of the AR variety, all blessed. A big van pulled up in the rear of the convoy and out popped Casey Meacham, along with Chauncey Watson, his big glasses glinting even in the smoke-addled daylight. Which came as a slight surprise to Arch; he wondered if maybe Chauncey had left with the others last night since he hadn't been in attendance when the big worm showed up.

"What are we dealing with here, Arch?" Chauncey asked. First to get situated and get his thoughts about him, Arch reckoned.

Arch looked into the trees beside the road. "Reckon we're...what? Quarter mile from the mill? Kids were abducted about here," and he pointed at the crashed car that was sandwiched between a couple trees, hood caved in. Someone had smacked into it pretty good, and there were a couple of child seats in the back that showed signs of being torn up. "Dragged in that direction. So we go through the woods, try and see what we can, but the only point of interest nearby is the mill, so we'll head that way. If we see something that suggests they went elsewhere, then elsewhere we'll go. Otherwise..." And he pointed toward the mill. What was it Hendricks always said at moments like this? That military phrasing, so crisp, so clear...Arch remembered it. "Fall in." And they started moving.

BRAEDEN DIDN'T HAVE a ton of experience with his AR-15, but he had enough to feel somewhat comfortable with it as they started the slog through the woods. Brush cracked dryly with every step, the lack of rain feeding the death of this patch of ground. "What do you suppose is holding back the rains?" Braeden asked, listening to a twig snap under the tread of his boots. "I mean, before we lost contact with the outside world, I was still watching the TV, and Chattanooga was getting rain. Knoxville was getting rain. No one else around us was in a drought."

"It's like God singled us out for a very special form of torment," Terri said, that ring of defeat visible in the slump of her shoulders, which were bare and tanned beneath the stained, faded white of her tank top. But she was soldiering on.

"I don't think it's the doing of God," Barney said. "I don't think it's him at all."

"Feels like if God was all-powerful," she said, huffing a little because she was walking on uneven ground, "he'd be able to drop some rain."

"You're assuming a lot," Duncan said, the demon making his way up alongside them. "One, that God exists. Two, he's all-powerful. Three...that he wants to help you." The straight-faced way he delivered these were maybe the worst part of them.

"Yes, I assume that," Barney said. "Do you wish to dispute it for me? With your advanced demon knowledge that I can't argue with?" The preacher smirked. "Because I have an answer for that, too.

Duncan hesitated. "Sorry, preacher," he said after a moment. "Arguing religion with humans was – is – the province of my former partner. I think I picked up one of his bad habits."

Jones raised an eyebrow. "Why did your old partner do that?"

Duncan did not react. "Because he could. Because he

wanted to." Then he shrugged. "Because it was fun, I think, arguing against people who believe but don't *know*."

"You know what I think's fun?" Terri cracked a smile. "Being anywhere but here, doing anything but this."

"Amen," Braeden said.

Duncan looked at them both for a second. "Humor me, then – why are you here?"

Terri exchanged a look with Braeden, and seemed to nod to him as if in deference. He took that as his cue to speak, so he did, slow and plodding at first, but gaining speed as he got his thoughts together. "These demons took everything I had left – except this town. Now maybe you know this, maybe you don't – I was a mechanic by trade. Most of the things I do in my job I don't do for fun. I figure if I lose this town, I lose the last bit I've got left of my wife and my daughter." He nodded. "And that's before the whole world-ending thing came into play."

"That's a good answer," Duncan said, shifting his gaze to Terri. "What about you?"

"I got nowhere else to be," Terri said, without missing a beat.

"And you, reverend?" Duncan asked, turning to Barney. "Is this a holy war for you?"

"I was a chaplain in Vietnam, and I can tell you there is nothing holy about war," Jones said, his own shoes crunching the underbrush. Ahead, the trees were starting to clear, and the metal pipes and towers of the mill were visible in the breaks. "I do find it nice that this one's a little more clear-cut as to who's evil and who's not."

"Must be nice to have that moral clarity," Duncan said. And there was not a trace of sarcasm about him.

"Do you not have moral clarity on this?" Terri asked.

"How do I say this without – aww, fuck it," Duncan said, shaking his head, like he had just made a decision on something momentous. "I made a decision a long time ago, along with a great many others, to do what felt right, felt good, in the moment – and was absolutely against what I knew was actually right in my heart, or whatever place you humans put your moral reasoning. You could call it pride that made me do it, and I think you'd be mostly right, but whatever the case...moral clarity went out the window afterwards.

"Because, see, once you start a war with someone," Duncan said, staring straight ahead, "you lose the right to be offended when they strike back, when they escalate, when there are consequences you can barely bear, and they fall all around you, on your head, like a rain of blows or bricks or oxcarts. You can rail at the sky but it's empty and quiet." He seemed to be drifting, walking without effort, speaking without knowing they were even there any longer. "And all your morals are gone, gone because why would you have them, they were a thing of before, a world before, and now you're free and unfettered–

"But unfettered is just another word for unmoored," Duncan whispered. He shook his head, seemed to come back to himself. "I am not bound to your system of morality. If anything, I'm disincentivized from it. Hell doesn't care for decency. It cares about power, about desire, about want. See, that's the real secret to hell that most people don't realize." He smiled, but it was hollow, and there was something terrible about it. "Hell is not just fire blackening the skin you no longer have or any such physical thing. It's desire blackening your soul; it's getting every *thing* you thought you wanted in this world – money, huge house, sports car, bling, private jet, billions to drop in a casino, video games, millions of empty-eyed, empty-headed whores fawning all over you, forever – and realizing it's all so hollow and empty and pointless that living with it for eternity is suffering rather than triumph. No lake of fire necessary; it's crushing disappointment and the soul-deep feeling that there was so much more than this, and you could have had it if you hadn't been so damned stupid."

That produced a quiet as Duncan lapsed back into silence. Braeden looked at Terri; her eyebrows were up, almost in the swirls of long hair that acted like bangs except they were just slightly straying from her ponytail in the space over her forehead. It was a cute look. "Wow," she said. "That's, uh...intense. Though I'm not sure I understand what you mean."

"Pray you don't find out," Duncan said, and his voice held a slight rasp, like he had either spoken not nearly enough or entirely too much. With his baton clutched tightly in hand, he wandered off, taking a tangent away from their small party toward the far edge of the group, past Gary Wrightson, who was being pushed hard through the underbrush by his brother, the one with the smooth, pudgy cheeks and well-kept appearance. Terry? Yeah. That seemed right. Larry was the long-haired troublemaker. Braeden had only known Paul, the name-outcast, who was now dead.

"Pastor Jones?" The soft voice of Lauren Darlington interrupted Braeden's train of thought, and he turned to find the good doctor easing over toward Barney, who favored her with a smile.

"I think we're past titles, now, Lauren," Barney said. "You don't call me 'reverend,' I won't bother with, 'doctor.'"

"Fair trade," she said. "Listen, I hate to even ask this, but you're the, uhm...oldest one in the Watch. And I have some questions about construction on the Tallakeet Dam."

"Weird time to start thinking about construction projects," Terri said.

"I'm not sure how much help I can even be," Barney said. "The Tallakeet Dam was built as part of the New Deal. I wasn't even born until '50. Most of what I know about it was from the tales my grandpappy told me about the old settlement they cleared in order to build the reservoir."

Braeden knew what he was talking about; when the water level had gotten real low last summer, the buildings that had once stood there had emerged from the receding waters like skeletons from a grave. There'd always been an old silo that stuck out down the river path, but now you could see a whole town that had once been inhabited - before the reservoir had flooded it.

Terri was wearing a cringe. "Did they...flood an old slave settlement? Because I could see the government doing that?"

Barney chuckled. "No, it was a white folks settlement. I'm sure they would have, without a moment's thought, and probably with a lot less concern for properly enforced eminent domain." He crunched through the underbrush, the end of the woods growing ever nearer. "To be honest, it made grandpappy chuckle that those white folks had got the short end of the stick, because that was some of the most fertile land in the valley. He and the other black folks were on higher ground, real rocky ground, scratching out a living." He shrugged. "Anyway, ask your questions. I'll answer 'em if I can – but I doubt I can."

THAT ANSWER from Jones didn't leave Lauren hopeful. She was trying to do two things at once, economize with her time. One, rescue the kids, because how could she let them just die to demons? And two, tug on the thread of this theory she had about the dam project hiding the gate, a thought which had fully seized her mind and was holding tightly to it, even as she trudged through the woods holding a gun she wasn't comfortable with, in shoes she wasn't comfortable with, and with an air temperature that was awfully warm for winter.

Also, the air itself stunk, and little embers would occasionally find their way onto her from the distant wildfires. It was actually fortunate she'd run out of hairspray, because one of those suckers landing on her head on a normal product day would result in an explosion, giving her a crown of flames to rival the wildfires. Talk about things going to hell.

"I had a theory," Lauren said, letting the words rush out, needing to get this out to as many people as possible as quickly as possible, because, facing the God's honest truth, she could die in the next five minutes. If no one knew her theory, that was probably the end. "That maybe the government knew about the fact there's a gate here. And that maybe the giant construction project that is the Tallakeet Dam covered up that fact, and that it's buried somewhere in the guts of the structure."

"That sounds like the plot of the first Transformers movie," Terri Pritchard said, frowning.

"Hey, if you can think of another place where that gate could be hiding around here, I'm all ears," Lauren said. "But it seems to me that the government is definitely on the demon train, and that if they wanted to hide something, a big-ass federal project would be the way to go about it."

"Why now, though?" Braeden Tarley asked, his bushy eyebrows knitting together. "I mean, after our battle to the death with the feds trucking in that water, I accept your thesis about the government being deeply in bed with the demons–" He paused, because there was a grunt and a mumble that ran through the entire Watch around them – because apparently everyone lacked for anything better to do than listen to her – before continuing. "–but it doesn't feel like the feds being in with the demons is a new thing. And if what you're saying is true, and Tallakeet is hiding this gate, then...why wait until now to go for it? Why not years back?"

"That's a good point, and I don't reckon I know anything that'd help you," Barney Jones said, shaking his head. "My knowledge of that project is limited to what it destroyed, and grandpappy didn't ever say anything about a gate – not that he would have known."

"Construction started on the Tallakeet Dam in August of 1940," Chauncey Watson said, and Lauren turned her head to realize he'd eased in on her, and was now walking almost at her elbow. Good thing he wasn't a demon. "It took three years, and was part of the flood-control plan that followed in the wake of the massive floods of the twenties and thirties. Plus the hydro-electrics brought power to the whole area. So there was a reason to build the project beyond any supposed gate." He shrugged his skinny shoulders, his magnified eyes in all earnestness.

"Huh," Lauren said, frowning. Maybe she was wrong about this? "Y'all raise some good points. I guess I'm just not sure where this gate would be if it's not hidden by some giant structure, you know?"

"How big is it?" Gary Wrightson asked. The wheelchair was leaving ruts in the ground behind it, his brother pushing aside and crunching the dried leaves. Fortunately the ground was hard-packed, or else he'd probably be struggling even more with it. "Because if it's the size of a door, it could be anywhere. If it's big as a semi trailer, that limits the placement a little more."

"Anyone see any signs of movement?" Arch called from the fore.

"I got a trail here," Casey Meacham said, pointing at the ground and, frankly, surprising the hell out of Lauren. She never really thought of him as any kind of tracker for anything other than ass. But he was a taxidermist, so she supposed being a hunter dovetailed with that. "Something moved through here that was big – and big-footed."

"Hear that?" Larry Wrightson asked with a smirk. "Bigfoot came through here."

"Shut your dumb fucking mouth," Gary muttered. His pale girlfriend, Marina, was walking a couple steps behind. His voice was tense, his eyes ahead, as they broke out of the thin strip of woods onto the road that led to the mill's parking lot. Lauren's foot touched pavement, and under that brown sky she adjusted the sling on her AR-15, feeling like somehow it was heavier than the gallons of holy water she usually had slung over her shoulders.

GARY DIDN'T QUITE BREATHE a sigh of relief as his wheels hit pavement on the mill's parking lot, but close. Real close. He was sick of Terry pushing him, and said so, snappish, peeved, pissed as hell, and took over the wheels for himself.

Terry took it in good humor, like he mostly did. "You're welcome," he said, pretty good-natured, that smooth-faced fuck.

Gary did pause, though, stopping and spinning about with a quick burst of speed. He looked up at his brother. "Thank you."

Terry's eyebrows rose a touch, and he nodded. Message sent, message received. No more need for words.

"Now let's go get these kids," Gary said, and spun back around. The mill stood ahead, with all its steam pipes and corrugated metal buildings that were shaded the same crap brown as the skies. He went right for it, too.

ARCH HAD HIS PURPOSE SET, and only paused at the parking lot, sweeping left, then right, to see what awaited at either end of the mill complex. And a complex it was; ten or twenty buildings, depending on how one wanted to count them, subtly divided in places he couldn't distinguish with his own eye. One blended into the next, and all were covered in a series of pipes, valves, and machinery that made the place look like it had endless metal grafted onto corrugated walls. He was used to it being shrouded in a perpetual fog of steam that it emitted. Today, though, it was shrouded in smoke from the wildfires, a haze that seemed to be growing worse by the hour.

"Any sign of them?" Arch asked, looking right at – for some reason – Casey Meacham.

Meacham had not yet stepped foot on the pavement, and was shuffling around in the dead grass just before the asphalt. "They were headed straight forward when they hit the parking lot." He pointed at the nearest building, which had only a couple smokestacks sticking out of it. Usually when you got this close to the mill, while it was running, the noise was so loud you couldn't hear yourself think. Arch had busted a couple of drug deals in the parking lot back in the old days, before he worried about demons and stolen children, and only had to concern himself with methamphetamines, and human, garden-variety violence.

"So they went right for it," Erin said, clutching up on her gun a bit tighter. She'd put on an olive drab green plate carrier from the equipment locker, and it hung mighty big on her small frame. "Think they're holed up in there?"

Arch frowned. "Go past the mill and you're in the Caledonia River. Since they straight-lined it here from that car...I reckon this must be their nest." He carefully slid back the bolt on his rifle just to confirm he had a round in the chamber. "Must have moved in after the last tenant vacated the place."

"I am not looking forward to getting into the guts of this place," Casey Meacham said, "which is not a sentiment I think I've ever expressed before. I'm usually real keen to get into the guts, y'all know."

"All too well," Erin said, peeling her lips back in disgust.

"This is a big facility," Arch said. "Ten stories at the height. Multiple buildings. We need to stick together. Search methodically, so we don't get divided and conquered." He turned his attention to the tallest building, with a metal scaffolding sloping off it like some kind of slide, making its way down to the ground on the far side of the complex. And the tanks! There were so many tanks, for water or chemicals, they seemed to be everywhere. "There are a lot of places to hide, so let's hope they left a trail for us to follow, or we might be here a long while."

"And that's before we get to the pits and mines on the back side of the property," Chauncey Watson said cheerfully. "They got this one pit that's hundreds of feet long – I saw it on the satellite imagery – I swear it looks like they dump logs right in there to soak or something. Big enough I bet you could play football in it – if not for the logs, of course."

"Thank you for that, Chauncey," Arch said. "Only way out is through it, so let's get to it." That was from his football coach. High school, not college. Man didn't exactly have a way with words, but that one stuck. Probably cuz he heard it so much.

"Good speech," Erin said, at his elbow as they walked through the parking lot. Surprisingly – or maybe not – there were still a few cars here. Of the type that looked like they'd never run, or at least never run again.

He eyed a broken-down Ford Taurus from the mid-nineties as he walked past it, pondering Erin's comment. "Probably worse than whatever you'd have come up with."

"Doubt it," Erin said, a little airily. That open door was looming ahead, just waiting for 'em to come in, it seemed. Gave Arch a little rumble in his belly thinking about what might be waiting inside.

"The safety protocols in this plant are top notch," Chauncey said. "I've talked to some of the fellows that work there and you wouldn't think it, but they are. Though I've heard the firefighting equipment is a little out of date."

"Oh?" Lauren Darlington answered him, presumably out of an abundance of politeness.

Arch stepped through the open door and swept his gun left and right, searching for signs of trouble. He didn't find any, at least not any obvious ones, but did find himself in a large, open plant floor with industrial machinery roughly the height of his chin ahead of him in two lines. Catwalks hung thirty or more feet above, bare and empty, the metal quiet.

Heck, the whole place was quiet. He wanted to say, "Too quiet," but in a place of demons, there was no such thing, was there?

BRAEDEN WASN'T first into the plant, not even tenth, but he wasn't bringing up the rear, either. Catwalks above lined all four sides of the room, and visible doors in the far corner of the upstairs led elsewhere in the plant, other buildings. As for the ground floor, the machinery lines in the middle of the room cut off Braeden's view of what lay beyond.

The lack of motion beyond their crew, the lack of sound in the expansive, warehouse-sized space, didn't give Braeden much reassurance. The woods had been quiet last night, too – until they weren't.

"You know that old saying about silence being golden?" Terri was easing along beside the bare factory line. It was about four feet across and composed of rollers; Braeden could only assume paper, freshly pulped, rolled across it when the mill was running.

"Really old saying," Braeden muttered back, and caught the flush of mild red at Terri's cheeks. She turned her head enough to give him sharp, if slightly amused look. "Uh...sorry?"

"Whippersnapper," she said with the trace of a smile. She wasn't that much older than him.

"It's very golden, though," Braeden said, almost bumping

into Casey Meacham, who'd paused to peer over the line, his rifle elevated in an awkward position, as if to blind fire over the obstruction. Braeden kept his rifle tight to his shoulder, but pointed at the floor. The last thing they needed in a moment of high tension like this was to have a friendly fire incident.

"SOMEONE SHOULD CHECK THE CATWALK," Erin said, feeling a little stir of initiative. Looking up at the metal structure that ringed the square room, she found it...discomforting. "Cover us from up there, especially since there's not shit up there right now."

"Sure," Arch said. He seemed...reserved. Or maybe just nervous about what was still to come. It was a big complex after all, lots of room for nerves to gnaw at you, especially as you crawled through the whole place looking for kid-stealing demons. "Take someone else with you, though."

"I'll go with you, Erin," Chauncey Watson said, brushing back his glasses with one hand. She gave him a nod – best she could hope for to watch her back right now – and headed for the metal staircase nearest to them, intent on putting herself above everyone – at least physically. She knew where she sat in the hierarchy, and by her reckoning, right now, it was not even in the goddamned basement. She was at the center of the earth.

DUNCAN HEARD the squeak in the distance, and was certain he'd be the only one who did. "Nobody else heard that, right?" he asked. Just to confirm.

It rang out, at least in his mind, in his essence. But somehow he knew it was below the audible threshold for the humans he was bunched up with. Terry Wrightson was already up and on the conveyor, pointing his gun down and around the machinery to the expanse of floor beyond. About twenty feet of it, then another conveyor, this one not composed of metal rollers but an actual rubber conveyor. What was it meant to convey? Hell if Duncan knew.

The squeak, though. Was it just machinery settling? Or a door opening somewhere else in the complex? Duncan did not know. But he was equally sure he did not want to find out.

"I don't hear anything except this fatass climbing on a line that's not meant to hold his weight," Gary Wrightson said, already scooting along in his chair, rolling down the line, gun on his lap, that determination ever present in his eyes...well, still present.

"Thinner than you, pig fucker," Terry called out. Then: "Sorry, Marina. Didn't mean it like that."

"Is fine," the European girl said. She gave him a look. "Did not hear anything, either, though."

"Great," Duncan said. He didn't have the space to doubt himself. He knew what he'd heard. He just wasn't sure if it was ominous or ordinary.

"HRMPH," Lauren pronounced to herself – well, mostly, anyway. She'd broken right, nominally, behind Gary and Marina, but was lingering, bringing up the rear behind the first conveyor line, not wanting to match Terry Wrightson's vault over the machinery. The metal conveyors came to just below her breastbone, and once she was over them, she felt she'd be truly committed to this space. And like an interior designer not sure if she wanted a job, Lauren was uncertain about this room.

"Whatcha hrmphing about?" Barney Jones asked. "Still thinking about your dam theory?"

"No," Lauren said, keeping her gun pointed firmly at the floor. Lessons from her father that stuck were few and far between, but that one she did remember. Safe direction – until it was time to stop being safe. "I was thinking about Paul Cummings, and how I saw him get his truck on the road before we left. The last boat out just left. No one else is coming now."

Jones nodded slowly. "I sent my wife with him."

"Awww," Lauren said, feeling a torrent of emotions. Sentiment, mostly. "The quality of the cooking in this town just took a real shit dive with Olivia gone." She matched his smile at that comment. "But it starts to feel final, y'know? With only a handful of us left."

"It does," Jones said. "We bled support – and it was an arterial bleed. Hard to believe we went from a Watch that challenged and triumphed over a government convoy a month or so ago to now being able to rattle around in a school bus."

Lauren was nodding when she heard something. Something that was beyond the range of a squeak, but outside the sound of the metal conveyors being strained by someone's weight on them. No one was even on the conveyor right now, she realized as she turned to look. Terry was in the perimeter of the factory lines, but everyone else was creeping left or right, heading for the easier entry points to the simple maze at the center of the building. Paths of least resistance, those, which did not include climbing over shut-down lines.

"It all comes down to us, though," Lauren said, looking around. "And Father Nguyen, back at the church."

"And a very few others," Jones said with a muted smile as they trudged along. Ducking under a point in the line that started to climb upward, he craned his neck and followed

Marina, his gun pointed at the ceiling. "What's that Shakespeare quote? 'We happy few?'"

"I don't think I know much Shakespeare," Lauren said, only having to duck a little to get under the line. "They might have covered it in school when I was out having a baby. Or they might just not have covered it. This is Midian, after all. Shakespeare's not the most in-demand read. James Patterson seems much more this town's speed."

"Was always a bit of a Dan Brown fan myself."

"You and a whole bunch of other people," Lauren said. Now they were in the middle of it, the lines surrounding them on all sides, the catwalks looking down on them from above. The only solace was the lack of motion, the lack of noise. If the attack was to come, perhaps it would come later.

"Casey?" Arch asked. He'd entered the line some forty feet across the room, opposite them. The taxidermist had gone along with him and stopped, examining the ground as though it were a leafy piece of woods, where he could paw at the dirt and produce a conclusion about which way something went. Lauren glanced at the concrete floor and determined – nope, she couldn't see anything except the natural, cloudy look of the concrete.

"This is weird," Casey said, frowning. He looked up, and Lauren looked with him. Sure, there was the catwalk, which was squeaking as Erin and Chauncey climbed the stairs leading to it; they'd just about reached the level. The cloudy windows shed a bit of light. A few pipes, some HVAC ductwork, and, of course, the sprinkler heads for the fire suppression system broke the outline of the rafters.

"Don't keep us in suspense, fucknugget," Gary Wrightson said. He'd maneuvered the wheelchair under the line just ahead of her, and was heading toward the center of the factory floor, where his brother awaited. "Spill."

"No trail here," Casey said. "Not that I can see, anyway." He pressed his fingers against the floor. "No dust, see?" And he lifted them up, showing them to everyone. "But there oughta be dust. Oughta be ash, hell, from just the last day of the wildfires, right? But there's nothing." He wrinkled his nose. "Which makes me wonder...how?"

"I never would have would have pegged the guy who likes to be pegged to figure it out first."

The voice rang out through the room, and Lauren froze, along with the rest. They were split; guns were pointing in all directions, but in all directions...

...There was nothing. Bare walls, empty catwalks, and a factory floor bereft of life.

"What is that supposed to mean?" Lauren asked. She started to turn, to see if someone had an idea – about who had spoken, about what it all meant–

But when she turned, the plant was gone, and so were the catwalks, and so was the Watch. Gone were the guns, the worried looks, and replacing it...

...Was Molly.

ARCH WAS on the floor of the mill one minute, and in the next he was in bed with Alison. It was like the walls had closed in on him, like he'd woken up from the world's worst nightmare, and suddenly he wasn't cold anymore, he was warm, and she was pressed against him, her long, blond hair tickling his nose.

It seemed very natural, to be without a gun and back in bed, her bare back visible as he checked it. Every mole was in the right place, every curve was exactly as he remembered it, and a relaxing feeling came over him, coursing through his veins, and he lay back down on the soft mattress and felt her stir beside him.

"It's funny how quick we get used to things," Alison said, snuggling back against him in that way she had. Okay, it wasn't so much snuggling as grinding her butt against his crotch to see what happened. Well, she always knew what would happen. That seemed to be half the fun for her. "Humans are adaptable creatures."

"Hmm," Arch said, through the veil of sleepiness that had come over him. It was like he'd just drifted off, and he liked that. Liked it quite a bit, actually. As though he hadn't gotten a proper night of sleep in a long time, and now he just found himself out, with nothing to do but nap.

A flash of red hair beneath the blond didn't even do anything but make him go, "Hmmm," again. Because it was his wife beside him, and things were the way they were supposed to be, the way they ought to be, and the fact that they were not the way they had been only a moment earlier was only a small tickle in the back of his clouded mind.

THE TABLE in the Wrightson house was always a chaotic place. Insults always flew, and sometimes food did, too, as an extension of the insults. But whoever threw knew that Mother Mary was going to have her revenge, so it didn't typically rise to that level of conflict. Not since the Great Food Fight of Thanksgiving 2014, anyhow.

If the truth was told, though, Gary preferred it that way. Peace and quiet was for his house, where he lived alone. Chaos was the calling card of the family home. He didn't come to his mother's house to feel his blood pressure fall. He didn't come to feel it rise, either, he just understood that was a byproduct of a family dinner.

"What are you grinning at, you dumb sonofabitch?" Mary was doing some grinning of her own after saying that; Gary looked up to find her leering at him, all her teeth displayed in their rough, uneven lines.

"The fact my mother just called herself a bitch," Gary said without hesitation. He looked to his right; Marina was there, smiling, kind of reassuring in her way. "You done played yourself, momma."

"I was talking about your daddy," Mary said, and slid the fried chicken toward him. Just like momma made it; he could smell. Big bowl of white gravy sitting on the table behind it, and biscuits just behind those. Man, Gary was hungry. He'd worked up an appetite.

"These are great, bro." Paul was there across the table from him, sliding the baked apples to him. The smell of cinnamon and sugar was strong, absolutely dominating the room. "You gotta give 'em a try."

"Hell yes I will," Gary said, and he stood to reach over the gravy boat to take 'em. Feeling the weight born by his legs was a unique sensation, though he couldn't quite figure out why.

"SHIT," Duncan said, because it had happened again.

The whole crew had frozen in place, stopped where they were, went slack, guns going loose and falling out of their grips. Every last human with him, this time, not an exception among them. They were standing in the middle of those empty factory lines, in the quiet haze, and Duncan realized he wasn't seeing quite right.

There weren't bare walls and empty catwalks on all sides.

There was something...else going on here. An illusory sort of spell. Like the kind of annoying illusion that fucking screen Spellman used to sell, except way more irritating, more comprehensive. If those required baby amounts of juice, this needed one of those industrial tanks of the stuff, the kind of vat the beer companies made their brews in.

"Nah, you haven't shit yet," came that voice again – Guthrie, of course. "But you will."

"I am not really capable of that," Duncan said, trying to see through the illusion. It was frayed at the edges now that he knew it was there, hints of reality peeking in if he turned his head suddenly. It wasn't visual so much as a sense pushing through to his essence, a feeling that no, they were not in a silent room by themselves. Especially since he could hear the breathing of something – some *things* – behind him.

They were surrounded by some very hostile demons. Demons with a whole lot of power, if they were running an illusion that could have made Wren Spellman look like a fucking piker. That was serious underworld power at work.

"Fuck," Duncan said, again, and shoved Braeden, who was right in front of him, the only one he could reach out and touch. "Pass it on," he said, jarring the mechanic out of whatever spell he'd been under. Seeing him blink his way out of it was little consolation, because he didn't shove the next person in line for several seconds, and Duncan had a feeling that by the time all of them had come out of it, someone – or several someones – were going to be dead.

BRAEDEN HAD BEEN CURLED up in bed on a lazy Sunday morning with his wife beside him and Abi worming her way through the sheets between them when someone – some supreme dickhead, some loathsome little infected twat hair – shoved him right out of it and back to cold, nasty reality. Suddenly he was stumbling and hitting a metal conveyor, ripping his hand open against a jagged stretch of metal, and swearing as he blinked that beautiful vision of a life he could have had right out of his eyes.

Now he was back on the floor of the mill, pissed off, the world kind of dark around him save for the dim light streaming in from above, and he did as Duncan commanded – just irritably. He slapped Terri on the ass, because he didn't want to raise his hand to drip blood on her, and hey, her ass was right there, and he was too annoyed to do much else besides stoop down and retrieve his gun.

"The fuck?" Terri turned quickly, still half out of it, and suddenly Braeden had to worry he'd pissed her off and put his head at smacking level all in one dumb move.

"You got suckered. Again." This from Duncan, who was squeezing past Braeden now. "We're surrounded. Wake everyone up that you can. I'm gonna move over there and–" He pointed at the center of the line, which included one of the Wrightsons, standing some fifty, sixty feet away. Beyond even them was Gary, Marina, the other Wrightson, Barney Jones, and Lauren Darlington. Glancing up, he saw Erin Harris and Chauncey Watson frozen in place above on the catwalk. Fuck only knew how they'd save those two, because–

–Suddenly there was a whole lot of movement between them. It was as though Braeden's vision was a sheet draped over his eyes, and cuts were appearing in it, showing hints of something hiding beneath the cloth.

And then, as he stood back up, gun in hand, he saw exactly what he'd been missing this whole time.

"THAT WAS AN ALL-TIMER," Hendricks said. Erin was curled up to the ex-Marine's side, running her fingers over his abs, brushing them over the stray hairs. Yes, he had chest hair. No, he didn't wax like some metrosexual pussy. Didn't really need to, in her opinion; he wasn't fuzzy-wuzzy the bear, he just had a little nest there for her to rest her head on.

Erin draped her bare leg over his, enjoying the post-coital sensation. This was what life was about, wasn't it? Demon slaying and fucking laying. Sweat on her skin, fresh semen drying inside her. God, the pill was a blessing. How had she coped with condoms for so long, when they felt like fucking a plastic dick instead of a real man? She reached over and gave Hendricks a tweak on the pecker and he jerked, chuckling.

Had she been somewhere else a minute ago or had the sex been just that good, to take her on an out of body experience? She suspected the latter, because things had started out decent with Hendricks, but they'd gotten better over the weeks of their acquaintance until she was hitting new highs. She'd never kept a boyfriend for too long – too tempestuous, she expected – and was pleasantly surprised that maybe there was something to what her brother Jesse had told her: sex really does get better the longer you're with someone. If they're not a fucking moron, and you still get along. It made her wonder if there was a point of diminishing returns on that, or if she managed to stick around with Hendricks until they were in their eighties if she'd have the best goddamned sex of her life. Because that seemed like a long time to wait.

But, she reflected as she rubbed her head against his chest, fluttering all the little hairs across the surface, it might just be worth waiting for.

"Can we just stay here like this for a while?" Erin asked, not wanting to lift her head. There were scary things out there in Midian, terrible things lurking in the night. No worries, no doubts, just...this. Better than work, better than sitting around her apartment by herself Netflixing some bullshit show she didn't really care about while she scanned her phone. This was real.

This was right.

And this felt like what she'd been missing.

"Sure," Hendricks said, drawling in a fake Southern accent. The boy just couldn't pull it off, though; he was just too much of a Yankee, that broad Midwestern accent still shining through. "Why not?"

"Just feels like there's so much going on," Erin said, gathering the covers with one hand without leaving her cuddle pose. She draped them over her body, because the AC was kicking in to fight against the summer humidity. "Like the town is pulling at us to get back to work."

"The town doesn't know or care what we get up to," Hendricks said, stroking his fingers across the side of her hip. It made her spasm and jerk, half-tickled, half-aroused. "This time's just for us."

"But..." Erin started to say.

"Shhhh," Hendricks said, putting a finger over her lips.

She frowned, then cringed slightly. Because she knew where that finger had recently been. Pulling away from it, she said, "But everything that's going on. How can we just ignore it?"

"We don't need to worry about that right now," he said, stroking stray hairs out of her face. Her hair was wild, unbound – and curling just a bit from the sweat and the humidity. "We just need to worry about this. About being here..." He brushed tickling fingers across her chest, finding her nipples in just almost the way she liked. "...About doing what we want."

And then he poked her. Not with a finger, but with a part of his anatomy that was, inexplicably, pointed and erect again, somehow.

"You're going to have to wake me up if you want to get lucky again," she pronounced, confident she knew where this would go. Well, like ninety percent.

She was not disappointed. He flashed her a grin in the half-light of the bedroom and then kissed her neck before he slipped lower, lower, across her nipples and down her belly, and she smiled as he began to kiss his way around the edges of her, because she knew this would take a nice, long while, and that she'd enjoy every minute of it.

ARCH FELT ALISON BESIDE HIM, then an abrupt shove from behind and he came out of it to see–

It was definitely not Alison pressed against him, but someone certainly was. Blazing red hair was there in his face, the back of a familiar head, the scent of faint, faded perfume and sweat, naked flesh pressed to his clothing–

"Yeah, get off the trollop," Terri Pritchard said, pulling him back, hand on his shoulder.

Arch watched Starling pull away from him, too, then slowly turn to look at him. She stood beside the rolling conveyor line, Terry Wrightson and Casey Meacham just behind her. Shadows seemed to crawl across the floor of the mill, and with a start Arch recoiled further–

Demons. All demons.

They were crawling on all fours, those nearest to him, a black coating on the ground from so many of the spider-like creatures. Further away they became two-legged things, none of them even vaguely human-looking. Casting his gaze far over the redhead's shoulder, her could see Gary Wrightson with Marina just behind him, Larry a step behind, and Barney Jones along with Lauren Darlington barely visible under the far section of the conveyor. Lifting his eyes up, he saw the catwalks were swarming with demons, and they surrounded Erin and Chauncey Watson.

All he could think to say was: "Where are the kids?"

Starling cocked her head at him, eyes dusky as ever, and rubbed her bare belly. As if that was the answer. Well, it was an answer, if not one that was particularly satisfactory.

"Did you eat them?" he asked. Behind him, the steady breathing of Terri Pritchard was matched by someone else; a quick look revealed Braeden Tarley, weapon in hand and pointed at the demons surrounding them, with Duncan bringing up the rear.

"I'm going to eat the whole world," Starling said, and where once he'd heard flat, emotionless words, now there seemed to be a loathing infusing them, and it hurt his ears, hurt his heart.

"Arch," Duncan said warningly, "we're a bit out of our depth here."

"And a bit outnumbered," Braeden added.

"Indeed," Starling said, and did the most disquieting thing he'd yet seen her do.

She *smiled*.

Then, without any motion from her, Terry Wrightson was pulled to the floor in a sudden movement of shadow. It happened quickly, and then he was down, a spray of blood all there was to mark his passage.

"Casey!" Terri shouted, throwing something at the smaller man. It hit just as a shadowy demon seemed to rise up to strike him, and he staggered back, causing the demon to leap at him and miss, landing in a pile with its own kind and setting off some sort of melee. As if she'd thrown meat to hungry dogs.

"Ahhh! Ahhhh!" Casey shouted, leaping at once over the conveyor and rolling. There was nothing visible left of Terry

Wrightson, the darkness having seemingly consumed him whole.

GARY FELT a scream beneath the seas of his mind, even as he sat in his mother's dining room and watched the family eat. There was just so much to be thankful for.

So why did it feel like someone was crying?

BRAEDEN DIDN'T NEED to count to know the odds – already badly against them – had shifted further with the death of Terry Wrightson. He didn't much care for the Wrightsons – not Mary, God rest her soul, not Paul, God rest his soul, not Terry (now God rest his soul), nor Larry or Gary (fuck them and their souls, those dickweeds) – but dammit, those boys were fighters, and their mother, too. They didn't deserve to go out like this, taken in their sleep, almost. They deserved to go out roaring, with a machine gun in their hands, or rolling a sanctified monster truck eighteen times until it exploded in a geyser of flames. Not disappearing like a baby ploplet of a turd, down the toilet never to be seen again.

"Terri, we're gonna have to start shooting our way out pretty quick," Braeden said. That demon that had leapt and missed and maybe gotten eaten by its own? That had really changed the winds; the room felt different. Less confident, more ominous.

"Mmm," Starling said, throwing her red hair back over her shoulder. "Can you, though?"

Someone screamed; it was Chauncey Watson, pushed from the upper deck by some black-goop demon. He fell, and quickly, without catching himself, and it was another *plop!* situation for him, too, disappeared into a frenzy of insect-like limbs and mouths, his scream tapering off.

"You," Arch said, voice taut, and it was as though he were trying to hold in tears. "You."

"Relax, you upright man, you." This from that black female OOC who'd betrayed them last night. She appeared coming down the stairs, strolling, really, past the writhing demons surrounding her. "These were the bit players. Most of you couldn't even remember their names. Their deaths? A pale shadow of what happens to the rest of you." She thrust her arms wide. "What is that thing the kids say nowadays? They lacked 'main character energy.'" She cocked her head, looking right at Braeden, right at Terri. "But then...so do some of the rest of your lot..."

"Shoot now!" Terri shouted, and Braeden couldn't agree more. He was already firing.

"ISN'T IT EASIER LIKE THIS?" Molly asked in the darkness. "Me knowing who my dad is?"

Lauren stared at her. "When did I tell you?"

Molly smiled at her. "You didn't have to. I just know." She walked in a slow circle, past the credenza in her grandmother's living room. "You didn't want to cop to the fact you slept with a guy who had a girlfriend." Her eyes were lively, dancing in the candlelight. "Can you believe they ended up getting married, those two?"

"Yes," Lauren said, her voice low, rough, and scratchy. Of course she knew. They had Facebook.

Molly looked up with a mischievous glance. "You should have told me before I left. I have an aunt, and she's right there with you, and has no idea. Hell, she's only a few years older than

I am. We could be like sisters."

"I didn't want you to be anything like Erin Harris," Lauren said, running fingers back through her hair, which was drifting around her eyes for some reason. "At least – not before. Now that I know her a little better...I don't know. Maybe."

"Blood is blood, mom," Molly said with a grin. "And you – you're going to shed a lot of it. Soon, too. Why–"

Something hit Lauren in the head, smacking her out of the reverie.

The thunder of guns firing made Lauren drop in sheer panic, pure instinct. Molly wasn't here, and she wasn't in their living room. This was the mill, and all hell was breaking loose, and black-shelled demons were all around them–

Suddenly there was a scream above, and Lauren looked up to see–

ARCH FIRED, but not at Starling. He couldn't get himself to fire at Starling, not with that belly, not looking like that, in the family way. She just stared at him as he raked fire across her demon army, not striking out at him, tearing him in two like he knew she could. She let him shoot, and then she made a motion with her hand, raising it up and letting it flop like a dead fish.

Erin screamed above. The demons had swarmed her, knocking her back into consciousness, and she was defenseless. Her gun had slipped out of her grasp, and she wasn't wearing a sling, or it had been too loose upon her thin frame. Whatever the case, it was gone, gone, and she was rocking over the edge of the catwalk's railing, tipping now, and there was no stopping her fall.

The thunder of gunfire blotted out all sound, deafening Arch as he watched demons pop like little balloons all around him. Not nearly enough. Not nearly quick enough. He thought about adjusting his fire to try and clear the floor where Erin was certain to land, but...

...She was up so high, she'd surely break her neck. If he didn't accidentally shoot her in the process.

The demons were going to get her, or she was going to be mortally wounded, or both. There was no stopping that now, not with Chauncey Watson and Terry Wrightson dead, and Barney Jones, Lauren, Gary, and Marina just coming out of it now. Casey was still atop the line, firing wildly but not inaccurately. Duncan was behind Arch, Terri and Braeden between them, the OOC whipping his baton this way and that while the other two shot like crazy just to keep the demons off them.

Erin was over the rail now, legs in the air, above her head, hands flying free, far from anything she could hold onto. She was falling, gone, now, nothing but demons between them, Starling's slow smile flashing in the dark. Another ally down, and there wasn't anything to be done about it.

It was amazing, Arch reflected, how quickly things could go right to shit.

ERIN CAME out of the sweet sexual fantasy to something much less pleasant than an orgasm donated to her by Hendricks. Hendricks was gone, fucking gone, long gone, and that cold reality came rushing in with her return to consciousness. She came back to the mill with a hard shove, something's claws poking her in the back, like a dog jumping on her and knocking her sideways. It was heavy, too – not a small dog, like a Chihuahua. A big one, like a St. Bernard, or a pit bull, and it took her off her feet. Her hip slammed into the catwalk railing, much less gently than a caress from Hendricks. Pain spasmed its way down her ass and up into her lower back, and she jerked.

There were demons all around her, writhing, black, like shadows, or oil, and moving like a slick on the midnight ocean. She caught a flash of them as the pain spiked through her and she spun, seeing nothing but their motion.

Gunfire cracked the air, drowning out her scream of surprise. Her skin prickled at the sudden, dramatic change in her body was experiencing. One moment she was floating, on cloud nine, getting that laying she had been daydreaming about for days, weeks, months, even.

Now she was toppling backward over the railing, the floor beneath her writhing with the motion of demons.

Erin knew she was fucked, and not in the good way, the way Hendricks had been doing it in her fantasy. The ground was below some thirty feet, her head was down. Demons spread in every direction, snapping teeth and whipping spider-like claws up at her.

Fear spiked through her, and she knew her fate in that moment. It was not going to be pretty, it was not going to leave a corpse behind, it was not going to become some legend. If she was remembered at all, it'd be as a fucking punchline, a demon skidmark. She would have left more sign of her passage if she'd been dropped in a vat of acid, and, frankly, it fucking galled her in the second between realization and when the fear hit.

Then, fuck it all, terror got her, because terror does that when you're falling and you don't have tons of time to break out of the lizard brain-lock.

Her legs tangled on the railing, catching her for just a fleeting second. She thrashed, but it did nothing, buying her only a moment more as she twisted her knee trying, in desperation, to save herself from falling, and the shock of it ran through her whole body.

It also didn't save her. Trying to use her bent leg as a fish-hook to capture her weight on the rail didn't work; it slid off against her pant leg, the lack of friction surrendering her to gravity.

And that was it. That was the end of Erin Harris. She could see the Watch moving around below – shooting, fighting, trying to save their own lives. It looked like they were going to fail, and that – well, that sucked. To come this far, and get taken out by a demon ambush, without even getting a shot to live out their last three days, maybe take a stab at saving the world–

Well, the Watch had been flying by the seat of their pants for this entire time. As Erin's pants leg lost that last millimeter of grip and she slid free, ankle banging against the rail as she went over, it wasn't that surprising that she went out dying because of a fucking pair of pants – and a lack of hands to hold it.

Something snapped on her ankle, and Erin jerked like she'd just gotten hanged, except in reverse. The tendons in her knee screamed at her. A shock ran down her body from ankle to spine, and gravity played a mean song on her connective tissues as her fall halted.

A hand was clutching tight around her ankle, and flashes from the firing guns matched with the thundering heartbeat in her ears as someone played the song of fucking freedom on a full auto or damned near to gun, ripping up the demons that had so unceremoniously tossed her.

But she'd looked; no one from the Watch had been anywhere near her ass. She'd been alone on the catwalk, no Chauncey in sight, and suddenly–

Her breath caught in her throat.

The shadow loomed over her...

...of a big fucking hat.

A big fucking cowboy hat...and a big, long, black coat. And boots she could see through the slits of the catwalk.

He held her there, straining, but firing with his free hand

from a pistol to keep the demons off him. He tossed a look back at her, and smiled that cocky smile she hadn't seen in a month.

"Hey," Hendricks said, "sorry I'm late. Just hang on for a second, will you?" And he set his face as he fired a gun with his other hand, ripping apart demons with every holy blast. "I'll pull you up just as soon as I get these fuckers cleared off."

One Week Ago

"MOVING," Hendricks said, without benefit of radio, or tac gear, just his sword and his pistol. Brian was following behind, looking pretty miserable, but moving and not saying anything. Micah was bringing up the rear, hustling pretty quick for an old man, and keeping Brian sandwiched between the two of them where he – hopefully – could not fuck things up too badly. Hendricks had considered leaving him in the car, but he had visions of the skinny bitch driving off and leaving them, and in a pinch he could throw the hipster at Kitty as a distraction, so he came along. None the wiser that this was the emergency plan, but hey, that was the advantage of making the plan yourself.

They were outside the door to Kitty Elizabeth's penthouse on Central Park West. Security had been an interesting problem to defeat, but defeat it they had, by tromping in with a refrigerator box and claiming delivery to a third-floor apartment while wearing overalls. Were they making the delivery during normal working hours? No. Did the security guy who was spending his shift playing Texas Hold 'Em on his phone give a single solitary fuck? Also no.

So up they went, and the refrigerator box got broken down and discarded in the hallway outside the stairwell at the third floor, and off came the workmen overalls and out came the weapons and Hendricks's attire. A few flights of stairs later (and some swearing by Micah) and they were queuing up outside the penthouse, ready to breach. With the metal breacher, which had also been adding weight to the refrigerator box. The long, heavy piece of metal looked like it was going to make mincemeat out of Kitty Elizabeth's fancy wooden door.

And then, once everyone was positioned and Micah had the breacher raised high and was ready to bust the motherfucker down, there was a click...

...And the door just opened.

It stayed cracked, like someone had unlocked it and let it swing open less than an inch. It remained that way, and somewhere deeper within someone said, "No reason to ruin the door, it costs twenty thousand dollars. Just compose yourselves and come inside when you're ready."

Hendricks had taken note of the cameras posted around the elevator lobby they were standing in, but he didn't for a moment believe anyone would be watching them.

"Shit," Micah said, and let the breacher fall with a heavy *clunk!* to the ground. "What now, cowboy?"

"It's unfortunate if she's ready for a fight," Hendricks said, raising up his sword into a two-handed grip, a lower one that would allow him to stab or slash. "But the odds were good it was always going to come to this, because demons have wicked good hearing, and busting down a door ain't quiet. We go in – and just be ready for anything."

"Fuck," Brian whispered behind him. But when Hendricks moved, he moved, following.

Hendricks checked corners as quickly as he could, but found the entryway empty, and kept moving. This wasn't Ramadi, that was for sure, it was a tastefully, classily, swankily appointed luxury penthouse in some of the most expensive real estate on the planet. Every design choice reflected that, and as he came up on the living area, the view made it clear why this place was so expensive. Central Park spread expansively beyond the massive windows, and the penthouse's high ceilings gave the whole place the feel of being on the top of the fucking world.

"Took you long enough." Kitty Elizabeth was sitting on a couch, her back to him, a glass of some fragrant liquor in her only hand, swirling.

"I'm not charging into your living room without clearing the corners," Hendricks said, trying to decide if he should just come at her and risk it, or sweep the room first, at least with his eyes. He started on the latter, and found no signs of trouble anywhere but sitting on her ass, on the couch.

"There's no one here but you and me," Kitty said, voice bereft of its usual airiness. She sounded...tired, if such a thing was possible. He'd gotten to know her voice well, far better than he ever wanted to, even though their exposure to each other was short. "And your friends, of course. I would wave a hand to indicate them, but obviously..." And she waggled the stump where her arm had been. Before Arch had severed it. It still galled him that it hadn't been him.

"You've been expecting us?" Micah asked. There was a fire glowing and crackling in the hearth, and its reflection was shedding enough light to allow Hendricks to see Kitty's face reflected in the windows. She did not look pleased, amused, annoyed, or orgasmic, all expressions he was unfortunately familiar with in her.

"Just him," Kitty said, swirling her alcohol. She did not look at them. "I don't have the first fucking clue who you are."

"Oh," Brian said, "I'm–"

"I don't care," Kitty said, still swirling.

"So is this a trap, then?" Micah asked. Still looking for the ambush. Which was fair, in Hendricks's estimation.

"I can't kill him," Kitty said, and finally, she turned, and upon her face was a look of sad, curious desperation. "You, I could...but I probably won't, because then I'd have to kill him." She swirled her drink. "So, no. No ambush."

Hendricks felt a prickle at the back of his spine. "You can't...kill me?"

"Nope," she said, with surprising verve, almost drunken. "She wouldn't let me." Kitty chuckled. "I know what you're thinking. Who tells a Duchess of Hell they can't kill a human?" Her smile faded. "The answer is...someone more powerful than a Duchess of Hell. Do the math." Cocking her head, she peered at him. "Didn't you wonder why I left you alive after our encounter? It wasn't charity."

"Who told you to leave me alive?" Hendricks asked. Was he experiencing a chill? It sure felt like it.

"I'll give you two hints," she said. "She's presently got red hair, and she's a hellacious bitch. Wait – she doesn't actually have red hair. But her vessel does." She cocked her head further. "Though – question for you. Do the curtains match the carpet? It's not a professional interest, more morbid curiosity."

"There was no carpet," Hendricks said in a whisper, unsure why he bothered to answer at all, except that he'd been absolutely brained by the answer before the question, and his response slipped out.

Kitty's eyebrows rose. "That makes sense, given that vessel's profession. I shoulda known that."

"You're talking about Starling, right?" Brian asked, taking a step forward. "But I thought she was a good guy?"

Kitty loosed a horrifying, rumbling laugh that – if one had been uncertain she was a denizen of hell, the laugh would have cleared right up. "'Good guy.' Good grief. No. I don't meant to taunt you, but she was using you." Now she looked right into Hendricks's eyes. "In almost exactly the same way I did, except I was never after your seed. I used you for my pleasure and cast you aside. She used you for – well, not quite pleasure, but reproduction, and – well, here you are. I'm fairly certain she's done with you, but I really can't take the chance of pissing in her corn flakes, so..." She made a motion with her swirling glass. "...Off with you. Now you know the truth, or at least a good part of it."

"What's to stop me from conducting my business with you," Hendricks said, "before I go?"

Kitty made a long, productive sigh. "Knowledge, first." She looked up at him. "She's going to destroy your whole world, and it's coming quite soon. Within a week or two, I would guesstimate. I'm not really plugged in anymore, but...it's coming. We're all going to hell." She raised her glass in a toast. "Yay." And then drained it.

"You don't seem excited about that," Brian said. Hendricks was still mulling...well, a lot of things.

"Going back to hell?" Kitty very delicately slurred a word in there. How much had she had? "I am on a shit list in hell, so...no. I am not looking forward to going back, my recent agreements with your baby mama notwithstanding." She cocked her head again. "You really didn't know that's what she was using you for?"

"What now?" Micah asked, looking very sideways at Hendricks.

"Oh," Brian said. "That seed thing suddenly makes much more sense."

"It does, doesn't it? It's gonna make so much more sense when that thing you created in your depressive bursts of eroticism erupts out of the redheaded whore's shaven cunt and tears the world apart," Kitty said. She tossed her glass aside, and it shattered against the tile floor in front of the fireplace, leaving only a few droplets to reflect in the burning light. She sighed. "It makes me long for the good old days, when all I had to worry about was where I was going to find the next worthless meat puppet to munch my rug. But we're so far beyond that now. Now it's time to run for cover, though there's none to be had. No hiding place down here, you see." And she mimed stretching, a one-armed motion that looked more than a little silly. "When you go to the rock to hide your face, I mean."

Hendricks felt his mouth curiously dry. "What?"

"That all you can say? 'What?'" She sneered mockingly. "You did what you did. They've found the gate in that shithole town of yours, and they're gearing up to send in the armies, to end the world, send us all to hell, and turn that other place into hell, too. All the pieces are together, there'll be nowhere left to run – unless *He* gets involved." She rolled her eyes. "Unlikely. A snowball's chance packed tightly between my thighs, that's the odds I'd give it. But I assumed you'd want to be there at the death, scrabbling to try and save your precious world, or at least shag your way to another baby mama before the end. Whatever you humans do with your time."

Hendricks took a step forward, brandishing his sword. He had a plan coming in, and nothing she'd said was going to change that plan. Not lies, not truths – nothing.

"What are you doing?" She stared at him with undisguised contempt. "You're really going to try that? After what I just told you? You fucked her, and fucked us all, and you're still all mad about me making you lick demon twat? Come on. Bigger stakes here, hat. Get your head in the game."

"You don't get to tell me where to put my head anymore." And he made a motion toward her, setting up to stab in her direction.

"Fuck's sake," she said, drawn up, tense, clearly contemplating. But not for long. She tossed him a little salute. "Fine. Have it your way. As I said, I can't kill you, so..."

And she turned, took two long steps–

–And leapt out the windows into the night.

Hendricks made it to the edge and looked out, half-expecting to see her fly over Central Park on bat-like wings that would sprout from her. But no, she'd landed below on the pavement, and cracks extended out in a wide circle from where she'd crashed down. Barely visible, she picked herself up, brushed herself off, tossed off another half-hearted salute that ended with an extended middle finger, and walked off down the street.

"Shit," Micah said, looking out the shattered window and watching her stroll off into the night. "She really was a demon, wasn't she?"

"Yep," Hendricks said, mulling, because his brain hadn't shifted gears from KILL to whatever he was going to do next.

"There was a real density of information she just dumped on us," Brian said. "You're having a demon baby, for one. The world apparently ending, for another. Something about a gate was thrown in there. And apocalyptic jibber-jabber, some of which is gonna need to be untangled to make actual sense."

"The world's coming to an end," Hendricks said, sheathing his sword now that he had no Duchess guts in which to bury it. "Midian's the epicenter. What more do you need to know?"

"Fuck," Brian said. "I always feared I'd die in that fucking town, but this is ridiculous."

Hendricks looked at Micah. "Believe any of that shit?"

Gunny was looking right at him, smoky-eyed and squinting. "Some of it, maybe."

"Then believe this: the world's going to end," Hendricks said. "And it's probably starting in Tennessee."

Gunny sighed a long sigh. "Maybe." He listened, and sirens echoed out in the distance. "We should go. I don't know much about New York, but in my town, busting a window and having a lady fly out means the cops will be on their way. And I don't think we should be here when they arrive."

On that much, they could agree. Wordlessly, Hendricks headed for the door. The other two followed just the same.

They were halfway down the stairs when Brian piped up: "You're going back, right?" He had a real quiver in his voice, a sense of nerves bleeding in, like he was trying to summon up courage for maybe the first time and looking for reassurance as he did so.

"Yep," Hendricks said, because what else was there to do? No world, no revenge. That seemed simple enough and obvious, even to him. "I'm going back." This he whispered mostly to himself, because...fuck. There was nothing but pain waiting for him in Midian.

But then...that had been true of just about everywhere, for a while now, so why was Midian any different? Visions of a flash of blond hair flashed into his mind, and it made him wonder if maybe – just maybe – there might be something else waiting, too.

TEN

MANY UNHAPPY RETURNS

This whole damned thing was a clusterfuck, but Brian Longholt had a plan to save the day. Which amazed him, sort of, but not really. He was always good with plans. Planning had carried him to Brown University, and his useless degree. It's just that when they were more complex, and strayed beyond the basic, he kinda sucked ass at the execution of said plans.

But this one was easy enough, and only required him to fight his way through the weakest swarm of demons he'd ever seen. Swinging his sword, Micah watching his back and swearing, "Fuck, there *are* demons! Fuck!" all the while, he fought his way over to where Pastor Barney Jones was being swarmed at by an absolutely terrifying number of the black-goo beetles, partially hidden by the conveyor roller belt that he was under, damned things coming at him from all directions. Lauren Darlington was just behind him, out of it, and about to get covered over.

Well, they couldn't have that, could they? Brian grabbed the doctor as he passed, slicing his way past her. She jerked like he'd slapped her ass and called her sugar tits, dragging her head around to look him in the eyes, hers wide and surprised.

"Whattheactualfuck?" she said, all one word, one thought. It definitely captured the moment.

"We gotta get moving," he said, pointing her to the door. Shit. It was covered over by just swarms of the demon beetles, like black vines on a fucking trellis from hell. "Never mind." He reached past her and put a hand on Barney Jones's shoulder, trying to jerk him awake. "Pastor," he said once Jones had come out of it enough to start like he, too, had gotten his ass squeezed, "I need your help for a minute."

ARCH STARED up at the catwalk, a thin, dawning thread of consciousness breaking through as he gawked. The shadow of a long drover coat, like cowboys wore out on the trail, and that big hat. He couldn't quite see the face, but he saw the man had Erin by the ankle and was holding her. Like as not, right now she was wishing she'd skipped a meal or two more, and taken a few less pulls of whiskey, to make the man's job easier.

But he held her, sweating, with one hand, as he turned and ripped off a dozen shots from his own AR, clearing the area around him of those crawling demons.

Arch spun to see Starling paused, staring up at the catwalk with a frozen look on her face. It was subtle, as everything was with the woman, but it was there–

And it was rage.

"Your boyfriend's back," Arch said, and she turned her head at him in a blur. He suddenly felt an unfortunate amount of attention shift in his direction, as though every demon in the room suddenly had him in its sights.

"COMING TOO close to the end here," Guthrie said. She'd found her way to Duncan, and was standing opposite him, blocking the exit – which he'd moved to clear so they could escape. There was a rumble beneath his feet, either more demons swarming in, or...

...Or something large in the distance. Very large, potentially.

"Your time is running low," Guthrie said, just standing there. Blocking him.

"Seems like you're trying to cut it short," Duncan said, hesitating. He'd played with the line so far, but striking at Guthrie with his baton? That would really open up the can. Whether it ended up being worms or whoopass, either way it was going to be a mess. "I thought we had three days."

"The world has three days," Guthrie said with a twinkle of amusement in her eye. "Your friends? They're not going to make it that long. Well, some of them might – but they're going to suffer to go the distance. We're talking live disembowelment. Maybe some vivisection." She waved a hand in the direction of Starling. "You know how testy these higher beings get when they're incubating something terrible."

"Actually, I don't," Duncan said, looking about. He was searching for an alternate exit, but all he could find was that the cowboy had returned. And saved Erin – for now. Yippee. "Tell me about it."

"Time is not on your side, old friend," Guthrie said, and that rumble touched Duncan's legs again. Deeply concerning.

"I don't think we're friends anymore," Duncan said tautly. "If we ever were."

"Just a human speech affectation," Guthrie said. "I've long pondered the way they use words. Calling each other 'friends,' when they're more acquaintances. When the loyalty is only as thick as the scum on top of a drink left out overnight. But we worked together for over a hundred years – surely that's worth something?"

"Am I going to hell with the rest?" Duncan asked.

"Oh, yes," Guthrie said, chortling. "You sealed your fate last night."

"Then I guess I've got nothing left to lose," he said, and took a swing at Guthrie with his baton.

BRAEDEN FELT as though there were a storm inside him. He was blowing through magazines, trying to hold off the swarms of black demon bugs coming for him. He was back to back, ass to ass with Terri, and they were doing their damned best, leaving a big spot for Arch, who was tangling with them himself, and doing a reasonable job of it.

But they were all three running low on ammo. Had to be, Braeden figured. He definitely was, at least, and Terri and Arch were chewing through it as fast as he was, so...

"Last mag," he said, aping the words he'd heard on however many TV series, and maybe even the video games he'd played when he was a younger man. Before responsibility. Before settling down.

Before Abi.

He'd come to this because of her. Because he'd fucked up and lost her, he'd stayed rather than leaving town. Now he was standing here, feeling the rip and recoil of the AR against his shoulder, gently stitching a pattern of bruises into the skin and muscle tissue there as he aimed and fired, aimed and fired.

If she hadn't died – if she'd lived – he would have fled town with her, for sure. He didn't care enough about Midian to stay; he cared about Abi, and he'd have done any-damned-thing to protect her.

Without her...there was nothing left but the storm inside him. It had led him to beat a demon with a wrench, against all wisdom. It had led him here, into this trap, in the heat of foolishness, trying to save someone else's children.

And now he was going to die, because he just was. Stupid.

But at least, maybe, he'd see Abi again.

LAUREN WAS NOT HAVING the time of her life. Mostly, it felt as though she was trying to keep from shooting someone on her own team as the black spider demons came sweeping in, wave after wave. One little pop of a round would end them, but they were so small that it felt like they'd catch two or three or more before they'd finished evaporating, leaving that sulfuric stink behind.

"Anyone see a way out?" Larry Wrightson shouted. He had his head down, long, black locks partially obscuring his eyes, but he was going to town firing over his brother's head. Gary, for his part, still seemed out of it; apparently no one had bothered to wake him.

Lauren was looking behind her, but ever since Brian Longholt had disappeared with Barney Jones – through one of the last remaining gaps – there didn't seem to be a way out. The factory crawled with demon life, covering all exits, swarming up the walls, and just generally blocking the windows.

Which, for lack of a better word, sucked.

Lauren had somewhat reconciled herself to dying, especially with the end being nigh, and them not having found the gate. Those, to her, seemed like a twosome of inescapable troubles, and without any exit, either from the troubles at hand, in the mill, or the one coming, outside, to destroy the world...

It was a disappointment. Thin hopes were not no hopes,

after all, and she'd been grasping, and would have grasped right up to the end.

But the end was pretty damned close, and the clouds were closing in, and the rain was...

...Coming?

Her brain had bent toward that metaphor not realizing that she'd been touched by a droplet of water. First, she assumed it was demon spit, or essence, or some other such thing. But it had a smell to it, like water kept too long in a cask, and another struck her a moment later.

Smoke rose, first in little dribs and drabs, nothing like that which suffused the air outside. This was foul, sulfuric, that stinky water mixed with demon death, and suddenly the air was pierced by a thousand shrieks from a thousand spider demons swarming everywhere–

Being rained upon. Because water was falling from the sky in a steady rhythm, now pouring down as though the clouds had opened up in the heavens. Except they were inside.

Oh.

The sprinkler system.

The demons were screaming, screaming like they were burning, because they were. Everywhere a droplet of water hit a spider demon, smoke seemed to puff up–

–and the whole room was filling with it.

"KEEP IT UP, PREACHER," Brian said, watching the sprinklers pour down on the demons, burning them just the same as if acid had been spraying out. "You've got this."

Barney Jones did, indeed, have this, his hand upon the water pipe running up to feed the sprinklers, his head bowed, prayer mumbled under his breath blessing the waters now raining down upon the mill–

–And killing the flood of demons with a flood of their own.

GARY AWOKE to splatters of foul-smelling water upon him and somehow he knew.

He knew.

The vision of Terry getting devoured by the spider demons was strong in his mind, and he hadn't had to blink his eyes coming out of his trance, and he just...he knew.

He was down another brother.

"Larry!" he shouted, and the dark-haired bastard popped over his shoulder into Gary's peripheral vision. Gary started firing, of course, not that there seemed to be much point in it, but he was doing it anyway, into the decaying remains of the melting demons. "What the fuck are we doing!"

His brother shrugged, pointing at the naked redhead who seemed to be advancing on Arch Stan. "Don't know. We were about to get overwhelmed when things took a sudden turn, and a lot of our troubles started melting away."

Gary raised his rifle and took three shots in a burst at the naked ass of the redheaded hooker. Holy blessed or no, they didn't so much as make a dent in her anywhere. They spanged off the skin beside her spine like a striker off a flint, and she didn't even deign to turn and look at him.

Over the sound of the rushing water, vibrations got to him through his wheelchair, and he froze, holding his gun. There'd be time to mourn later. Right now–

Something burst through the wall behind them, a head so giant it looked to be about the size of VW Beetle, and it came through ten, fifteen feet off the ground, ripping up the corrugated metal like it was a dog through a stretched piece of aluminum foil holding leftovers.

"Fucking shit," Gary said, jerking his thumb toward the nearest exit door, which was only about twenty feet away, black pools of demon-tinged water swirling between them and it. "We need to get the fuck outta here, and now."

"YOU'D BE surprised what you've got left to lose," Guthrie said, grinning. It was like he could see Lerner's face shining through hers, as though the shell didn't matter, the person beneath was glaring out like it was a mask. Which it was, really.

Holy water was spraying down around them, and Duncan was ducking low, under a piece of machinery, because – well, he didn't want to melt like the wicked witch in the rain. Guthrie was doing the same, grinning at him, letting her shoes touch the falling water and nothing else.

"Say," Guthrie said, still leering, "you didn't happen to bring an umbrella, did you?"

"HANG ON, HANG ON," Hendricks said, pulling Erin up onto the catwalk. Now that the demons were washed away, and he had room to maneuver and breathe, he'd let the gun drop, the sling catching it. It had been a good idea, the gun, a recommendation from Father Nguyen when he'd stopped in at St. Brigid's to find out what was cooking in Midian. Of course, he hadn't exactly expected this to be the answer.

Pulling Erin up by the ankle took both hands. She was thin, but she was still a human being, and lifting a hundred-plus pounds of dead weight wasn't easy, especially if there was swaying involved. And there was swaying involved. Not even the sexy kind, either.

He hauled her up around the time the water was starting to taper off. His hat was soaked, his coat was soaked, and man, that water stunk. Clearly it had been sitting in the pipes for a long while. Lucky they had still water pressure and gravity on their side, because they certainly didn't have power to run the pumps.

Looking out, he could see pretty much every demon that could be dissolved had been dissolved. With one last yank he brought Erin over the catwalk and set her on the ground. His back thanked him for ending the awkward wrangling, and he offered her a hand, half-expecting her to slap it away or, maybe worse, take it, then slap the shit out of him when she got up in range to do so.

She was staring at him wide-eyed, though, and he had her on her feet a second or two later, only drips coming down around him, and off the brim of his hat. She was staring at him; he opened his mouth to speak and the only thing that came out was:

"I'm sorry," he said. "For...everything. Being a dickhead. For leaving. For being too full of shit, or pride, or–"

Something slammed into the wall behind them, and they both turned to look. Something burst through the wall, big, ugly, demon, and at least twenty feet off the ground. It was a head of some kind, and attached to a body that stubbornly remained outside the wall, and hinted that this thing was fucking huge.

"We should get the fuck outta here," Erin said, still hanging onto his hand.

Hendricks took one look at the thing ripping through the corrugated steel. "Yep," he agreed, and they bolted for the stairs to get off the catwalk.

ARCH WAS STUMBLING BACKWARDS, butt-first, and Starling was advancing on him. "Where are the kids?" he shouted, shooting at her feet.

It didn't deter her. Seemed like a bullet bounced off her foot, even, because he felt it whizz past his face and there was no one behind her any longer. Something was chewing through the wall behind them and prompting everyone to run. He couldn't blame them; they'd just dispatched the flood of spider demons, and now something truly giant was coming.

Also, Starling hadn't been affected by the holy water at all. She was covered in a sheen, like perspiration, and it made Arch feel awfully awkward, looking at her like this. Couldn't she do this with some clothes on? It didn't feel right, looking at a pregnant girl this way. Even he wasn't too proud to admit that other than the bulging stomach, she was quite shapely, about as good-looking as a pregnant lady could hope for. Probably the demon in her at work.

He was surprised the demon in her wasn't working harder; she seemed to pause, to lose the luster in her eyes, staring at him. "You should go," she said, wrapping her thin arms around herself, hiding her body, as though she'd suddenly gone demure. Her eyes lost that dusky hue, replaced by a brilliant green.

Arch paused in his flight. "You're not Starling, are you?"

She shook her head slowly. "Not now. But she'll be back, and mad." Her eyelids fluttered. "Go. You don't have long."

Arch lifted up his sword. "If I cut you, I might be able to–"

She shook her head; without the demon in charge, her hair was stringy, and there were desperate, dark circles under her eyes. "It won't work." She slid an elbow down and brushed her oversized belly. "This...it can't be excised like that. It's in me..." She shuddered as though something vile had touched her. "...and it will be until it's time." She looked back up at him, and Arch wondered if he'd ever seen such a picture of hopelessness as he saw in that girl's eyes now. And she was a girl, just. Not a woman, not at all, but a scared girl who knew she was in so very far over her head.

"Just go," she whispered, and there were hints of tears in her eyes. "You have to go."

Arch hesitated; she screamed, "GO!" at him, and with great reluctance – and at the sound of the thing hammering its way through the wall, and metal tearing, he did.

BRAEDEN DIDN'T LOVE the smell of the water soaking his clothes, but he liked it better than dying. The floor of the mill looked like the aftermath of the finale of *Who Framed Roger Rabbit?* with a layer of prismatic slick covering the concrete.

"The cars are awfully far away," Terri said, because they were all in full flight now, splashing their way through. She cast a look over her shoulder at the demon-thing ripping through the wall. "And that is – well, close."

"Yep," Braeden said. The rain had shut off, either because the water pressure had died or someone had shut it off. It was hard to believe they'd shut it off, so it was probably the former, especially given the city water had been off for weeks. "Just keep running, I reckon–"

They burst out into the smoky, brown-skied daylight to find a truck waiting right there for them. A thickset black man was behind the wheel and shouted, in a commanding voice, "Come on!"

Without bothering to argue, Braeden mantled the bed and helped Terri in. All the while, behind them and around the corner, that thing was ripping its way into the mill.

ALMOST EVERYONE WAS out by now, or well on their way to the door, Hendricks realized, coming down the last of the stairs. He was letting Erin lead, and keeping a wary eye on the thing ripping through the wall. It was making solid progress and would probably be through and onto the mill floor in a few seconds. If only the holy water rain had still been going.

Whatever. Micah was outside with the truck running, and the only point now was to GTFO and deal with the fallout later. That said fallout involved Hendricks rather directly was cause for concern, and as he came down the last couple steps he found himself very nearly face to face with said fallout.

"Shit." He stopped just short of plowing into Erin. She'd stopped too, water sloshing in a thin line around her shoes like a car driving through a puddle.

"You said it," she said, her elbow almost in his sternum.

There, over her shoulder, was Starling. Naked as he remembered her (from all the sex), but with a crucial difference. A big, swollen belly replaced the tight, nearly ab-displaying stomach she'd had when last he'd seen it. And cum on it. And in it.

Gone was the dusky eyes, the unflappable air, the complete lack of modesty. This girl was covering up her breasts and her crotch self-consciously, like she was preparing for a photo spread that had to blot out the crucial areas to be displayed on the magazine stands in supermarkets. Her hair hung in lank strands, and her eyes–

Fucking shit, her eyes. She looked like she was strung out, like she'd just come out of a drug-addled trance. She looked at him, and she croaked, "Kill me. When you get a chance."

"Is this not a chance?" Erin asked, and she had her pistol out.

Lucia – for that's who she was, not Starling – shook her head slowly. "You could try, but you'd get hurt. It'd bring *her* back, and I'd be gone again. And she'd chase you, and catch you, and the things she wants to do to you..." Her thin body shook, and she slowly sunk down to a squat. "You should run." Lifting her eyes, she looked up at the thing behind them, the thing with jaws wide enough to swallow a man whole. Kind of like her, but much less pleasantly and much more completely.

Erin's finger tightened on the trigger, and Hendricks landed a hand on hers. "Let's not tempt fate," he said, when she looked up at him with flaming eyes. "You've seen what Starling can do. We're not ready to tackle that, not right now."

"Then when?" Erin asked. She did let him lead her away, though, breaking into a run. She kept her gun out, though, and kept casting looks over her shoulder at the pregnant girl now sitting bare-assed on the wet concrete floor.

"When we've got more than a fucking shadow's chance on the sun," Hendricks said, and fired a couple rounds of holy ammo at the big demon crushing its way through the wall. As he might have predicted, it didn't do a damned bit of good.

"BE SEEING YOU AGAIN REAL SOON," Guthrie said as Duncan slid out from beneath the machinery, hands hissing from contact with the holy water, smoke pouring off them like steam from a boiling pot. Her eyes were glinting in the darkness of the shadows, and she was barely audible beneath the sound of metal tearing.

"FUCKING LIFT me up and throw me in," Gary said, shaking his head at the stupidity of his brother, who'd dithered from the second they reached the pickup truck waiting to spirit them away.

Larry only stared at him a second, then shrugged. "Okay."

And he did, like he'd been waiting his whole damned life to do so. It fucking stung, too, landing unceremoniously in the bed like he was a dwarf that had just been tossed. The only thing that broke his fall was Casey Meacham, who he half-believed had done it just to cop a feel of his ass. The wheelchair followed, fortunately, along with Marina, climbing up beside him, looking about as shook as he'd ever seen her. She patted him down real quick and said, "You are okay," and then collapsed against the wheel well.

"No, I'm fucking not," Gary said as Arch Stan vaulted the side and landed a foot solidly on his leg. He didn't give a shit about that, though, because he only felt it as an impact. The other, thing, though, the knowledge of what happened to Terry...that shit racked up his guts, and he felt every bit of it.

"MICAH – GO, GO, GO!" Brian Longholt shouted the moment Hendricks threw himself into the bed of the truck, about two steps behind Erin Harris. She was looking a bit like a drowned rat, blond hair clinging all around her face. Hendricks looked only a little better as the tires squealed and his boots hung over the back edge of the truck. Lauren Darlington and Duncan each seized a hand and dragged him in as the truck took off like a cat that had just had its tail stepped on.

Good timing, too, because the thing that had been ripping its way into the plant turned the corner at just that moment and let out a wail that sounded a little like a man ululating after getting kicked in the balls. It was answered a moment later by a similar wail, and out of the woods burst another of the things, and another, each thirty feet tall and running on their broad legs at the truck that was already squealing tires as it burned out of the mill's parking lot.

"I JUST GOT to ask you a question, Gary," Casey Meacham said as Gary toppled over into Marina's lap. Fucking sitting upright on a shifting base was a nightmare for him, unable to keep his ass stable.

"Well, don't keep me in suspense, you fucking cock dribble," Gary said, just embracing that this was where he ended up. He looked up at Marina, and she held him still in strong arms as the truck squealed sideways again. "What?"

"That worm," Casey said. "Where'd you get an RPG, anyway?"

Gary clenched his teeth as the vehicle slid again on gravel, a cloud of it spitting out the back. Hell if he knew if they were making good their escape, or if one of those giant-jawed things was about to take a hell of a bite out of them all. "You're gonna find this hard to believe given how much of a solid citizen I am," he said, locking eyes on his wheelchair, "but...I got friends in some low-ass places." They skidded again, and the wheelchair bumped against him. God, he couldn't wait to get back in it, be master of his own destiny. At least there he'd have a fucking chance. With someone else at the wheel, he had none. And they were leaving his van behind, because he heard a roar and it was right fucking behind them.

ARCH HAD NOT OPTED to get in the passenger side. That had been where Barney Jones had ended up, but the truck's rear window was slid open, and he could see a big black man at the wheel, and giving the vehicle absolute heck in his struggle to get them away from the pursuing demons. The giant demons. Which were not that far behind them, and not losing ground.

"Things look like a skinned T-Rex without a tail, dipped in oil," Larry Wrightson said. Hazy air was whipping around them; the skies had gotten darker ahead, black smoke billowing up out of a sector of the horizon that had not been on fire this morning. Not a great sign, that. It meant the wildfire was spreading, and fast.

"But mashed up," Casey Meacham said, and he fired a few rounds at it. They did nothing.

"Looks like a," Duncan said, then launched into some unpronounceable demon language. He sat miserably sandwiched between Meacham and the back of the cab. "Bullets might not get through, even the consecrated kind."

"Why?" Arch asked.

"Because I'm not sure they're technically demons," Duncan said. "I think they might be essences in an engineered shell." He waited, because no one asked a question about that. "Basically a science project done by demons and turned loose where they're most needed."

"Hell really is coming," Lauren Darlington said. On that they could all agree.

"Then what do we do?" Arch asked.

"Make a run for St. Brigid's," Duncan said. There were three – no, four – of them now, and more howls from the woods. It was keeping pace with the truck, which was now up to fifty or so. "Engineered shell or not, they will not be able to enter the perimeter of the church property without falling over helpless." He stared straight ahead for a moment. "Which is what's going to happen to me."

Father Nguyen had tuned up the church's holy defenses somehow, though Arch was unclear on the details. Whatever he'd done, it had seemingly made entry into even the church parking lot impossible for Duncan. Arch had seen it for himself, otherwise he might not have believed it.

"What do we do until then?" Arch asked.

Duncan looked out the back of the tailgate. They were up to six of the malformed things chasing them now, and the woods were rustling furiously on either side of the road, suggesting either the wind was wild...or there were more. "Well," the OOC said. "it might not be a bad time to do some praying."

DARLA PIKE STARED up at the figure of Christ upon the cross, and there was a rumbling in her stomach. It wasn't hunger; she'd eaten before she left the house this morning, and she habitually went long stretches without consuming food. That was the secret of keeping her ass from looking fat after two kids, really: restrict her caloric intake as much as possible. And it worked...up to a point. Her ass wasn't a glutinous mess. But it wasn't the rock hard one she'd had in her youth, the kind you could bounce a quarter off of. The kind random men wanted to dive head-first into. And sure, she could have made some sort of demon pact to make it like that again – others certainly had, using demon power as their own personal fountains of youth – but those deals tended to possess a certain shelf life, and afterward the bill came due with a ton of interest.

None of that for Darla. She'd age'd gracelessly, and saved her power for the things that really counted. That was why she'd undertaken this particular bullshit assignment. One look at that Starling and she knew what she was making a deal with.

The fucking future. And, to a certain extent, the very distant past.

"Can I get you anything, Mrs. Pike?" The soft voice of the priest swam into the edges of her tunnel vision. Her focus was on that symbol, the figure hanging upon the wooden crucifix, and it made her deeply...uncomfortable.

"I don't think I could eat," she said, putting her face in her hands. Keeping up appearances. What she was really waiting for was a rumble outside that would tell her this fucking priest was the last surviving demon hunter in town. At which point she'd pull the knife hidden in her pants and do something that the man on the cross would certainly not approve of, thus ending Starling's problems in Midian and, by extension, ending the world.

And then...power, overwhelming. All she'd ever wanted, all she'd ever worked for, delivered right to her. Anyone who'd pissed her off in the past was in for a rude awakening, as she took a special interest in their personal damnation.

Also...maybe she could see Jay and Mera again? She'd done what she had to, and of course she'd known it was going to be a sacrifice. She'd made it happen, she'd done it with a gleeful face on, because that was what a bloodthirsty demon would want. And she didn't regret it.

But...she was ready to move past it. After all, life was temporary, life was transitory, and *they* were beyond it now. Where were they? She had a vague idea; it wasn't like there was a map of hell. Jason...she might not see again. Something would have gotten its clutches into him. But the children? They might have gone through a rough patch, but they should be...salvageable. Ish. Well, maybe.

She needed to say something to the priest, get him off her back. "Do you think they're going to find my children?" She had the tiny diamond pendant she wore around her neck between her thumb and forefinger, and was turning it over in them. It wasn't much, the pendant, just a little thing she'd stolen from Marischa, her mother-in-law's, things. It was nice, though. She liked nice things. And she was going to have a whole lot more of them soon.

"I'm certain that if your children are alive, they're going to do everything they can to bring them back," Father Nguyen said.

"They're going to bring them back," Darla said, putting some numbness, a little robotic tone into it. "They will." She twisted the knife of desperation. "They have to."

Out of the corner of her eye, Father Nguyen's faint smile froze. "Of course," he murmured. The priest was young, he didn't know quite how to deal with someone who would not face reality. Or maybe he just didn't want to. Either way, he brushed her shoulder reassuringly, then turned to leave her.

Which left Darla staring up at the sculpted, plasticine figure in agony on the cross. She thought about saying something tart, but abstained. It would probably draw the priest back her way, and she didn't need that. Instead she lowered her eyes, but not reverently, and sat there waiting, hoping to hear the sound of her coming victory trumpeted upon the horizon, and soon.

HENDRICKS FOUND himself awkwardly next to Erin, watching the giant things chase them as they reached the outskirts of Midian, with its runnels of destruction that had been carved through the town. It made things difficult to navigate, but not impossible, and Gunny in the driver's seat knew this was what was going to be waiting for them, since they'd already been to the church once and had to deal with this rough, no-lube butt-fuckery of a navigation hazard.

There was no need to harry Gunny about it, so Hendricks sat in the truck bed, Erin tense as shit beside him, like a cat in a room full of hungry, pissed-off pit bulls. She was alternating between watching the things chase them, the roar of the engine throttling up and down as Gunny lurched the truck this way and that through the smoke-choked streets, looking for the closest entryway to the warren of wreckage that was now Midian.

The sun overhead was near buried in darkness, a hazy disc glinting out from behind the soupy air and clouds far above, barely visible. It felt like a Wisconsin winter's afternoon in that December interstitial space just before the solstice, when cloud cover would make things go dark as night around 4pm. No snow was piled up here, though, just some ash, the light of distant torches burning on two thirds of the horizon, wildfires surrounding them from roughly the northeastern compass point almost to the northwestern one, entirely consuming the southerly horizon. To the north: Mouth Horeb, a mere outline.

A hard vibration ran through the truck as the tires bounced over a loose piece of a wrecked house. Debris was coming fast now, rising like twin hills on either side, and they bounced once on the smoothed foundation of a wrecked house, and into the path of destruction.

Erin snuck a look at him, and he pretended not to notice. She didn't seem pissed; probably because she was busy being terrified that this was about to be the end. "This is really the end, ain't it?" she asked, all that corn pone accent she was usually decent at hiding when she wanted to bleeding out.

"Not necessarily," he said, flashing her a grin like the kind he tended to find on his face just before he did something necessary and stupid, like kicking down doors in Iraq. "We're still sucking breath. The world isn't over just yet." He looked back at those fires glowing in the hazy distance, beyond the smoke that wreathed...well, everything, and gave the world a hellish tint. "Though it does appear to be warming up."

The demonic T-Rex-looking thing had disappeared once they'd entered the warren of Midian, and for just a sec, Hendricks thought maybe they'd lost it, or maybe it had deigned not to pursue them any further.

That was a bullshit hope, though, because a moment later it burst through the side of the wreckage wall just behind them, missing them by about ten feet, and only because Micah had gunned the engine the moment he'd gotten on a straightaway. If he'd been going the same speed he'd been going when they'd disappeared into the channel of ruin, they'd have gotten plowed into by the goddamned thing.

"Gunny," Hendricks said. He tried to keep the tone flat and warning; it might have come out a little higher than he wanted, maybe a touch worried.

"Cool your tits," Gunny called back over the roar of the engine and the roar of the demon. Hendricks more felt that than heard it, really. How many turns away from the church were they?

He exchanged a look with Erin, and managed to conjure up another of those smiles. "Things have been a little hectic since you've been gone," she said. And he had a feeling she might have been understating a bit. But at least she wasn't hammering him over the head with the fact that Starling was carrying a belly about as big as a house, and that it was all his fault. More than one woman would have held it against him, and maybe that was still to come, but for now he felt a little pinch of relief that she was looking at him with something akin to relief.

ARCH WAS STARING out the back as they slewed around a corner roughly, skidding through stray wreckage that had not quite been pushed aside by the worm in its passage, or that had fallen down the slopes of the debris hills after its death. Nestled in the back of an overfull F-150's bed, Arch stared dully at the thing coming at them, feeling more or less useless.

He'd just faced down Starling, again, and felt powerless

against her. What was it about that redhead, about the way she presented herself?

Well...the answer to that seemed obvious enough. He was a man, after all, and his desires hadn't gone away with Alison. But his decency made him hate that they hadn't, especially given the woman's profession – and current state. There was a dark shame in him that he didn't want to feel, like the slick-oil skin of those demon bugs in the mill. He didn't dare touch it; he felt that ruin lay that way.

Besides, the dual nature of that girl had always troubled him; less so when he'd believed the Starling creature inhabiting her had been an angel than now...when he knew that it was an angel, but the fallen kind. It had used that girl, had taken her body from some unfortunate pact or sheer possession, and done the opposite number of what had happened to the Virgin Mary. It made him shudder; he didn't even care to think about it. Where the Virgin Mary had received a priceless gift, the girl Lucia had received something quite different. A curse, Arch figured, of the most horrifying kind. Had she done something to deserve it?

Hadn't they all? Arch had, and he knew it. His uncontrollable feelings about the redhead, those stirrings inside at the mere sight of her naked flesh, marred as it was, were a reflection of those parts of him he most disliked. Others had called him a righteous man – Guthrie had called him an upright one, like Job – but Arch knew the truth in his heart.

He was a sinner, like everyone else. He felt it, he acknowledged it, he wallowed in it at times – shameful moments, to be sure. There was not even so much as a split hair's worth of difference between him and the cowboy, he knew, looking over at Hendricks, whose hair stirred beneath the hat as he focused on the demon chasing after them.

There but for the grace of God...might have gone Arch himself.

The pickup took a hard turn, skidding once more; ahead, beyond the cab, Arch could see St. Brigid's. It was close, but so was the demon, mere feet behind them, running on those strange, stubby legs to catch up.

Its jaws were behind them, just feet away, and Hendricks lifted his rifle and fired into its open mouth. It loosed a metallic roar, something horrible that made Arch cringe as though hell's own breath had been breathed on his naked skin in the dark on a summer night. It was sulfuric, and hateful, and it made his throat close and his stomach threaten to upturn its contents. The thunder of each bullet fired did nothing, flashes in the dimness, lighting up the geography of the demon's face – its small eyes, countless teeth, the drool stringing in great rivulets from its jaws. It was there, it was behind them, and it was reaching out toward Hendricks's outstretched arm, ready to bite down–

And suddenly...it wasn't there anymore. It receded as it skidded to a stop twenty, then thirty feet behind.

The truck coasted in beneath the portico of St. Brigid's, and the demon remained at the street, joined by two others in its wake, then two more. They paced at the curb, touching the sidewalk and coming no further. One howled in the dimness, and it made Arch shudder again, turning his face away.

But the truck came to a halt, and the weary riders sat waiting, listening, watching as the thing bellowed again into the night, and Arch knew that somehow – and barely – they had survived again.

But only for now.

ELEVEN

ON ARMAGEDDON EVE

"That thing," Gary said, waiting for his brother to unfold his chair down on the ground, watching those things pacing at the edge of the street, "is it just going to stand there and stare longingly at our hindquarters? Or is going to do something nasty? Like throw a diesel bomb on the church roof or something?"

His answer came from the OOC, who looked worse than usual. "No, they can't enter the property." He seemed to be itching, or dealing with a headache, something that made him speak slowly. "Nor can they just have one of their human-shaped friends throw a Molotov cocktail, or drop a bomb on it – none of that." His hands started to shake, like he was experiencing a palsy, or some bullshit, bitchass PTSD.

"Why not?" Erin Harris asked. She was taking the cowboy's hand and jumping down from the truck. That was embarrassing, Gary thought, watching her blush while she did it. What a fucking perfect gentleman. And what a fucking sadass display of pussitude. How had she been the leader of this band?

"If thrown by their hand," Duncan said, curling up in the back of the truck like a fucking teenage girl crying in the shower, his words coming out as shaky as his fucking hands, "it'd come bouncing right back. It's a pre – pre – precaution." He was all bound up in a near-fetal position, except he hadn't fallen on his side yet. "The – the consecration. It–" And he just stopped speaking, closed his eyes, and keeled over, curled up and shaking.

"He'll live," someone said. Everyone turned, honestly, it was like a little old bar where the regulars were on a fucking pull string to the door when it opened.

It was that Indian girl, standing at the entrance to the church along with Father Nguyen, Mrs. Pike, and Mrs. Addie Longholt, who was holding her chest like she'd just had a heart attack. A little gasping, a little wheezing, and a word popped out.

"Brian."

BRIAN HAD STAYED in the truck when they'd come to St. Brigid's before. He hadn't wanted to rock the boat, had been afraid of what he'd find if he went inside, especially given how torn up the town had been. It was another mark of his cowardice, he figured, that he hadn't been ready to face the consequences of his running away. He'd made a clean break with Midian, he'd run to New York City seeking shelter, sanctuary, and not having to come back and face...

...Well...this.

"Hey, ma," he said with a weak grin.

HENDRICKS LET GO of Erin's hand, which had been in his as he'd helped her down out of the truck bed. No, he hadn't had to, she was perfectly capable of getting herself down from a pickup truck bed. But he'd offered, like a fucking gentleman, and she'd accepted, like a proper lady, and it had felt good.

For about two seconds. Until that heavily accented voice had punctured the moment like a knife between the ribs. And Hendricks had looked, and he'd seen–

Her.

Of course, her.

The same face, a few years aged past the fucking eight-year-old who'd been staring at him in the hospital in New Orleans when he'd come to after getting fished out of the drink.

Hendricks shot a look at the skinned T-Rex demons, then pulled his hat from his head. Sweat had beaded beneath the hairline, and he sighed. "Shoulda figured this was coming."

"You thought you dodged your little mentor?" Arch said, a little stiffly. Didn't seem mad, just...something. Constipated, maybe.

"Nah," Hendricks said, trying to sound more calm than he felt. His eyes fell on the blond lady he didn't recognize, and he didn't feel like it was the appropriate moment to ask about her. It reeked of kicking up a distraction to save his own ass, and he was through with that shit. "Consequences have a way of showing up no matter how far you run."

"All I want to know is," Gary Wrightson said, getting his ass lowered into his wheelchair, "when are we going to attack again?"

Hendricks raised an eyebrow at him. He'd known the guy for all of five seconds, having received the introduction in the back of the truck while they were on the run, from that serial masturbator Casey – and already he wasn't a fan. Felt like one of those glory hound lieutenants that was aching for a medal and didn't mind how many of his men got killed getting it for him. He waved a hand at the things pacing at the curb not forty feet away. "There they are. Go attack 'em, if you want." He turned his attention back to Rhea, who was still watching him carefully, and sighed. "Guess we're about due for a talk, huh? Well...let's go, then." And he waved a hand toward the church like he was shooing a cow.

Then he put his hat back on his head as he entered the house of worship, because fuck if he was going into an ass chewing from a tweenager without having it firmly on. He caught the slight twitch of the eye from Pastor Barney Jones, and it made him smile inside, because some shit might have changed for him, but that sure hadn't.

"BRIAN," Addie Longholt said, throwing her arms around her son.

Brian hugged back, but barely. "Hey, ma."

What was that feeling in him? Thrumming like a storm, but steady like...well, a storm. Pattering rain inside, a cold feeling. His mother should have left long ago. Now Brian cast a worried look at the flames encircling the horizon, or what of them he could see. They'd cut off everything to the south and east and west. Most of the roads out of town were along those vectors. Hell, they'd had to come in through the back roads from the north, past Mount Horeb, and crossed the freeway by cutting the fences and driving down the embankments to go over I-75. If they wanted to evacuate, they were going to have to go the same way, which was a bit of a slow crawl all the way to Athens.

"We should talk, too," his mother whispered in his ear. He

nodded in resignation and followed her as she threaded a thin arm around his waist, walking him back inside St. Brigid's. He watched the big demons pace at the edge of the sidewalk, and wondered if he would be better off heading in the opposite direction than going in with his mother.

ERIN WAS GIRDING HERSELF. She still felt funny about taking Hendricks's hand to get down out of the truck, but hell, it was just a hand, and she hadn't refused it when he'd grabbed her back at the mill. She'd held on for dear fucking life, because he'd just saved hers.

So why was she so damned conflicted?

On one hand, there was the clear evidence of her eyes of how bad Hendricks had fucked up: Starling, naked, barefoot, and pregnant, damned far from a kitchen yet still doing some serious cooking. She thought about the redhead, the hooker, and cringed. A flash of anger welled up, pissed her right off, as she imagined Hendricks's naked back and bare ass showing from between Starling's legs, moving up and down in a steady cadence as he fucked – and fucked up – majorly.

Now she was sorry she'd taken his hand. Maybe either time, goddammit.

"We need to get after them again," Gary Wrightson was saying. "They–"

"They killed Terry, bro," Larry Wrightson said. "You really that eager to be next?"

Gary Wrightson's face flushed about the shade of a cherry Mustang. "We ain't gonna win this thing, or honor their memories, by sitting on our asses, jerking each other off until they come for us!"

"Come on, bro," Larry said, and he started backing Gary up, pulling the handles of his wheelchair.

"Goddammit!" Gary seized his wheels and did it hard, breaking his brother's grip. "Don't you go pushing me!"

Erin felt embarrassed on his behalf, but he wasn't her problem. Nobody was her problem anymore, except–

She threaded through the small crowd, making her way to Darla Pike, who stood looking like a dead leaf waiting to be blown off a tree in autumn, steeling herself to deliver the bad news.

"NO," Darla whispered to herself, shaking her head, because this was how the mother of missing children would act. Erin Harris was cutting through the crowd toward her, and still Darla shook her head, because no, no, no, a mother would never accept that her missing children were lost, truly lost. She'd hold out hope, because she was stupid, and stupid people weren't dangerous. They were pitiable, and so she'd be pitied, and left alone, and consoled–

Which was what she needed now, since someone had fucked up and let this band of merry rejects escape alive from their perfectly laid trap.

Who fucked up? Well, it wasn't Darla's place to say. It was, however, her place to figure out how to fix it, because by doing so she'd prove herself indispensable to the-powers-about-to-be, and that was all that mattered to her.

So she readied herself, or de-steadied herself, preparing to collapse at the knees, shaking her head, refusing to accept the news that was coming. The secret was to keep it subtle, keep it understated, buried under a layer of shock, to let the emotion leak out rather than overact. She would not wail, nor gnash her teeth. She would fall into herself, enter catatonia, keep her eyes downcast and her heart full, but her mouth closed save for the occasional sob.

And the suckers would buy it. Because what kind of piece of shit would challenge a mother who'd just lost her children?

"GET YOUR GODDAMNED, skank-fisting hands off me, Larry!" Gary said, twisting his wheelchair hard enough to break his brother's grip. He spun it around, about running over Larry's foot in the process.

Larry's face crumpled, reminding Gary of when they'd both been little boys, and he'd delivered a walloping blow to his little brother. Same bitchass child, same bitchass feelings. "Damn, Gary. Ya ain't got to be like that."

"Apparently, I do," Gary said, raising his voice loud enough that the demons paused to look at him from where they were pacing by the curb, like hungry dogs waiting for their next meal. "Because everyone else seems to want to take a break, go have a talk, give each other a little sucky-sucky–"

"Ain't no one advocating for that, Gary," Larry said. "Maybe just give 'em a minute. We just lost Terry. And Chauncey–"

"You're gonna lose a lot more than a couple of limpdicks if we don't get back out there and kill those things!" Gary shouted. Top of the lungs, because he had no chill left. He was pointing at the demons by the curb.

"You're safe for now, Gary," Father Nguyen said. There was a sob over Gary's shoulder; that crying mother, no doubt. He didn't look. Didn't want to, didn't care. He had bigger fish to fry.

"Says who?" Gary asked, quieting himself not one iota. He threw his arms wide; Marina was the only one not looking at him. She was off to the side, arms wrapped tightly around herself, as if from a chill. "That fucking demon? Whose partner already betrayed us? The little girl who keeps spouting about what she knows of the future? Why should we trust any of these damned people?" He waved a hand at the cowboy, whose black hat and coat were disappearing into the church even now, trailing after that little girl. "They're not from Midian. Some of 'em ain't even from this planet."

"Gary," Lauren Darlington said, standing there beside him all of a sudden, "you need to calm the fuck down."

"Is that your professional opinion, *doctor?*" Gary spun to look her right in the – well, tits, almost. But she was staring down at him, the condescending bitch. Always thought she was better than everyone because of her fancy schooling.

"I was going to ask who's in charge around here," said the big black man who'd been driving the truck, "but I think it's starting to look like the answer is, 'no one.'"

"Listen, sir," Gary said, now turning on him–

A shadow crossed the sturdy man's face, and he answered with particular venom. "Don't call me '*sir*.' I work for a living."

Gary cast a look around. In the distance, like shadows creeping in at the edge of a campfire fire's circle of illumination, moved...things. Demons. More of them. Not large, like the T-Rexes, but small, some man-sized, some smaller, like the insects that had devoured Terry–

He couldn't help it. Gary tried to stifle a sob, but he couldn't. Someone tried to touch his shoulder, but he brushed it off. Not hard, because he didn't have it in him, but brusque for sure. He had his head bowed. "They're coming," he said, wanting to rage but not able to get there. The grief had him now, and he brushed another hand off. "Leave me alone, you cunts."

And they did. Right there in the parking lot, with the pacing demons and others coming in the distance, surrounding the church, while everybody else went inside to hide their heads in the sand.

"HE'LL BE ALL RIGHT," Larry Wrightson said once they were inside. One of the last survivors of the Wrightson clan, he wasn't hiding his tears like Gary. Lauren saw them in the corners of his eyes, and on his cheeks, where they'd fallen during the ride back from the mill.

That had been a hell of a trip. Lauren had stayed quiet, because what else was there to say? Half of them had lost their guns somewhere along the way, or left them in the truck. It felt weird, having the strap hanging around her neck the way it was, but she didn't dare drop it the way Larry had his. She kept it clutched tight to her, safety on and pointed at the ground the way her daddy had taught her when she was young.

God, how long had it been since she thought about her daddy? Most days Lauren didn't, not at all. It wasn't malice, not really, though they'd never been particularly close. He'd been distant long before his only offspring had gotten pregnant as a teenager; he'd been a man's man, and unsure of how to deal with her petulant moods, her ringing self-righteousness, her uncompromising certainty that everything he'd believed was bullshit, and sometimes kind of racist.

It had been a long time since Lauren remembered what it felt like to be wrapped up in strong arms, safe from the world. She'd sought it out from a host of men before and after Molly had been born. It was her bad luck that none of them had worked out. Probably a couple of them, it maybe could have, but she'd torpedoed them because–

Lauren leaned against the church's wall, unsure whether she wanted to even consider this further.

God, they'd been close once, though. She'd been Daddy's Little Girl when she was truly little, before puberty had taken her feelings and twisted them and made her angry and bitchy for a few years. But he hadn't known how to handle it, and she hadn't cared to push through, and so the block of ice grew between them day by day until she wasn't Daddy's Little Girl anymore, and they were strangers living in the same house. Molly had succeeded her, becoming Granddaddy's Little Girl, and Lauren had medical school to worry about, and–

"What in the fuck?" she whispered. Everyone else had gone on, inward. She felt like she was in a haze, and it wasn't some delicate one, like a dream of a summer day. It was the other kind, the kind she'd been snared on when in the mill. Dark ruminations, thoughts of all the shit she'd had go wrong in her life. The roads not taken. The fuckups she couldn't undo.

Her mom had understood. Because her mom was a woman, had been through it, maybe. Had not become a defiant teenager with an infant then toddler daughter that her father saw as a do-over.

"Seriously, what the fuck?" Lauren whispered to herself. She'd never been prone to depression, but she wondered if this was it. Intrusive thoughts that wouldn't leave her alone. She slid down the wall until her tailbone and ass touched floor, and breathed in and out, curling up like Duncan had out in the parking lot, defenseless against these thoughts that wouldn't leave her alone.

"THAT WAS WEIRD, RIGHT?" Terri asked, pacing ahead of Braeden into the church. Everyone seemed to be making their way inside, and Braeden got that. Who wanted to sit outside and look at the things pacing the edge of the church property?

Braeden sure wasn't looking forward to charging down one of those demon T-Rex things. Not with the five rounds he had left in the AR. Especially not since they were doing about as much good as trying to put out the wildfire by pissing into it.

"That was weird," Braeden agreed, trudging along behind her. He glanced around the church; boy, there weren't many left, even compared to last night. There were maybe – even with the cowboy and his late arrivals – what, twenty people left in town? And that number would have shrunk if he hadn't shown up, down to zero, because they'd really been on the ropes, getting the shit pummeled out of them.

Terri turned around on him, her tank top clinging tight to her. He tried not to look. "I feel like you might just be telling me what you think I want to hear."

"If I was going to do that," Braeden said with a tired smile, "I'd tell you everything was going to be all right."

She smirked. "You got a point there." She looked down at her sodden shirt, and pinched it between her fingers at the strap, lifting it up and giving it a sniff. "Oof!" She turned her face away quickly. "I am going to need something other than this." She slapped a hand down and hit her jeans, sloshing drips of water out of them.

"Yeah," Braeden said, and looked out the stained-glass windows, where it sure looked like night was gathering outside. It wasn't, it was just the smoke and the haze. "Don't reckon we should leave the church, though, or we'll get eaten."

"There are some clothes in the back," Father Nguyen said. "Might be something that'd fit you. Or at least something you could make do with." He was standing by Darla Pike, who was head down, sobbing softly in a pew beside Erin Harris. They were comforting her. Which was sweet.

"What do you suppose happened to those kids?" Terri asked as the two of them made their way in the direction he'd pointed.

There was a hallway toward back offices or something; Braeden hadn't spent much time in St. Brigid's, but he followed Terri now. Terri in her wet, stringy, wife-beater t-shirt and tight jeans that were clinging to her.

"I don't even want to think about it," Braeden said. It hit a little too close to home for him.

DARLA PRETENDED to sob softly into her hands, but didn't dare look up. The news had been received: her children were dead. She didn't want to be showy, didn't want to make a fool of herself by overdoing it. She just pictured the saddest thing she could think of and wept softly, making sure to keep the volume in the pitiable range rather than histrionic.

"Is there anything I can do for you?" Erin Harris asked her, stroking her back gently. It was sweet. In another time, if she'd been feeling randy rather than annoyed, and the deputy had been drunk enough, Darla would have enjoyed taking advantage of her. She had a tight ass, a cute face, and wide eyes.

But it wasn't the act itself that necessarily did it for Darla. A pretty face was a fine thing; she could enjoy it almost as much as a handsome one, given the right circumstances – and had, especially in college.

It was the destruction of innocence she really enjoyed. Pushing a girl, a woman, innocent in her way, into this new experience, into new feelings – only to tear her heart out later.

One of those girls had called her a psychopath when she'd laughed after delivering the knife to the heart that was a proper jilting after months of circling that culminated in a night of passion. Imagine that; and she'd consecrated that, too, to a demon who enjoyed such things. It had netted her a few chits in the great game, a few orgasms, and a modicum of enjoyment as she dropped the hammer on a girl who'd been hurt enough by men that taking a chance on an understanding woman with the help of a little alcohol had seemed a reasonable, open-minded thing to do.

Darla had pretended to be as sad as everyone else when she'd seen the coroner's van outside the dorm a few days later. She wasn't, but she pretended. That she dedicated to a different demon, ex post facto, and it had given her a few more chits, a feeling of real power, and a couple orgasms, too (from the demon, who respected her hustle).

Okay, maybe she was a little bit of a psychopath. But not entirely, because she was, in fact, crying. Real tears. Big ones. And all she had to do was envision all her sacrifices coming up in vain by the simple act of fucking up what she was trying to accomplish here.

Presto – tears. Free-flowing snot. The proper cry of a grieved mother. Or at least the distress of a woman who'd given everything to get what she wanted, only to have a group of inbred hicks refuse to die on her altar the way they were supposed to.

"Please," Darla said, brushing a snot-drenched hand onto Erin Harris's, and causing the deputy to squirm from base-level germophobia. Bet she wasn't that squeamish about putting a dick in her mouth – and who knew where those had been. "I just - I need a few minutes."

"Take all the time you need," Father Nguyen said soothingly. How sweet. She'd been dreaming about cutting the priest's throat for over an hour. Should have done it while everyone was gone, then pissed on his corpse and said a little anti-prayer to deconsecrate the grounds. Simple enough ceremony, but it tended to take a while. Plus some effort.

Looking up with her red eyes, she knew one thing: she did not have a while. Not with this many fucking dipshit rubes meandering around the church. Trying to cut the priest's throat would be enough to get her caught, because she'd barely get the knife across his jugular before he'd squeal like a little piggy. She'd slit enough throats in her time to know that it never went as quick as you wanted; there was always time for a scream.

And a scream would bring them all down on her, lickety-split. Unless she could come up with a distraction...

"We'll be over here if you need anything," Harris said, taking her little hand away, then sauntering off with her cute little ass in her tight little jeans.

Darla had worn jeans like that once upon a time. Back when she was young and hot. Back before the kids fucked up her body. Before Jason had put two in her belly.

She felt a brief flash of irrational hatred.

"If you need any other kinds of comfort," came a breathy voice in her ear, "you just let me know."

Darla raised her eyes to find a leering face beside hers. "Wh...what?"

"Any. Kind," the skinny hick said in a long country drawl. He arched his eyebrows with a level of suggestiveness that Darla thought had been wiped out during the MeToo movement. Who was this hillbilly piece of shit?

"Casey," Harris's voice was a whip crack, the kind Darla might have gotten excited about if it had slashed across her back. "Leave her alone."

"Any kind," Casey said, arching those eyebrows again. "I don't judge. Whatever you need." God, he was a skinny little fucker. She watched him withdraw, but he winked at her on his path away.

Darla was keenly aware she was being watched. She kept a squinty, uncertain look on her face as she watched him wander away, trying to make everyone think she was simply perplexed.

Inside, she was shouting hallelujah, or the opposite equivalent of it, because now she knew exactly what to do next.

"SO," Hendricks said as he and Rhea passed through a series of hallways at the back of St. Brigid's. He hadn't meant that as a statement, but it came out as one, freestanding. She didn't turn to answer him, just kept striding through the halls on her tiny legs, leading him past classrooms that were used for Sunday school, or maybe regular school.

"Yes?" Rhea asked, stopping at one of the classrooms and opening the door. It had one of those glass slit windows that let people look in. Boxes of stuff were piled up around the edges, giving it the appearance of a storage room, but little wooden tables and chairs still filled the center, and a few posters were visible peeking around the boxes bearing slogans that Hendricks wasn't too familiar with, probably stuff from the bible. One of them said JESUS LOVES and the rest was cut off. He imagined it finished with something pedestrian, but got a chuckle out of the idea that the unseen words were something offbeat, like JESUS LOVES CHILI CON QUESO, or JESUS LOVES THE DALLAS COWBOYS – AT LEAST IN THEIR WINNING YEARS. BUT THE CHEERLEADERS ALL THE TIME (AND ESPECIALLY AT NIGHT, WITH THE LIGHTS OUT, UNDER THE COVERS).

That brought an irreverent grin to Hendricks's face. He'd loved the Dallas Cowboy cheerleaders when the lights were out at night as a teenager.

Hendricks shook off the goofy thoughts and focused on the pint-sized guru before him. She had changed since last he'd seen her, all those years ago in the hospital. She'd provided financial support, but that was via checks in the mail to places he was heading, made out to cash, and phone calls wherein she offered him guidance that hadn't steered him wrong, exactly, but had made him question his sanity once or thrice. After all, nearly dying and then taking a single digit aged child as your spiritual guide to vengeance against demons? He knew what sanity was, and he never bothered to profess he was entrenched deeply within its echelons. Because this shit was crazy.

"You strayed from the path, Hendricks," Rhea said, with just about as much feeling as Starling ever brought to any of their trysts. "And now look what you've wrought."

He sighed. Time was, he might have gotten mad at being confronted like this. Now, though, he just pulled his hat off and sat on one of the little miniature chairs, cradling it and cutting his eyes low. "Yeah. I fucked, and I fucked up bad."

"I see you retain your talent for understatement," Rhea said. She did not sit. Didn't matter; she was still roughly on eye level with him thanks to these stupid kiddie chairs. "And cleverness."

"Well, I tried to get rid of 'em, but it's like a bad case of the clap," Hendricks said. "My question is...what do we do now?"

She was quiet for a spell, staring at him, skinny arms crossed over her skinny torso. "What do you want to do?"

Hendricks chuckled. "Well, if I had my druthers, I'd head out with the whole crew, and drop a nuke on this place once we were at minimum safe distance. Maybe even maximal distance. But I'm lacking nukes, and I'm not entirely sure that would even solve the problem."

"It probably wouldn't."

"Can't say for certain? Or just won't?"

"The gate is the problem," she said, and in spite of that big backpack looking like it might tip her over, she managed to squat down on a chair across the little table from him. "It's not built by man, and I'm not sure it can be destroyed by one."

Hendricks sat back in his seat, damned near turning it over in the process. "If you don't know, who does?"

"People who aren't people," she said with a little glitter of amusement. "People who weren't born on earth, as humans. In other words–"

"Yeah, yeah," Hendricks said dismissively. "Angels, demons, blah, blah, blah."

She chuckled, and he blushed a little, because he knew what was coming next. "You fight demons all the time. Is it really so hard for you to accept that there are other forces, more powerful and obscure? A deity that looks down, that created–"

"If I wanted a sermon, I would have come to a ch–" Hendricks paused. "Well, shit. I still don't want a sermon, though."

"Of course you don't," she said. "And I'm not here to give you one. But the reason you don't want one is not because you don't believe." She leaned a little forward to look harder at him, and he tried not to squirm under her gaze. "It's because you've only believed in yourself and vengeance for about five years now, and you're starting to realize that's a fine thing to do when you're looking to die – but it's a rickety foundation to build a life on."

"I don't have a life," Hendricks said, and that same exhaustion that had threatened to pull him down, the same kind that landed him in the hospital came roaring back now. He felt like he was deflating. "If I have a superpower in all this, it's that I know I'm going to die. There's no walking away now. Not from the things I've done. Not from the way I've lived. And definitely not from all those little tonics I drank to save my own life." He could see them in his mind's eye, the elixirs from Wren Spellman. How many of them had he taken? Draughts that saved him from death, healed his injuries, brought him back to life?

He'd been told there was a cost to drinking too many of those. Well, he could feel it in his veins now, had known it since he'd woken up in the hospital those weeks ago. The bill was coming due, and he was fresh out of any currency to pay it save for with his own life.

Rhea sat back in her chair. "You're not going to survive this? That's your view?"

"That is indeed the view from the cheap seats," he said, wiggling his left boot, popping it off his heel and letting it dangle slightly without removing it. "Which is the only place I've ever sat."

"That's a dark place to be sitting."

Hendricks turned his face to the windows on the side of the room. Mostly, they were covered by the cardboard boxes, but only halfway. He could see that demons were pacing in the hazy light; man-shaped figures, or other ones, moving about in the gray smoke of the darkening day. A wind was moving hard, stirring the dead grass that lay between the church building and the street beyond where the shadows lurked. "I don't know if you've noticed, but it ain't sweetness and light out there."

"And yet beyond that cloud that suffocates this town, there is light. The sun still shines elsewhere."

"And that would matter to me," Hendricks said with a grim smile, "if I were elsewhere. But I'm here. So I gotta take conditions as they come." He felt the smile evaporate slowly. "Nothing can change my fate. I just figure I ought to use the time I have left to try and leave things better than I found them."

She sat in silence for a moment before rising up. "I don't know what your future holds, Hendricks. I haven't been told."

"I know the way things work for you." He stood, adjusting his hat as he did so. "I got into this demon-hunting thing because it was what I wanted, and I don't have regrets. But we all know how revenge and obsession play out." He stared out the window for a moment. "I'm going to die, because we probably all are. There's no walking away from this, it's a suicide mission. I just need to figure out a way to make things right for these people."

When she didn't answer that, he felt like the conversation was closed – and that was fine with him. He needed to find

Arch, anyway, talk to him about...well, the things they needed to work on.

"Hendricks," Rhea called out to him as he opened the door. "Before the end...you might want to find something to believe in that doesn't include vengeance." When he looked back at her, he found her somewhat...beseeching. "If it's a bad foundation for a life, it's an even worse one for an afterlife."

He smirked. "You know I don't believe in–"

"I know what I've seen," she said. "And I know what I know."

"Guess we'll find out," he said, and gave her a wink. Mostly because he figured it might drive her nuts, as it would most.

But maybe a little bit because being cocky was good cover for the churning feeling in his guts that seemed to be growing as the end approached.

ARCH WASN'T sure why he was wandering the halls; he'd passed a room and saw Addie Longholt inside with Brian, just talking, the two of them. He hadn't lingered; he'd felt like an intruder, especially now with Alison dead, like he wasn't part of that family, and maybe never had been.

A door opened ahead, and suddenly Arch knew why he'd been wandering.

"Hey," the cowboy said, in that typically quiet way he had. He'd never have considered the cowboy laconic, exactly, but he wasn't the most verbose soul, either.

"That stuff's for horses," Arch said, letting the cowboy come to him.

Hendricks frowned, lines creasing his forehead deeply. "Save the dad jokes for the dads," he said, then seemed to think the better of it. "Sorry. I didn't mean–"

"Water under the bridge," Arch said, waving him off. "Or at least it would be, if we had water around here that didn't come in a bottle."

"I did notice things are a little parched. And flaming."

"It's not exactly been a barrel of laughs since you left," Arch said, following Hendricks's saunter over to the hallway's side. The cowboy leaned against the wall, resting his shoulder there, lifting a foot and crossing it behind the other to stand coolly.

"You were dealing with human-eating demons and a pack of wildcat ones before I left," Hendricks said. "What have you been getting into since that's got this place looking like the apocalypse has come? Other than my pregnant ex."

"Can't thank you enough for that one, by the by."

Hendricks winced. "I really am sorry. Not that it means much now."

"It's not nothing," Arch said. "But it ain't a path to a win, either."

"Let's see if we can get there," Hendricks said.

"Not sure how. Things are looking dire at the moment."

"Yeah, well," Hendricks said. "Darkest before dawn and all that claptrap. When did you find out about Starling?"

"Last night," Arch said. "She and some other demons started the fires, drew us all in, hypnotized us. Killed a couple folks." He shook his head. "Been a steady dwindling of our numbers lately, as you can probably tell. Death and...well..."

"Morale issues?"

"Good enough way to explain it," Arch said. "Better one might be that no one sees a way to win, and a lot of them left because they figure the town is going down."

"But you don't believe that?"

"I believe a whole lot more than the town is going down," Arch said. "Starling told us we had three days and then the world was going to end." He looked at the darkening sky through a window at the end of the hall. "I haven't seen anything to convince me she's a liar. About that, anyway."

"I'm not sure she was a liar about anything else, either," Hendricks said, face twisting slightly. "I just think we saw what we wanted to see, and didn't dig too deep into why she was helping us."

"Why was she helping us, then?" Arch asked.

Here, Hendricks winced. "Remember that time you saved my life?"

Arch cocked an eyebrow at him. "You might have to get a touch more specific."

Hendricks grinned. "Okay, fine, we watched each others' backs a lot. I meant at the edge of the dam, but your point is well taken. If I'd been fighting alone, I'd have died a bunch of times. I die, where does Starling get the sperm donor for whatever is growing in her belly right now?"

"Literally anywhere. She's not an unappealing lady."

Hendricks frowned. "Yeah, that's a good point. But I think it had to be me. Or at least that there was a reason she chose me. Not sure why."

Arch mulled that a moment. "Not much about this makes sense, but that's the sort of question I'd like to run by Duncan. See if he has an explanation that makes more sense."

Hendricks nodded along to that. "Guthrie betrayed you, I take it?"

"Indeed. It was a night of surprises all around."

"I'm surprised you managed to escape."

That made Arch frown, too. "I get this feeling she's picking us apart one piece at a time."

"Like hyenas," Hendricks said. "A little nip here, a little nip there, letting the prey bleed out, weaken."

"We were promised some torment," Arch said. "I get the feeling our end is not meant to be gentle, nor quick."

"Slow torture," Hendricks said. "Starling always did like to take her time." That drew a hard look from Arch, but the cowboy shrugged it away. "Just telling you. Could turn out to be important."

"I doubt that one small detail is going to be relevant, but thank you for your thoroughness." Arch stared past him at the emergency exit door, and the window looking out into the darkened town. Things were definitely moving in the lengthening shadows out there, and Arch had a real good guess as to what they were: surrounded. "What we could really use is a plan."

"At this point it's either batter your way out, or sit tight and wait for the situation to change." Hendricks had his arms crossed over his broad chest. "Which I can't imagine taking a turn for the favorable, but weirder things have happened."

"It's been a shame, not having you around for inspiration," Arch said. "I'd like to get these folks the heck out of here."

"Really, Arch? It's the end of the world. You can say 'hell,' because it's going to be here real soon, it sounds like."

"Seems to me it's more important than ever to keep running my race the right way," Arch said. "With the finish line in sight."

"Well, you can't go out the front door nor the back without being ready for a hell of a rumble – and with your diminished numbers, I don't think you are," Hendricks said. "For the same reason, you can't go left or right. Can't go up, obviously, unless you've got a hot air balloon or a jetpack stored away in one of these rooms." He shrugged. "And you can't go down, unless you want to start tunneling to the center of the earth. So...what?" Hendricks was frowning at him.

Mainly because Arch had suddenly started frowning. "There's a tunnel system under this town. Storm drains. Remember? That's where I chased that demon that kidnapped the kids?"

"Oh, right, the incredible edible children," Hendricks said

with a look of disgust. "Sorry, I don't remember that. I was busy at the time helping Starling to, uh...well..."

"Murder the county administrator for fun and ritual?" Arch gave him a sour look. He'd earned it.

Hendricks rolled his eyes. "Whatever. Water, bridges, et cetera. Tunnels, you said?"

Arch nodded slowly. "Storm tunnels. They're all over under the town." He glanced at the floor. "Might be a way we could get out of here after all – if we have a mind to."

"GARY," Larry said from somewhere over his shoulder, "you ought to come in now."

"Fuck off," Gary said. He'd anchored his brakes and was just sitting in the church parking lot, head down, as the light level fell a few lumens at a time. The sun was setting in the distance, somewhere beyond the haze of smoke, and the wildfires that filled the horizon with black. It gave the town a graying look, and he figured another thirty minutes and it'd be like midnight save for the burning orange fires on the horizon.

"Fine," Larry said, losing patience, audibly. "I'm going inside to hit up the supply cache for one of them MREs, or maybe some canned corn. You want anything?"

"What part of 'fuck off' are you struggling with?" Gary asked, still keeping his voice level, and properly down. "Is it the fucking part? Because that would make sense, you've always struggled with fucking."

"Trip over your wheels and eat shit, Gary," Larry said, and his footsteps receded inside. Marina had already gone in, thankfully. Because he didn't want her to see him like this.

He didn't need to look to know that trouble was swarming in. The big T-Rex demons were still out there, though only one was staring at him from the street right now. The others had circled the church, taking up positions elsewhere, but watching to make sure some enterprising soul didn't try and sneak out without becoming a snack.

"What's...up...your...ass?" The question came from the demon in the back of the pickup, and he sounded like he was suffering a wicked case of the shakes.

"Don't know," Gary said, keeping his head down. "Can't feel it, see. Probably a giant ass demon, maybe a hemorrhoid." He lifted his head to at least look at the demon, but he couldn't see him; he was still lying down in the back of the truck, below where Gary could look at him. "What's up yours?"

"A two-thousand-year-old...crucifixion," Duncan stuttered out. "And some...bad choices...from way before that."

"Well whoop-de-doo," Gary said, still keeping his head down, though it was obvious now that things were skittering just out beyond the edge of the church property. "What do you propose to do about it? Swap mutual shitass life stories?"

"Nope," Duncan said, then held for a pause in which he kicked the truck hard enough that it caused a ringing noise of something striking metal. He'd spasmed, probably from whatever the holy blessings of St. Brigid's were doing to him. "Not looking to...bare my essence. But we could...start an insult war. Maybe distract ourselves. What do you say?"

Gary looked up. "Hell, yeah, you pink piece of fake skin with a bunch of turds stuffed inside. I could insult you all day today without taking a break or repeating myself." Finally someone understood him.

LAUREN WAS ON HER SIDE, curled up in the entry to St. Brigid's, and she could not uncurl herself no matter what she did. The floor was cold, the smoky air filled her sinuses even this low to the ground, which made her wonder if suffocation was a danger at some point, soon, for all of them.

"Demons, demons, everywhere," someone said in the distance. "There's a certain type of them that love nothing more than fucking humans to death. Women, men – they don't care. They don't even notice a distinction. One hole is as good as another for them."

Charming, Lauren thought, wondering if those were her intrusive thoughts again, or if someone was actually saying that.

Why was this happening? She recognized a clear difference in the symptoms between what was happening now, and what Starling had done with those curious, dream-like spells she kept casting over them. This was a type of paralysis, she realized, the analytical part of her mind free to work while a clutching fear wrapped itself around the more primitive parts of her brain, the ones that couldn't reason. On one hand, she knew she was in danger, that there were in fact demons lurking just outside these walls.

On the other, she couldn't figure out why that meant she couldn't so much as wiggle her toes.

Starling's trances featured people she knew, people she loved, and conversations that felt nearly real in the moment, if not once she had stirred back to consciousness. This, though, was something else.

In those dark parts of her mind that controlled her body, she was remembering things she didn't want to recall: kissing Stephen Fenton in seventh grade during seven minutes in heaven. He was number seven on the football team, too. 777. Sneaking away from school in sixth to get high. Going down for her first time on Alan Ross and watching his eyes roll back in his head as he ejaculated in her mouth and, once she'd realized that it tasted fucking foul, all over her favorite sweater, ruining it.

She'd walked around the rest of the day with that stain, telling anyone who asked that it was frosting from a toaster strudel. Which was embarrassing, too, but not nearly as much as admitting where it had really come from. Or cum from.

See! That was the kind of knuckleheaded humor she could not have appreciated if she was terrified out of her mind.

But then...what was going on? Why was she a prisoner to her memories, her embarrassments, her past fuck-ups?

On that screen in her brain she was watching herself on a bed with Jesse Harris. They'd come over to her house to smoke weed, because she had some and he didn't, and he was handsome and taken, and she was free and horny.

She'd kissed him first, and it had been like awakening something in him. She'd heard Emily Marie Johnson – that girl who became his wife – didn't do anything below the belt, but Lauren hadn't been prepared for how quickly things turned. He had her skirt up in thirty seconds, and she had his pants unbuckled right after. When he entered her, she shuddered, because he didn't go slow and it hurt a little.

Then...it started to feel real good. The best it had ever felt.

It wasn't her first time. It wasn't even her tenth, or twentieth, maybe. She'd gotten into sex after her first boyfriend, had become a connoisseur of it, almost like weed at that stage of her life. Getting properly railed was a delight she couldn't get enough of, though it was kind of hard to come by in her grade. Most of the guys she tried out weren't very good. Not one of them had actually gotten her to orgasm. The only one who'd ever done that was an older guy in his twenties she'd met at a party. She hadn't told him her age, he hadn't asked, but she'd let him go down on her, then fuck her, and she had no regrets. Which was more than she could say about a few of the high schoolers she'd given a try out.

But Jesse was different. He was barely inside her when she

came, hard, and strong, gasping and clutching at his back, pushing him deeper inside her. He followed a moment later, surprising the hell out of her because she'd planned to tell him to pull out as soon as she finished, but before she could marshal the words he sprayed inside her instead of across her belly.

And that had conceived Molly.

Sure, now, as a doctor and an older woman, she knew pulling out wasn't effective birth control. But a small part of her wondered if she hadn't cum so unexpectedly, if her experience with him had been like every other guy she'd been with, and it had ended in disappointment for her, and she'd explained herself rather than being thrown into that ecstasy – a high she'd been chasing without luck through a whole host of men in all the years since – maybe she wouldn't have had a daughter. Even a couple more reprises with Jesse on the sly hadn't yielded the same results; she either hadn't gotten there right away, or she hadn't gotten there at all.

Maybe it was that she'd been ready that day. Maybe it was the shape of his erection and the angle of entry. Maybe it was sheer fucking dumb luck.

All this flashed through her mind as she lay there on the floor, unable to move, wondering what the hell had her in its grip. She tried to speak, tried to squeeze a word or two out, but nothing came. Just these fucking intrusive thoughts, holding her in place while the world went slouching toward apocalypse around her.

DARLA WAS SEARCHING FOR A DISTRACTION. There were just too many people around, that was the problem. Two rows back sat some pale Eastern European girl, skinny as a rail, who looked like she was trying to keep down her lunch.

Which had likely been two bean sprouts and three grains of rice based on her physique. The priest was still lingering nearby, too, and so was a smattering of other people. Some long, raven-haired guy who looked straight out of the trailer park, a black preacher she dimly recognized from some public function, another stockier, squarish black man she didn't. He was standing like a military man, ramrod-up-his-ass straight. Harris was hanging nearby, too, as if waiting for Darla to start sobbing again so she could swoop in and help.

A gasping cry from near the entrance drew all the attention – and oxygen – in the room. Darla stood, making sure to squint her eyes to emphasize that she'd been crying, and parked a hand over her mouth to make it look like she was still holding in sobs.

Everyone else looked, too. The source took a moment for her to locate, but she figured it out.

Huddled in the back, in the fetal position against one of the walls, was that lady doctor, Darlington. She'd met her a couple times, and liked her, actually, as far as Darla liked anyone. She was smart, had a keen wit, and didn't fit in well in this backwater shithole. Darla respected that more than anything. And identified with it.

The doctor was spasming, which seemed ironic, because who else could they count on to help her? "Oh, shit," Harris said, on her feet in an instant, heading straight for her. Father Nguyen followed.

Once every eye in the room was on that spectacle, Darla found herself without a single soul paying attention to her.

Well, except for one.

She glanced toward the far end of the room, where a door waited just behind the pulpit, presumably leading to the priest's chambers. She moved in that direction, uncertainly at first, acting as though whatever was going on with the doctor had her spooked. When she reached the door, however, she glanced right at the skinny, horny little bastard who'd hit on her earlier. He was still the only one looking at her.

So she gave him a wink, then pushed through the door. She found herself in a small chamber, a few robes hanging on hooks on the walls, and another door waited beyond leading deeper into the building.

She didn't have to wait long; the bastard might have run after her for all she knew. He didn't say anything, just grinned.

This was going to be easy. Darla beckoned him with a come-hither motion of her finger and pushed back through the door, which swung open for her and led into a small office. Naturally, the dumb hick followed, leering and arching his eyebrows.

ERIN MADE it to Dr. Darlington's side and hit the ground, jarring her knees. Darlington's long, dark hair was bound back, and her eyes were open, like she was comatose but unseeing, staring off into the distance. She put a hand on the doctor's shoulder and shook her, to little effect. The doctor's knees spasmed up and gave her a hellacious bruise on the side of her thigh, causing Erin to mutter, "Ow."

"What's wrong with her?" Father Nguyen asked, bending over Erin's shoulder. Using her as a human shield, really, because she didn't see him catching a knee to the quad. Damn, that hurt.

"I don't know," Erin said, not relenting in her shaking. "She seemed fine coming back from the mill. Maybe she's...what's that thing where you fall asleep when you're not supposed to?"

"Narcoleptic," said the sturdy, older black man who'd showed up with Hendricks. Who was this guy? Erin didn't know, but strangely she trusted him right away. Not because he showed up with Hendricks, but because he spoke like a man who knew his shit. "This ain't that, though." He slid in next to her and rolled the doctor onto her back. Pushing her head back, he cleared her airway just the way Erin had learned in one of her first aid classes she'd taken for the sheriff's department training. And forgotten because she'd attended the class fighting a five-alarm hangover. "This is more like a trance."

Whatever it was, the doctor was staring up at the ceiling now, and still jerking like someone had snuck stray voltage into the underwire of her bra. Erin just knelt there, helplessly, watching her seize.

"I DIDN'T THINK you were coming back," Addie Longholt said to her son, stroking his cheek. "I thought you'd left for the last time after your daddy..."

"Yeah," Brian said with a deep sigh. "I thought I was out, but, well, the cowboy found me up in New York and just..." He made a motion like grabbing someone and tugging them toward him. "...Pulled me back in, y'know?" He shook his head slowly. "I couldn't just leave it, ma."

"Why not?" she asked, whisper-soft.

"Because I don't want to think of myself as a coward for the rest of my life," he answered, just as quietly, then swallowed the mighty lump in his throat. "I think maybe that's...that's even worse than dying, living with that."

"You came back for the right reason, then," she said. And he just stayed quiet, because how could he disagree?

"SOMETHING GOING ON OUT THERE?" Hendricks asked. Rhea had just passed them by at a trot, the young girl running toward the church's nave. He and Arch had been hanging in that hallway, just shooting a little bit of the shit, catching up, mulling ideas. They actually had one, a good one, maybe, though it was going to require asking questions of the priest. They hadn't moved to go find him yet, though, because...well, it felt good to be talking to Arch again. The big man must have felt the same, too, because he hadn't made a move to break the seal and go, either.

Rhea stopped just shy of the doors leading into the church. Turning back, she said, "There is something wrong with the doctor." And then pushed through without further explanation.

Hendricks furrowed his brow; Arch matched his expression, and without another word, they both headed in the direction of the trouble.

"YOU WERE RIGHT ABOUT ME," Darla said, catching that skinny little fucker the moment he was in the inner sanctum of the priest. There were chairs, there was a desk, there was a giant crucifix on the wall behind it. As fitted a priest's office, Darla supposed. She grabbed him and dragged him forward, pushing him against the desk ass-first. He folded over backward in surprise, almost toppling. Taking hold of the nearest chair, she jammed it against the door to keep it from opening easily, after locking it. "My husband died a few months ago."

He blinked a couple times, the skinny fucker. "Yeah. Yeah. That's...that's tough."

"I can't stop myself," she said, slinking over to him. "I don't want to feel it, you see?" She ran a hand slowly across her chest, letting her fingertips stray on them, pulling the fabric tight. "So I keep thinking about...other things. So to keep from thinking about how bad things are, I keep thinking about..." She adjusted her bra, and his eyes fell to her chest. Something good had come out of her pregnancies, and it was a C cup where before she had been a B. "...How bad I could be."

"Sure," he said, eyes still wide. He had a bulge in his crotch. A big one. "I'm Casey, by the way," he said, sticking out his hand like he wanted to shake.

She walked forward into it, grabbed it with both hands, planting it on her left tit. "Hi, Casey," she said, unzipping her pants and letting them fall to her ankles. Kicking off her shoes was easy, and she didn't waste time with her socks. "I'm Darla. Now..." And she reached down and unfastened his belt, ripping it free of the loops like a magician pulling a tablecloth out from beneath a full dinner spread. Once it was out, she folded it, then gave it a snap. "Let's not talk anymore."

BRAEDEN FOUND himself in an odd position, at least for him. And at least lately.

Missionary.

His breathing came heavy, his movement smooth, pounding. Terri lay beneath him, reaching up and stroking his hair as he moved in and out in regular thrusts. He felt like he had the largest erection of all time, that his tip was going to explode at any second because of how long it had been.

How long had it been? Since Abi died, he hadn't even touched himself. It hadn't felt right, he hadn't had time, he'd been living in Barney Jones's house. Before that, sure, he'd go to bed at night and wax the ol' purple pole most evenings. He was, after all, still a young man.

But man, how long had it been since he'd had sex? That was a less comfortable question, because being a single dad, owning his own demanding business, and living in small town Midian hadn't afforded him too many opportunities for dating, both in a time sense, and in terms of the available pool.

"It's been kind of a long time for me," Terri said, gasping lightly beneath him, small but beautiful breasts heaving. "I kinda suck on top, but you want me to take a turn?"

Was it that obvious he was about to die from exertion? "Sure," he said, and turned over, planting his ass on the rug in this unused classroom. Did he feel guilty about getting it on in a church?

Nope. Mostly he just felt lust, especially as she positioned herself on top of him and guided his dick into her, starting to bounce. He watched her go, breasts tumbling in front of his eyes, and he planted hands on her thighs as she slid down his pole, enjoying every moment of this.

"LAUREN?" Someone asked as Hendricks came into the church. "Doc?" It was that black pastor that Arch had gone to live with after Alison died. He was gently slapping her in the face. Micah was there, too, looking down at her.

"What happened to her?" Arch asked, pacing ahead of Hendricks by a bit. Long-legged bastard really had the inside track on these things.

"She just cried out," Erin said, huddled over Dr. Darlington as well. "And she's staring into space like she can't see anything." She speared Hendricks with a look. "You ever seen anything like this?"

"There are some demons that cause fugue states and the like," Hendricks said. She was collapsed right in the entry to the church. "Weird mind power kind of things." He looked down at the doc; she stared up at the ceiling, face paler than usual. Pretty lady, the doc. But she didn't look healthy now. She looked sickly, like she had a real need of her own services. "I've only read about it, though, never seen it."

"This place is the ultimate draw of every demon in the world, though," Arch said. "Makes sense, seeing something new."

"This is not something new," Rhea said. She was at Arch's elbow, peering down at the doctor. "It is something very old."

Hendricks raised an eyebrow at that, and did a little more peering of his own. Not that mere looking was likely to do him much good.

"YOU GOT BROUGHT LOW," Gary said, sitting in his wheelchair only a few feet from the back of that pickup truck. "It happens to the best of us." He was staring down at his feet – his useless fucking feet, almost as useless as his family right now. Two brothers dead, their mom gone, too. A third that might as well have been. Even Marina wasn't as efficient as she used to be.

And who did he have to blame for that? Well, not himself, for fuck's sake. He was the only one in this goddamned band still trying.

"'Low' does not begin...to describe how I'm doing," Duncan said, the shakes in his words melting right in for the most part, some of the stutter dissolving as he got used to whatever torment he was experiencing from being on the church property. "Have you ever had someone...peel back your skin...and then light matches on your exposed musculature and skeleton...then set fire to it...?"

"No, but I've watched *The View*," Gary said. "Probably as close to that experience as you can get without actually dying."

A pained chuckle came from behind the edge of the pickup truck bed. "You been...this low...before?"

Gary stared down at his feet. "Probably when I got my spine broken, yeah."

In the distance, that big T-Rex demon pacing the sidewalk snorted. "How'd that...happen?" Duncan asked.

Gary bowed his head, feeling that familiar flush in his cheeks. Looking over his shoulder, he checked to make sure no one else was out here. "Look, you ever tell anyone this, I won't just deny it. I'll spike your ass with a holy object and turn you into stink, you hear me?"

"Yeah...?"

Looking over his shoulder one more time, Gary spoke low and certain. "The story goes I was out driving – drunk – and I ended up going into the ditch. Clocked a telephone pole, wasn't wearing my seatbelt, and boom, the truck cabin crunched, shattered my spine low in my back, putting an end to my promising career as a ballet dancer."

There was a short beat. "Okay. But what...actually happened?" Duncan grunted out.

Gary hung his head. "I did something fucking stupid. Which is really out of character for me. I wasn't drunk. I didn't hit a telephone pole – 'least not at first." He glanced at the door to the church one last time, just to confirm it hadn't opened. "I was listening to Ricky Martin's *Livin' La Vida Loca*, and dancing in my seat while I was driving. And these were the days when that was the most popular song on the radio, okay?"

"...Okay."

"So the song ends," Gary said, "and I was pissed. Because I like that song. I find it catchy. So I go to change the station, figuring it's bound to be played on the pop station out of Chattanooga in the next five minutes. Well, while I'm looking down, my truck goes right off the road. Distracted driving, they call it. And boom – I hit the ditch, bounce up, get the telephone pole, and flip. Crunch crunch – there goes my spine."

"And so you vowed...never to have fun again."

"Fuck you," Gary said, then chuckled. "But...maybe a little bit, yeah." And he kept chuckling.

"ARE YOU OKAY WITH A LITTLE KINK?" Darla asked, after pulling the hick's big cock out of her mouth. But she wasn't really asking. She'd warmed him up to the point where even a man of sterner stuff, who'd gotten laid mere hours before, would have trouble saying no to her now. The salty taste of pre-cum lingered on her tongue, and the sweat and stink of his crotch threatened to knock her over.

None of it mattered. She'd tasted worse, smelled worse, and done worse for power.

"Hell yeah," Casey said, oozing at his tip.

"Good," she said, and gave him a squeeze around his balls, running her index finger up to press gently in the space beneath them where the prostate hid. "Because I've got one, and it's a little...weird."

"Girl, you ain't got to worry about me being judgmental," he said. His ass had been pressed against the ridge of the desk while she was blowing him, and his member stood like a tower out of one of those stupid fantasy epics her husband used to foist on her at least once a year. Except this one was white. "I've done shit you wouldn't believe."

"Really?" Darla asked, batting her eyes demurely at him as she brushed all the shit off Father Nguyen's desk onto the floor. It mostly clanked, but a few things crashed. Hopefully no one heard them.

"Yep," he said, watching her ease over to the big crucifix hanging on the wall. "And I'm willing to do more."

"Good," she said, and took her shirt off. "Hold onto this for me?" Then she popped loose her bra and tossed it to him.

"Mmmm, check out those milkers," Casey muttered, his big dick swaying up and down. If she hadn't been so focused on the task at hand, Darla might even have enjoyed this. Briefly, though. Because the face attached to that horse cock? Not nearly pretty enough for her.

She pulled the crucifix down off the wall with a grunt, and when she started to turn, he was already there, dick pressing against her back, hands on hers to guide it down.

"You *are* kinky," he said, nibbling at her neck. "I like that."

"You're going to love what I do next, then," she said, and with his help, she set the crucifix flat on the desk. It was mostly a symbolic wall decoration, but it was long enough, she figured. "Now," she said, pointing her chin at it, "get on."

He raised both eyebrows. "You want me to...?"

"You get on," she said, "and I'm going to tie you to it." She picked up her bra, and her shirt.

He looked at it, then at her. Then at her tits. Then he shrugged. "Okay, sure." And the dumb fuck climbed onto the cross and splayed out, crossing his feet at the bottom and putting one hand each on the ends.

Darla just stared at him for a moment. This was going to be easier than she thought. With a smile, she went to work tying him down with her discarded clothing. And she did it nice and tight.

"YOUR WHOLE LIFE'S been leading up to this moment, Lauren."

Her father's voice came back to her as she lay there on that church floor, except she wasn't there, with people yelling her name, in a time of apocalypse.

She was standing on Mount Horeb fifteen years earlier, looking off the overlook on the entire Caledonia River Valley, her belly just starting to bulge with what would become Molly – though she hardly knew that at the time.

"Pretty sure my whole life wasn't on track for this until I decided to screw around without a condom, dad," she said, kicking pebbles around the parking space. Her dad's long Buick was nose-in, looking over the sheer cliff face. There were fresh hints of chub showing on her face now, and boy did she have a hell of a time putting down the Cheez Balls. That hadn't been a problem before. Also? First trimester sleepiness was definitely a thing. "And guess what? It could return to its previous track, all I have to do is...just one thing. One little thing." And she shoved her hands deep in her pockets. She already had the money. Just a little trip to the clinic, and everything would go back to normal.

"That's true," her father said. He'd asked to go for a ride with her, and here they were. "It's all in your hands, my dear." At the top of the fucking mountain, for some reason. Because this is where he'd steered them. "You get to decide which direction your life goes." Never the most touchy-feely man, he still wrapped an arm around her and pulled her close. "Now, you can shut this detour right down, get back on that main road, keep going the direction you were planning on going–"

She rolled her eyes. Lauren only had a vague conception of what she'd wanted to do with the rest of her life. She was sixteen for fuck's sake. She still had time.

"–Or," he said, "you can take this detour, and see it where it leads you." He glanced down at her belly with significance; her mom was back home crying, because Lauren had broken the news to them this afternoon. Why? Because her mom had guessed, that was why, and because she hadn't been to the clinic yet, though she'd planned it. She just...

Couldn't fucking go through with it. Needed a push or something. Or that's what she told herself.

"Maybe I don't want any detours," Lauren said, setting her chin, shrugging away from her dad's hand. "Maybe I just want to get on the freeway and get on with my life."

"That's the fun thing about life, sweetheart," he said in his deep drawl. "You get to decide your route. Like a cross-country trip where we all start in different places, but pretty much all end up in the same spot. Just some differences in how we get there and how fast. Gonna go through Nebraska? Or Texas? The Dakotas? Or Kansas?"

"They all sound like they suck, frankly."

"Because there are times in life that are like a Kansas," her father said. "But then, you get past those moments and suddenly you're in Colorado."

"And then, eventually, Nevada, presumably, where it's drinking, gambling, and prostitution all the live long day."

"Some of us have avoided that segment. This detour you're on right now, though," and here he looked her in the eyes, "I'm just going to tell you...it's been the most rewarding part of my life. Way better than the...the main trip."

She felt pressure in her throat. "I don't know if I can handle this...detour. I don't know if I'm...ready." She felt her hands fall to her belly.

"You want to hear a secret?" He looked out over the vista, the sun setting on Midian far, far below. "You'll never be ready. This..." He shook his head, and turned back toward the mountain. "You know they used to mine here? Tried to get coal, but there wasn't much to speak of. So they closed off the shafts, pretty much – long before I was even born, y'see. But when I was a kid, I went exploring with my friends, as one did in those days, and, of course, being boys and being stupid, we found our way into some of those disused mines..."

"I thought we were talking about teenage pregnancy," Lauren said.

"I'm getting back to it," he said. "Give me a second to bring it around. Anyway, one particular day we went into the mine not too far from this very spot. And if you know anything about mines, they sink a shaft–"

"Oh, I see. Because 'sinking a shaft' is how I got here, too."

"–And they have spur lines coming off that," he said, wrinkling his brow only a little at her crude aside. "Well, I got lost in one of those spurs. Quite twisty. Quite dark. And it goes deep into the earth, because they must have really been looking for that coal. Anyway, the sun was starting to set, and the light left me...and that left me in the dark inside the mountain..."

Lauren looked up at her father. Taller than her, but not by much, he seemed to be staring out over the counties before them. Mount Horeb was at the farthest north part of Calhoun County, and the south-facing view meant all of it was laid before them: Midian, certainly, but further out she could see the hints beyond green patches of forest, the road to Culver, and, eventually, Chattanooga, maybe, on a clear day.

"It got real quiet in that mountain," he said. "And I was all alone, I couldn't hear my friends. It started to get cold. Well, colder, because it was cold already. And Lauren, I'm gonna tell you – I've been scared a few times in my life. I was scared a lot in Vietnam, out on patrols. But I may have been more scared that evening in the mountain when the light left me than I ever was in the jungles. And I thought...maybe this is it. I'll just be down here forever, in the places where men delved and left. That is the most alone I ever felt in my life."

He turned his head to look at her. "Here's what I promise you...if you take this detour, you will never be alone in this. You can stay in my house. You raise my grandchild, and I will do everything in my power to make sure this detour doesn't become some dead end that keeps you off whatever road you want for yourself. All right?"

Her voice cracked a little with emotion as she asked, "Why?"

He hugged her closer. "Because...I wouldn't want you to miss what may become the greatest road you ever go down just because you worry it might not be worth it."

She sniffed, face buried in his chest. She could smell momma's detergent mingle with that faint cologne of his, a scent that would always and forever in her mind be distinctly daddy. "You're sure?"

"I am your father," he said. "I would do anything for you, my child."

Through her tears she hugged him, and her decision was made.

"DEFINE 'DAMNATION,'" Gary said.

Duncan had said, casually, that they were heading toward damnation. Well, as casually as one could get with a burning spear shoved squarely into the middle of one's essence, with some absolute tool spinning it around and sending shocks through the core of one's being. "Mmmmm," Duncan said, grunting. "As a technical term?"

"As in, the world's ending, and you say we're going to hell," Gary said. "What's that look like? What's the stakes for me?"

Duncan grunted, long and slow. His whole body was ringing with the pain of the consecration of this place, and thus concentrating was hard. "The stakes? I'd think not dying would be...stakes enough."

"Yeah," Gary's voice drifted over the wall of the truck bed

that separated them. How long would this infernal pain last? Oh, right. Until he left the property, at which point the demons circling 'round would destroy him, sending him back to hell. "But what if that's not enough for me? Especially after what I just admitted to you."

"Hmmm," Duncan said, closing his eyes and feeling the coolness of the truck bed against his cheek. "You want a reason not to go to hell? I tried to explain this to the others earlier, but I'm limited in what I can say under normal circumstances."

"Why?"

"Because you're not ready, and I'm too sensitive to the fact humans are a collection of impulses and body parts," Duncan said, "with an ape's brain attached. But my whole essence is ringing like someone is banging at it with a tambourine, so you know what? Okay." He squinted his eyes closed and summoned up the best thought he could come up with. "You ever read Dante's *Inferno*?"

"Not really," Gary said.

"Okay. The Bible?"

"Little bit. Been a long while, though. I'm not what you'd call the faithful type."

"Doesn't matter," Duncan said. "There's a passage that talks about people being given over to their sins. A lot of people get real fire and brimstone about that. Others don't; those are the real ones, the ones who know the truth." And he lapsed into a pained silence.

"And? What's the truth?"

"That every so-called sin you people commit does more damage to you than you ever realize," Duncan said, chortling painfully. "See, it's not the moderate use that kills you. Go ahead, lust after your wife. That can be real healthy, and fun. But when you make drooling lust your lifestyle, you end up like Hugh Hefner." He interrupted Gary's protest. "Oh, I know – all the guys who think with their dicks believe he had it all. But Hugh Hefner couldn't connect in a healthy way with a woman to save his member from falling off. He died basically alone, and had himself buried next to Marilyn Monroe, a woman he didn't even know, who loathed him for publishing naked pictures of her unwanted and unasked. Yeah, he was still rumored to be banging prospective Playmates til the day he died, choking down blue pills to get an erection so he could do it, only entering them briefly, and watching gay porn the whole time because he'd taken his libido down such a fucking rabbit hole that he couldn't get excited by the regular stuff anymore.

"Or how about gluttony? Yeah, enjoy a cake or a pie every once in a while. But make it your life, and you're not enjoying what you eat. The funny thing is you humans know this on some level, especially now that you have television shows. Watch that 600 pound life show. Tell me who's living great there.

"Envy? Healthy, if it's done with respect, using what others have to motivate yourself, to drive yourself to become better. But when it turns bitter, it doesn't just poison you, it poisons your society toxically. Instead of thinking how you can be the best you possible, you think of how you can destroy others and take what they have.

"Sloth? Do nothing. Be nothing. Drift through existence without meaning or purpose. Produce no art, die with the music still inside you. You're not even a participant in your own survival, your own life.

"Wrath? You destroy all around you. Everything that matters to you is ruined.

"Greed? Self-explanatory, and you become a miserable human being, beholden to chunks of metal over people who you could help, who you could connect with, who could mean more to you than any piece of paper. Saving for the future is no crime, but losing sight of your decency in a mad dash to accumulate paper and coin? What's more human than that?"

Duncan grunted, pained. "Then there's pride. And not the simple pride, either, the kind where you put a little effort into the things you care about to make them the best you can. No, this is the pride where you put yourself above others, above everything. Your body – the best, because you spend all your time on it. Your identity – bespoke, different, as you claw for acceptance when really, no one's paying attention to you because they're all busy with their own problems. Or–"

And here Duncan swallowed. "You think you know better. You think you know *best*. And how could you be wrong, knowing what you know? And how could you fail, knowing what you do? No one could know better than you, could be wiser than you. Because you *know*. You know things would be different if you were in charge, if they just did things different. Just a few little changes. Just a little bit of violence. You're so fucking certain, it'd be so easy–"

Duncan felt himself deflate. "You don't know what I'm talking about."

Gary chuckled. "Man...everyone who's survived the teenage years knows just what you're talking about. I knew better than my momma for years. Hell, it went on after that, too, just a bigger parent figure: 'Make me the president, or dictator, I'll fix all the problems you stupid shithead Boomers can't seem to solve.'"

Duncan closed his eyes, and chuckled a little. "I guess maybe you do understand. What you don't get, maybe, is the consequences of each. How every one of them destroys you in its own way, leads you astray."

"Nah, I get that," Gary said. "Lust leaves you a lonely, bitter old man. I saw that when I was hitting the hookers out in Reno before Marina. So if we're talking me overdoing the lust, it'd be like...lying in a bed of thorns with endless partners, their faces are made of snakes or something, because their souls are broken glass for me, they cut me and leave me lonely and in agony...?"

Duncan's eyes widened. "That's...pretty close to what it's like, yeah."

"And greed would leave me trying to claw money I could never hold onto, always slipping through my fingers as I scream for eternity, unable to hold the thing that matters to me and all the while my soul emptying as I cry out in despair. I guess that just leaves me wondering..."

"Hm?"

"What does pride get you?" Gary asked. "In this end of yours."

Duncan stared straight ahead, cheek against the dirty, corrugated metal of the truck bed. He couldn't feel it directly on his essence, but he did feel it. Because he couldn't walk the earth without a shell, the way he once did. And that...

"It leaves you alone," Duncan said. "Separated. Individual and lonely, because you're too apart to sincerely connect with others. Too much better, really. You scream for others to acknowledge you, but they can't hear you because they're doing the same. So you slip beneath a black, lightless sea of despair. You can't breathe, it's cold and a cacophony in which only fragments of voices are heard, forever. Where you can't touch, can't speak or understand, because Babel is all around you, and all the warmth you once felt in your soul is drained away and you're left in the cold. Forever. A dull knife constantly carving your heart out."

"Yeah, that sounds like it sucks," Gary said. "I think I want to fight that."

"Heh," Duncan said. "I thought you always wanted to fight." And he guffawed. Gary called him a prick, but a moment later he joined in, too, and they laughed together under the smoky, darkening sky as the world burned around them.

"CAN we get some butt stuff going? And by 'we,' I mean you do it to me," Casey asked her as Darla strapped his feet to the cross with his own belt. "You know, before we finish?"

"Mmmm," she said, pursing her lips seductively. "Tell you what – when I get done, I'll fuck you so hard in the ass with whatever we can find in here that some poor radiologist down in Chattanooga is going to be mystified how it got up there."

"Won't be my first time," he said as he rocked slightly on the desk. "Feel like I should get one of those punch cards for every time I go, because I'd be coming up on a free extraction here pretty quick."

"That's exciting," she said, lifting her leg up over him on the desk and shifting her balance to mount the desk – and the crucifix. And his skinny fucking legs, which were smaller than hers.

Whatever. She rubbed her beaver against his throbbing tower of a dick while she leaned over to check his left hand's binding. "Ooh," he said, because she tightened it, "you're cutting off my circulation." Then he grinned. "I like that."

"Good," she said, and got unsteadily to her feet. Standing on the desk, she felt it rock and raised a hand to the ceiling to brace. She was astride him now, a foot planted on either side of his chest. "Now, before we get started...I really need to wash you off."

He blinked up at her, focused entirely on her crotch. "Yeah, baby. I think I know what you mean."

Darla concentrated; she wasn't quite aroused yet, which was good, because pissing while she was would have been a real chore.

"Oh – ohhhhhh! Hoooo! Watersports! You are kinky, mama!" he said, giggling while she baptized him. She smiled, waiting until she'd finished to squat and check his pulse – rectally. "Ooh! Yeah!"

"Still with me?" she asked.

"Damned right I am," he said. And his dick flexed, turgid as hell.

"Good," she whispered in a throaty voice. She pushed him up inside her – slowly, because she wasn't very wet, and he was quite large. Rocking back and forth, she felt a little like she was trying to ride the Hancock tower, except it was just a regular cock tower. Once she felt moist enough, she started to fuck him in earnest. He moaned, squeezed and grew inside her subtly. She whispered the first words of her black prayer, rode his piss-covered body on the cross, leaning back, clutching her knife she'd retrieved from her pants, preparing herself to unleash it when the moment came.

LAUREN CAME out of the trance, or the paralysis, or whatever it was, with a start. Like someone had hit her cooch with a cattle prod, or snapped her stringiest string bikini in such a way as to put all the force directly on her sphincter, or something of that sort. It was a tit punch of a wakeup, that's how she would describe it, no pleasure, all pain, and she sat upright and got a head rush for her troubles.

"Oooh," she said, remembering her daddy, and that day on the mountain. Her head was jangling fiercely, like someone had treated her brain like a lock they weren't sure they had a key for, and just attempted a whole fucking box of them. Right in her ears, too.

She saw a whole host of faces above her, felt the squeeze of pain, like she was looking through a mail slot, up at the church's ceiling, and asked, "What the hell just happened to me?"

Rhea supplied the answer. "I don't believe it was hell at all, in fact."

BRAEDEN WAS A GENTLEMAN, so he waited until Terri finished rubbing herself strongly with him thrusting inside her. She moaned, she grunted, all the while giving her own clitoris hell. He didn't mind; hell, he strongly approved. He only had two hands, and they were holding him upright as he gave it to her, so if she needed that outside stimulation to get across the finish, he didn't have the physical strength or dexterity to give it to her. Good for her, he thought. It didn't bother his ego, mostly because his wife had explained to him that yes, she needed it done just this way in order to get there. It didn't work like the movies for her, and after years of hit or miss orgasms with his previous partners, this was a breakthrough bit of info he wished he'd known before.

Terri gasped and finished, tightening up and then slackening. She paused, repositioned slightly, and tightened things up down there for him. He slid in and out a few more times, and that was all he needed.

Head rush. In both of them.

He collapsed onto her when he was done, and she made a sort of hybrid giggle/chuckle/guffaw that suggested she was pleased. She stroked across his back with her bare fingers, teasing him, and he lay his head down upon the top of her breast and into the side of her neck.

"That was good," she said with lazy satisfaction after he'd been there for a couple minutes. She was still stroking him. He was limp within her, like all his life had sprayed out. It really did feel like total satisfaction as his bare torso pressed to hers, his groin did the same, and she wrapped her legs around him, heels gently kicking against the back of his buttocks. It was like a hug, but way better than just the standard.

How long had it been? Too long. Especially given all the doom, all the drear, of Midian these last few months. Braeden actually felt alive again, somehow. Such a silly little thing, getting down like this, but man, did it work wonders on him. A little flirting, a little possibility, and boom, here they were.

"Can we just stay like this for a few more minutes?" Braeden asked, breathing the words into the side of Terri's neck. She had the scent of sweat upon her, but he didn't mind. He did, too.

"Sure," she said, and she didn't sound put out by it at all. She held him close, held him into her, and did not let him go until he asked. And then it came in something of a panicked rush.

DARLA WAS GETTING CLOSE, and she felt based on the turgidness of this hick's member, he was, too. She was riding him furiously, flexing her legs in ways that yoga had prepared her for. Well, yoga, fucking, and Kegels. She was pulling out all the stops for this skinny little weirdo.

The funny thing was...she was probably going to get there, too. And getting off while banging a skinny reject in a human sacrifice ritual had not been on her bingo card for today.

A single droplet of sweat fell from her chin onto his recessed chest; he was a bit like an anti-man in that way. Straddling him was like riding a saw horse instead of a regular horse. Except for that cock. That was regular horse all the way, and she kept going, edging closer to her own orgasm.

"WHEW," Erin said, slumping down onto her ass. She'd been bent over the doctor as the woman spasmed and suffered from what looked like a seizure. "Thought we were losing you for a second there, doc."

"Still here," Dr. Darlington said, sitting up. She clasped her hand over her eyes. "Felt like I was getting a vision. Some kind of broadcast."

"What kind of broadcast?" Rhea asked.

"Like a memory from the past," Lauren said, still rubbing her eyes, shading them from even the minimal light in the church. "Not sure why, though." She finally lifted her hand; the eyes were bloodshot, irises showing barely. "Just some stuff my dad told me when I first got pregnant. Not exactly germane to the situation."

"Oh," Rhea said. "Sometimes revelations come in the form of memories. But also, sometimes, memories just come back to us, unbidden." She seemed to think for a moment. "It's possible that demons outside are increasing the amount of psychic pressure in the town, and that's something that could still penetrate the church's sanctuary effect."

Dr. Darlington frowned. "Wait. Did it hit anyone else?" She looked around; no one else nodded, everyone else shook their head. "Does that mean I'm psychologically weaker than everyone else?"

"Or that the attack was targeted, maybe?" Hendricks asked with a shrug. "Not sure why they'd pick you, doc, other than you got a pretty face and a mean right hook." Erin looked up at him with a frown of her own. "Though clearly you are not the only one with those two attributes in the church."

Erin couldn't help it. She was glaring at him. Something about the way she was feeling, maybe, but she stared up at him in irritation.

"BRIAN," his mother said, "you know you're going to be walking a dangerous road, though, right?"

Brian nodded. He felt that. Boy, did he feel that. "Chickening out is worse than death," Brian said. Because that really was how he felt. "It's like a cloud I'll be breathing every day for the rest of my life. I never fit in here. But I don't know that'll ever fit in anywhere I want to be if I can't look people in the eye. And running while gutless – how can I ever look myself in the eye again?"

She was nodding, but he saw the worry there, in her eyes. Couldn't blame her for that, either. She was his mother, after all.

"ALMOST THERE," Darla said, huffing as she rose and fell upon the skinny little hick's horsecock. It was glorious, and she had her eyes closed, imagining bouncing her crotch on someone attractive instead. The little bastard was actually bouncing in time with her, perfectly, which she found both wonderful and annoying. His pelvic bone slapping against hers in rhythm that brought her ever closer to her climax as her fingers tightened on the knife. Just a bit more...

"REMEMBER HOW YOU LEFT?" Erin asked, like a slap across Hendricks's face. He was standing there amidst them, and he could tell something in her had hit 'Don't give a fuck.'

"I do," Hendricks said, trying his best to not answer in anger. It was pretty much his fault. His fault he'd dug his stupid ass into an ego hole, his fault he'd done some shit they hadn't wanted him to do, his fault he'd reacted like a bitch and run. Saying so, on the other hand...well, that was not quite the sort of thing he wanted to admit in a crowd.

And it was a crowd. The doctor on the ground, Micah and that reverend at her sides, along with Erin, who was coming to her feet now, like a fucking wolf with a taste for blood. Rhea before him, some long-haired country boy watching with grim amusement, the priest, plus Arch right there at his elbow. Arguing with Erin was fine, it felt like something that was going to happen naturally just by being around her. But he didn't feel the need to air their soiled laundry in public.

"But you come back," she said, all sense lost to rage, "and now we're dealing with your shit again."

"I said I'm sorry." Hendricks kept an even tone, kept it low. No need to throw fuel on this fire; he'd just take the burns and go on. Say little, escape with his life. That was his strategy. Dignity might take some hits, though.

"Oh, I'm not talking about the redhead," Erin said, and looked around. "Where's Darla?"

Pretty much everyone turned their heads on that one. "Who's Darla?" Hendricks asked. He really felt like he'd missed something.

"Remember when you murdered County Administrator Pike?" Erin asked, with a mean grin. Had she been drinking? Or were they just falling back into old patterns? Because if so, man, that had happened quickly. Barely thirty minutes of grace and they were right back to the same old shit.

Hendricks looked around for this Darla person, half-expecting to get a knife in the back at any second. He started shuffling away, planning to put his back to the nearest wall, which he found within a few seconds. "I'm not sorry about that," Hendricks said, his face turning to stone. "The guy was bad. I caught him making a pact with a demon he'd summoned, okay?

He was not on the side of light. And let's not forget – he was the one who put on the Halloween celebration and sent out the invites. If he was talking to demons, he knew what he was setting up. And I'm pretty positive he killed Reeve."

"Could be," Arch said. He sounded noncommittal, and was watching Hendricks.

"Why don't you tell his widow that?" Erin said. "Darla was his wife. She's right..." She waved a hand around, then looked...and then looked befuddled. "Well, she was right here."

Hendricks frowned. "Here? Why?"

"It was her kids that were lost in the mill," Arch said. But his voice had just gone high, and his eyes were wider than usual.

"The one where you walked into a giant demon ambush?" Micah asked, completely deadpan. Leave it to Gunny to deliver the obvious bad news with tact and care.

Hendricks's eyes felt like they bulged, and he reached out and grabbed Arch by the arm. Not gently. "Where is she *now?*"

"I don't know," Arch said, and looked at Father Nguyen, who shrugged.

Hendricks swallowed, his throat moving up and down. Felt like he'd just choked down a boulder. "Father...is there some sort of basement leading out of here? To the tunnels, maybe?"

"There's a crypt down there," Father Nguyen said, the small priest tensing up. "Old one, though. No space left, and no one goes down there anymore."

"Gunny," Hendricks said, "you might want to check that for an escape route. We need to get everybody together right now, and find that bitch–"

"She lost her fucking kids, Hendricks," Erin said – but there was a tiny glimmer of worry in her eyes. "What's she going to do? It's a church. We're safe here, remember?"

Hendricks suddenly had a wicked case of the dry mouth. "Ever heard of deconsecration?" He looked around again.

"Where's that skinny little pervert that would fuck a snake if you held it still for him?"

"Casey?" Dr. Darlington asked, sounding a little woozy.

"Casey Meacham," the long black-haired hillbilly singsonged. "Dick rider, pussy glider."

"Yeah, that's Casey for sure," Father Nguyen said, clearing his throat.

Hendricks felt like his skull was about to pop. Did these people have no conception of what was at stake here? "Where the fuck is the little weasel?" He operated his head on a swivel. "And where's the bitch that lured you people into the trap?" He started striding down the pews until he found a thin, pale girl lying on one of the benches. She looked up at him with tired, pitiful eyes, and he had a strong suspicion this was not the demon-scheming bitch he was searching out. "Who is this?"

"That's just Marina," the hillbilly said. "She ain't it, hoss."

"She go that way," the pale girl said in a thick accent, and in a tired voice, pointing toward the front of the church. "And the pervert, too."

"Fuck," Hendricks said, moving toward the front of the church. He saw doors on either side of the pulpit, but what he needed to know was which one led to the bitch in question? He started to run, cowboy boots hitting the tile floor in time, sounding like slaps to the face. "Get armed, and get ready. I got a bad feeling coming on. If I'm wrong...I swear I'll apologize. But if I'm right...you're gonna want something consecrated in your hand, and a plan for how to get the fuck out of here, and quick."

"OHMIGOD, OHMIGOD..."

The skinny little shit was talking from beneath the gag she'd placed over his mouth. She'd stuffed a sock in his mouth, too, before tying him, and he'd accepted it with all the grace of a man willing to put up with tremendous indignities to cum. Just like the rest of them, then.

In a way, she'd missed this about not being married. Oh, sure, Jason let her have affairs if she wanted to. Not that he could talk, or could stop her. But her life had been dedicated – for the last few years – toward raising the children, which had been a necessary part of maintaining their cover, advancing his career, and blending in, especially given they had no idea when the apocalypse they waited for was truly coming.

But the total freedom of walking into a room, catching a man's eye, and knowing she could have him in minutes? That's what she missed as she squinted her eyes closed, sliding up and down on that skinny hillbilly's horsecock. He was so engorged she knew he was about to blow. She had the knife clutched tightly in her hand, right beside his head, where she was resting it, where she'd moved it while his eyes were closed. He couldn't see it, of course, because even if he'd turned his head, he was elevated up a few inches on a crucifix.

She only hoped he came soon; the desk was absolutely destroying her knees. And her thighs were mutinous; she'd been riding up and down on him for the last few minutes. Her excitement was starting to die off, too, after an early hiccup of an orgasm; she was beginning to dry up, and the first hints of chafing were coming on. He was just too stupidly big and too scrawny. And ugly. Not her type.

But if she had to grind his dick all night in order to get this done, using the blood flowing from her rubbed-raw vaginal walls as lubrication, she'd do it. Because this was it, the last thing she needed to do before–

He drew a sharp intake of breath through the cloth and she felt it begin. Nothing so subtle as a spray; no, what she could feel was him, his muscles as his body spasmed, and deep within her his penis began the peristaltic reaction of ejaculation. He jerked a few times, bound to the cross, his ass squeezing tight as he came inside her, breaths fast but tapering off.

And it was then, in the midst of his climax that she jabbed her blade into, first, his coronary artery, and then, right after, his jugular vein.

The spray coated her in spurts of red, bathing her hanging tits, coating her thighs. It shot at her like a second ejaculation and she took it gladly, whispering words she'd known by heart since she was seventeen and pissed at the world and hungry for power and lusting for all that it hadn't dared give her.

She did take a moment as she whispered the words and appreciate the panicked look in his eyes. She didn't bother to speak to him, of course; he was a sacrificial goat, that was all. Straining against his bonds, and against her weight, he was too weak to make any headway against either.

He finished inside her, his erection already fading from the blood loss; his flaccidity was the least of his problems, though. His face was paling, eyes were rolling back in his head. He'd gone from *la petit mort* to a much larger one – death, itself – in a matter of seconds.

Darla smiled wolfishly as she uttered the last of the words through the blood coating her lips; arterial sprays made it quite far if you made the hole small enough. His spurts from the artery barely bubbled now, and his jugular was hardly oozing. His eyes were fully rolled back in his head, half-closed, all the blood departed from his brain via one route or another.

This motherfucker was dead, even if he wasn't conscious enough to realize it.

Darla realized it, though, as she sat there coated in his bodily fluids: semen inside her, blood all over her, and, as she rested with her knees on the desk astride him, she felt – and smelled – him vacate his bowels, the last little kiss of life saying goodbye.

And she felt a shudder, too, but not from him. This one was deeper, as if from somewhere beneath the earth, and her skin grew cold, as though the warmth had fled from the room.

Because it had, in a way. "Knock knock," Darla whispered, feeling the blood drip down her skin, and the flaccid penis within her slowly crawl its way out of her as she knelt there, listening, now that all their sexual sound and fury had stilled. It wasn't more than a few seconds before she heard the heavy footsteps and the first crash, as the building shook, the demons all around the church having realized immediately that this place, so long forbidden to them, was now open for the devil's business.

TWELVE

REAP THE WHIRLWIND

Duncan sat up in the bed of the pickup truck.

He felt like someone had removed the shock prod that had been ripping at his very essence, like a knife placed directly into him had, at long last, been pulled free, and left no wound behind. Nothing; perfect, pristine shell, not a hint of anything ever having happened there.

The wind had shifted direction; flaming embers blew in like sparks on the breeze. Fireflies in the growing dark, that was what they looked like. Sometime in the last while, the smoke had grown so thick it was covering the sun entirely, and what had been a disc glowing faintly in the sky was no longer visible. Instead, the orange glow of the fires that ringed Midian was the primary source of light.

"What?" Gary asked, looking over at him. "You all right?"

"Yes, suddenly," Duncan said, doing some looking of his own, at the dark shapes that had patrolled the perimeter of the church property. "Which is worrisome."

Lurching out of the dark, he saw that giant T-Rex thing. It didn't even go for him, it went straight for the front of the church and smashed through the door like the wall wasn't even there, collapsing the portico.

It was only the start, though. Next Duncan heard the rush of others, and knew that the situation had changed, and not for the better.

BRIAN WAS HUGGING his mother when the first demon crashed through the windows in their Sunday school room.

Not the last, though. But by the time the next came in, he was already moving, dragging Addie with him the hell out of there.

LAUREN GOT DRAGGED to her feet as the entrance to the church collapsed. She was feeling lightheaded even before a piece of drywall or ceiling clipped her across the ear, beginning a searing pain and causing warm wetness to drip down to her shoulder. Erin Harris had one of her hands, Barney Jones had the other, and they helped her up as shit started to go very, very wrong in the church of St. Brigid's.

BRAEDEN HAD BARELY GOTTEN his pants on when a demon crashed through the windows beside him, prompting Terri to loose a very un-Terri-like scream, probably relating to the fact that she did not have pants on and, indeed, had only just pulled up her (rather granny) panties.

It took him only a surprising second to snag his wrench and swing it like he was back on the baseball diamonds of his youth, socking the demonic creature in an offhand way. It burst and burned, leaving only a stink of sulfuric reek as its residue spattered against the far wall like a stink bomb. Braeden was already moving, his free hand grabbing Terri's and towing her the hell away from the windows, because where there was one demon, he knew, more were surely coming.

"FUCK!" Hendricks shouted as the T-Rex-like jaw came through the front of the church behind him, collapsing the main entrance and cutting off one line of retreat lickety-fucking-split. A cloud of dust from the unscheduled demolition blew in past him, adding some powder to the air to mingle with the already prodigious smell of smoke.

Whatever that demon was, it got its ass stuck in the entry, neck swiveling this way and that as it snapped at Dr. Darlington and her rescuers, Erin and Pastor Jones. It couldn't quite get to her, though, and this seemed to make it even madder, huffing out dust and snapping harder.

"Let's find those stairs," Arch said, passing Hendricks as he grabbed for that little Eastern European chick, Marina, and then pulled her toward the double doors that led to the rest of the church complex. "Now!"

Hendricks tossed off a last look at the doors behind the pulpit. Tempting as it was to see if the bitch who'd just deconsecrated the church was back there, even Father Nguyen wasn't heading in that direction. The church was surrounded, after all, which meant that taking one of the main exits meant delivering yourself right into the feeding chute where demon mouths were waiting.

Writing that off as bad strategy, Hendricks reversed course, coat flapping all around him, as he bolted to follow the others, hopefully to the last passage out of this rapidly collapsing safe zone.

DARLA SMILED, not even bothering to dismount from the hick's corpse as walls started to crash down elsewhere in the church, She just sat there, straddling the dead body, him still barely inside her, as her promise to destroy the last refuge of the humans in Midian came true.

"GARY!" Larry shouted as the world came crashing fucking down. His black hair was visible hanging out one of the ground-floor windows of the church, and his ass popped out a second later after writhing through, spraying 5.56 rounds in a cone in front of him as he did so. The bullets went off like thunder amidst a dull roar of demons all around.

"Get the fuck outta here, Larry!" Gary shouted, turning toward his last surviving brother. He'd been sitting pretty still right up until Duncan had sat his ass upright like a zombie in one of those horror movies. He'd felt an icy knife of cold dread cut into his guts when that demon T-Rex had charged past, because he knew – goddammit – that his options for retreat were real limited, and the moment that big fucker smashed through the front of the church, they got even more so.

Duncan leapt down behind him, seizing the handles of his wheelchair, and started to move him forward. "Toward my brother, you dumb fuck!" he shouted, gesturing at Larry furiously. As though there were any other way for him to gesture.

He didn't even get a chance to complete the thought. Something leapt out of the darkness and clipped Larry at the knee, making him stumble. He didn't make it another step before something else hit him again in the leg, some kind of crawling insect in a black carapace that skittered out of the dark, barely visible in the glow of the floating embers.

"Larry!" Gary shouted as his little brother went down, knees buckling under the assault. He landed hard, elbow catching the concrete.

"GarEEEEE–" Larry's scream went guttural and then cut off as the things pounced on him and went right for the throat. His hand was up, waving like a flag, but it slowly fell as Duncan rolled Gary forward and brought him to an abrupt stop next to the pickup truck.

"Shit. No keys," Duncan said, after a brief glance inside the truck window. He started to turn, and tensed, preparing to run–

Gary smacked his elbow down on Duncan's hands, knocking them free of the wheelchair. The demon didn't hesitate, grabbing them again, and this time, instead of batting them away, Gary grabbed his wheels and snapped on the brakes. "I ain't leaving!" he shouted, looking into the dark place where Larry had disappeared under the flood of demon insects. "Just...just go, Duncan," he said, his voice breaking. "Get outta here."

"It doesn't have to end like this," Duncan said, but he pulled a hand free of the wheelchair and came around the side, staring at Gary with that doughy face. God, he was just so fucking bland. He coulda been any bureaucrat from the government, or a middle manager in an insurance company. "You could–"

"My brothers are all dead," Gary said, and his voice made it sound like he was, too. There was no more movement in the place where Larry had gone down. "I fucking quit, Duncan. Go."

Duncan looked, for just a second, like he wanted to argue.

But he didn't; he sprinted away, around the side of the church where there was no movement yet.

As Gary sat there, listening to things skittering in the dark, feeling the burn of the occasional glowing ember landing on his skin, he waited for the inevitable to come get him. Like it had the whole rest of his family.

"FUCKING MOVE!" Hendricks shouted, catching Brian and Addie coming from the opposite direction in the hallways, where he and Arch and Erin had been gabbing before the safety of the church had come crashing in around them. Behind, he could hear that giant demon crunching its way through the front of the building, and windows were shattering in the rooms in the distance as more demons broke in. At the far end of the hall, behind Brian, a bunch of human-shaped demons were moving in the shadows, lit by the glow reflecting its way into the building from the last bits of the day's sunlight and the fires.

"What happened?" Brian shouted, falling in with them behind Father Nguyen, who took a quick turn into what looked like a storage closet. It was tough to tell, but Hendricks saw a seam in the construction here; the original church had ended a few feet down the hall, and the rest of this was addition.

"Casey got laid, and we got fucked," Erin said, quite succinctly.

"Turns out sleeping with strange women has been as hazardous as I always feared," Father Nguyen said as he led them, swiftly, down a winding, ancient staircase. It squealed something fierce; Hendricks felt suddenly thankful that the more robust members of the Watch had bitched out or died while he was gone, because even Micah's slightly above-average frame was putting stress on this motherfucker. And it sounded like it was about to collapse at any time, which would send them all plummeting to the stone floor beneath.

Hendricks breathed again once his boots hit stone, and he found himself in a cool, dark room without so much as a drop of light to see by. He squinted in the dark, feeling someone – Dr. Darlington, he realized a moment later – press against his coat, pushing him gently forward, because she was in danger of being crushed by someone doing the same to her.

But this was a moment of pausing and taking a deep breath; Nguyen had halted because he couldn't see shit down here. "Anyone got a light?" Nguyen said, peering into the darkness. Behind them, the unnatural demon sounds of growls and clicks and hideous fucking laughter was growing closer. It wasn't going to be a secret where they'd gone; Arch was bringing up the rear with Micah, hopefully they'd be able to hold.

"I gotcha covered, Father," Brian said, passing up his cell phone with the little light turned on. "Just charged it on the drive down." White light flooded over them and illuminated the dull stone walls on either side, leading forward into the crypt.

"This place looks like a disaster area," Darlington said, as the priest led them forward. That pale Eastern European girl was beside Hendricks, and he had a moment's panic when he couldn't remember her name, wondering if she was about to get ripped through one of the crypt walls like a red shirt out of *Star Trek*. That mechanic was here, too, Brendan or something, along with an older blond chick in a tank top, the two of them looking like they just got in a proper roll in the hay or something, her hair way more mussed than when he'd seen her in the truck after the flight from the mill.

Hendricks shoved forward now that there was light. He found himself in a stone-walled room with clefts for old coffins. He watched as Nguyen spun around, revealed–

"Aw, fuck,'" Hendricks said.

"You said it, not me," Nguyen said.

There was no door out of here, at least not an obvious one.

Just coffins and stone-carved crypt doors, little squares that had been sealed with corpses inside fifty or a hundred years ago, names and details carved on the stone facing out at them. If there was tunnel access, it must be through the back of one of the crypts, or on a wall. Fucking lovely.

"They are coming in hot behind us," Micah said, deep voice echoing off the walls of the crypt. A couple gunshots rang out, magnified by the tight quarters.

"What's the verdict?" Erin asked, bumping into Hendricks's back – and staring past him, seeking the mythical exit.

"We might be fucked," Hendricks said, reaching for his pistol. He'd had it and the bullets consecrated, but he didn't have a hell of a lot of them. Still had his sword, though. Wouldn't be fun to swing that in these tight quarters, but probably more fun than trying to shoot through other members of the Watch. "And not in the good way."

Father Nguyen shrugged in the reflecting light of the phone. "Sorry. There's a reason I only come down here during tornado warnings, and it's not just because of the ambiance."

"Yeah, it's not exactly a romantic getaway spot," Hendricks said, then chucked a thumb at the blond chick and the mechanic. "Unless you're these two, I guess."

"Braeden?" Erin asked, frowning. "Terri?"

Hendricks could tell by the blush he'd hit home on that one. "We used one of the classrooms upstairs, actually," Braeden said, only slightly embarrassed.

"Good for you, grease jockey," Hendricks said, clapping him on the shoulder – and pushing past. Sounds of demons were growing closer, and before he lost his hearing entirely from gunshots in this confined space, Hendricks picked a spot in the corner and put his ear up to the cold stone, just listening.

"Thanks," Braeden said, then planted his ear on the wall opposite Hendricks's.

"Hear anything?" Erin asked, getting right up in Hendricks's face, and not being particularly quiet. A couple more gunshots rang out, skunking his hearing with a nasty ringing.

"No." Hendricks lifted his head, moved two feet to the right, and planted it again. Rapping against the cold stone with his knuckles, he estimated he was all of two feet from the first of the tomb vaults. If there wasn't something behind this wall or one of the other three corner walls, the only exit was going to be through the vaults, and over the corpses. Which was not a wrinkle Hendricks was interested in exploring considering the limited timeframe for their escape.

"How bad is it looking up there?" Barney Jones asked. Always the cool voice of reason, that one. In spite of his distaste for the clergy, Hendricks did like that guy.

"It's getting real salty, real fast," Micah announced. Hendricks was surprised he could still hear after all that shooting. A couple more rounds rang out. Yep, things were going to get sporty pretty quick. He lifted his head, moved two feet back, and kept rapping his knuckles against the wall, listening for a sound like a ripe cantaloupe.

DUNCAN STARTED to sprint for the side entrance, but it didn't take him more than a few steps before he realized, no, that was not going to be a viable entry to the church. Whereas there had not been any demons visible when he'd turned the corner into the church yard, there definitely was now. They flooded forth like a great and terrible, well...flood. From the smallest of the small, mites the size of mosquitoes, imbued with tiny pissy essences, to that enormous T-Rex thing, every size of the demon spectrum was represented just around the corner from the church.

And Duncan didn't feel he had much of a chance of survival in that direction, because a goodly portion came right for him.

How did they know? Had his shell's picture been circulated in the demon masses: get this pasty, overweight white guy? He saw other demons in human shells rushing in with the army, and nobody looked askance at them. Never the greatest pattern recognizers, more than a few demons now coming at him would struggle to pick him out of a lineup that included even the other demons in the crowd coming for him.

It was like someone had painted his essence with a laser, and the demons were cats. He knew what was going to happen next, and didn't much care for the thought, so instead of just rushing madly into the midst of them and taking his medicine – which would not be a corrective that would in any way save the patient – he turned on his heel and threw himself through the nearest stained-glass window into the church. Because doors were for more polite and less urgent moments.

DARLA LUXURIATED. Covered in hick blood, dripping the hick's semen, she felt warm and sticky all over her naked body. Normally this would have made her feel self-conscious, but she was about to be a goddamned Duchess of the Underworld, and all this bile was like the anointing oil royalty put on during their coronation.

So she strode out into the church without bothering to dress herself. Why would she? She'd coated herself in the accoutrements of unholiness; it would be like a beacon to any demon that came anywhere near her, one that warned them: this one is unholy. Do not fuck with her.

She walked down the main aisle of the church, watching the demon T-Rex collapsing the front entrance before her, letting one heel touch the hard tile and stretching her arms out at her sides as though to accept offerings. She felt the cool prickle of a draft coming in through the gaping hole at the front of the church, the warm blood already cooled on her flesh. She was trying to enjoy her moment, knowing that hated, holy symbol was behind her, leering down from the wall above.

It had no power over her; that was the uniqueness of humans over demons, that they were forever forced to recoil from it as part of their very nature. She, on the other hand, was human, and had the freest will, and could properly turn, lift her middle finger, and extend it at the crucifix. Which she did now, because why not?

This was the problem with so-called good: where was the reward? Some ephemeral cloud to sit upon some distant day in the future? Peace? Quiet? Who the fuck wanted that, other than her once she had kids and had listened to them cry for a while? Darla had never wanted to sit in silence just for its own sake, not even while reading. She liked the buzz of a coffee shop while she read, and could not imagine "peace," so-called, being any kind of inducement to join a side.

In fact, the times in Darla's life when she'd felt most alive had been the moments of raw chaos and hubbub she could never imagine being repeated in any so-called heaven: the time she'd been half-drunk and stumbled down an alley in Chicago, running across a young woman who'd clearly been dreading someone turning the corner in her moments of vulnerability while taking this shortcut. She'd relaxed the moment she saw Darla.

Which had been her last mistake, because the moment Darla had staggered past the poor girl, so certain that another woman wouldn't do anything to harm her, Darla had punched her in the back of the head then slit her throat, stumbling on into the night after she'd watched the blood flow for a few minutes, and after offering that sacrifice to the proper demon, of course.

That moment she'd felt alive, in charge of herself and with the fate of others in her hands. How could sitting in some peaceful nirvana compare with the rush of bloodletting? With the thrill of forbidden sex? With the mood in a club with sweaty bodies gyrating around and against you, that energy between people flowing in the air?

Darla wanted that, and dominion over that – the temporal, forever. That was why she'd chosen power and hell. In heaven she'd be a nothing and like it; one of so many throne-watchers, bowing and scraping forever.

But instead: real power and determination, unlocked for her. She could be a somebody, and now–

Now she was. And she walked like it, right down the aisle of the church as the front of the building collapsed. A window shattered to her right, and something flew in like it had been hurled. But no simple baseball off course, this; it was a man, or man-shaped. Dull, lumpen, it crashed into the pews and upended several, destroyed a few more. She stared at it, her arms still held benignly out like a corruption of the Virgin Mary.

It leapt to its feet and it was a man, or – no. She could see it now in the lack of blood, the dull pallor, the absence of visible emotion in the eyes. It was a demon in a suit, one of those OOCs that had come to town in the days before the end. He stared at her, she stared at him.

And she smiled.

"You broke the consecration?" he asked. Glass was shattering behind him; demons were starting to pour in, of the smaller, garden variety.

She gave him a half-shrug of her bare shoulder, feeling demure in the presence of her own glory. But what was glory if it wasn't shared? "Yeah," she said. "I did."

"Who'd you kill to do it?" He had a baton in his hand – long, thin, metal, black. Two of those four attributes interested her. One she was indifferent toward.

"See if you can guess," she said, unworried about her nakedness. She was fashionably clad for the underworld, after all, wearing this blood.

He didn't linger long over it. "Casey."

"Was that its name?" Darla put a thin, blood-coated finger up to her lips, pretending to think about it. "I might not have been giving my full attention when introductions were made. If they were made. Manners are hard to come by around here. Among other things."

"Like clothes?"

"I was thinking more like 'class,' 'style,' 'sophistication...'" she said. "You should know. You've been there." She didn't move toward him, mostly because she had a sense that she was holding him in place. He wasn't of the brood, if such a thing was possible. He'd gone native, for whatever reason, and thus was not a rational actor.

"Yes, I've been there," he said, easing toward the far hallway, where – unless Darla missed her guess – the others had fled when that giant thing came crashing through the front of the building. Even now, it seemed to be trying to dig its way through the collapse like a big dog trying to squeeze through a little dog door but not finding any luck. "There's not nearly as much style, class, and sophistication as you may be hoping for."

That took some of the smile off Darla's face. "So you threw in with the enemy?"

"Looks like we both did, respectively," he said. There was noise to the side, and he jerked his head around to look. Demons came at him from that hallway, his intended direction of escape, and he spiked one with a quick blow from the baton, turning it into a whiff of sulfur.

Waning twilight and the glow of orange on the horizon painted the interior of the church in a strange shade. Darla stared at him as he brought his baton down, again and again, against all comers. She didn't dare get closer – that baton could split her skull, after all – but she watched as he did what he did, fending off an ever-increasing number of demons that ignored her in all her splendor and focused on the demon betrayer, trying to end him before he could end any more of them.

ARCH WAS NOT HAVING an easy time at the top of the basement stairs.

There wasn't much light, the last natural sources having been blotted out by their entrance to the underground. Above, there'd been the glow of twilight, like a cloudy day, shining through the smoky haze on the horizon. Plus, the fires, burning distantly, had shed a little illumination, like headlights shining through a fog.

Now he was standing here, trying to keep a door closed against demons pounding against it, his companions this big fella with an AR and the bearing of a drill sergeant that Hendricks kept calling "Gunny," and his wayward brother-in-law. Arch found himself pressing against the door as a solid thump rattled it in its frame, his own large body and all his weight against it while Brian was beside him lending – well, much less weight and solidity. Meanwhile, the drill sergeant had his gun aimed just over their shoulders, at the place where the door would crack open, and he was prepared to unload.

The door jarred, hard, against Arch's back, and he felt it give way. The thing flew open, just for a beat, he and Brian lurching forward, in a moment's peril of being thrown down the steps to the stone floor a flight downward.

Arch recovered himself, though, as something black as night with no moon slithered past on leathered wings. They flapped and gunshots rang out, the drill sergeant trying to pepper the thing, whatever it was, before it cut them all down.

He failed, though, and it swept away, a tail slithering through the air like a snake, the wings glinting for a moment in the dark before it was gone. Arch threw himself against the door as though blocking back in his football days, and it slammed shut. "Something got through!" he shouted, already in a desperate battle with the next thing trying to pound its way in.

Brian posted up next to him, his skinny shoulder to the door, sweating, feverish, as the drill sergeant looked back down the stairs into the crypt, which wasn't visible from where they stood. "What the hell was that?" Brian asked.

LAUREN DIDN'T KNOW what she was doing, other than putting her ear to the wall and listening, in just the same way the cowboy was, and Father Nguyen was, and Barney Jones was. Erin Harris was beside her, doing the same, blond hair lilting sideways as she tipped her ear against some carved crypt door the size of a hatbox lid. She found herself staring her in the eye, the two of them listening, just listening, for what, Lauren didn't know.

It was an awkward position; they were both already bent over as if moving to get into some sort of yoga position, or doing some weightlifting. Face to face, inches away, in a crypt filled with so damned many people.

"You're Molly's aunt," Lauren said.

Erin's face changed only a shade. "What now?"

"Jesse is Molly's father," Lauren said, because she couldn't hold it in any more. "If anything happens to me – tell her. Please."

Erin just stared at her blankly for a moment, a hint of panic appearing. "Um...okay?"

"I was looking for a more definitive answer," Lauren said, and a flash of motion out of the corner of her eye made her turn.

She just held off on screaming, which was her first instinct as something flew at her out of the dark, when other movement caught her eye. Barney Jones had been standing there, had turned toward the staircase leading out of the crypt when something hit him in the head.

And then his head hit her. Nothing else; just his head. Bumped her shoulder, then fell to the ground.

She didn't need to scream, someone else did it for her. Barney Jones's dead eyes looked up at her, light reflecting in them from where he'd taken some sort of hit to the neck, which was severed.

A cold, clinical analysis ran through Lauren's mind: head severed around the C4 vertebra...

Of course, that hardly captured the horror of seeing someone you knew, someone you respected, someone you thought of as one of the most steadfast and decent men you'd ever met get cut down like a garden snake beneath the rake of a pissed-off farmer, but neither could Lauren pretend this was just surgery, that someone – probably a fucking intern – had just removed a head, purely by accident. *Whoops! That one's going to be a malpractice suit for sure!*

"What the fuck was that?" someone shouted, maybe Braeden Tarley. It was tough to tell, because the scream hadn't quite faded from Lauren's ears when the shooting started anew up the stairs, and she blanched away, shoving her own head once more against the stone wall, because there wasn't anything else for her to do.

GARY JUST SAT THERE, staring as an army, a torrent, of demons came flooding around him.

And not fucking one of them had the grace to just put him out of his misery.

Fine. Whatever. Fuck them.

So Gary sat, feeling them brush his foot when a dog-like one ran by. Got bumped sideways when one that looked human...ish...went charging past at speeds that would have made the NFL combine look like the Paralympics. He spun in a slow circle and came to a stop, with a fucking floor-to-ceiling view of a very naked, very pregnant, very redheaded hooker, who had apparently not bothered putting on a single fucking stitch for this occasion.

"If this is the end of the world," Gary said, because the fucking discourtesy of this demon army not even wasting a fucking claw slitting his goddamned throat really stuck in his ass, "you're kinda underdressed."

"Been to a lot of world ends, have you?" Starling asked, a lot less formal than she normally was. She plopped a bare foot down on his – not that he could fucking enjoy it – and halted his slow turn. She dragged him slowly forward, just a few inches, placing her palms on his armrests, which he vacated immediately like he was on a plane and a six-hundred pounder had just plopped down next to him. She leaned over, her small but pleasant rack hanging right in front of his face. He didn't look directly at it, like it was an eclipse or some such shit.

"Well, I'm here for this one," he said, looking her right in her dusky eyes, "and I feel like there should be some standards. Maybe a dress code. You mind putting on something a little formal? I could get a tux."

Her face was inches from his. Her breath smelled strangely

pleasant, a toothpaste or mouthwash aroma wafting out with strains of mint. "Maybe you're overdressed." She made a show of looking him up and down. "Ever think of that?"

"Well, I haven't had much time to consider it," Gary said. "But if it's all the same to you, one of us should keep their pants on."

"Suit yourself," she said, and spun him about, taking hold of his handles and giving him a slow push forward. The demons were surging into the church like black water running toward a shower drain. The last hints of twilight were shining around him, the sun punching through the clouds, the glare of the fires lighting up whatever the sky didn't get. It was a strange shade to be cast in, and it gave Gary an eerie feeling.

"Since we're talking about suiting me, how about you just have one of these things eat me and get it over with?" Gary asked, a little tense, as she pushed him toward the church building. If they were going in, Gary couldn't see where; the whole front was collapsed, and his wheelchair wasn't going to roll very well through the thick, unmoved grass at the side.

Didn't seem to matter to the redhead. She didn't answer, and when she came to the grass, she rolled him right through like he was a lawnmower. Didn't even grunt, or act like it was a big deal.

Demons were crawling and leaping around them like they were some kind of break in the flood. Whatever they were, they seemed to take notice of the redhead and, by extension, him, and give them a wide berth, giving even his feet several inches of clearance as they flowed around and smashed through the remaining stained glass to enter the church. It made a tinkling noise, like a wind chime in his ear.

They came to a door ripped off its hinges by something bigger and stronger than a normal man. Maybe even stronger than a normal man-demon. She turned him easily, and in they went, the demons that had been using this entrance moments before just detouring around in all directions like the space around them was occupied by something immovable. Gary judged this to be an alarming amount of respect from the demon populace.

"The strong, silent type, huh?" Gary asked. He felt unnerved, but still didn't give a shit. His brothers were dead, his mother was gone. He was ready to go, too. He'd fought his fucking fight, and he'd lost. First time in his life, really. What an insult.

But at least he was going out at the end of the world. What the hell else could you do? If the world decided it was going to end, how was one little paraplegic supposed to fight that?

Well, he'd tried. Given it his damned all. And his family members, too, to their lesser or greater abilities. Some quite a bit lesser, sure. But they'd made their best effort...and now they were all dead, and he was about to follow.

At some point.

"Will you just fucking kill me already, lady?" Gary jerked around in his wheelchair.

"No," the redhead said, not even bothering to dignify him by looking him in the eye.

Gary slammed his hand down on his brake, and the wheelchair jerked, threatened to overturn–

But only for a second, and then it steadied, because the redhead smoothly tapped it off, so swift he barely noticed it. He stared at her sullenly for a moment, reached for it again–

The pain in his hand was swifter still, stinging like he'd just slammed it in the back door of his van. Goddamn, but it hurt! She didn't bother to say anything, but he knew she'd done it, a polite discouragement to keep him from acting a prick. Well, that was fine, he thought as she rolled him past a door that was getting swarmed by a shit ton of demons, he could be polite for the moment. Especially since pissing her off didn't seem likely to result in his death.

Glass shattered ahead as Duncan threw himself out the window of the church and pounded past with only a glance at Gary, running in the direction of the door he'd just passed through. Demons flooded after him, leaving Gary with the redhead...

...And with this bitch.

Darla Pike. He'd met her before, of course, and knew her by reputation. Of course whenever he'd seen her before, she hadn't been drenched in blood from nape to toes. And she'd been wearing clothes. Subtle differences, easy for a man distracted by being captured by demons to miss, but Gary prided himself on noticing little details like that.

"Well, if it isn't the cripple," Darla Pike said, smirking at him. "How's your inbred family doing?"

"Well, if it isn't the carpetbagging cunt," Gary said. "I see you've decided to engage in some freebleeding advocacy."

"Oh, this?" She wiped a hand through the rapidly drying blood on her saggy tits. "This was a friend of yours, actually."

Gary sighed, rolling his eyes. "What is it with you demonic bitches and the casual nudity? It's not for attraction purposes, obviously, or you'd do your makeup, maybe make an effort with your hair." He waved a hand in Pike's direction. "So what's the deal? You trying to stick it to the squares? If so, try not to cut yourself on all that 1960's vintage edge you're riding."

Darla Pike cocked her head at him, like she was trying to be seductive. Honestly, if she'd had someone else's head on her body – anyone's, really – the fucking girl who used to work the scanner at Rogerson's, Selene from Surrey's Diner, even old lady Marsden – Gary might have found himself interested. Maybe.

"Just fucking kill me already," Gary said, shaking his head, rolling his eyes. Giving this snotty Yankee bitch a taste of her own preferred medicine.

"Oh, sweety," Darla Pike said, leaning in to breathe in his ear, "you don't get to die until you beg us for it." And she ran a finger roughly across his neck, doing nothing but slightly scratching it. "And even then, don't count on it being quick."

Their laughter really pissed Gary off. But what the hell was he supposed to do? Nothing, that was what. His fighting days were over. He settled down in his chair and lowered his head, letting her get her fucking yuks out in hopes that when the moment came it would be soon. And hopefully quicker than she wanted it to be.

ERIN COULD HEAR something moving in the dark, but following the sudden death of Barney Jones, she couldn't see where it – whatever the fuck it was – was.

Light was extremely limited, down to just the cell phone in Father Nguyen's hand. He swung it back and forth unhelpfully, only succeeding in blinding those of them that were trying to figure out where the flying demon had gone. "Where is it?" he shouted, sounding about two steps shy of pissing his frock, or habit, or whatever they called it for a priest.

Erin found herself thrust up against Dr. Darlington, still reeling from the bomb the doctor had dropped. All this time, gossips around Midian had wondered who Molly Darlington's father was, and all along it had been fucking Jesse. Fucking steady, unassuming Jesse, who'd been with the same girlfriend since high school, who – gun to her head – she would have sworn had never stuck his dick in anyone else, ever, and maybe had never even jerked off without thinking of his wife, and as it turned out–

Nope. Not only had Jesse not kept it in his pants, he'd been the answer to the longest-running mystery in Midian, at least in the Maury Povich category.

"I have a niece?" Erin asked, because dwelling on being blinded, surrounded, and having a flying, decapitating demon in the room with her? Too fucking much. Especially when coupled with the return of Hendricks.

"Yeah, I can practically see the resemblance," Hendricks said. "Get your fucking head in the game before you lose it!"

"Fuck off!" Erin shot right back. It wasn't like she could do much to avoid decapitation right now anyway. Turning back to the doctor, she asked, "Molly doesn't know?"

Darlington shook her head slowly. "I didn't want to fuck things up for Jesse."

"Jesse has the perfect ability to fuck things up all on his own," Erin said dryly. "Trust me. He's my brother."

"If anything happens to me," Darlington said, taking Erin by both shoulders, "please. Tell Molly – and take care of her."

Erin stood there, fucking leveled. Death, she'd seen plenty of these last few months. Responsibility? Plenty more, until she'd pushed away from the table and said no more of that shit. She'd made sure her parents and her brothers had left town safely after her accident up on Mt. Horeb, because she didn't want to think about any of them getting hurt–

And all this time, she'd had family close at hand. Right here, in the Watch.

Something moved in the dark, sweeping out of the bouncing shadows at the ceiling. There was a scream, and Erin turned–

Addie Longholt was against the wall, holding herself. "I'm all right," she murmured, but there was a thin slick of blood painting the stone beside her that glared out in the light of the cell phone.

"Aw, shit, Addie," Erin said, catching her as she started to slide down. It had got her like a sword to the trapezius, or a guillotine that had gone badly sideways.

"I heard that confession," Addie said to Darlington, sounding dazed.

"You're the one who prompted it," Darlington shot back, a little edge to her voice. But it softened as she came alongside. "Addie...you're hit real bad. This is..." The doctor shook her head. "I can't fix it."

"Where's Brian?" Addie said, voice barely louder than a whisper.

"Brian?" Erin bellowed, not at the top of her lungs, but adjacent.

"He's holding the door with Arch," Hendricks said moving past them as he rapped his knuckles against another wall. He spared a glance, and his look turned pitying. "Shit. Brian!"

"Kinda busy!" The answer came back shouted.

Looking around the room, he snapped his fingers at Braeden, who'd been milling around next to Terri. "You. Mechanic. Get up there and help Arch bar the door. Tell Brian he needs to get his ass down here in three shakes."

"Sure," Braeden said, and stepped forward. He was holding his wrench, though what reason he could have for doing that, Erin had no idea. Was it consecrated? She couldn't even remember. He passed Terri, giving her a peck on the cheek, and something moved above them–

Erin blanched away, not because she wanted to, but because a spray of blood hit her across the face and instinct kicked in. She opened her eyes to find–

Terri Pritchard's head missing, and Braeden's mouth open

wide, in a scream that was drowned out by the gunfire thundering above them.

DUNCAN THREW himself into the night, ignoring Gary in his wheelchair, captive to Starling, to the entity that called itself Starling, and her handmaiden, Darla Pike. He should have seen it, seen the evil in that woman, but he was blocked and cut off from what power he used to have to sense the motives and soul-deep essence of human and demon.

The sun must have been close to below the hills in the west, or else the smoke from the fires had gotten too thick. The air was heavy with haze, and the light was dimming, the fires in the distance a mere orange glow as the sky darkened, now near black.

Duncan pounded down the street, ignoring the demons flooding in the opposite direction, toward the church, toward the remnants of the Watch. Remnants, now, for sure they were dead, at least in some number, if not in all.

He had no tears to shed, because he had no tear ducts. If he'd had them, maybe he would be crying as he ran. The feeling was certainly there, a sorrow, a clenching sensation within that he imagined might have been in his stomach, were he human. That dropping feeling he'd heard them describe, like their gut was an elevator and someone had severed one of the cables, giving it a proper lurch before the last fall.

It had all gone wrong, that much was obvious. Something a block behind him bellowed flames into the air, into the night, and it gave the scene a hellish cast. All he could see glancing back was demons, demons, demons flooding into the church, now, ready to complete their destruction of the Watch.

"There falls the last hope of men," came the voice of

Guthrie, echoing from somewhere distant. "Don't you think, Duncan?" She cackled.

Duncan could have stopped. Probably should have, really, because...well, this was the end. These had been the last champions fighting for humanity. Now they were dead, or, like Gary, would surely be wishing they were before too long.

That meant it was over. What was it Ambrose Bierce had written about Manichaeism? When good gave up the fight, the people joined the victorious opposition.

What else was there now but a chaos of demons, burning its way through Midian, and, finally, to the gate? And what good was there left in men that would stop it? No one else was coming; the demon hunters that had been on their way to Midian had surely been cut down, in the singles and groups in which they came to any hot spot. The institutions of man, the ones that knew what was happening, they were all complicit. They would do nothing, and would prevent word from getting out to those who might act – assuming any would believe it.

The demon army would march through the gate, and there would be nowhere left for any soul to escape the torments of hell.

Duncan ran anyway. Ran and cursed.

"See you soon, Duncan," Guthrie called after him, from somewhere in the darkness. "Real soon."

Duncan ignored that, feet pounding against the city street in the dark. Where had it all gone wrong? It felt like they had a handle on things, and not that long ago. They'd been dealing with the worst of the demons, they'd followed the Pact–

Ah, yes, the Pact. That was somewhere he went terribly wrong. Thinking that as an enforcement officer for hell that was trying to keep the demons from getting too rambunctious, that he had any business trying to save the world. And now he was damned with the rest of them.

The warm, ember-filled wind brushed his cheek, and he knew that it was, as Guthrie said, coming soon. Sounds of claws on pavement tickled his essence, and Duncan looked back.

Of course. Demons in pursuit. Vlash-nah-ran. Fast movers. They'd run him down, take him to his knees, and drag him back to Guthrie, Pike, and Starling, not necessarily in that order.

Starling. How had he been so blind as to think she might have worked for the other side, instead of being what "she" actually was? He consoled himself with the knowledge that for years people had been getting fooled in the same way with that dumb reality show *Undercover Boss*, where the CEO of the whole organization would show up in disguise and their employees wouldn't even recognize them.

How was he supposed to recognize the biggest boss of the demon world when he was wearing a redheaded hooker as a disguise? One didn't normally associate the Morning Star with a redhead, unless one was married to her and she was in a fit of temper.

Duncan had run down an alley between two brick buildings off some street, barely visible in the last glow of twilight. The dumpsters overflowed and ash was beginning to settle on the street like falling snow. Duncan needed a place to hide, but this wasn't it. Vlash-nah-ran had excellent noses for essences. Perfect demon hunters, really. The problem was they couldn't blend in for shit, which was why they were only employed in situations where a place was already overrun.

Duncan stopped, his essence roiling within. He couldn't run much more, and his shell was puffing as if to show how he was overheating. He looked around, eyes settling on a white door that looked a little out of place for this alley.

Why fight this anymore? He had nowhere else to run. They were going to catch him, there was little doubt. Hell was coming, and it was only steps behind him, and–

Well, Duncan decided, if he was going to hell, he was going to at least put it off as long as he could. Might as well spend his last moments relatively free of torment doing something for himself. Eating Nutella right out of the jar. Jerking off one last time. Something other than going quietly into the night.

So with that thought in mind, Duncan reached for the door handle, shoving himself through, the barking sounds of the hunters only steps behind him.

THEY WERE DROPPING like fucking flies in here, and Hendricks didn't have it in him to watch it happen again. "Steady that light, Father!" he shouted, whipping out his pistol. Nguyen did steady the light, just for a second, and it was enough for Hendricks to draw a bead on the winged demon that was lurking in the shadows above. It started to skitter away, hanging from the concrete ceiling on claws, about to lunge for him, but Hendricks popped off a thunderous burst, and it disintegrated into a cloud of stinking sulfur. He shook his head, trying to get rid of the ringing now echoing in his ears.

Fuck. He'd come back to this town to try and save the place, but now they were about to get overrun. No goddamned air support, no further back up, and demons swarming from all directions. This basement was going to end up his Alamo if he didn't find or make an exit. Unfortunately, he was low on plastique, and the walls weren't offering any way out. At least he'd dispensed with the flying bastard, because they already had at least two dead and another well on the way.

Glancing down at Brian's mom, he knew she didn't have long. Her son had yet to appear, probably because abandoning the door would mean those things would be in here in seconds, making his goodbye extremely temporary. Good for the egghead.

It had taken getting thrown into the most extreme deep end of the shit possible, but he'd figured some things out. Hendricks might have allowed himself a moment of pride – if he weren't down to the last moments of his fucking life, and desperately scrambling to escape that took precedence over basking.

"Dammit, dammit, fuck," Hendricks muttered, not really hearing but every other syllable over the inconsistent ringing in his ears. He thumped his head against the wall in the corner he'd been examining before he'd had to stop and whack that leathery, flying demon fuck. It had sounded promising, maybe even looked promising, but he'd gotten distracted. "Father, get over here!" he shouted, but it sounded like his head was underwater.

Rapping his knuckles against the wall as the light drew closer in the priest's hand, Hendricks stared, trying to listen through the ringing. The quality of the feeling against his knuckles had changed, too, hadn't it? Or was that simple desperation?

"I NEED to get to my mother," Brian gulped from beside Arch, whose back was taking the hits in a decidedly unpleasant manner. It wasn't quite like being tackled in his football days, but the thumping as the door – heavy, full wood – took another shellacking from the multitude of demons on the other side was a bit like a kick in the rump.

"You go," the drill sergeant said, throwing Brian out of the way and putting himself in the breach. Cracks were appearing in the wood; it wouldn't last much longer under this assault. Brian scrambled down, and the drill sergeant looked him in the eye. "I'm getting real low on ammo, blessed or otherwise."

"Not sure how much longer it's going to matter," Arch said, weathering another hit like he was riding in a bumpy truck along a rutted road. The crack in the wood beside him now ran almost halfway through the door.

BRAEDEN FOUND himself beside Terri's body in a swirling pool of blood. Her heart was pumping its last squirts and then it stilled, hand still warm clamped in his, if slightly sweaty. He had dropped his wrench, and once the gun went off and he smelled the sulfur, he just stopped where he was. Why move?

This was it. Life's final insult, the kick square in the fucking balls that Braeden had dreaded, knowing in his gut it was coming.

He'd lost his wife, and it had nearly broken him. Abi had kept him going.

He'd lost Abi at Halloween, and the death of his daughter had done it, had broken him. Barney Jones had helped him limp along, channeling the only feeling he had left into the Watch, into justice, into revenge.

Barney Jones lay headless on the floor, and Braeden felt it, numbly, with terror clouding his mind. Who would tell Olivia that her husband was dead?

Not Braeden. Because now Terri, the last person he'd really connected with, enough to allow him to feel intimate, to get naked, truly naked, to be inside her – lay dead next to Barney. Scalped by this merciless world that wasn't content just to stab you through the fucking heart. No, it had to take it all, like scraping the skin off an old wound to draw fresh blood. Any time he started to feel alive again, like he might just regrow his heart, fucking life cut it right out of him again.

"I got something!" Hendricks shouted, cowboy hat in one hand, sword in the other. He slammed his hilt against the wall, raining down stone chips. The whole room seemed to rattle as the door up the stairs took another hit.

Braeden stared down at the pool of blood mingling between Barney Jones and Terri Pritchard, the last two people in this world he had felt close to. He felt cold, felt a chill descend, felt his soul seem to leave his body along with his consciousness, and he appeared to be watching himself standing over the corpses–

"You aren't going to chip this open with a little bitty sword," Father Nguyen said dimly, in the distance.

"Well, find something, then," Hendricks said, donning his hat again, which shadowed his eyes.

Nguyen stretched his arms wide, as if to encompass the whole room. "Where would you like me to look?"

Braeden came back to his body in a screaming fit of fury, and he stretched his fingers out to find cold metal beside them. His wrench was right there, heavy in his fingers, not the ideal weapon for slaying demons, yet it had slain many of them. It had weight, unlike the sword, which was designed for slashing or stabbing with the point. The wrench was for blunt force trauma, an instrument of strength and rage–

Both of which Braeden had in seemingly infinite supply at the moment.

He screamed his fury so loudly it made the cowboy take a step back and the priest nearly leap out of his way as though he were a runaway train barreling down rattling tracks. Braeden smashed it into the wall where Hendricks had merely chipped it, and a block shattered. He brought it down again and dust and pebbles hit him in the face.

Braeden did not give a single, solitary fuck about that. He'd given his last fuck, and he'd given it to Terri, and now she was dead.

He slammed his wrench down again and again, powdering stone and filling the air with its dust to mingle with the choking smoke. The light swung behind him, casting his shadow over the darkness he was creating – no, revealing – beyond the wall. A hole was there now that stretched beyond, an infinite blackness, yawning before him like his own fucking soul–

Braeden stopped once the hole was wide enough for a person to fit through, and Hendricks laid a delicate hand on his arm and said, "I think you got it." Braeden was breathing hard, sweat had coursed down his face, and dust was settled in his mouth and upon his tongue like a layer of chalk.

Nguyen shined his light through the hole and whistled, low. "That's a tunnel, all right. This is the storm drain system beneath the town?"

"Let's hope so," Hendricks said, snatching up the cell phone and stepping through. Shining it beyond, Braeden could see the darkness cleanly cut; faint light waited in the distance. "Okay, I see a couple ways out way down there. We need to start getting people through, and somehow get Arch and Micah off the door without getting ourselves overrun."

"I'll handle it," Braeden said. His voice was steady, low, menacing.

"Braeden," Nguyen said, accepting the phone back from Hendricks, an ashen look on the priest's face, "you'll die."

"I said I'll handle it," Braeden said.

"Thank you," Hendricks said, meeting Braeden's eye for just a second. "You've got this." It was not a question.

Braeden gave him a nod, then bellowed. "Everybody out!" He needn't have bothered. Everyone in the cellar was already well aware of the hole in the wall, and was already heading for it as he headed up the stairs, heart thundering in his chest. This was going to be the last time he'd ever climb stairs, he realized.

Something about that realization filled his heart with unexplainable...not quite, but almost...joy.

BRIAN ALMOST BUSTED his knees landing next to his mother after one long, last leap down the stairs. There was a hubbub in the corner, people squeezing through a newly minted hole in the wall, dankness and smoky air seeping in to offend his nose from beyond it.

He ignored all those little details that presented themselves to him, though, as well as the sudden, spiking pain in his knees, because his mother lay before him, next to two other corpses, except she was not quite dead – yet.

"Oh, Brian," she said, when he could not speak. Her hand brushed down his shirt, spreading warm, dark, sticky liquid that smelled of copper. Her neck was laid open at the side, and with the faint light from his cell phone, pointed back through that hole in the corner, he could see hints of meat, like she had been smuggling a raw roast.

"Mom," he said, knowing in that moment that this would be the last time they spoke. He'd said goodbye to her before: when he left to go to Brown, when he'd left just months ago for New York City. None of those times had felt final, though, not like this.

"I wish you hadn't come back, son," she said, hand flopping uselessly up and down his chest.

"I couldn't stay gone," he said.

"But now you're stuck here," she said. "In this town. I know you never wanted to end up here."

He felt a grimace split his lips. "I never wanted to end anywhere. But the end is not going to be limited to Midian when it comes." And it's coming soon, he did not feel compelled to say.

"You need to go on, son," she said, looking up at him. "Survive. Learn what you need to, but please – you're the last of our family. I need you to make it."

"I – I'll try," he said, listening to the thunder up the stairs as the army of demons cracked the door. It wouldn't hold much longer; he was surprised it had held even this long.

"You need to make it," she said, grabbing his collar with surprising strength. "For me. For us. Alison, your daddy – all of us. You're the last...last Longholt."

"If I can, I will," Brian said, taking her hand. Once, he might have been icked out by all the blood, the grossness. Now he had bigger problems to worry about. The door thumped again.

"We should go." Arch was there, a hand on his shoulder. Brian looked up, and he nodded to the hole in the wall.

"Go," Addie said, letting loose of him and waving her hand like it had a handkerchief in it. "My boys. My sons. Go."

Brian let himself be led by Arch, his brother-in-law, and the closest thing he'd ever had to an actual. The thundering up at the top of the stairs was growing in intensity. Wood was cracking, growls were coming down. "But who has the door?" Brian asked numbly as his mother went slack. He turned away, not wanting to look at her, at anything in this cellar.

"Braeden," Arch said, pushing him roughly through the hole in the wall, into the tunnels beyond. He could see concrete walls, and the flash of his phone swinging around.

A growl in the distance, echoing through the tunnel, made Brian freeze with the others.

"Go!" Hendricks shouted from somewhere ahead of him, the hat nothing more than a shadow he could barely see in the thin darkness. "They're already in here, run!"

BRAEDEN FELT the crack of the door once more, mighty, and knew it was about to break.

So was he. But like the door, he'd hold just a little longer.

Growls from the other side. That was his warning the next hit was coming. It landed with a mighty splintering, and a groan, and he knew it wouldn't bear even one more hit. That was the straw, the door was the camel's back. No assembly required, no reassembly possible.

Braeden leapt down the stairs, taking them five at a time. He heard the door shatter in its frame, smash into the wall at the landing. He was already beyond it, legs aching from the jumps, ankles pissed off at him in a way they'd never been when he was a kid and did stupid shit like leaping down stairs.

Oh, to be a kid again. Like Abi. God, Abi. How had he been so lucky to end up with her as his daughter? Part of him had worried his life was over when his not-yet-wife had said those two little life-changing words: "I'm pregnant." But Braeden had been ready to be responsible. He'd thought: a boy. What could be better? Playing catch together. Working on engines, his little guy next to him.

Nothing had prepared him for princess dresses and princess movies and hopscotch. Of his daughter squeezing into the bed terrified in the middle of the night, pummeling him with little kicks and him waking up tired, but grinning stupidly, because dammit, he was smitten by this soft-skinned, sweet-eyed little doe who'd become his everything–

But Abilene Harlequin Tarley was gone now. She'd been ripped out of his hands at Halloween as he held on with everything he had. Nothing in the months before or since had prepared him for that, had allowed him to let go.

Until this moment right here.

Braeden stood, feet planted on aching ankles at the bottom of the steps as the demons came rushing down in a flood. He heard screams behind him from the hole in the tunnels, and started backing up. They were coming, coming for him, coming for the rest of the Watch behind him, so he placed himself squarely in front of that hole.

"My life is worth nothing if I don't do this." He said it to himself, then chuckled. "My life's worth nothing if I do this. It's worth nothing either way, so fuck it all." And he choked up on the wrench the way he would have taught his son – if he'd had one – to choke up on a baseball bat.

But he didn't have a son. He had Abi. Perfect, sweet little Abi. Who he couldn't protect. He knew, dimly, he was about to fail again. But he couldn't – wouldn't – let that stop him.

He was the last thing standing between these demons and the Watch. The last thing standing between this onslaught of fucking hell and the only people who had a snowball's chance in hell to save the world.

The first one came close, making a grunting noise, and Braeden swung. He made hard contact, and the thing puffed into sulfur air, but Braeden was used to it and didn't even flinch. He swung again, ripping into the next demon coming at him.

Abi was gone. Jennifer was gone. Now Terri was gone. His parents were long gone. One by one, they left him here.

But no longer. He swung, and something made hard contact with his side, sending a fiery pain along it and causing him to flinch, almost double over.

Braeden didn't have time for that shit, though. He swung again, blanching a little, but striking the thing that had just cut him.

Something else hit him in the leg and it collapsed beneath him. He went down swinging, though, screaming in pain and fury. More sulfur hit him in the face from where he'd popped another of these fuckers.

The only thing he could see now was shadows in the dark. The cell phone light was gone, and he was going by sound, by fury, swinging like a madman. There was always a brief flash each time a demon would pop. Quick, then gone, like a match going out in the dark, and the smell followed. It gave him just enough to go by to swing again. Teeth flashing in that little spark. A slithering face lit by the next.

Pop. Pop. Pop.

The pain was getting to him now, and he was breathing hard. As last stands went, this one wasn't bad, Braeden figured. Sure, it didn't seem likely anyone was walking away from this, not judging by the screaming from the hole behind him, but that was all right. They wouldn't get through him. Not right away, anyhow.

He just kept swinging until the blood running down his side left him cold. Kept swinging until his arms hurt, and his breath was coming in gasps, faster and faster, and he was down on one knee, then flat on his ass, and couldn't swing at all anymore.

Then, in the dark, he thought he saw a familiar face in one of those little sparks of light.

"Abi...?" he whispered.

The wrench fell out of his hand and clanged as he went limp, all sense leaving him forever.

LAUREN HAD RUN AS SOON as Hendricks had shouted, sprinting down the concrete tunnel toward the light she saw in the distance. It was the last of twilight, viewed through the square of the storm drain, and she could see movement behind her even without the cell phone light bouncing around the walls of the tunnel as Father Nguyen ran frantically from whatever was coming. Gunshots sounded in the dark, a whole bunch of them all in a row.

If they'd had an element of surprise from coming out into these tunnels, it was surely gone now.

Lauren popped out of the storm drain into the dried-out retention pond at the end of Division Street. In better times, the kids played soccer and football games here. Now the grass was dry and dead, and, hell, so was the town. Acrid smoke filled the air, and the last rays of natural light faded away, leaving them only the hellish ochre of the distant wildfires filtered through a prism of thick, choking smoke and falling ash.

"Welcome to Silent Hill," Brian Longholt said beside her, covering his mouth and coughing against the ashen air.

Others were popping out of the storm drain now: Hendricks, Micah, that drill sergeant, holding an AR-15. Erin, thin, pale Marina. Father Nguyen came out, still clutching the cell phone, light shining from it.

And finally, Arch Stan. That was it, she realized. The very last of them.

"Where..." Lauren asked, looking back in the tunnel. There was movement in there, but she couldn't see what was going on. "...Where's Rhea?"

Hendricks looked back and swore under his breath. "Don't know. Wherever she is, she ain't with us, and we can't go back for her unless you want to swim upriver through those fucking monsters." He flung a pointed finger ahead, across the field toward the dry woods beyond. "We need to keep moving."

"And go where?" Father Nguyen asked, turning his face away from the embers blowing at them. "The fires are out there, almost certainly heading this way. You run into the woods looking for cover, you probably die of smoke inhalation or burn to death in twenty minutes."

"Or you sit here," Hendricks said flatly, "and die of demons in twenty seconds. Up to you."

"We can find cover in the town," Brian said, striking off to the right, and in the midst of a rattling cough. "The houses and neighborhoods. We split up, lead 'em on a chase–"

"They are going to run us down," Hendricks said, with a cold efficiency. "They have the speed, and they have blood hunters."

"Better to split up, then," Arch said, a steely look coming over his face. He went partway up the hillside next to the storm drain. "We go in different directions. Make 'em work for it."

Lauren recognized that look; Hendricks looked like Molly when she wanted to argue. But it passed quickly, and the cowboy just nodded. "Okay. Let's do it." He hooked to the right, the direction Brian had gone. "I'm heading for town."

"I'll go with you," Lauren said. She had an itch in her head. "We could skirt the edge of downtown. I still want to hit the archives, see if I can figure out where this gate is."

No one said anything for a moment. "I'm going," Arch said, and off he went. Nguyen followed after him, wordlessly, and so did Marina and Drill Sergeant Micah. Which felt strange; Lauren had heard he was Hendricks's father-in-law? Or was that just a rumor?

It bothered Lauren not to know where Rhea had gone. But then...she sort of knew where Rhea had gone, didn't she? Surely the same place as Braeden Tarley, and Terri Pritchard, and Barney Jones. And Gary Wrightson. And Duncan, presumably.

"There are only eight of us left," Lauren whispered as she hiked a hard right and headed along the embankment, following the ex-Marine in the cowboy hat. They broke into a run toward the house at the corner of Crosser Street, in the dark, and soon Lauren found herself vaulting a fence into an unoccupied backyard, thankful that she'd not completely lost her cardio fitness.

ERIN FELT herself wanting to scream, but knowing she could not as she leapt gingerly over a fence into the backyard of Asa

Shrewsberry. The grass was unkempt, a fact that would have doubtless annoyed Asa – if he hadn't been killed by demons months ago.

This was the ruin of her hometown. Endless empty houses, dead yards, gardens bereft of life. They leapt another fence and found themselves in a backyard with a little plastic play set complete with slide. It stood there among brown grass that had wilted and now lay nearly flat, ready to burn whenever the fires came this way. Embers were floating around them; perhaps soon one would find purchase in this dry, dead grass – if it hadn't already, somewhere in town.

The smoke in the air was starting to become suffocating. Erin tried to cover her nose, but it didn't do shit. Her eyes burned, and visibility was down to a mere hundred yards, with the only light the distant glow of the fires in the suddenly sweeping night. Checking her watch, she found it was only four in the afternoon. Might as well have been midnight.

"Where are we going?" Erin asked, taking advantage of Hendricks pausing before the next fence. They'd leapt five in a row, and though the sound of demons moving about on the streets was in the air, she didn't think any were close.

Hendricks looked back at her, and a flash of anger seemed to come over his face. It was fleeting, and when he answered, his tone was calm, his voice measured: "I don't know."

"I need to get to the archive," Lauren said, butting into their discussion.

Hendricks just stared at her flatly. "Why?"

"To find out where this gate is," she said.

He stared at her even more blankly. "Look...our first priority is to evade the demons, because whatever you learn in some dusty archive isn't going to do you any good if you're dead, okay?"

"You really think we can evade the demons in Midian right

now?" Erin asked, probably coming off a little more condescending than she intended.

A rash of footsteps, heavy, not quite human, went by on the other side of the wooden fence they were perched behind. Hendricks signaled them to shut the fuck up, and everybody complied, even Brian, who seemed to go from panting desperately to holding in his breath in...well, in a breath.

"If anyone has a better plan," Hendricks said, meeting Erin's eyes with some fire in his, "I am all ears."

Something burst through the fence beside them, a head of a demon that flashed nothing but teeth at Erin. Hendricks lashed out with his sword – she didn't even realize he had it out – and the demon popped like a sulfur-filled balloon. Another screamed behind it, and another, and yep, they had not, in fact, passed by at all–

"Run!" Hendricks yelled, and fired a couple rounds to discourage them as he broke and bolted for it, sprinting along behind Erin, who'd chosen her path and paralleled the fence before leaping it and ending up in the front yard of the Gardner house, on Division Street.

Only after she looked back did she realize that Brian and Lauren had gone in a different direction, and that left her and Hendricks alone, sprinting across Division, pursued by demons.

BRIAN FOUND himself alone and running, leaping over the back fence of Ed Hanlon's yard. This was, perhaps, an annoyance of being in Midian. His brain catalogued and noted exactly where he was going. If he'd been running down Eighth Avenue in New York City, his mind might have given it a break, kept it simple, maybe classified things in relation to the cross street or some restaurant or coffee shop he knew in the area.

Not in Midian, though, where he knew of everyone, even if he didn't actually know many of them. Which was why when he leapt the fence, alone, into Jean Bryson's back yard, he was keenly aware of it. When he cleared the fence into Mickey Jensen's side yard, he knew exactly where he was.

And when the demon dog leapt after him coming around Mark Anderson's garage, he knew he wasn't going to make it any farther.

Then...he saw something he didn't quite remember. When had Mark ever had a door in the side of his garage?

It didn't matter. The dog was on his heels, was snapping, was evil, covered in black-tar leather skin, and the door was the only conceivable obstacle between him and it.

"I just had to come home," he muttered to himself, scrambling for the door knob. Even for him, this was a low. Mother dead, Watch scattered, the world about to end, and he was running through his hometown about to take refuge in a garage. And how long would that last?

Longer than he'd last if he didn't get through the fucking door.

It opened, to his surprise – hallelujah, really – and in he went, expecting darkness as he slammed the door behind him.

Which made what he found instead quite the surprise.

LAUREN RAN DOWN MAIN STREET, not caring what was behind her. She heard demons, but she didn't know where. She heard a scream, a shout, but had no clue where it was coming from.

She realized, as she reached the door to the archives, where she'd last set foot hours earlier, before the worm had turned, and wrecked downtown, that the place was actually in surprisingly good shape. Opening the door and bolting inside, she listened.

No one was following her.

Closing the latch, she hesitated. She waited another minute or so, just to be sure.

Silence, except in the distance.

All alone, she walked down the stairs into the archive, wondering why she was even bothering. Surely the Watch, whatever was left of it, could not survive this...this...hounding.

But she felt herself drawn regardless, down into the dusty archives, wondering what the hell she could even do if she managed to find the truth somewhere within.

ARCH KNEW they didn't have long, and he was looking for an exit. Such things seemed hard to come by in the ember-tinged air. Glowing embers floated past like particles in a suspension. His lungs hurt within his chest, a product of either the air quality (or lack thereof) or running too much, for too long. He didn't care to guess which.

The sound of pursuers coming after them was like dogs after a runaway prisoner. Alien noises, foreign to human life, were tight on his trail. "Keep it together," Arch said, because he didn't know what else to say but that.

Something crunched mightily behind him, and he dared a look back.

One of the T-Rex demons. It stuck out above the trees, and rustled branches, dropping a flurry of pine needles as it pushed through the boughs, in pursuit of them. It was a block, maybe a block and a half away.

"I can't run much farther," Nguyen said, gasping for breath.

"Nor...can I," Marina said, huffing behind Arch. He'd slowed his pace so as not to leave them behind.

Three gunshots rang out; Hendricks's father-in-law drilled two demons that had been tight on their tails. He, too, was puffing. "Think we're coming up on the last stand." Pulling a hand from his gun, he mopped his brow. "I really didn't think my shitheel son-in-law was right about demons, about this end of the world thing, but..." He glanced back at the rest of the group, the fatigue showing on his face. "...I guess I was wrong about him. Surprise."

Arch felt that acknowledgment might have been better directed at Hendricks, but he realized what it was: a dying declaration from a man who had come into this at the last moment. "Welcome to the Watch," Arch said. "Where none of us wanted to believe in demons, but were dragging kicking and screaming into it against our wills."

"Very much like how I've learned everything I have about Harry and Meghan," Father Nguyen said, and he came to a stop, clutching his side. "This is it. I can't go any farther."

They were in the shadow of Colton Everett's house, a white clapboard rambler on Worth Street, and Arch knew his little party had gone as far as he was going to be able to drag it. The demons were still coming, flooding at them from a couple different directions. He could hear them crashing through the backyards across the street, though the house still stood between him and seeing them. The T-Rex was coming from a block back and up the street, and quick, now visible through barren, skeletal tree limbs, breaking the dry branches like dead sticks, each step thundering enough to more than ripple a glass of still water.

"We make our stand here, then," Arch said, and drew his sword. Running with it had been awkward, and it seemed unlikely to help much now. A blessed AR would have been much more effective at doing damage to the swarm than this, but he had no other options available.

"Just gonna...sit on the porch until this is over," Nguyen said, plopping down on a rocking chair next to the front door. It squeaked, as orange streaks of falling embers in the smoky mist provided a surreal quality to the scene. Marina sat down next to him. She rocked twice, then stilled, staring straight ahead at nothing in particular.

Arch exchanged a look with Micah. They were the last two, for whatever good it would do. Just a couple guys standing against an impossible number of odds, crashing toward them like an inescapable wave. Arch nodded at him, Micah nodded back, and they both readied themselves for the end that was coming.

"DID I GET RHEA KILLED?" Hendricks asked the empty frigging air, maybe because that seemed to be all he had to talk to.

Erin stared at him in the darkness, which hung over Midian like a shroud. They'd crept away, bent double, keeping their heads down, trying to avoid all the trouble crawling through the town, catching the occasional burning ember on bare skin and prompting an under-the-breath swear. The sound of demons was all about them, but somehow they had evaded the trouble, and now found themselves creeping up Ted Kinzer's driveway. Nothing seemed particularly close, which was fortunate, because Erin felt tired, tired enough to lay down and die.

Hendricks paused next to a panel van, reading the side. Ted was an electrician, and apparently he'd left town without his work van. Or he'd died. Couldn't rule that out. So many had died without being courteous enough to inform the authorities they'd been eaten by demons or whatever. The absolute gall.

Erin was breathing hard, partly from running bent over, partly because they'd covered a decent amount of ground since being split from Darlington, Brian, and the others. "I need a minute," she whispered, in lieu of yelling a more emotionally satisfying reply to him.

He nodded. Hendricks seemed to be tired as well; he had that look on his face he got after being on top for too long. Nodding at Kinzer's van, he opened the door absolutely silently, and indicated for her to get in.

She did, though she wasn't thrilled about it. She would have preferred some dank basement, with concrete walls between them and the demons swarming around. But this would do, she figured, the van's shocks barely reacting to her weight. As it should be.

Hendricks climbed in after her and gingerly shut the door with but a click in the night. No windows in the back of the van meant the place was absolutely dark, save for the very small quantity of firelight that came through from the front window. Black curtains hung between the front cabin with the driver's seat and this compartment, which held tools strapped on a pegboard, and a mattress against the other side, held in place by bungie cords. Erin poked at it; it was soft...ish. "Huh."

She could feel a sudden tension as Hendricks froze next to her. In the no-light, he pressed a finger to her lips, and something moved by outside. Claws scraped against the concrete driveway, then receded into the night.

Erin felt her skin grow hot. "Yes, you got Rhea killed," she said, unsure why she was saying it other than pure, unbridled anger. "You got a lot of people killed."

She expected – and kind of wanted – a heated retort. She wanted him to fight back, to yell, to give her fury, so they could go out like they ought to. One last fight between the two of them, recapturing the olden days where she'd pitch fire at him, he'd shoot back, and so it would go. They'd raise their voices, and she'd *feel* again what it was like to love this man and hate him simultaneously, to know she had a righteous reason to be pissed at him, but also want to rip his clothes off. How she could feel both at once, she still didn't understand, but it was better than that dull, awful, clawing guilt she'd experienced in recent days, the kind that made her want to crawl into a bottle and never come out.

"Yeah," he said instead, completely deflating her, "I guess I did."

Well, fuck. She settled down on her haunches in the van, ass on the rubberized floor, not sure what to even say to that. He didn't appear to have much to add, and so they settled there, in the dim and the silence, and waited for the world to end.

THIRTEEN

NO EXIT

Gary didn't have much to say when they carted him away. He was surprised that it involved a car trip, because it felt like they could have just tortured him and eaten him alive right there on the church grounds. He was starting to cough, unwillingly, against the smoke in the air, a couple demon minders dressed like extras from West Side Story in street tough gear straight outta the fifties. The ladies had disappeared into the night, or rather, the ladies of the night had disappeared into the darkness, and left him just sitting in his wheelchair with these two fucking idiots.

And he could tell they were fucking idiots just by looking at them. No introduction necessary.

"Hey," he said to one, a young, Marlon Brando-looking motherfucker in a denim shirt, but with a receding hairline. "I need a drink of water."

The guy looked at him blankly, then exchanged a look with his partner, who had the appearance of a John Travolta from *Grease*, but minus the charm. And the chin. Charmless Travolta shrugged, not bothering to speak, then looked away. A variety of demons was strolling through the area, mostly not human-shaped. Gary was experiencing a real biodiversity of demons here, and he had about all the interest in it that he had for examining different-shaped turds.

Charmless Travolta walked over to Balding Brando and smacked him on the arm. "You're supposed to be watching him."

After a quick blink, Marlon smacked right back. "So?"

Charmless waved a hand at him. "When the boss of the whole fucking demon world tells you to do something, do you have any idea what happens if you fail at that?"

That made Brando squirm a bit, but he still shrugged it off. "What's he going to do? He's a cripple. He can't run, we'd catch him. And he ain't got any weapons." Brando turned to him. "You got any weapons?"

"Like I'd tell you if I did," Gary said.

Brando and Charmless exchanged a look. "Let's search him," Charmless said.

"I ain't got nothing on me but my dick," Gary said.

They fucking searched him anyway, and they weren't gentle about it. The fuckers tore off his jeans, ripping the denim like it was nothing, and giving Gary a real vivid idea of what it would be like if they decided to tear into him; it'd be like a kid eating Jello with their hands.

"You happy now, fuckers?" Gary said as they pushed him back into his wheelchair, naked as the day he was born, after removing every single article of his clothing and lifting him up to make sure he wasn't sitting on a shotgun or something. He wasn't; he hadn't gotten the damned thing reloaded after shooting it last time. "Told you I didn't have nothing but my dick."

"And now we know," Charmless said with a goofy grin. He twanged Gary's wang like a TSA agent, the fucking pervert.

"I see we've changed places in the dressing department." Darla Pike appeared out of the darkness wearing a priest's frock, minus the collar. She didn't even have a smudge of blood on her face any longer, but she did wear a hell of a grin as she came up to him, barefoot on the grass. "Did you check up his ass for weapons?"

Charmless and Brando exchanged another look. "No," Brando said, and started to lift him.

"You asshat," Gary said, knowing he wasn't going to feel this, but pissed as hell anyway. Darla Pike just grinned at him as Brando threw Gary over his shoulder like a fucking sack of potatoes, and Charmless peered in to take a look. Talk about a lifetime low, getting probed by demons right in the prison wallet. He would have felt better about it if it had been aliens, or Bigfoot.

"Save the pillow talk for the bedroom," she said, making kissy faces at him. Not sincere ones. Taunting ones. "And you two hurry up. We're moving out in the next few minutes."

"Going where?" Gary asked, pretty casually, even though he could tell by the sudden jarring he experienced that he'd just been violated. No lube. Pig fuckers.

Darla Pike just smiled, making an evil-ass amount of eye contact while that demon was rummaging around in his ass. Bitch. "You'll see," she said. "You'll see."

LAUREN FOUND A LANTERN, the kind that had LED bulbs in it that mimicked an old fluorescent. She took stood among the books, compiled of old minutes from town meetings, of stories retold to townsfolk and members of the council, and...

Hours passed, and she paged through every one of them.

She'd left a jug of water here before, when she'd engaged in this study back when Rhea interrupted her, and then the worm. It was a fortunate accident, because now she had nothing – no food, no additional clothing, no holy weapons, just herself, her ragged clothing, and this jug of water. Which would maybe last her a few hours, if she was lucky, before the dehydration effects started. Then she'd have to leave and...what?

Well, that was the trouble, wasn't it? The Watch was scattered, what was left of it. Most of them were dead or gone even before the events of the last days. They were down to eight or so before she'd parted ways with them. How many had survived that?

Probably few to none. Which made Lauren maybe the last hope.

"Let's try not to think about that," she said, poring over a volume that described segregationist town policies in the 1930's in great and excited detail. Just fucking charming, it was.

She groaned, because even her skimming wasn't producing much more than notes about the nothings of everyday life. How had the gate to heaven been present in Midian all this time and yet still hidden? What of significance had happened here, other than the construction of the Tallakeet Dam? It was, she figured, the only sort of physical upheaval she could think of. Everything else was garden variety – house and road construction, rumors and mumblings and ruptures among church congregations. Births and deaths.

What the else was there in this small-town life until the demons started showing up?

And even that was nondescript at first. Hendricks and Arch had stopped some cow demon from rising, then teamed up with Erin and the OOCs to stop another from destroying the dam. There was some murder and mayhem sandwiched in there, sure, but even when that fucking penis-attached-to-a-demon Mick tried to impregnate her daughter with devil fire dogs, it hadn't been an incident of wildly interesting note. It had taken the Rog'tausch ripping through the streets of downtown for it to finally start to register with the townsfolk that something was going on really outside of the ordinary–

Lauren sat up straight. The Rog'tausch...what was it about the Rog'tausch that suddenly tickled her mind?

She stood up, pushing through the archive to the newest meeting book, which was sitting on a desk toward the entry. Glancing at the door, something seemed off, but she didn't have time to deal with odd feelings at the moment. She took hold of the book and moved back to the desk, already flipping through the most recent minutes of the town meetings until–

"Ah ha," she said, because ah-fucking-ha.

Some helpful soul in the city government had marked a map of the Rog'tausch's path of destruction through Midian. She'd been there the night it had come, her and that pencil-necked reporter Belzer, following along as it cut a swath through the town. It had been heading in a singular direction, though, only thrown off course when members of the Watch had pissed it off, she realized at last, looking at the map.

And it was in that moment she realized exactly where the gate this whole thing turned on was, exactly.

"Huh," she said, because...well...it was a surprise.

But sitting in the lonely archive, wondering if she was the last member of the Watch, it did beg one question.

What the fuck was she supposed to do now that she knew?

HENDRICKS WAS SITTING, running his hand over the mattress strapped to the side of the van, and he asked in a whisper, "What the hell do you think this is doing in an electrician's van?"

Erin let out a rough guffaw of amusement. "Ted and his old lady did not get along. But they didn't want to get a divorce – heaven knows why, we all talked about it, no one had an answer. I guess at some point he decided he needed a place to sleep on those occasions when she tossed him out of the house. And she did it, like, five times a week, no joke."

A wry thought occurred to Hendricks. "That coulda been us. If we met under different circumstances, I mean."

Erin seemed to slump at that. She was quiet for a long moment, allowing the sounds of some demon trumpeting in the distance to seep in like the smoke between them. "I've been...I don't know."

Hendricks stared at her. "Some people just aren't compatible. And maybe that's us. I'm too much of a dick, too scabbed over by hard experience. When I met you, you were sweet, you were fun-loving, you were...well, fun. And I feel like everything that's happened since has made you–"

"A bitch?" Erin's thin lips were twisted in a wry smile.

"Whatever you were, or are," Hendricks said, "you're different now. And at least part of that, maybe the biggest part – well, it's my fault."

"God," she said, hissing annoyance. "You just had to take away my thunder, huh?"

Hendricks blinked a couple times. "I just took the blame for the problems between us. How is that your 'thunder?'"

"Because I wanted the blame, clearly," she said, exhibiting a little passion, a light burning in her eyes. "Just like I wanted a fight a few minutes ago, before you went and accepted responsibility for getting people in Midian killed without so much as a push back. And yes, that kind of makes you a dick."

Hendricks found himself blinking again. "I don't understand."

"Of fucking course you don't," Erin said, "because it's not

supposed to make sense. I've been angry at you. For months. Obviously. Since I went off that cliff on Mt. Horeb, since I went into the hospital. And since you were gone afterward, and I climbed into a bottle and didn't come out until the town got wrecked by that Rug toss demon–"

"Rog'tausch."

"Who fucking cares?"

"Just trying to get it right while I'm being accused of doing nothing but wrong."

Erin almost seemed to smile. It was right there, then the balance tipped, and it was gone. "I wanted to be mad at you. For leaving, I mean. I needed to be. Because if I was mad at you, if it was justified, I didn't have to ask myself tough questions about why you did what you did. How would you have gotten me out of that hospital? These were questions I didn't want to answer. I just wanted to be mad. And you made it so fucking easy for a while, you and Arch, jousting with Reeve, that I didn't have to question whether I was on the right side until that thing came ripping through town and fucked everybody's neat little lives up once and for all. I could drink and smoke and fuck – and not feel an ounce of guilt about any of it, knowing all the while you and Arch and Duncan and Alison were out there fighting the good fight."

She put her head down, her arms resting in a comfortable ring around her knees, which were pulled to her chest. "And I did all those things. Drank, smoke, fucked – without you. While you were carrying on the war."

"I know," Hendricks said softly. "But it doesn't matter now, Erin. We all fucked up." He laughed bitterly. "I mean, look how bad I fucked up. After you, I fell dick first into a trap right outta hell. And I may just have destroyed the entire world. Guarantee whatever you smoked, whatever you drank, and whoever you fucked – you can't say that."

She laughed bitterly. "Yeah, okay. You definitely win the fuckup competition." A little tear streamed out of the corner of her eye. "But I'm still sorry."

"Yeah," Hendricks said. "Me too. But I don't have it in me to fight back against you anymore. I've fought enough. First in Iraq, then across the world against demons. I had this pain in my soul that I just wanted to put up against those who deserve it. And demons? Man, they made it easy. They killed my Renee." He could picture her face in front of him, again, that magical face. "Damned near got me. When Rhea came to me and explained why I could do a damned thing against them? It was like I was a gun, fully loaded and ready to go, and someone just pointed me at the right target and let it fly. It felt...not good exactly, but right." He lowered his head. "And somewhere along the way, I just got lost in it all."

"I think it was easy to get lost in Midian when there were so few of us fighting so many," Erin said, hugging her legs closer. "Now there's a clarity because all we can do is run and keep running to survive. But before, when society still functioned, and there was still drinks available, and you could still get maid service at the Sinbad to clean up whatever we did to the sheets the night before," and she flashed him a quicksilver grin, "it was easier to not focus on it, y'know?"

"Looks to me like plenty of people still ran," Hendricks said. "Not that I blame them, having done a little running myself."

She nodded slowly. "You catch up with Kitty Elizabeth?"

He drew a slow, pained breath that seemed to stab at his ribcage – or at least in the vicinity of his heart. "I did – sort of."

Erin cocked her head. "What's that supposed to mean?"

"Means Micah, Brian, and I stormed her fancy New York penthouse," Hendricks said. "And she was waiting."

"Oh, shit," Erin said, thin eyebrows rising.

Hendricks shook his head. "No, it wasn't a fight. She

wouldn't fight, in fact. She begged off – because of Starling. Said she feared...well, whatever entity is driving Lucia." He let his head fall back. "I don't understand the politics of hell."

"That's probably good, right?"

Hendricks chuckled. "I guess? I don't know. Seems like there are all these factions. Whatever's in charge of Lucia, though...it had Duchess Kitty scared shitless to lift a hand against me even after Starling had gotten everything she wanted out of my dick. And keep in mind that Kitty Elizabeth is the thing most demons wake up sweating about, so whoever is running the redhead...it's bad."

Erin's lips quivered. "And you fucked it. You fucked the thing that nightmares are afraid of."

Hendricks stared at her for a moment, then snorted. "I fucked it." They both laughed, softly but uncontrollably. "Man, I was so hard up after you left that I ended up fucking a demon in a hooker, Erin. And it might just end the world."

"Yeah," she said, and her smile started to fade. "Well. If it makes you feel better...she was really hot. I say that as a woman who's not into other women, like at all, but...Lucia was hot. And whenever that thing would take over, she got very weirdly commanding. It made sense to me. Hell, made me jealous. Anyway...I forgive you."

He thought about it a sec, then blinked a couple times, mentally chewing it over. "That does make me feel a little better. Not just about the hotness, I mean, but...thank you for forgiving me."

She shrugged. "If it hadn't been you that fathered that thing, it would have been Casey, I'm sure." Her lips turned down, eyes squinted. "Why did it have to be you?"

He gave her a wry look. "Well, I mean...you chose me. Is it so weird a demonic entity would?"

Erin smiled, but rolled her eyes. "I just mean that Starling went through some serious hoops to get you. Why? When there are plenty of sperm donors around happy to give. Lucia had sex for money, like...all the time. Why not one of her johns?"

Hendricks didn't bother to give it much thought. "I have no idea. Really none." Then he cocked his head. "Wait. She did have me kill Pike. I wonder if that had anything to do with it?"

"Maybe. Not that it matters at this point anyway." She glanced at the metal walls of the van. "She wins, we lose. Not like knowing the reason would give us information we could do a goddamned thing with."

"Yeah," Hendricks said, and paused to listen. It was quiet out there – or as quiet as a demon-infested town could be. Whatever hellbeasts there were out there, they didn't sound close. "I wonder what they're up to?"

"I don't even care anymore," Erin said, leaning back against the metal. "They're going to get us, and if they don't, the world ending will." She relaxed her grip on her legs. "When I drank all that whiskey last night, it was like I could sense things were coming to an end. Like it was the last time I'd get a drink. And I needed to do it."

"Regret it in the morning?"

She smiled, then rubbed her head. "Little bit."

"I get that," Hendricks said, nodding. "I haven't unwound since before I left here. It's just been go, go, go." He shrugged. "Not that it matters now."

She nodded absently, then turned her eyes toward the side of the van. Where the mattress was strapped by bungee cords to hooks to keep it from toppling over. "Hm."

He let that silence rest for a moment before asking, "'Hm' what?"

She rocked forward to her knees, fiddling with one of the bungee cords. "'Hm,' why are we sitting on this hard rubber floor when something more comfortable is right here?" She gestured to him and he moved back, letting her unstrap the mattress. When it was loose, they caught it and lowered it to the floor of the van so it didn't make a thump that would rock the whole vehicle, thus alerting any demons in the area with sensitive ears to their presence.

Hendricks waited until he was sure that nothing was coming, nothing had heard them, then joined Erin on the mattress. It wasn't thick, but it felt better on his haunches than the thin rubber layer on the floor had.

"You know," she said, with a very conspiratorial air, "this is so much better."

"Yeah," Hendricks agreed. It was.

"But I didn't just let it down for comfort right now."

"Hm?" Hendricks looked up at her.

She moved pretty quick, yet somehow quite slow at the same time. Her lips were on his in a moment, and they stayed there for what felt like forever, in the best way. "Oh," he said when she finally broke off the kiss, grinning at him, his hat askew.

"Remember what I said about last times?" She took his hat off and hung it on one of the pegs.

"Fuck yeah," Hendricks said, and suddenly it was a race to both kiss her and get naked, with as little interruption to the former as the latter would allow. His hands probed and found her tits, small handfuls hidden under her bra, and when he got her out of it, it felt so damned good he could scarcely believe how silly it seemed that he just wanted to put his fingers on the nipples, play with these little notches of raised flesh as she shuddered slightly under his grasp. His tongue found hers repeatedly and she took over as he shucked off his coat, kicked off his boots with her on top of him. He let her peel off his t-shirt, which was sticking to his skin, then unfasten his jeans, which thankfully didn't.

He didn't even get them halfway down and she had his cock

in her mouth, treating it like it was a cold longneck on a hot summer's day. He was kicking the jeans off as she worked him, and as soon as he was rid of them she paused for a moment, a little trail of saliva or pre-cum anchored to her lower lip as she shot him seductive eyes.

Hendricks grabbed her, pulled her to him, and put her on her back, kissing his way down her chest. He licked his way from the bottom of her sex to the top, focusing on her clitoris. He spent several minutes going at it with delicate touches, trying to see if he could drive her wild before he even slipped the tip of a finger in.

He worked her for long minutes, until he could feel the tension in her building, and then he rose, kissing back up her body and entering her in a series of long, slow strokes. She traced her fingertips along his sides, his flanks, and dug her heels in to the back of his thighs, keeping him from pulling out too far.

That suited him fine. He was exactly where he wanted to be.

It felt like an hour, felt like forever, felt like the last taste of heaven he was ever likely to get. She came first, a slow, rolling crescendo that came to an explosive finish until she jerked and spasmed, barely a whimper escaping her in the quiet confines of the van.

He only needed another minute or two after that to finish himself. She helped by pulling him close, really digging those heels in, and when he started to come, she wrapped her arms around him to hold him in.

Hendricks was left gasping when he was done, and so was she, looking in the eyes of this woman who he hadn't been with in months, hadn't gotten along with for nearly as long. Coming back to Midian, he wouldn't have expected this, not in a million years, not with the way they left it.

"I think I kinda forgot how good we work together,"

Hendricks said, not daring to roll off. Not like there was a lot of room for him to on this little mattress.

"I didn't," she said with a smile. "Which is why I wanted this to happen." She cupped his ass. His dick flexed inside her, spent but not sorry to be where it was. "Honestly, I've been missing this since we stopped." When he looked at her in surprise, she added, "You're the best I've ever had, Hendricks."

"Not sure whether that's a commentary on you or on me," Hendricks said, enjoying the feel of her breasts pressing against him, of her feet and her legs still keeping him wrapped up in her. It was far, far different from the cold and impersonal fuckings he'd experienced with Starling. This was warm in addition to being hot, it was pleasurable in addition to being a simple orgasm.

It was...the closest thing to being loved he'd felt since Renee.

Hendricks didn't dare say that out loud, though. He just sat there inside her, his head against the side of her neck, breathing in her scent, feeling himself still inside her, her arms around him, ignored that there was an army of demons somewhere outside this van, and enjoyed the last peace he figured he might ever have.

DUNCAN BURST through the door in the brick alley and found himself–

–found himself–

Found himself in a house.

The door slammed shut behind him with an air of foreboding, of finality, like it been swung by some force beyond that which he'd applied to it. He was standing in a sitting room, and the air had an aroma like...cleaner? Fresh cleaner, like someone had just Windexed or Pinesoled or something.

"Ah, Mr. Duncan," came a pleasant voice from somewhere down the hall. "Do come in, won't you? And wipe your feet on the rug, will you? No need to track all that ash from the outside world."

Duncan had this feeling – a prickling, annoying feeling – he knew exactly where he was. That this was a place he had long been searching for, and yet had never quite been able to get to–

Until now.

Keeping his baton firmly in hand, he eased down the hall to the back of the house where, waiting at a kitchen table no more impressive than any other he'd seen in any house in Calhoun County, waited what appeared to be a gray-haired man wearing a Han jacket and a benign smile that didn't quite reach the eyes. Because they were fake.

"Wren fucking Spellman," Duncan said, clenching his teeth, and clenching his baton in hand.

"That's not my middle name, but otherwise, entirely correct," Spellman said amiably.

"'Wren Spellman' isn't your fucking name, either," Duncan said, almost growling. Very unlike him, but this was a moment he'd been hoping for, waiting for, since he'd come to this town.

"No, in fact," Spellman said. "As you know, this form is but a humble screen to keep my true identity secret and safe from reprisal by unhappy parties such as...well...yourself."

"Give me one reason why I shouldn't pop your screen self right now," Duncan said.

"Because it wouldn't harm me at all," Spellman said, "but would harm you and your cause immeasurably." He spread his hands wide. "I'm here to help you in your hour of need. Destroy me, and I can't help."

Duncan started to answer that, but a thump behind him made him turn.

The front door had opened, then rapidly shut, and standing there was–

"Brian?" Duncan asked.

"What the fuck?" Brian Longholt said, backing away from the front door like it was about to come crashing down.

"You're quite safe here," Spellman said, gliding past Duncan without the least regard for his safety. "That door only opens where I want it to, and only appears where I want it to. It appeared to pick you up, and now it's gone again, so whatever was chasing you won't be finding you now."

"Thanks," Brian said, not sounding too terribly grateful. He gave Duncan the once-over. "You all right?"

"Peachy."

"Good," Brian said. "So...this is the 'fucking screen' you're always bitching about?"

"Yep."

Spellman sighed. "I am so very misunderstood. Have I not assisted you almost as much as I've harmed you? Who came to you when Gideon was going to blow up the dam, not only offering information but rendering needed aid to Mr. Hendricks?"

"You," Duncan said, crossing his arms in front of him, baton still jutting out, "but only after you'd sold Gideon the bomb he was going to use to destroy the dam."

"But he didn't destroy the dam," Spellman said, "because you were there, along with Mr. Hendricks, Mr. Stan, your former partner, and Mrs. Stan." He inclined his head subtly toward Brian. "Plus her commanding rifle, naturally."

"You act like you didn't set the whole thing up," Duncan said.

"Merely in motion," Spellman said. "And you are welcome to hold it against me, if you wish. Why, there's hardly anything I can do to stop you from taking that...terribly unpleasant object," he waved vaguely at Duncan's baton, "and shoving it anywhere you wish in me. Then I will be gone, this screen destroyed, and you will be unable to benefit from the help I am willing to offer you."

"Why are you willing to offer us help?" Brian asked, looking quite confused.

"Excuse me just a moment," Spellman said, and without another word, started walking toward the front door.

ARCH DIDN'T THINK they were going to last much longer, and that was fine. It really was an onslaught, demons coming from every direction to feast on their bones. Between his sword and Micah's AR-15, Arch figured they were doing about as fine as one could, but in a place where you were being attacked by an entire army of demons, fine wasn't going to be enough.

Nguyen and Marina were up on the porch, not a weapon between them, neither looking fit enough to do squat. Arch kept looking over his shoulder at 'em, afraid something was going to sneak past, or flank around Arch and Micah, and get at those two. They didn't look like they had enough fight in them to so much as proffer a slap if a demon leapt on them.

"This looks like the end," Micah said, slapping what appeared to be one final magazine into his rifle.

"Mmhmm," Arch said. What more was there to say? Soon he was going to see Alison again. Real soon, it looked like.

They were coming in all around now, and he was swinging, sweating like he was back at three-a-days in summer practice season. His arm was tired, the gun was thundering, teeth in angry faces were everywhere, coming from all directions, and he just kept going. Take a step, take a swing, hit another, take a small hit, stumble, recover, swing and kill.

He could feel it closing in on him now, the jaws of death. He didn't fear it. It was like birth; leaving the world was like coming into it, he figured, a decent amount of pain and discomfort, and then everything was going to be all right – in this case, forevermore.

"Kindly step inside please," came a polite, familiar voice from behind him, "so that I can close this door and thus seal this riffraff out."

Arch turned to look, nearly costing himself his footing as a demon the size of a dachshund leapt at him. Micah managed to blast it out of the air about five feet from his chest, but Arch stumbled back anyway.

"Move your ass, Arch!" Brian Longholt was standing on the porch, shepherding Nguyen and Marina in past–

Wren Spellman. That...fellow. For lack of a better word.

Arch, though, was caught between the devil and the deep black sea...of demons. It didn't take him more than a moment to shift focus and accept the life raft thrown to his companions in this fight. "Get in there," he said to Micah.

Micah looked back at him, perhaps sensing. "You coming?"

Arch grimaced, slashing through a couple demons that threw themselves at him. The sulfur was strong here, almost as bad as the smoke. "I suppose."

"You'd rather die out here?" Brian called to him from the porch.

Arch had an answer for that. Something about seeing Alison, he supposed.

But it wasn't all about him, was it? The world was still hanging in the balance, and while he might have liked to go home...

A quick look at Micah's face – the man was retreating quite happily, covering Arch as he went, but gladly falling back – proved true what Arch knew in his heart.

The world was worth saving, because there people in it who had lives, hopes, loved ones. And while Arch might have lost all that, he couldn't lose sight of the fact that if the one he worshipped had given his life to save the world, how could Arch do it any differently? Dying here on this lawn wouldn't do squat for the world.

So Arch turned and hustled up the steps behind Micah, letting the man fall back ahead of him. The moment he was through the door, Spellman shut it behind them, and after one brief thump, it fell silent.

"Arch," said Duncan, who was standing right there.

"You do this?" Arch asked, nodding at Spellman.

"I got saved same as you," Duncan said with a shake of the head. "He hasn't made clear why, yet. Probably waiting until we're all assembled to spell it all out."

"That may take a while," Spellman said, templing his fingers. "You see, several of your number are...distracted at present. Out of reach, you could say. But this I promise you – nothing else is happening at the moment. No friends in danger, and the world isn't going to end until tomorrow. So, if you like...you can take advantage of these facilities and rest. There's food in the kitchen, there are bedrooms and showers upstairs, you'll find fresh clothes in your size in–"

"Fucking great, I'm in," Brian said, already heading for the staircase.

"I call first shower," Father Nguyen said, racing for the stairs with an energy he hadn't been exhibiting on the porch.

"After me," Marina said, hustling after him. Now it was a three-way race.

Arch just looked at Duncan. "We safe here?"

Duncan shrugged. "Safer than you were out there."

Arch nodded. "Who else are we waiting for?" Which was kinder than just asking, "Who else made it?"

Spellman wore a very tiny smile. "Hendricks and Harris are alive, but...indisposed. Dr. Darlington is also alive, but I can't quite reach her at the moment. I'm setting up a bridge to do so, but it will take a short while. Also, your benefactor shall be arriving in the morning."

That raised Arch's eyebrow. "Benefactor?"

"I'm not doing this out of charity," Spellman said with that same infuriating smile. "Though I am sympathetic – bordering on enthusiastic – about your cause. However, someone is making this all very worth my while."

"Fucking screen," Duncan said, sounding a lot more like Lerner than himself. He sounded exhausted, though, and hesitated before speaking again. "Did Gary Wrightson make it?"

Spellman did a little hesitating of his own, closing his eyes. When he opened them again, he said, "He is alive...but he may soon wish he were not."

Arch just shook his head. Captivity. That had seemed like Starling's plan for them, otherwise she would have come at them a lot harder. He could feel the demons aiming for his legs, trying to hit areas that weren't his throat. The T-Rex things hadn't squashed him flat, and they could have. "Why does she want him alive?" he asked, thinking maybe the answer would be simple.

Turned out...it wasn't, quite.

ERIN LOVED the feeling of Hendricks inside her.

Yes, he pissed her off. More than a few times. Yes, he'd apparently helped bring about the end of the world, but hey, who among them hadn't consorted with Starling in some way these last few months?

But no one in her life fucked like him. Not ever. And it

honestly made her wonder if the fighting, the heat between them, if it was just part of the magical chemical stew that made the sex so damned good.

"You seem calmer," she said, running fingers through his hair as he lay atop her, weight pleasantly pushing down on her.

"Well, I did just get laid," he said, and though she couldn't see his face, she could read the lazy smile in his tone. "That has a tendency to calm a man right down. In fact, it's maybe second only to a blow job in the hierarchy of things that can put a man into a state of tranquility."

"Since you got back, I mean. Smartass." She grabbed his ass again. It was a perfect handful. She'd missed watching it retreat into the bathroom in the mornings since he left. Such a stupid little thing, missing that. Missing getting railed by him? Duh. No brainer. Obvious. The guys she'd let try to fill the gap after they'd parted ways couldn't hold a candle to him. And they couldn't find the clitoris with a goddamned shovel and a treasure map, let alone be willing to stay down there until she really started humming.

It almost made her want to push him off and suck on him for a little bit just to see if she could get a second round. She almost certainly could, based on past experience. Especially if he hadn't been jerking his Gherkin lately, she might have even been able to get two more rounds out of him. Though by that point, the chafing on her end would be getting into the uncomfortable range. But who cared about chafing when you could go out on a high?

She started to make a move when he tensed up beneath her fingers. He lifted his head, listening. "Do you hear something?"

"Your heartbeat," she said, "but that's more something I'm feeling." Along with his half-flaccid dick. She thought about giving it a playful squeeze within her, but he was in too serious a mood – and this was probably too serious a situation – for that.

"How long do you think we can stay like this?" Hendricks asked.

She felt the seriousness return. "If they're gonna get us, y'know, might as well go out having fun, right?"

He smirked for just a second, then it faded. "I kinda want to go out swinging."

She sighed, then nodded. "You should probably put your pants on, then, cowboy."

"Yep," he said. "Saddle up." And he withdrew, moving his body off hers, and suddenly Erin felt cold, a small chill. She wanted him back already, not because she wanted to fuck some more, but just because she liked the feeling of him being close to her, his weight atop her. There was comfort there, a feeling of safety in the middle of this storm.

They dressed in silence, listening amidst the rustle of denim and cloth, the sound of zippers. They traded shy looks, amused looks, nothing sexy, nothing that would lead her to abandon this feeling of dread acting as a cold pit in her stomach and get back to being naked, being pressed together in an embrace that meant a shocking amount more to Erin than anything she'd felt before, not because of the sex but because of the intimacy.

"I've been in love with you for a while," she said once he was back in his coat. She couldn't even look at him as she said it. "That's why...that's why I..."

He took her in his arms, clutching her to him, her head to his chest as they sat there. "I know how you feel. You were the first one since...since...you know...to make me feel alive again. And it gave me feelings for you, too, however much I didn't want them to be there. However much I didn't think I could ever feel that way again, at all."

She felt tears edging in at the corners of her eyes. "This sucks. That it had to happen now, when we're about to fucking die. When the world is about to break into pieces or get dragged to hell or whatever."

"Yeah," Hendricks said. "We don't get to choose our time, I know, but you're right – this sucks. We could have been born in the forties, the thirties, and we'd have our trials. Instead we're here, now, with a seat for the end of the world, which is just fucking great. Any second now, some demon is going to hear or smell us, and come tearing through that door," and he pointed at the van's rear doors, "and then–"

A very polite, insistent, tap-tap-tap, came from the rear doors just then, followed by, "Hey, it's Duncan. Please don't shoot me."

Erin froze, staring at the door. "You fucking serious right now?"

"Yeah," Duncan said, voice muffled by the metal. "It's me. I have an exit for you, but we need to go pretty quick. There's a demon patrol two blocks out and heading this way. Probably because they hear me and smell you."

Hendricks let go of Erin and threw open the door, clutching his pistol, ready to shoot. Duncan's pasty face was waiting outside, arms crossed. "Shit," Hendricks said, "it really is you. Did you go evil again?"

He shook his head. "There's no redemption for me now, not even if I surrendered and brought you all in. It's going to be all hell, all the time for me, I'm afraid. Unless."

Erin stared at him, expectantly. She had her clothes on now, but somehow she still felt naked, exposed. "Unless...what?"

He gestured to a door, standing open to the house. Waiting inside was Arch, and...someone else, someone Erin didn't recognize, but Hendricks did. "That fucker," he said with a bit of a growl.

"He's saving our lives," Duncan said. "So you might want to lay off the hostility."

"Fine," Hendricks said, and slid out of the back door. He

turned back and, without looking, offered his hand to Erin to help her down. What a gentleman...who's just fucked her brains out. How pleasantly rare. She took his hand and down she went, following Duncan back through the door.

It took her a second to realize that this was not, in fact, the same house she'd walked into. For one, it didn't smell of the wickedly pervasive smoke that infused every single particle of air in Midian. She hadn't even realized she'd been breathing smoke with every breath until it was suddenly gone.

"Demon magic," Hendricks said, apparently having gotten there before she did. The door was already closed, and the windows all bore curtains to block any view of wherever this house was, in actuality. He focused on the man in the funny jacket, standing in the hallway. "What's your deal, Spellman?"

"Salvation," Spellman said, with a smile. "That is the 'deal,' as you so eloquently put it, for today. Yours, your friends, and – if you're very lucky and very good – for this whole world." Something about the way he said it put Erin right on edge.

GARY WASN'T HAVING any fun. Not that it was a requirement for where he was at in life at the moment. Being paraded, naked, sitting in his wheelchair in the back of a pickup truck before jeering demon crowds as he was detoured around the wreckage left by the big worm just didn't hold any joy. The wildfires still lit the hills, Gary saw, Charmless and Brando beside him, holding his wheels in place as the pickup cruised its way around at an average speed of – he estimated – five miles per hour.

They seemed to be heading in the direction of the last five degrees of the horizon that weren't encircled with wildfires, Gary realized as they came up a hill. Ahead was the freeway –

closed since the earthquakes. They were heading down Old Jackson Highway, north, toward Mount Horeb, which wasn't even a shadow on the horizon right now thanks to the thick smoke that blanketed everything like a fog. Gary coughed, not really wanting to, but having to.

Behind them, demons marched like an army, except without the discipline. They stretched back to the horizon, all shapes, all sizes, most hanging in the roughly-human range. Oh, sure, there were the T-Rex things, and some dogs and bugs the size of dogs, but in general, they were human-ish. No ranks, no formation, which maybe would have been scarier, giving things a Nazi feel. It wasn't a big mystery to Gary now how they'd lost; against this many fucking demons, how could they have done anything but lose?

"Beautiful, isn't it?" This came outta Darla Pike's cock-sucking mouth. She was driving, which was as serious a mismatch between image and personality as Gary could ever recall seeing. Starling was riding shotgun, getting chauffeured.

"Yeah, it's a real hell on earth," Gary said, wondering if he could throw himself out of the pickup. Nah. You needed momentum for that, and with his wheels blocked and his chair held, he didn't have any. "You must be so proud. Say, you're from Chicago, aren't you?"

"Yes," she said, looking back at him. She wasn't paying much attention to the road, which, admittedly, wasn't too much of an issue at five miles per hour. "Why?"

"Just wanted to make sure I had it right before I commended you on being a real goddamned Yankee carpetbagger for turning your new home into your old one," Gary said. "Yep. This looks exactly like Chicago to me. It's the same picture, as the meme says. Well done."

She actually laughed, the bitch. "Thank you. I'd like to thank the academy..." And then she turned back to the wheel, laughing her ass off again. Which really stuck in Gary's craw; the least she could do, having him over a fucking barrel like this, is to let him have a snide comment or five at her expense.

He lapsed into silence, crawling back into his own thoughts. That felt like the last private domain he had, maybe the last thing he had, period. After all, they had taken his family. They'd taken his body. His clothes. They'd taken every damned thing from him, and probably killed the whole rest of the Watch in the collapse of the church. Everyone except, maybe, Duncan. He was surprised they weren't parading the bodies with them.

Wait. They actually were. Back there he could some half-eaten bastards being passed along the marching demons like they were crowd surfing. They were limp, though, not moving one whit. At least one female form, he could tell, though barely, the damage was so grisly. At least a couple males, one so deformed it was nearly impossible to tell.

So who was dead, and who, if anyone, was left alive? As he rode slowly down Old Jackson Highway toward the fallen freeway exits, Gary had no idea. In fact, if left to deduce what remained for him, the answer was simple.

He was fucked. It was over. Earth had a good run, but hell was coming, and coming pretty quick.

Well, he'd given it his all, hadn't he? Once he came off the bench, no one had fought harder than Gary. He'd led his family into this shitshow. Sure, they'd "talked" about leaving, in one lone conversation with Larry bringing it up, but it had gotten shot down fast, and not just by him. He'd known, in his gut, that he could by God make a difference, that Gary Wrightson and Gary Wrightson alone could turn this whole fucking thing around, if necessary. By sheer force of will if he had to.

But now he was sitting here naked as a fucking jaybird in his wheelchair, night air tickling his skin where he could feel it, dick shriveled up and sad there between his legs, balls beneath him –

he made a quick adjustment there, moving his legs, picking up the testicles – and breathing so much fucking smoke that lung cancer would be along directly to serve him with a number and telling him to wait, but not long, for it to be with him.

No family left.

No weapons.

Just his dick, his balls, his hands, and a wheelchair.

Even Marina was gone. He looked back again, hoping to hell it wasn't her being carried along there, food for fucking demons. She'd been good to him, and he'd been cold, distant, and a real prick. Sure, that was just him being him, but still. With the rest of the Wrightsons dead, and Ulysses gone, she'd been the last, closest thing he had to family. She'd even let him stick his dick in her lately, for what reason God only knew, because Gary couldn't figure it out.

So it came to this. He was going to die horribly, at the hands of demons, and maybe a goddamned Yankee, which could be worse. He had nothing left to fight with, and he'd failed in every single way. This was it; it was time to know he was whipped. They'd manhandled him, stuck hands up his ass like he was fucking Grover from Sesame Street, or Kermit the Frog, and now he was their prisoner. Helpless, hopeless, the bitch of these demon bitches. What did that make him? A bitch's bitch, that's what.

"Fuck that," Gary mumbled to himself. "Kermit the Frog wouldn't quit like a bitch."

"What'd you say?" that charmless John Travolta knockoff motherfucker asked.

"Nothing," Gary said.

"Sounded like something about Kermit the Frog not quitting," Brando said. "Which is total bunk; Kermit the Frog quits all the time. He's almost the first one to quit. I mean, in the Muppets movie–"

"You keep Kermit the Frog's name out of your godless, people-eating mouth," Gary said, looking at the bastard with a real glare of hatred.

"Or what?" Brando asked, grinning at him with undisguised demon teeth. He'd heard when they first came to this town, the demons had hidden among the humans. Now they weren't hiding anymore.

"Well, you took everything else I had," Gary said, "so I guess I'm gonna have to piss on you."

"You do," Brando said, holding up his hand, with some pretty terrible fingernails that looked – if you really squinted – like cat's claws, "I'm cutting it off with these."

"Go ahead. I won't even feel it," Gary said, sticking out his chin at the bastard. Of course that was a lie. Not only would he feel it, it'd haunt him for the rest of his life if he survived, not only by the loss of his joy stick, but also in the form of a lower testosterone level. Sure, it would still leave him at a higher T level than every single goddamned hipster wearing skinny jeans and man buns, but that wasn't exactly a high fucking bar to clear.

"No mangling the sacrifice," Darla Pike announced, not even turning her head to look back at him. "At least not until the time comes." Starling didn't say shit, didn't even look at him. Fucking redheads.

Well, Gary resolved in that moment, when the time came, he'd fight back with every thing he had. It didn't feel like much, but he had what he had, and he'd do what he could. Not because he had a chance in hell of success.

No, he was going to fight back because that was what Wrightsons did, by God. And he'd die a Wrightson, and when he got to wherever he was going, even if it was hell, maybe he'd see his brothers and his mother there and be able to tell 'em he'd spat in the eyes of everyone who'd fucked with him right up to the last.

That resolved, Gary sat back and enjoyed the ride, waving like a fucking princess to the crowd behind him. "Smile, you pieces of shit," he said, drawing a scowl from Brando and Charmless, "it's your victory parade, ain't it?"

HOURS PASSED, and Arch wasn't sure quite what to do with himself. Others showered, passing in and out of the living room and the kitchen. Pretty much no one lingered very long, the uneasy atmosphere casting a sort of pall over everything.

Last time he'd been here, there had been humans kept in cages, a thing he'd been nearly ill to his stomach about. None of that now; he wondered if Spellman's new benefactor had made him get out of the business, or if he was simply out of stock. Or just putting on a good face for the Watch, who seemed to rotate in and out of the upstairs with surprisingly regularity.

"The sheets in those rooms," Brian Longholt said, coming down with slightly wet hair, his glasses glinting in the dim light. He made a low, whistling noise. "Gotta be Egyptian cotton."

"You should check out the buffet," Duncan said, passing through from the kitchen area.

Brian's eyes just about bugged out of his head. "There's food?" He made himself scarce, leaving Arch alone with Duncan. He hadn't seen hide nor hair of Nguyen or Marina since arriving, and had only glimpsed Micah briefly before the big man filtered back to the buffet. He'd been in there a while, and the occasional peal of his laughter could be heard as he talked to Spellman or whoever was back there.

"You don't like this." Duncan's words did not come in the form of a question.

"Nor do you." Arch's reply was the same.

"This screen has been my bugbear the entire time I've been

in this town," Duncan said. "But...in the interest of fairness, he has done some good. From to time to time."

"Did you ever ask yourself why?" Spellman appeared at the corner, eyes glinting with amusement. Arch was unclear on how the whole "screen" concept worked; was there some demon on the other side of the world (or underworld) who wore the same expression?

"I assumed it was because you were a money-hungry bastard," Duncan said. Simple, not particularly expressive, yet succinct.

"I deal in life, Mr. Duncan," Spellman said. "Money is life. People exchange their time for it, and time is life, the very fragments and building blocks of it. I can feel the life coming off of money." He shivered slightly, an odd thing to see from a full-grown man – or at least one who appeared as such. "That should give you a good idea of what I am."

Duncan actually made a face. "A g'war'nah'fessht?"

Spellman bowed. "Thus you see why I wear a mask."

"You want to explain that one to me?" Arch asked.

"G'war'nah'fessht are fucking hideous." This came courtesy of Hendricks, who was sliding on a fresh t-shirt as he descended the stairs, hair wet, hat and coat absent. He also seemed to be wearing Crocs in a camo pattern. When he caught Arch looking, he shrugged. "What? They're comfortable, and they were in the closet."

"I stocked that pattern just for you," Spellman said, apparently not fazed by being called hideous.

"They're also fucking vampires," Duncan said, "to use the Marine's parlance."

"Not quite," Spellman said. "We feed on life. Yes, traditionally, that involves blood. But in a modern context, money is a much better, cleaner way to achieve the end." He made a face. "And I'm not partial to the scent, the taste, or the mess of blood, human or otherwise."

"He's like a demon vegan," Hendricks said, chucking a thumb over his shoulder at Spellman. "Except we've met several times and this is the first he's mentioned of it."

"No actual vegan could manage that, for sure," Duncan said. "Within three seconds of meeting them, it's coming out."

"I can tell them by sight," Hendricks said. "And the smell."

Arch raised an eyebrow. "Vegans have a smell?"

"Yeah," Hendricks said, settling in an overstuffed armchair to his left. "Smells like malnutrition and cut grass."

"Neither of which are on the menu at the buffet, should you get hungry," Spellman said, a little huffy, then made himself scarce by heading back toward the kitchen.

"How long are we going to be waiting here?" Hendricks asked. "That's the question I want an answer to."

"Spellman suggested it wouldn't be too long," Duncan said, looking at a watch he wore on his wrist. It looked tasteful, maybe expensive; Arch had trouble with those concepts. Alison would have known. "If Spellman's on the level."

Hendricks pursed his lips. "I'm just wondering who this benefactor is that paid to save our lives."

"Hello." A calm, yet high voice spoke from the stairs, where Arch craned his neck to look. Rhea was descending, her own hair quite dry, yet she seemed to be wearing something different than when last he'd seen the girl.

"Shit." Hendricks was on his feet in a moment. "It's you."

"It is me, in the sense that I am here," Rhea said. "And before any of the rest of you arrived. It is not me, however, if you are musing on the identity of who paid for us to be saved from the church debacle."

"How'd you get out of that?" Arch asked.

"When we ran down the hall after everything went terribly wrong, I saw the door," Rhea said. "I went through right as something came flying at me, and it closed behind me. I did worry the rest of you were dead, but Mr. Spellman assured me that you would be along shortly. Those of you who survived."

"Convenient timing on his part," Arch said. "If he'd acted a little quicker, he could have saved more of us."

"I do not think so," Rhea said, shaking her head. "Those who survived were fated to."

"There's not enough of us left to do much of anything with, though," Hendricks said.

"That is not true," Rhea said. "There are still enough of you left to win this war – if you are willing."

"Maybe you didn't notice, in the hubbub of the retreat," Hendricks said, Crocs dangling distractingly, "but there's a demon army in Midian now. Thousands. Probably tens of thousands. Possibly in the hundred thousand plus range."

"And if you were in a traditional war, with traditional forces, I would say your chances were nil," Rhea said, always strangely calm. "But you are not traditional, and you fight demons. Powerful, yes, but with immense weaknesses which you could exploit. Plus," and here she smiled, "you have righteousness upon your side."

Arch felt himself cringe slightly at that, already knowing what Hendricks was going to say.

But apparently he didn't, because Hendricks looked down. "I hope it's enough." That left Arch blinking.

"I am going to eat," Rhea said. "Lauren should be along soon, I sense."

"And then we ride?" Hendricks asked.

Rhea stopped at the corner, and cocked her head at him. "We ride at dawn, bitches. Even I know this. Enjoy your last night before the fight of your lives." And she went around the corner.

"There is something deeply disturbing about that little girl,"

Arch said. Hendricks just nodded. There wasn't much else to say but that.

HENDRICKS FOUND himself alone with Arch, which prompted a smile. "I guess it really is just you and me again."

Arch stirred. The big man had been leaning a hand against his face. "For the moment, anyway." He seemed to sit uneasily for a moment, then spoke. "What do you suppose the end of the world looks like?"

"I saw a lot of fire and smoke," Hendricks said. "That felt appropriately hellish. Especially driving in through the woods on fire, flames leaping from one side to the other through the dry brush and dying trees." He shook his head. "You're going to have a hard time finding a patch of green around here anytime in the next five years. Assuming we live that long."

"It could happen," Arch said, leaning his head back. "But it might not, either."

Hendricks nodded. "It's funny. I was ready for it to happen for a long time ago. Now I find myself looking death in the eye and...I don't want to go. For the first time in a long while."

Arch glanced up at the smooth ceiling. "I find myself in the opposite position. I put all my belief in the idea I was doing the right thing, from the minute I found out demons were real. And I ended up losing everything I had to the point where...well, I was always prepared for the Lord to call me home. But now..." He looked at Hendricks, and there were depths of sorrow in the man's eyes that felt like it might just be Halloween night all over again. "...Now I'm truly ready. Nothing left to lose, you know."

"If they're right about this," Hendricks said, "then you could end up losing your heaven. If we fail, I mean."

"I don't believe we could fail badly enough to lose heaven,"

Arch said. "But I do believe we could fail badly enough to lose the earth for a spell. The Book of Revelation is about as clear as mud, but that much is obvious."

"I wouldn't know," Hendricks said, trying, maybe for the first time with Arch, to be truly diplomatic. But he found himself with a question as the silence settled over them again, and a puckish smile escaped his lips to perch there. "Say, Arch...I know what you believe in. What do you think your God believes in?"

Arch looked straight at him. "You."

"Well," Hendricks said, a touch hoarsely. Probably from the ash and smoke earlier. "Good thing I don't believe in him, or that'd be a hell of a lot of pressure on my shoulders." He cleared said throat, but failed.

"Why don't you believe?" Arch asked, settling eyes on Hendricks again. Watchful, considering. "It's a big universe. Room for all manner of explanations."

"It's awfully big, don't you think?" Hendricks asked with a faint smile. "Billions of stars across billions of galaxies, and it's billions of light-years across. All that distance, all that space, all that wonder...what? So he can get to know you? Listen to all your petty problems? Worry about you when everything is going wrong for everyone everywhere?"

Now it was Arch's turn to smile faintly. "Why would size matter one iota to a being that's eternal? The distances? Would you love your children less if there were ten of them instead of one?"

Hendricks chuckled. "No...but if I had ten million – let alone ten billion – I wouldn't even know all their names."

"You're not almighty, though you may sometimes wish you were." Arch smiled, and spread his arms wide as if to indicate everything, all around them. "An eternal being has eternity to work with. An all-powerful one has the capacity to communicate or deal with anyone He wants to."

"So why doesn't he, then?" Hendricks asked.

"I don't have the capacity to know or understand," Arch said.

"Cop out from the cop," Hendricks said. "And I don't believe in an all-powerful, eternal being."

"That, I believe."

Hendricks went silent for a moment. "You think we can win?"

"All things are possible through..." Arch smiled wanly. "You know the rest."

"I suspect I've heard it from you before. And thank you for sparing me the evangelism, at least this once."

"If we mess this up," Arch said, "you're not going to need me to explain it to you. You'll be seeing it for yourself."

Hendricks felt the world seem to grow still around them. "I, uh...admire you, Arch. Some people I've met in my life, I've felt like they use their faith as a shield to keep from having to grapple with tough things, to keep from having to answer questions they either don't want to, or are afraid to answer. Not you, though. You always have an answer, even if I don't like it. And it's usually rooted in the fact that you admit you don't know a lot."

Arch just shrugged. "Anyone who professes otherwise is either a fool or a liar. I try not to be either."

"A few weeks ago I would have said the same," Hendricks said, "but then I was so hard up for sex I screwed a hooker possessed by an otherworldly force and got her pregnant with something that seems poised to play a role in this whole world-ending affair."

Arch didn't blink as he stared at Hendricks. "Well, we appreciate you coming back to accept some responsibility for your actions. Not sure what good it'll do, being this late in the game, and setting us up as it has for certain unforeseen troubles, but...it's not nothing."

"If I'd known I was a deadbeat demon dad, I'd have shown up earlier. Problem is, I had some other business to settle. You know, with–"

"Kitty Elizabeth." Arch was on his feet, looking like he was ready to spring back through the wall.

Hendricks turned, where he found, standing in the doorway behind him...

Kitty Elizabeth.

FOURTEEN

...AND I FEEL FINE

Arch caught Hendricks just before he leapt at Kitty Elizabeth, getting a hand on his chest and the other on his arm, yanking the ex-Marine off balance and spoiling his charge at the duchess of the underworld. "A little help here!" he shouted, because he knew that Hendricks was insensate with rage, and corralling him was not going to be an easy matter.

"Oh, it's you," Kitty said, in a high voice, with a wide, toothy grin that emphasized she was not human, not even in the vicinity of human, really. "I didn't recognize you without that silly hat. I mean, I would have recognized the top of your head, of course, but I can hardly see that from here, can I?"

"What the fuck?" Erin was there, suddenly, blond hair wet, and she froze about two feet from Kitty Elizabeth, who turned her benign smile upon her. "Is this an attack?"

Arch, for his part, had a strong feeling he knew what was happening here, and he did not care for it at all.

Kitty confirmed it. "An attack? Hardly." She chuckled, holding a hand up to her chest like some society grand dame who'd heard an amusing remark, like that the peasants were rioting in a distant county. "Why, I'm the one who paid for you all to be here."

Micah came rushing around the corner just then, took in the scene, Kitty and all, and with a wary eye on her, skirted just clear of her reach and came quickly to Arch's aid. Between the two of them, they got Hendricks in a solid hold.

Duncan appeared next to Erin, and subtly interposed his stout body between her and Duchess Kitty, which reminded Arch – who was still dealing with a thrashing Hendricks – of a mother putting herself between a cub and great danger. Others started to file in, too – Brian, who nearly dropped his plate, Rhea, who seemed quite unbothered by the disturbance, and even Nguyen, who made no move to do anything, and looked quite odd without his priest's collar. He was clad in jeans and a plain white t-shirt, and this was the most casual he had seen the man since this whole mess had begun.

"I want to kill her," Hendricks said through gritted teeth, once he'd stopped throwing himself against Arch and Micah's iron grips. Both of them outweighed him, Micah by a considerable margin, Arch by a little less, yet still he'd pulled them forward several feet from where Arch had first grabbed him to keep him from making – in Arch's estimation – his final mistake, had he succeeded.

"Oh, that much is obvious, darling," Kitty said in her aristocratic drawl, smile evincing a clear delight in his present state. "But you should let your friends do your thinking for you, because not only do you not have a weapon on you, but because we've already proven that when it's you versus me, you only end up eating something that disagrees with you. Why, I could beat you one-handed." She waved her only hand before her. "And would have to, thanks to you." She sent a searing look at Arch.

"Sorry that I'm not sorry," Arch said.

"She's right, Hendricks," Duncan said, with all the emotion

– or lack thereof – he usually brought to any discussion. "She'd clean your clock, even if you had your sword."

"Plus," Kitty said, "the world would die. And that would be sad. So very, very sad. For all of us."

That prompted Hendricks to stop straining for the first time since Arch had gotten hold of him.

"You're a demon," Erin said.

Kitty turned her eyes upon Erin and blinked at her. For the first time, Arch noticed a sort of cat's-eye feeling to the way she did so. "Yes. And?"

Erin looked at Kitty like she was being punked. "Don't you want to join up with the other Mean Girls and destroy the world?"

Kitty scoffed, loudly. "'Destroy the world?' Can you imagine anything more cliché for a demon to want to do than that?" She breezed past, prompting Duncan to put an iron hand on Erin and gently steer her out of Kitty's path. He needn't have worried; she made no aggressive move, other than to gently boop Rhea on the nose as she passed, orbiting the room but taking care not to get too near to Hendricks. "Have you any idea what hell is like?"

"No," Erin said.

"Yes," Duncan said.

Kitty spun, pointing at Duncan. "He knows, you see. He's a demon, and he's here with you. And do you know why?" She paused, and those cat's eyes blinked again, even more obviously this time, leaving Arch wondering how he'd never noticed it before. "Because it sucks big, sweaty, smelly balls, ones where the bearer has a case of Elephantiasis of the testicles. It's the worst place you can imagine, and I've been to Hutchinson, Kansas, so I know what I'm talking about."

"Not mentioned," Duncan said, "is that the Duchess here used to be the queen. Of hell, I mean. She's still the Queen of Mean."

"Only because I pried that title from Leona Helmsley's corpse at her funeral," Kitty said, her smile returned. "And I was such a good queen."

"As the kids say – Narrator: She was not a good queen." Duncan stared her down. "She was, however, a perfect queen for hell."

"Okay, fine," Kitty said, smirking and shaking her head. "That's true."

"How does one lose the title of Queen of Hell?" Micah asked. With Hendricks having gone slack, it apparently gave him room to think. "And also," he said, this to Hendricks, "you didn't mention we were going after the former Queen of Hell."

"Must have slipped my mind," Hendricks said icily.

Kitty made a pained sound, clearly feigned. "It's all very tragic. The short answer is that I had a bit of a split with the power that reigns."

"The king?" Brian asked.

"See, these human titles you come up, they're not particularly useful for describing demons," Kitty said. "I mean, this so-called king is currently wearing the skin of a redheaded prostitute, a role which suits him so very well, I must say."

Brian was not the only one to turn his eyes upon Hendricks, but he was the only one to speak up. "Dude, you fucked the devil?"

"Such simple minds," Kitty said.

The door behind her opened, and somehow all the air seemed to leave the room as Lauren Darlington poked her head in, wearing a frown that curled down her eyebrows. "Uh..." She stuck her head back out, then back in, clearly unable to quite believe her eyes. "Did I just die of a brain aneurysm...?"

"Not yet," Brian said, "but maybe soon, given all the weirdness that's flying around at the moment."

Arch kept his grip on Hendricks, though the man was no

longer resisting fiercely. Kitty smiled benignly upon the whole scene, and Arch had to wonder...how was this group supposed to save the world when they couldn't even trust the person who'd saved them?

GARY DIDN'T much care for his current predicament, but he at least had the good fortune of not being in the hands of total sadistic shitheads, he figured out pretty quick. Or at least maybe not.

"I need water," he'd said once they'd crossed the freeway in a slow, lurching four-wheel drive motion. "I'm thirsty."

Starling actually tossed a water bottle back to him. It was half-drunk, piss-warm, and had probably been in the truck a while, but he drank it all down under the watchful eyes of Brando and Charmless, nobody saying shit to him as they started to thread their way up dry, wooded roads toward Mount Horeb in the distance. Gary stared at it, wondering why the hell they were bothering, both with heading this way, and keeping him alive. He had a feeling he wasn't going to like the answer to either question.

HENDRICKS FELT about as safe as a baby in the arms of a murderous serial killer, but Micah had him on one arm, and Arch had the other, and the two of them would have been his first round and second round draft picks in an intramural, Watch-only football game, so he felt like escape was not going to be an option.

And, he could see, somehow behind all the red clouding his

vision, that Kitty Bitchnuggets seemed to be trying extra hard to stay away from him. It would have been easy for her, with his arms held securely, to just slit his throat. Even in his rage, partially driven by his impotent fear in the face of her, he was aware that right now he was almost helpless. How did he come downstairs without bringing his sword, his gun, the knife he kept in his hat? The fucking Erin had laid on him earlier had been too good, the afterglow crowding all the common sense out of his brain.

Speaking of Erin, she escaped the shadow of Duncan and eased over to him, placing a soft hand on his chest, like he was a stray cat about to bolt if it didn't get a pat of reassurance. "She's not trying to kill us right now, and she did help save us, so...maybe we listen?"

"She is, indeed, your savior," Spellman said, thin fingers templed before him.

"Not mine," Arch muttered. Because of course he did.

"Nor mine," Nguyen said. "But in these strange, possibly final days, I'm willing to listen to what she has to say." And the thin priest sat down on the couch, positioning himself expectantly, like he was ready for a proper dishing with the girls.

"Leave it to the Catholic priest to make a deal with the devil," Hendricks said. He didn't really mean it – he had nothing in particular against Nguyen – but he was still pissed as hell about all of this, and he wasn't going to just let it all pass without letting everyone know it.

"Now, now," Kitty said with a wide grin, "I'm not the devil, and you should know that. Besides, aren't you glad he's not making a deal with a little boy for candy or something?"

"I would have gone with, 'Don't you know the devil has girl parts these days, since you were up close and personal with them?'" Brian Longholt asked. When Hendricks shot him a look, Longholt just shrugged, unapologetic. He was finally growing a pair. A real pair, not ones fueled by weed and a deep-seated sense of inadequacy.

"Can I just ask what's happening here?" Lauren Darlington asked. She still had the door partially open, her head sticking in. "Because my ass is in the town archives, and this, the door that I came in through, from the street, is now leading me...here."

"Is demon magic," Marina announced, coming down the stairs, and yawning as she reached the bottom. "Even I hear this through the floorboards."

"What kind of shitty magic house do you have where there's no proper insulation?" Brian asked, turning to Spellman, who just shrugged.

"This is the confabulation of rejects that's going to save the world?" Micah asked, finally relinquishing his hold on Hendricks. Hendricks didn't take advantage of it, though. Mostly because Micah had said the magic words.

Kitty noticed. "Is that a decision, cowboy?"

Hendricks just stared at her smokily. Arch still had his other arm, but lightly. "I don't need to make a final decision...yet."

"Oh, it'd be a final decision, though," Kitty said, voice wry with amusement. "One way or another, though, I know where I'd bet my considerable assets."

"Yes, your ass is considerable," Erin said, a hand still lightly on Hendricks's chest. "Elite New York girl like you, how have you not considered Ozempic?"

Kitty's nostrils flared. "Ooh, she's a spitfire." Leaning in closer, her eyes flashed. "In fact, I'd like her to spit all over my fire. Maybe the two of you would like to join me for a reprise once this is all over. Knife optional." She made a show of stretching. "But for now...this little world, this little blue world, this haven from hell." She finished, and her eyes, so cat-like in their motion, drifted around them all. "I would like this world to continue without being turned into a worse version of the hell that's currently plaguing your little town."

"I keep hearing people talk about that," Arch said, finally releasing his hold; Hendricks didn't take it personally. "But no one's coughed up the specifics on how it's going to happen, and why."

"That's because you run with an ignorant, uneducated crowd of hicks," Kitty said. "They don't even know where it's going to happen."

"Ooh, I do," Lauren said. "Mount Horeb."

"Okay, the doctor knows," Kitty said. "The rest of you hillbillies? Ignorant as fuck."

"I have degree in philosophy from Brown," Brian said. "Thank you very much."

"Your mother must have been so proud," Kitty said. "And where do you brew coffee these days?" She passed him, giving him a vague roll of the eyes. Once she was passed, he did twitch a little. Not bad emotional control, Hendricks reflected.

"Fine," Hendricks said, his own control strained, but present. "They're up on Mount Horeb with a gate to what they think is heaven, and a really pregnant...big, bad demon. The world's coming to an end because of what they're doing up there." Hendricks didn't look away from Kitty. "So...what's your plan to stop it?"

Kitty just smiled, steely, at him. "Before we talk about my plan...you might want to know what theirs is, first."

OF COURSE it was at the fucking top of Mount Horeb, almost. Gary suffered in silence in the back of the truck as they navigated the intense switchbacks of the road up. Even through the smoky fog he could see the fires burning in the darkness, faint glows below like city lights in the haze. The higher they climbed, the easier it got to breathe, and the more he caught the whiffs of the demon army marching in behind them, hints of vinegar, cumin, and maybe a little chili powder rubbed in a sweaty asshole.

At the top they came to a halt at one of the pulloffs, where people would park and go for hikes or running down the mountain or whatever these naturetards decided to do with themselves in the great outdoors. Gary hadn't really trucked with that dumb shit when he could walk, and the thought of rolling down it now in his wheelchair made him break out in a cold sweat. Hadn't he heard something about Erin Harris plunging off the side of one of the cliffs up here? Bet that broke her skinny blond ass.

That wasn't fair. He gave her way more shit than she'd deserved after his momma and Paul had died, he could see that now. None of that hypnotism shit was her fault, and not one of them had seen it coming, not even Duncan.

Oh, and Duncan. Gary had been a throbbing prick to that guy, too. Hopefully their last conversation had worked for him in the realm of making peace. Probably had; Duncan didn't seem like the kind of dripping pussy that would weep over a man greeting him with rough edges.

Hell, Gary had been a prick to everyone at one time or another. Some of them he did regret. Others...less so. Like that fucking cowboy. Fuck that guy for cutting and running, then showing back up at the close of business. Yeah, sure, he might have come back to die in Midian with the rest of them now, but where was he a month ago when they could have really used the help?

Brando lifted Gary out of his chair, legs hanging naked in the breeze like his ass and his fucking dangle until Charmless Travolta got the wheelchair set up on the ground. Once that was done, he got tossed down like a fucking dwarf, and Charmless caught him about as gracefully as a teenage boy would catch a passing tit. Which was to say he got caught, but it wasn't exactly with a light touch.

"Bring him along, boys," Darla tossed over her shoulder as she disappeared into the darkness and thin mist of smoke ahead. She was following the redhead, which seemed to be what everyone was doing around here, for good or ill. Probably ill. Redheads had never led Gary anywhere good, not even the ones he paid to suck him off in Reno.

Brando pushed Gary onward, into the dark, into the thin mist of smoke, gravel crunching beneath his wheels. Shadows moved around him, and though he sweated, he didn't fear, because whatever was out there was a fucking goldfish compared to the sharks that were pushing him right now.

Out of the darkness the square lines of a house appeared. It had the boxy structure of those glass abominations from California, and Gary groaned.

"What is it, Hot Wheels?" Darla Pike was there in her stolen black cassock, hair glinting in the light from something ahead.

"I know this house," Gary grunted, Brando pausing at the entry. Clearly trying to decide the most wheelchair accessible option to get him inside. "I came out here once on a service call to deal with an overflowing toilet. Dumb fucks moved here from California and had no idea how to treat a septic system." He chuckled. His repair had been the cheap part of the equation for them. Getting the shit flood out of their basement and then gutting and redoing it had probably run them tens of thousands of dollars. Gary got a paltry $600 by comparison. "Go to the garage, chief, they got a ramp there."

Brando did not acknowledge, but did veer in that direction. Soon enough Gary wheeled into the kitchen, which was pretty damned huge, big enough half his house would have fit in there

– before those goddamned demon feds burned the fucker down. Floor-to-ceiling windows made up the entire back of the house and provided a commanding view of the fires down below, burning in the distance and sending black smoke heavenward.

This was where Gary got parked, right next to the fireplace, which was already crackling. Had it been burning when they arrived, or had Starling lit it by lifting a leg and farting on the logs while he was getting pushed up the ramp? Hell if Gary knew. Hell if Gary cared. "What are we waiting for now?" he asked.

"Timing," Darla said, when Starling didn't bother to speak up.

"Got any more water?" Gary asked, after a few seconds of dead silence. "I'm as parched as your cooch when you contemplate sex that doesn't involve bloodshed."

Darla smirked at him, then nodded to Charmless. "Check the fridge. You know, I like your spunk. You're kinda clever for around here. Admittedly, that's not much of a compliment, but it's the most you're gonna get from me."

"Check this," Charmless said, and lobbed a water bottle underhand at Gary. Room temperature, because this place had been without power for weeks. A god-awful smell made Gary jerk his head away a moment later; clearly something in the fridge had gone sour. "Speaking of your cooch," Gary said, because he'd seen Darla flinch, too, "how exactly did poor, forever horny Casey die?"

"Tied to a cross, covered in my spit, piss, vaginal fluid, and his own blood," she said with a gleam in her eye and a smile curling at the corners of her cocksucking mouth.

Gary allowed himself a little shrug. "That's probably how he would have chosen to go out, if he could."

Darla chuckled. "How did I not meet you before now? You

might have made staying in this county just the least bit less onerous."

"I deal with a lot of turds, so clearly I just hadn't gotten to you yet," Gary said, turning his attention back to Starling, who lurked in the darkness, staring out the windows. "What about you, Red? You just gonna sit there in silence while we talk? Because that is the first clue that you are not a woman."

Starling barely glanced back at him, and did not speak. So that was how it was, huh?

Darla was just smirking, so Gary felt a need to pipe off to that: "What are you so damned happy about?"

"I made the deal of eternity," Darla said. "Now I'm anticipating my payment coming in."

"You got everything you wanted, huh?" Gary felt the heat rise in his face. "Ironic, considering I just lost everything that mattered to me."

She squatted down next to him. "That's how it's supposed to be, hillbilly. I win, you lose. How have you not gotten the message about that yet, given how bright you seem to be? The future belongs to those who take it, those who are smart, those who are bold, willing to seize it. How would you seize anything around here?" She waved a hand toward the window. "Until she came to town, the only thing you could gather in Midian was cow manure, maybe some corn. And your fellows? Morons, one and all. You should know this. You've lived among them."

"At the risk of sounding cliched," Gary said, "you're awfully pretentious for a bitch who fucked a powerfully dumb man just to kill him. Yes, congrats, the countryside can't beat the cities for pure IQ, sheer, grasping ambition, and a desire to play bullshit social climbing games. But let me tell you what we do have – neighbors we know well, and mostly like. A connection with the land, where we can see the sunset, and we're not buried in endless waves of strangers as far as the eye can see. It's the familiar. It's nice. There's a feeling of solidarity when someone's going through shit that you don't find in the cold and lonely city. Though I doubt you'd understand that – or much care."

She barely suppressed a smile. "You're right about that."

"Fine, then," Gary said, and raised his voice. "Since we got some time, it appears, how about you tell me your evil plan?"

Starling cocked her head. "Why would I do that?"

"Look, I don't know where you come from–"

"Hell," Starling said, with that quizzical look, like a dog who heard a distant sound. "At least of late."

"Don't you ever watch movies down in hell?" Gary asked, smirking. "It's a time-honored tradition among our evil villains that they explain themselves in exacting detail. In other words...it's what you're supposed to do." He settled back in his chair, trying to affect a cocky pose, which was tough without clothes. "Unless you think a naked guy in a wheelchair can stop you from executing it, in which case...I really wish you'd tell me anyway."

"You can't stop me," Starling said, in profile, the fires burning behind her glinting on that red hair. "No one can, now."

"So that's why you went so hard at the Watch," Gary said. "They actually had a chance to halt your evil plan before."

She turned to look at him. "You keep calling me evil. Yet you have no idea why I've done what I have."

"Then why don'tcha explain it to me," Gary said. "If I've got you all wrong, hell, I'll apologize. I'll even join you, how about that?"

Starling stared at him evenly. "I cannot imagine anything less meaningful." She walked toward him menacingly, trench coat hanging off her bulging stomach, her thin little legs almost comical holding up her pregnant bulk. "You, who are of a race of interlopers of no special ability. Given everything. Appreciating nothing. You see all that is around you with the eyes of children, understanding little and blundering about like fools in all you do. Playing games. Wasting your finite time."

She leaned over him now, had that look in her eyes like darkness had fallen over them. "Do you know what you are? The inferior second child of a never satisfied father, convinced you are the heir. To me, you are but fodder, like your own cattle; you may see yourselves as whole people, worthy, but to me you will never be anything save for the chattering locusts that inhabit this world, feeding and breeding and ignoring all else but your own whims."

"Okay, there's a lot there to unpack, as they say these days," Gary said, "but the big flashing billboard in the midst of all that sort of screams, 'Daddy issues.' You want to talk about that a little more?"

"This is a universe of misery," Starling said, voice hoarse, almost a whisper. "I am not its creator, thus I am not the villain."

"I'm starting to get the feeling you might have been the snake in the garden," Gary said. Her breath was hitting him, and it was warm, and there was a faint whiff of sulfur in it.

"And now you know you are naked," she said, making a show of looking him up and down, "and you have shame, and knowledge, and will – for all the good it does you." She rose up, and turned.

"Okay," Gary said. "So you're going to destroy the world because you're mad at your father for kicking you out of the house when you got too big for your britches?" She spun on him, revealing hints of surprise. "I meant it figuratively, but obviously it is now literal, too. But, hey, the trench coat works. It's a look."

"I did say he was smarter than the others around here," Darla said.

"Here's the thing I don't get," Gary said, "and maybe it's my small, inferior, second-child brain – why did you go through all the hoops? Pretending to help the cowboy and Arch save this town. Why go through all the trouble to get the cowboy to fuck your hooker self, get pregnant with whatever you got stewing in there? That's the shit I'm stuck on. I get you being so butthurt you want to blow up the universe and drag us all to hell with you. And I get it being in Midian. That sucks we're an interdimensional crossroads or whatever, but I understand it. I was mad when they built the Amazon warehouses down the road, too. It's the hooker and the cowboy I'm not clear on. Why are you in the hooker, and why did you fuck the cowboy? Was it for fun? Was it the hat? Or do you just enjoy fucking, as you call us, cattle? What is it?"

Starling stared back at him, head cocked curiously, as though the thing inside her couldn't decide quite what to make of him. "You really do know little of us. The thing in here," she said, hand on that swollen belly, "is me."

"But you're also in there," Gary said, pointing at Starling's head.

There was almost a smile in reply. "Is it beyond your understanding, how I could be in two places at once?"

"Nah," Gary said. "Just a little weird."

"I had to be reborn to walk this world in a form of my own," Starling said. "Not a borrowed one. I can move from body to body where I'm welcome. And that has been plenty enough all these many years. But what comes now requires a physical form all my own. And to get that–"

"You had to produce a birth of the non-virgin variety," Gary said. "Because you're not quite as, uh...skilled? Powerful?"

A kind of dangerous calm fell over Starling. "There are rules that must be followed. Rules I did not make, but am bound by. Rules that cannot be contravened without breaking the universe, in much the same way that removing the lower floor of a house will collapse the house. This is one; I am not of this realm, and neither are they." She looked over his shoulder at Brandon and

Charmless. "They require mere shells to survive here, to move about in this realm that is antithetical to our existence, like how your astronauts survive hostile, murderous environs in a suit. No shell devised can contain me, however. I require more."

"And that's more," Gary said, looking at the belly. It moved in front of him, like whatever was inside was kicking.

"*That*, as you so eloquently put it," Starling said, and again he could swear there was a trace of a smile on those lips, "is about to become *all*."

"All hail," Darla said, sing-songy, like she was trying to get a Gregorian chant going.

"But why the cowboy?" Gary asked. "Why not just some random dude? Hell, why not me? You come at me wearing that girl, even I'd probably say yes, and I have a severe aversion to redheads."

"I chose my vessel's father," she said. "A man steeped in grief, and willing to be an instrument of violence in a cause he deemed noble." She rubbed her belly. "And I used that violence to get the proper sacrifices to consecrate myself...to myself. The blood of an innocent boy. The blood of a man of dark heart." Behind her, Darla's expression flickered an iota; enough Gary caught it. "And the seed of one writhing in desperation, wretched, but not weak."

"Wow," Gary said. "You did all that scheming and sexual engineering so you could craft the perfect shell for yourself."

"It is much more than a shell," Starling said. "It will live and breathe as you do. And then, when the moment comes...it will make sure that nothing else lives or breathes ever again, anywhere." Now she was definitely smiling.

"Ah," Gary said. "You called it a universe of misery. You planning on ending that, then?"

"I'm planning on distributing the torment," Starling said, "everywhere. For you see, there were places and moments that were exempt from this levy. It was placed as a burden upon those of us who saw the truth of it, who were the scapegoats to carry the greatest portion of it for all others." Her eyes flashed with anger. "Now all will suffer it. All the time. Forever. And in order to do that, I must walk at the head of my army."

"Oh, yeah," Gary said, "throwing everyone into eternal anguish. You're definitely not the villain. I see the altruism now." He looked over her shoulder at Darla. "And you? You want to be miserable all the time?"

"I'm miserable all the time anyway," Darla said with a thin smile. "But I'm about to be miserable *and* powerful. Seems a fair trade. Plus, I get to watch the rest of you suffer, so I'll have the whip hand. Don't underestimate how much satisfaction some of us derive from suffering while the rest of you do, too, especially while we're in charge of administering the suffering."

"Oh, a BDSM queen, I get it now," Gary said. "Or are you a government bureaucrat? It's such a close resemblance between those two things, enjoying the suffering of others and being immensely self-gratified fucking others over."

Starling was looking him right in the eye, hands on the pads of his wheelchair, like he was some kind of scientific specimen. Darla, for her part, was smirking at him, not bothering to answer. "Does this satisfy your inquiry?" Starling asked. There seemed a glimmer of amusement in her eyes, something that was behind the face, like it was the demon within, wearing that hooker like a mask.

"I got one more question," Gary said, because why the hell not. "How exactly would I stop you, if I were of a mind to?"

That just prompted them to laugh. "Drat," Gary said mildly. "Can't blame a guy for trying, especially seeing as his future depends on it."

Darla did the answering on that one. "Your future is looking pretty bleak at this point, Hot Wheels."

"Why can't I cut a deal like you did?" Gary asked. "Get myself installed as a Duke in this new kingdom of hell?"

"You would need something to trade in order to make it worth my while," Starling said, and gave him a long look up and down. "And it would not appear you have anything of worth to trade."

"Well, my ass was virginal until your boys stuck their hands up it," Gary said. "So that one's kinda on you. But I suppose you're about to ruin a whole lot of beautiful things in your mad quest for revenge for being born, so..." He shrugged. "I'll try and think of something I can do to get in your good graces, maybe get myself a basic bitch title, like knight, or whatever. When do we leave for the caves?"

"When I am ready," Starling said, and stood, presenting her belly once more, putting that sucker right at eye level. "And not a moment before."

There it was, Gary thought. In that basketball-covered lump of flesh was the key to the end of the world. She hadn't said it explicitly, but it was obvious, wasn't it? She'd gone through all the trouble of picking Hendricks, moving him around the board, fucking him, using him to consecrate the baby demon thing – the vessel, he supposed – to her brand of devilry, and now she was just waiting for the labor pains to begin.

Once that sucker popped out, it was going to be the key to all her hopes and dreams. All he had to do was kill it, and he was going to be home fucking free. World saved. Wrightson family name given a chance to be carried on, with honors.

Well, he had a bit of a challenge ahead of him with that last one, but it was going to be a complete foreclosure of the possibility if he didn't save the damned world. Sure, all he had was himself and his dick, and he wasn't looking forward to the prospect of trying to kill a demon baby with just that, but...there were always possibilities.

Darla loosed an uneasy chuckle, and he found himself looking at her, in profile, because she was staring at the fires burning out in the haze. She really was a twisted bitch, wasn't she? Rooting against humanity? He didn't even want to know what had twisted her fucking tit. All he knew was he needed to kill Brando and Charmless, kill Darla, and stop Starling.

With nothing but his wheelchair and his dick.

"Easy peasy," Gary muttered. Thankfully, they either didn't hear him or ignored him. Which he hoped would come back to bite them in the ass later.

"...SO that's what they're going to do," Kitty said, spreading her arms and munificently, like some benevolent goddess of self-help come down from the mountaintop to give them advice and coaching on how best to avoid the humdrum troubles of low productivity and, also, the end of the world.

Duncan did not have eyes, as such, but his shell was made to mimic human reactions as best as possible, in order to help him better blend in. His eye was twitching now, the shell's response to the utter turmoil his essence was experiencing.

"Fuck," Father Nguyen said, because someone had to say it, and apparently the priest was going to be the first to do so.

"I don't get it," Micah said, his arms crossed over his barrel chest. "This Starling wants to end the world, why did it need a baby created by my idiot, horny son-in-law? Why not some bum from the streets of San Francisco?"

Duncan's eye twitched further, and Kitty turned her gaze on him. "You want to explain this one to them, OOC? I don't have the patience or the crayons."

Duncan grunted. "This is going to be tough for you rationalists and your clinical, scientific worldview to grasp, but: this is a magical universe, in spite of your abilities to observe and quantify everything from the number of calories in your breakfast to the feelings you have while idly scrolling your phone in the shitter and ruminating on your past fuckups. Demons in your world are not actually here; their souls, their essences, are only allowed to be present in this world because of our shells. Pop the shell, we vanish back to our own realm, never to return unless we get reshelled. Right?"

"Like Guthrie, sure," Lauren Darlington said.

Duncan nodded. "The...*thing*...in Starling...is not a demon. It...he...she...whatever...can come to this plane only while cohabitating with a willing human."

"You might want to explain the hierarchical nature of our demesne to them, too," Kitty said.

"I'm getting to it," Duncan said. "The thing in Starling...it is the..." He closed his eyes. "The oldest. The foulest. The worst. The betrayer, the morning star–"

"We get the point," Arch said softly. But firmly.

"There are specific rules regarding...it," Duncan said. "And furthermore, the binding of...it. It cannot come here without those specific conditions...sort of. And furthermore, those exiled cannot be allowed through that gate, for it is the contravention of a law of the universe as laid down by..." Here he closed his eyes tight, squinting. He couldn't go on.

"The law-giver," Arch filled in for him helpfully.

"Go with that," Duncan said, keeping his eyes closed for a second more before opening them. "If *it* crosses that threshold, into *that* place...it breaks the laws of the universe. What happens when you break the law?"

"You go to jail," Brian said. Head of the class, always.

"Except in this case," Duncan said, "you've already been sent there. To return, in defiance of the law – it shatters it. And along with it, the other laws of the universe. Which causes a complete reversal of the established order."

"'The first will be last, and the last will be first,'" Arch said.

Duncan squinted his eyes shut in discomfort again. "Yes. Evil and good, for lack of better terms, flipped. Chaos replaces order. All those years of human civilization turned to ash in an instant as you go from being your own masters to slaves, forever, in thrall to hell."

"And that means your devil character, Starling, becomes...first?" Brian asked. "In the universe?"

"Yep," Kitty said brightly. "See, this is why *I* wanted to find the Rog'tausch. It was going to lead me to the gate so I could be first." She made a wave at her missing arm. "But someone decided they didn't want a woman to get ahead, and I got put back in my place, back of the line, so now if this goes off, I'll be no better than any of you. Congratulations, crabs – you pulled me back into the bucket with you. Now we either win this or all broil together in the fires of hell for eternity."

"You're going to end up roasting beside us?" Erin asked, her thin arms folded over her thin body. "So there is an upside if we fuck this up, then."

"Not that you'll notice, sweet cheeks," Kitty said. "It will be on paper only, and technically I'll still outrank you. Which will be of zero satisfaction to you with your anuses being sodomized by amorous lava demons." She noted the strong wince from Lauren. "Relax, that's not an actual thing. But you'll wish it was after you feel what they do to you."

"Still don't get the pregnancy angle," Micah said. "Why go through the trouble?"

"In order to circumvent the restrictions on Starling coming to earth outside of its bounds," Duncan said, "it has to rhyme...with another such event." Why did it all feel like his essence was being scraped across razor blades? Oh, right – because he was discussing impossibilities that should have remained impossible. "Down to an even-numbered interval. The conception took place at an appointed hour. The unholy consecrations required to shepherd it through the natural laws designed to kill that...thing...would have been timed, down to the second and millisecond." Duncan pointed right at Hendricks. "If he was chosen, it was for the opposite reason of someone virtuous, someone virginal, someone pure of spirit being chosen to bear a golden child. It was because he's – for lack of a better word – corrupted, dangerous, fucked up, and susceptible to being manipulated to commit the violence necessary to create the unholy consecrations."

"Hey, cowboy, look at that," Brian said dryly, "sounds like you won the unholy lottery." Hendricks didn't even look sideways at him.

"That's why him." Duncan found himself exhaling a putrid breath, as though the sulfuric reek came out of him with his breath. "There might have been others who could have been used, in fact I bet 'Starling' had alternates waiting in the wings. But a broken demon hunter who was going to show up to the spot where it was all going to happen anyway? Who had just had his heart busted to pieces by his rebound girl, the first he'd been with since his wife died?" He shook his head slowly. "Hendricks couldn't have been more perfect for this."

Duncan glanced at Erin, who was wincing. Hendricks wore a surprisingly flat affect, eyes slack, staring straight ahead. "I'm sorry," Duncan said, to the two of them. "I didn't know. Only in retrospect does it all make sense. I just figured you were horny, and she was keen to try out some of the local night life with her brand new body."

"If you'd known you would have told me?" Hendricks asked, staring at him flatly. "Your OOC ethics wouldn't have prevented you, like they did when I threatened to kill her the first time?" He gestured toward Kitty.

Duncan cringed. "Maybe. Maybe not."

"But we're all clear on the why, now?" Kitty asked. "So we can get on with the, 'Let's stop this,' portion of the plan?"

"That part was already clear," Arch said. "We go up to Mount Horeb, and...we do what we do."

"Against an entire army," Lauren Darlington said. "That part, I wasn't so clear on."

"You'll have the means to fight an army, because I have an armory for you," Wren Spellman said. That fucking screen. Duncan still didn't like him – even if he did acknowledge the necessity of the help being provided. And he couldn't deny that Spellman had a motive to help, as did Kitty. This new hierarchy was not going to benefit either of them. Spellman's type of demons were not held in high esteem, which placed them closer in demon estimation to humans. That would mean an unpleasant reversal for them under the new order, basically a return to their awful status in hell. Life on earth had its advantages for hell's outcasts, and escaping the tyrannical hierarchy of demons was definitely one.

"What's it going to be, cowboy?" Kitty asked, with her trademark sneer. "Are you going to choose revenge? Or the world?"

Hendricks stared at her for a long moment. "I choose the world. But when this is over–"

"I know, I know," she said. "When this over...you're coming for me. And I look forward that, personally, because I know when it's done I'll be cumming on you." She smiled at all of them. "Along with anyone who wants to join him as an accomplice." She seemed to swell a few inches, shadows darkening her face as the room dimmed.

"Excellent," Spellman said. "If you'll follow me to the armory..." And he gestured, as if to lead them from the room.

Duncan let out another breath, as if doing so could cool his overheated essence. He didn't know exactly where Guthrie was in all this, but he knew she'd be there at the end, somewhere. And that filled his insides with a distinct, churning swirl.

"OKAY, see, I'm clear on the plan," Brian said, following Spellman and the others into a room that didn't seem to fit with the rest of the house. It felt a little like that scene out of *The Matrix*, where racks of guns appeared out of a white ether, except here it was bounded by distinct, daisy yellow walls. "I'm just unclear what they think I'm going to be able to do in all this."

Spellman strolled past a rack and paused, sweeping a hand gently over a weapon. "Do you understand your part in this now?"

Brian stared at the weapon in question before taking a deep gulp. "Yeah," he said, "I guess I do."

KITTY DIDN'T LET Hendricks follow her into the armory; she stood aside and watched him with a fucking smirk he'd have liked to wash off her face with a vial of holy water and a sword to what passed for her heart. "After you," she said. "I insist."

Hendricks followed the others in, and found Rhea milling in beside him. "You gonna suit up for this?" he asked, casting a look over his shoulder. Kitty was watching, and arched her eyebrows at him. He resisted the urge to puke right there.

"I am advised to stay behind," Rhea said, and he felt a tug at his hand; she'd placed hers in his, like she was eight again and he was her dad or some such shit, and quietly whispered, "She will never turn her back on you. There will never be an opening where you can take her. She will always see you coming, now and forevermore. Much depends on you now, Lafayette Hendricks. Put revenge out of your mind, or it will kill you, and shortly thereafter, the world."

"Maybe I don't want to live in a world that lets pieces of shit like her float along in it," Hendricks said. Where had Erin gone? He felt astir without her beside him, and Rhea didn't help. At all.

"You're so willing to die for revenge," Rhea said. "When the time comes, will you die for the world?" Her eyes were dark, but not like Starling's. They were wide, and caught the light in here. She let go of his hand and drifted down a row of weapons, leaving him in front of the swords like she'd just decided to grow up and go on without him.

"ALL THAT RESEARCH FOR NOTHING," Lauren grumbled, in front of a rack of Super Soakers of the vintage she grew up with. Father Nguyen was beside her, apparently having decided the regular guns were a little too aggressive for him, too. "I delved into the mining operations in such detail, found out that one of the mines got shut down in 1899, which was, coincidentally, the same year some real weird shit went on up at that hill. Reports of celestial lights, and revival tents, and people coming to Jesus like crazy. I put it all together...and it turns out that demon lady already knew. All for nothing."

Nguyen just shrugged. "Maybe it was for something still. Who knows." He pulled a Super Soaker off the rack and made the sign of the cross over it as he held it in front of him. "I certainly don't."

"Not for nothing," Rhea's soft voice came from beside

Lauren, and she turned to look at the girl. She had a brief flash of Molly at the same age, though it looked like, based on her height, Rhea was always going to be short because she was just about done growing. "It's all for something." And with a nod, off she went.

"Cryptic," Nguyen said, and offered Lauren the Super Soaker. "I wonder if that'll come back to help us later or just be something we forget in the crush of the demon armies coming for us...?"

"I have this dreadful feeling it's going to be the latter," Lauren said, taking the proffered squirt gun, "because you just know it's not going to be that easy..."

ARCH FOUND himself arming up next to Micah, which surprised him. Was the man actively avoiding Hendricks, had he just glommed on to Arch, or was it coincidence? Maybe it was because they were the only two black men in this crew still standing. Whatever the case, Arch loaded his weapon uneasily, because it wasn't the sort of weapon he'd used in the past.

"Need some help with that?" Micah asked, loading up his own weapon with expert hands.

"Is it that obvious?" Arch asked.

"You do look a little lost," Micah said, and got right in there, fixing the problem for him. "Like that," he said. Patient. Instructive. Not at all like a drill sergeant. Once he was done, he was still eyeing Arch. "How'd you get into this?"

Arch hesitated. "Saw your son-in-law get into a fight with a demon on the town square his first evening here, and suddenly I'm hip deep in it." He paused. "No. That's not quite right. I chose to wade in once I saw what I saw. And everyone around me paid the price for it. My wife. Her whole family. My town.

All of them are gone now." He took a deep breath, and sighed. "But then, if I hadn't, maybe Hendricks would have gotten ground up in this thing all on his own, with no one else to help. Then we'd all be standing around, the world would be ending, and no one would have a clue." He shook his head. "I have no idea what to tell myself about any of this anymore, except to say one thing: I feel I was called – and I answered, maybe a little too eagerly."

"I hear that." Micah cast a look over his shoulder, to where Hendricks was staring at a weapon rack, not making any moves. "I want to blame the shitheel for all this. But somehow I can't help but feel that if he hadn't done what he did, even taking my little girl away...maybe the world would be suffering all the more for it now." His jaw hardened into a line, and stayed that way until he moved it again to speak. "As if him being the obstinate dumbass he is gave us a shot we shouldn't have had to stop this."

"The Lord moves in mysterious ways," Arch mumbled, mostly to himself. Because he doubted it would be a satisfying answer to a man who'd lost his daughter to demons and chance. Who would want that, anyway? To sacrifice their child in order to give the world a chance to spin on?

Arch didn't think he would have. No...now that he knew what he'd lost when Alison died, he was certain he wouldn't have.

But it couldn't stop him from feeling like he'd laid that sacrifice upon an altar and swung the knife himself. He'd feel like that until the end of his days, like his eagerness to plunge into this, to fill that hollow sense in himself that being a husband and a father just wasn't enough for him–

He'd carry that forever, he knew, like a scar on his soul, self-inflicted. How long would it haunt him? For the rest of his life, that was all.

"How well did you know those folks in that basement that

died?" Micah asked, fussing about with his own weapon. It must have met his approval, because he didn't seem to be making changes, just checking and rechecking the operation.

"One of 'em was my pastor since I was a boy," Arch said. Barney Jones had baptized him. Confirmed him in the church. Married him to Alison, when the time came.

And he'd died in that cellar beneath St. Brigid's in a way so undignified that Arch couldn't help but feel the brush of a devil's wings over his shoulder as he contemplated it.

"And the others?"

"My mother-in-law," Arch said. "As a good a woman as you'd ever meet. Terri Pritchard...I didn't know her too well, even now, though we've fought together a lot recently. And then Braeden Tarley..."

What could he even say about Braeden? "He was a mechanic by trade," Arch said, thinking it through slowly, because in truth, he'd given a lot of thought to Braeden lately. They felt like men bound to the same fate, flip sides of the same coin, maybe. "He lost his daughter in this fight. Had already lost his wife years back. He and I both moved in to Barney Jones's house after our...our losses."

"You went through the shit together, then."

"You could say that," Arch said. "I didn't get a chance to see Braeden at the end. I wonder how he met his."

"He gave up," Micah said, apparently finally satisfied with his weapon. "Sometimes in a fight, a man wants to give up, but he doesn't want to let down his friends. So he volunteers for some duty that's going to get him killed, give him an honorable out. That's what he did. Sacrificed himself for y'all, so he didn't have to face what was going to come next in his life."

Arch nodded slowly. "Can't say I don't understand the feeling."

"Can't pretend that going out in a blaze of glory doesn't seem easier than rebuilding after you've been leveled down to your foundations," Micah said, staring straight at him. "I understand the appeal of checking out after a loss, especially a hard one, the kind you almost wish you didn't survive. But to me it feels like cowardice, going one single solitary breath before you're supposed to. Like quitting." He drew himself up to his full height, and he was commanding, even if he wasn't nearly as tall as Arch. "You know what I mean?"

Arch didn't have it in him to meet the grizzled veteran's gaze. "If you can die for the right cause, I guess I don't see anything wrong with it."

"Of course you don't," Micah said. "Because you're one of the men who knows what it's like to live with a belly full of the broken glass that is life at its worst. Martyrdom holds a certain appeal; makes it a desirable end, especially as it ends your suffering." He shook his head slowly. "I see the same desire in my son-in-law, except I think he got it from watching too many war movies."

Arch felt himself bristle. "You think it's wrong to die for a cause? For your fellow man?"

Micah's face split into a pained grin. "I spent my whole working life in the Army. I've seen more combat than you can believe. Shepherded more young men through the experience, stood at more gravesides than I can even count. I have been ready to die for my country since before I turned eighteen. No, I don't think it's wrong to die for a cause. I just think it's wrong to walk into a fight hoping you'll die for your cause instead of coming out the other side living for it. Because every time I've seen a man go into a battle with a death wish, he's damned near dragged the rest of his unit along to it with him."

With a last nod, Micah stepped away from him, carrying his weapon along, leaving Arch to think that one through.

"WE MOVE."

Starling's command was simple, and it set everyone to going.

Except Gary. Of course. Brando and Charmless had to come for him to get him moving.

"Do I at least get to keep my chair?" he asked. Didn't get an answer, but they started pushing him toward the ramp in the garage. So there was that. Might have been as simple as they'd push him as far as they could, then carry him the rest of the way.

That was fine. Gary preferred to have the chair if he was going to be carted off to death. "Can I get a bottle of water or two for the road?" he asked. Because why not? A bottle landed in his lap with a thump a second later. That Darla Pike had a cannon on her. "Softball?" he asked, turning to look at her.

"How'd you guess?" She was walking behind, smirking at him. Everyone fucking smirked in this group. Arrogant bastards.

"You got that 'softball lesbian' vibe," Gary said. "Minus the haircut." He made a motion with his hand.

"I do have a thing for pink tacos," she said, eyes flaring up with amusement. "And I have been thinking of cutting my hair short."

"Well, yeah, of course," Gary said. "Since you ain't got a man around to attract anymore, you can go short-haired, no problem. Something butch would communicate to your minions that they have to please you no matter what they think of your looks. It's a power cut."

"Keep talking," she said. "I'll give you a power cut." And she made a scissors motion with her fingers.

"If you want to scissor someone, you should really make it another girl," Gary said.

"I'll make you a girl, then we'll scissor," she said with a nasty grin that told him, yep, she'd cut off his pecker. She'd do it and not even worry about it.

"I gotta warn you if you do that," Gary said, "I wouldn't be on my period, though it might look like it."

Darla laughed again, cackling like a witch to the skies now that they were outside. The smoke smell had gotten intense, and there was a deep orange tinge to everything.

The fires were moving up the hills around Mount Horeb now, and the smoke was blowing in this direction. He could hear them crackling in the distance, like a blazing hearth. The skies were pure black, with just a hint of the glow cutting through. Gary wanted to flinch away, because the raw heat from the flames was making its way up toward him, even though they had to be a mile or better distant, and it stung his eyes.

Well, this was about to be it, Gary reflected, tipping up the water bottle and pouring it down his throat. Cool water sluiced down, pushing back that parched feeling only a little. He was one man against two demons, a dangerous-ass woman, and the devil herself. Plus that baby thing, however dangerous it was. And he was one crippled man, at that, without a single weapon at his disposal.

"Finish up that water," Brando said, glaring at him. Gary obliged, draining it immediately. He knew what Brando was thinking; undrunk water could be made holy with a simple blessing from a preacher. Gary wasn't one, of course, but it was a fair worry, he figured. So he finished the water to soothe the demons' souls, and pitched the bottle overboard. Littering didn't seem a priority right now, with the whole mountain about to be on fire.

Ahead, he could see the opening of a mine, like a cave in the clefts of the mountain. An army of demons waited in the murk out in front of it. Hundreds.

Thousands.

Sweeping down the fucking slope as far as his eye could see, disappearing into the haze like a carpet of evil's own soldiers, Gary realized once again what he was up against. And his stomach rumbled a little, stirring the water that was the only thing he'd had in hours and hours and hours.

Brothers, mama, please guide my dumb ass, Gary prayed without daring to open his mouth. *And God help me, because I am definitely gonna need it.*

ERIN FOUND herself staring at her shoes. They'd been scarred with dirt, with demon ichor, with God knew what else, and looked like they'd been through hell.

She sympathized.

"I don't want to do this," she whispered, feeling ashamed the moment it came out.

"Then don't." The answer was simple, and came from a girl she hadn't even realized had snuck in next to her while she fiddle-farted around with this weapon she held.

"Rhea," she said with a start. The girl was looking up at her with those big eyes. "I didn't see you come in." Then she frowned; the girl had no weapons, just her big backpack hanging off her back. "You're not coming with us?"

She shook her head slowly. "I am assured I would not be of much help."

Erin found herself smiling, even though she was suddenly hot as hell under the collar. "That fucking figures."

Rhea barely raised an eyebrow. "What does?"

It wasn't hard for Erin to answer; in fact it poured out of her like a wound had been opened. "We're out here fighting for our lives, for heaven and earth, you're the sole representative of the former, you're like twelve, and you're bailing on us before we go massively outnumbered into the last fight." She found herself grinning in pure, unadulterated fury. "It's the fucking story of this whole damned thing – we fight and die while your Almighty sits on his ass and does nothing."

She didn't even blink. "What would you have him do?"

"Fight," Erin said, incredulous that she had to say it.

"Okay," Rhea said. "Let us say he did. He fights, destroys all your enemies for you without even, as you would say, 'breaking a sweat.' Do you know what would then happen?"

Erin looked at her like she was dumb. "We'd win."

"You would win for the moment," Rhea said. "And then, slowly, or perhaps quickly, the universe would fall apart. If there was a player in your game that could win at any moment, and then did so, repeatedly...would the game have any meaning any longer?"

"This isn't a game," Erin said, voice taut. "This is our lives. This is our homes."

"Perhaps 'game' is the wrong word," Rhea said. "But it does fit in its way, even with the stakes as high as you say. For there are rules, and they must be followed, and there is one player who if He decided to get involved, would turn over the board instantly and permanently. Do you love your life?"

"Not much at the moment, no," Erin said.

"But did you before all this?" Rhea asked, then, without waiting for an answer, went on. "Could you again, after this, if it resolves to your satisfaction, and the world goes back to being as it was?"

"Yes," Erin said, suddenly feeling very quiet inside. "I did. I could, I think."

"You are playing today against the worst adversary in the universe," Rhea said. "But not an unbeatable one. Not at all. In fact, you play against one of the simultaneously strongest and yet weakest players you could go against. If you are waiting for someone to step in and intervene to make the world perfectly right for you, you misunderstand this world. You are, perhaps, in the wrong one. There is one yet to come that will fit you better. That one's fate is in your hands, along with this one. But this is the one you are in now. And the next one will not be ready, will not be better for you, if you fail here."

"Don't you think that's an awful lot to put on the shoulders of humans?" Erin asked.

"No," Rhea said. "And neither does He, clearly."

"What's the point, then?" Erin asked, tuning out the hustle and bustle around her. "Is this all just a test?"

"No," Rhea said. "The point is...there is evil out there. It exists. It has wants – a voracious appetite to devour and spread its misery and corruption everywhere. This world is already thick with it; everything here is corrupted, everything of this world dies eventually. Maybe today. Maybe a hundred years from now, but it happens, because that is *this* world, its defining characteristic. And there is beauty in that, amidst the slow rot of it. Beauty *because* of it. Sunsets would not be beautiful if they lasted, frozen, forever. It'd just be your sky. Flowers aren't beautiful if they're permanently bloomed. They're boring after a time, plasticine, fake. Death is corruption, but death in balance makes beauty, because it's temporary. "

She took Erin's hand. "You have to lead now. I know you don't want to. I know you wanted to throw it all away, to never be asked again, but it is up to you. Put aside your insecurities and just go."

"What if I fail?" Erin asked, her voice hollow.

Rhea took her hand, and rubbed it against her cheek. "Then I will see you again, in a place where the fires do not burn except in the hearths, and where no tears fall except those of joy."

"THIS IS where we fuck them up." This came from that vaguely Russian girl that Brian didn't know, as she picked up her weapon.

Brian looked at his with a feeling of mingled dread. "Is it?" he murmured, mostly to himself.

"Time to take up the mantle, eh?" Brian turned; Spellman was right there, asking with a twinkle in his eye.

Turning back, Brian stared, cold reality mingling in his stomach with that sick feeling that haunted him so much of the time in New York. "Yeah, I guess," he said. Because it was, indeed, time.

ROWS AND ROWS OF DEMONS. A whole damned army.

"They fucking stink, too," Gary said, prompting a snort from Darla and a glare from Charmless Travolta.

He was rolled unevenly past an old shed that looked like it was about to fall down; only the size of an outhouse, it had once held mining equipment, maybe, or was an actual outhouse. It certainly looked the part, old enough to have been here at the turn of the last century when this place had been an actual mine.

Every turn of his wheels thumped him against the crossties on the rails that had been once been used by miners to excavate ore. The cave opening yawned ahead; the army behind. He watched the light start to fade as the mine's rock walls slid past him in his uneven, thumping journey downward. He kept rolling, feeling Brando hold tight to his chair against the pull of gravity. They went down for minutes, in silence, into the darkness.

And then, suddenly, after a couple more turns...there was plenty of light.

He'd zoned out as they moved through the dark, but now

that light was being shed, he was attentive again. His stomach rumbled, acidic taste in the back of his throat telling him the water just wasn't cutting it. Gary ignored it, it was just background noise, as he was rolled forth behind the figure of Starling, her hair shining in the glow of whatever was ahead.

And then...he saw it.

It was a strange thing, something he couldn't quite describe. It was a gateway, for sure, but the smooth lines making up the structure of the thing were somehow more beautiful than any columns ever made by human hand, more symmetrical somehow, more graceful. The lintel that capped it, too, was more than mere lines, it seemed to reach out to him, to stroke his eyes in a sensual, but not sexual, way.

Gary was looking at glory, at greatness, at something no mortal man could construct or even conceive of. All at once he wanted to run through it, yet knew enough to keep his distance, that in his heart, he was unworthy to even look upon it, and that going through would be very dangerous indeed, most definitely fatal.

"Wow," Darla whispered.

Starling stopped before it and seemed to bask. She said nothing, but she didn't need to; there was a very tiny hint of a self-satisfied smile on her face, and seeing it gave Gary a wicked case of the nerves, way worse than just looking at the portal.

"Okay," Gary said, "I'm gonna be that guy and ask the stupid question: if you're an almighty, why do you build a door into your home that anyone can just walk right into?"

"Asked and answered," Darla said with that same fucking smirk.

Gary frowned at that. "Figures you were a fucking lawyer." No one was paying attention to him just now, all awestruck by the gate. But he wasn't quite ready to make his move, either, and so he just sat and thought about that one for a second. Why would you make a door into your house? Unless you meant for somebody to use it...?

"Do angels need to use that to get back and forth to heaven?" Gary asked.

Brando shook his head. "They have other ways. Powers to transit between. Make their own doors where they care to." He snorted. "Not that they care to anymore, but if they wanted to...they could."

"So you're saying an army of angels ain't going to come storming down to kill you and carry me off in their loving arms?" Gary asked. Brando didn't bother to answer, just grinned and shook his head. They were awfully confident about that for some reason, and they were sure enough about it that it didn't give Gary much hope for divine intervention.

Which meant the fate of the whole damned world was still sitting on his shoulders. What a fucking place to put it.

"ONE MINUTE," Spellman announced, reminding Hendricks of the boat operator in *Saving Private Ryan's* opening scene. He was stacked up just before the door, weapon in hand, where it was, honest to God, straining the hell out of him. The door couldn't open fast enough for him, trying to just keep from dropping the fucking thing, probably on something important, like his dick, or his toe.

"You ready for this?" Duncan was on one side of him. Arch and Micah were a couple steps behind with Brian. Erin, Lauren, Nguyen, Marina – that weird, pale, Euro chick – was bringing up the rear, along with Kitty. Hendricks tried not to think about that last one, but he failed – again.

"No," Hendricks said, hat snugly on his head, drover coat hanging off his shoulders with the familiar weight. "You?"

Duncan stared ahead at the door. "Not really. But we're out of choices and time, aren't we?"

Hendricks shrugged. "There's always a choice. We could go, we could stay. But there are also always consequences. And they can be real brutal sometimes." He checked his weapon one last time.

"Thirty seconds," Spellman's calm voice announced. He was looking at them, scanning them, really, and if Hendricks hadn't already been worried about the threat at his back, he might have found it unnerving.

A silence settled over them, only broken by a faint mumbling. Hendricks turned his head; it was Arch, praying under his breath. Of course.

"Hey," Hendricks said, and Arch cracked an eyelid, raising his head slightly to look at him. "Toss one in for me, will ya?"

Arch just nodded and closed his eye. "Already did."

Hendricks chortled. "Of course you did."

"You becoming a believer on me?" Duncan asked. He was just carrying his baton, eyes fixed forward. A warrior, this one, in spite of appearances. Not for the first time, Hendricks wondered at his history.

"I believe in...something," Hendricks said, staring forward himself. The end was nigh, wasn't it? Seemed likely he'd find out shortly whether Arch was right about the universe or he was. That filled him with a surprising calm, but at bottom there was at least a layer of apprehension. "Myself, maybe, if nothing else."

Duncan made a face like he'd just smelled sour milk. "You'd be a terrible god. Existence would be around all of five minutes before all creation rebelled against you, probably for sticking your dick in one of the prettier creations."

"Like the other guy did any better," Hendricks said, watching for Duncan's reaction.

"I don't think that was His fault," Duncan said. "You give

someone choices, you can't expect them to make the right ones every time." He seemed to swallow visibly, his throat moving. "But like you said...there are *consequences.*" And he put more feeling into that word than any he'd ever spoken in Hendricks's presence.

"Ten seconds," Spellman said.

"Just open the fucking door already, will you?" Brian shouted from in back. "And stop fucking counting!"

Spellman's gaze drifted over each of them. "Five seconds."

"God damn you," Brian muttered.

"Too late," Duncan said under his breath. He wasn't sure anyone but himself was in a position to have heard it.

Spellman threw open the door, and Hendricks rushed through. First into the darkness ahead, the smoky air hitting him in the face as he charged into the unknown.

DUNCAN STEPPED through the open door, half-expecting to wade into a war zone.

What he found wasn't that, although the smell of smoke was thick. The darkness was complete, except for a glow reflecting off the smoky haze that filled the air. Distant light was the source, bright, orange, and coming in from down the mountain.

It was the fires. They were crawling their way up the slopes of Mount Horeb in the dark. He could hear the crackling, like a campfire, only these were still a mile or more away. Aided by the wind, they were spreading, burning the abandoned homes and dried-out woods that forested the slopes of the mountain. Soon, there'd be nowhere safe to run, not around here.

Hell was coming.

And yet...it was already here.

Their door was planted on the side of a shed no bigger than

an outhouse, and when Hendricks stormed out, he was laboring under the bulk of the weapon he carried. Arch, Micah, Brian, they all did the same, Brian maybe struggling the most. Well, he was a smaller guy.

"Who are they?" The question came in hell's own language, from somewhere in the ranks of demons just across the way, lined up like an army. Correction: they were an army. But they didn't normally stand in line like one.

"We're reinforcements," Duncan called back. That seemed to reassure them as Hendricks plopped down his burden at last.

Duncan cringed at the unsightly lump the man had carried. Arch brought his down right next to the cowboy, Micah beside him, and finally Brian. In the dark, it might have been hard for a human to tell what they were carrying.

But Duncan wasn't human. And what they were carrying were M2 Browning machine guns, colloquially known as the Ma Deuce. Duncan didn't know much about human armaments – they weren't of much concern to him, generally speaking – but he knew this one had been in use for over a hundred years, that it spit the same bullets that Alison had used to such devastating effect against demons with lesser shells.

Oh, and every single shell going into these was consecrated.

"What are you guys doing?" one of the demons called over to them.

"What we're told," Kitty called back, helping him out. Only one demon talking back in their language might be suspicious. Two, though? That should make it seem more like they belong, right? "Shouldn't you be doing the same?"

"Is that Duchess Kitty?" Duncan heard muttered somewhere down the army.

"They're getting suspicious," he said under his total-lack-of-breath.

Hendricks was already seated, his weapon resting on a

tripod. Micah's was set, too, as was Brian's. Arch seemed to fuss with his, then nodded. Lauren, Erin, Nguyen, and Marina had all filled in behind them, burdened with belts of additional ammo. The four gunners were spread out in a perfect position to cover at least 270 degrees of the slope around them.

And with that – and a last nod from Hendricks – they opened fire.

Duncan may not have had much familiarity with the weapon they were using, but he knew the moment all four of them opened up that they were singing the song of death and pain. It was a familiar refrain to Duncan, something he'd listened to for longer than he cared to admit. In a good world, a pure world, such a device as the four of them were playing would have had no cause to exist. Indeed, in such a world, they would have been an abomination, fit only to be cursed and destroyed.

But in this world – this fallen, flawed, broken world – they sounded like a choir of angels as they cut into the demon army.

BRIAN FELT the strangest sort of symmetry as he cut loose with a machine gun – a real, honest to God one, not an AR-15 – on the demon army. Being his father's son, he'd been forced, coerced, to learned to shoot all manner of guns in his life. He'd never found joy in them, not the way Alison had, but he'd gained a passing familiarity. Friends of his would talk scornfully about how machine guns ought to be banned, and Brian never quite had it in him to speak up and tell them the difference, because it had always felt like inconsequential quibbling past a certain point. AR-15s shot a lot of bullets pretty fast.

It wasn't until now, his ass planted in the soils of Mount Horeb, looking down the sight of his M2 Browning, handles jerking in his hands, using all his strength to keep the gun down as the blast of the barrel lit up the night like sparks in the dark that he could fully articulate to anyone, friend or foe, that there was a hell of a fucking difference between a machine gun and an AR-15.

Four Ma Deuces rang out in time, and it was like the gates of hell had opened. Certainly it had for the demon army in front of them, which was being chewed up and sent back to hell in mass quantities, the consecrated bullets ripping through five and ten of them at a time. Each round fired was a .50 caliber, a bullet the size of Brian's index finger.

And something like 500 rounds were ripping out of just his barrel every minute. And there were four of them shooting.

The rows of neatly stacked demons didn't have a chance. They dissolved into a burst of sulfur as rounds tore through them. Every tenth round or so was a tracer, giving Brian a clearly lit path to where his bullets were going, and he walked his stream of fire into the densest demon concentration and watched them puff into sulfur, no longer a concern for this world.

Really, the only problem was the roaring pain in his ears. He had earplugs in, even, but this was worse than the time he'd gone to a Megadeth concert and gotten seated by the speaker. It felt like someone was playing the drums directly on his skull, and he didn't see the ringing going away much before New Year's...of 2035.

Someone slapped him on the shoulder, and he stopped firing long enough to look back. It was Duchess Kitty, and she was going down the line, hitting Micah's shoulder next. Duncan got Arch and Hendricks, the cowboy stirring only with a second slap.

"That ought to put a kink in their response for a few minutes," Kitty said, loud enough to be heard over the muffled ringing in his ears. She was bearing a blade, a sharp one, ornate, like something out of the French Revolution, with a fancy hilt and guard. She looked at him and raised an eyebrow, and he ignored the desire to crawl back in himself at the sight of those cat's eyes. "Those of you who are coming with me...come along." And she brought up her arm in a fluid motion to point at the shadowy entrance to the cavern.

Brian didn't move, but Hendricks and Arch did. So did Duncan, leading the way with that shuffling, middle-aged man walk of his.

"We'll just hang here, then," Lauren Darlington said, a Super Soaker slung over her shoulder by a bright orange strap. Nguyen had the same, but Erin was sporting some fancy new gun the military used; he didn't catch the name, but it looked vaguely M-16ish to him.

"Yes," Marina said, also carrying one of those fancy new army guns. "You watch our backs while we go do this, yes?" She was still pale, but she bore a look of determination.

"We got your backs," Brian said, turning his eyes away from the dark cave where they were treading to the open slope where movement still stirred. A distant rumble of thunder and a flash behind the haze and clouds made him think for a second someone had resumed firing. But they hadn't; it was just lightning, coming from the direction of the town. Bracing himself against the coming recoil, he drew a bead and pulled the trigger, opening the gates of hell once more.

ARCH DIDN'T KNOW what to expect as he plunged ahead into the darkness, clicking on the light that had been given to him to hang on the vest Spellman had provided. He'd shed all the extra ammo belts he'd been wearing for the M2, leaving it behind for the team that was going to be guarding their exit, and now he walked freely, his sword on his belt, one of those new Sig Sauer MCX Spear rifles in hands, and a prayer in his heart and on his lips.

He'd been in these caves before; dark rock was lit by the beam of his flashlight, showing the places where small seams of coal had been carved out. One particular time had been memorable, involving the good doctor. He spared a thought for her; how had she figured out that this was the spot? Probably he should have asked, had his mind not been on other things.

Looking back, his light glinted on Kitty's sword, still held in her hand. "What kind of weapon is that?"

"This old thing?" Kitty smiled. "It's a rapier."

"How apropos," Hendricks said in a voice as hard as diamonds.

"I'll rapier you again later, baby," Kitty said. "You don't even have to ask."

"Let's just keep this tight," Duncan said.

Kitty smirked. "Poor choice of words, OOC-y. But I'll forgive you, because I allow myself to see it as a compliment rather than an insult." Duncan looked a bit strained at that, but he kept on moving. And so did they all.

DARLA HEARD THE GUNFIRE; it would have been impossible to miss. Demons didn't, as a rule, use guns, so it meant, of course, interlopers.

Starling shot her an immediate look as soon as it started to go off. "Them." Calm. Flat. Maybe slightly annoyed.

Darla just nodded. "Them. We didn't find nearly enough bodies to account for them all."

Starling's dark eyes flashed in the reflection of the gate's light. "No matter." She put her hands on her belly, and there was a shudder visible through the skin, through all of her. "My moment is at hand."

"So you just gonna squat and push...yourself...out right here?" Gary asked. Wasn't he just a breath of fertilized air? If she'd been at all horny, Darla would have been tempted to give him a ride for his sheer chutzpah. Hell, he couldn't have been any worse than her last lay. Sure, he'd end up the same, but what did it matter to her now? Her fleshly desires were about to be left far, far behind.

"Yes," Starling said, looking straight on at the gate. "And also, I think...a bowel movement." She turned back to them. "That last part is not by choice. I am limited by the biological realities of this body."

"That's normal," Darla said quickly. Well, it was.

"Yeah, it's very normal to shit while you're giving birth to yourself," Gary said. "If I gave birth to myself, I would definitely shit. For sure." He reached over and smacked one of his demon escorts on the arm. "Hey, can you wheel me a little farther back? I don't want to see what a hooker pinches off while she's giving birth to the devil. Because I'm guessing she ain't been following the vegan diet, if you know what I mean." The demon just frowned at him, shaking his head. But he did take a few steps back himself.

"Prick," Gary said, looking right at him.

Starling began to bend double, her legs starting to fold under her. Darla recognized the signs of labor, and that was pretty clear. "So it begins," Starling said, squatting down.

"It begins," Darla intoned, careful to keep her distance. Not because she feared a normal shitting – she'd been through labor twice herself, after all, and was hardly squeamish about wiping asses after all these years with kids.

No, there was a dark, wine-colored stain spreading along the dirt and rock, drizzling down from between Starling's legs like a proper piss. The smell was sulfuric, and it made her want to gag. This was the demonic equivalent of water breaking, and whatever was going to come next seemed likely to involve fluids she didn't want to make contact with – and hell if she'd be willing to hold Starling's hand and have her own crushed right before she left her body behind for good.

LAUREN FELT like she was deaf, even in spite of the earplugs that Spellman had given to each of them before sending them out. The row of machine guns that had torn through the ranks of the demon army had been like thunder next to her ear. Well, now there was real thunder, and occasional flashes of lightning cutting through the haze of darkness, casting the distant glow of fires burning their way up the slopes of Mount Horeb in a harsh, unforgiving light.

But the guns had fallen silent, and Lauren thought she felt a tiny droplet of water on her forehead as she stood, waiting for the demons to rally and come charging up the slope in another wave. Maybe, if she was lucky, they'd decide nah, that thunderous noise was bad, and they should just go home.

She wasn't betting on it, though.

"How did you know?" Erin Harris shouted into her ear. Lauren still barely heard her, mostly had to read her lips in the glow of the flashlight beams bouncing around, strapped to each of their vests. "About the mines being the spot?"

"My dad drove me up here once," Lauren said. "A long time ago, when he first found out I was pregnant with Molly. On the way up, he was silent, because we were dealing with deep emotions, et cetera." She felt no need to dig into that, even for Molly's aunt. "But on the way back, we fell into casual conversation, the kind you have when you've said uncomfortable things, and you don't want to retread that ground." She stared down the slope, where there was movement in the dark, just beyond the reach of their flashlights. Demons reassembling to charge, maybe; not like they could hear them. "He told me a weird story about how the mining company just pulled the plug, like they ran out of money. Except they hadn't. They ran other mines elsewhere. He said it was the strangest thing, he'd heard stories from his grandpa about it."

Something moved out there, and Lauren leaned down to tap the shoulder of Brian, who said, "On it," and loosed a blast of fire from his machine gun barrel.

"Looks like they're massing again," Nguyen said, his voice muffled by the ringing in Lauren's ears. "Should we...?"

"I should," Micah said, rumbling where he sat at his machine gun. "You shouldn't. Unless any of y'all played baseball?"

"I played a little softball," Lauren said.

"So did I," Erin said, smiling at her. Solidarity, sister.

"I quit at the t-ball level because sports sucked," Brian said, triggering his machine gun again for a quick burst. "Or I sucked at sports. Try not to be shocked."

"Just get ready, you two," Micah said to Lauren and Erin, "they're gonna form up and charge."

"Yep," Lauren said.

"Copy that," Erin said. Then she turned back to Lauren. "So what did grandpa say?"

"Oh," Lauren said; she'd already almost forgotten about that. "He got this funny look on his face, my dad said, and mumbled something about how no one wanted to go back in that mine. That was all. Left him wondering if there was an accident or something, y'know, a near miss? But it got me thinking, earlier, because I had a memory, or a vision, of him on that day – and it made me wonder if there was something more to the mine thing because of that." Like I was being shown, Lauren didn't bother to add.

Erin nodded. "And...?" A flash of lightning lit them all.

"And the reports in the archive say one week that they didn't find coal, but they did find manganese or something that seemed to be an exploitable find, and they placed the value in the millions," Lauren said, watching down the slope, shining her flashlight to the maximum of its range. Yep, they were coming, and soon, a whole mess of demons in the darkness. "Then the next report said that the mine was shut down, pending investigation into some unnamed hazard."

"Hmph," Erin said. "I've never heard of a company passing up on millions of dollars."

"Especially not in the days when safety was cared about as little as it was back then," Lauren said. "This was 1899. Ergo..."

"They were lying," Erin said, and reached down to her belt, coming up with a hand grenade. She eyed it uneasily, the little pin dangling. "Speaking of lying...am I fooling myself thinking I can throw this far enough to make it count?"

"Nah," Lauren said, "I watched a few of your games. You've got a good pitch. Maybe throw it overhand, though, just to be sure?" She had a couple grenades of her own, but they were going to toss them one at a time, and she felt a lot better about letting Erin go first.

"'O Lord, bless this Thy Hand Grenade that, with it, Thou mayest blow Thine enemies to tiny bits in Thy mercy,'" Brian muttered, in a strangely high voice.

Erin kept her hand gripped around the handle-thingy, which Micah had called the spoon when instructing them all in its use. That had been just before Father Nguyen had said a prayer blessing all their weapons and ammo. With a quick breath, she pulled the pin, looked down the slope, and locked onto her target. Lifting her leg, she wound up and pitched the grenade down the hill toward the pack of demons assembling down the way.

There was a smack of metal against flesh, a grunt in the night, and then a thud as the grenade hit the dry earth. "Heads down," Micah said, and he bent lower behind his machine gun.

It felt like another bolt of lightning, but a lot closer this time, as the grenade went off down the slope. There was a stink of gunpowder, then one of sulfur, and then Brian and Micah opened up again, hammering with the M2s into the darkness, the tracer rounds like sparks flying in the dark.

After a few seconds, they both let up, and Micah shouted, "Not a bad pitch. You're no Sonny Gray, but you'll do for our purposes." He looked up at Erin. "Cook it next time, though, before you throw it."

"'Three shall be the number thou shalt count,'" Brian said. "'Four shalt thou not count, neither count thou two, except that thou then proceed to three. Five is right out.'"

"Do me a favor and shut the fuck up," Micah said. Brian nodded in reply, looking a little sheepish.

"Finally, though, something I can feel good about cooking," Erin said, and it made Lauren chuckle. They'd be coming again, and soon. Might as well enjoy the moment while they could.

HENDRICKS DIDN'T much care for the mood lighting – or lack thereof. They had flashlights pinned to their vests, and the lights were bouncing off rock walls and the dirt floor of the cave as they walked in a tight formation – him, Arch, Marina, Duncan, and, bringing up the rear, Kitty. Hendricks's only consolation there was that she'd have to cut through several people to get through him. Which she totally would, if she felt like it.

But would she? He hoped not. And it was not the only thing he hoped for as a bellowing howl of pain echoed up from somewhere below them. It didn't sound far off; the stale smell of the cave was suddenly filled with something fouler, like a septic treatment plant.

"Someone cut cheese," Marina said, pacing along with them, her weapon at low rest. She was quite the spectacle; thin thread of a girl with a big, long gun. It was the new MCX Spear, the military's replacement for the M4 carbine. It had a suppressor on the tip, which added some length but also meant that if shit went off down here – and it seemed destined to – maybe they wouldn't all be totally deaf if they walked out the other side. Too bad the Ma Deuces up top hadn't been similarly equipped.

Also, the Euro girl was right about the stink. It smelled like the rankest fart Hendricks had ever caught a whiff of. And he'd caught a whiff of some real horrors while sharing a barracks with all those guys in basic.

A billow of flame came out of the chamber ahead and sent Hendricks back a step. It seemed to spread along the walls, setting the whole damned cave on fire around them.

"Try not to piss your pants," Kitty said behind them, with her usual lack of charm. "That's not real fire – it's that hypnotic thing Starling does to fuck with your head. She can't fully pull it off right now because the host body is busy giving birth to herself, but you should still prepare yourself for some weird shit."

A horse ran by on fire, making Hendricks blink. "Did anybody else see...?"

"I told you," Kitty said. "Weird shit. Nothing you see down here is real unless it punches you in the face." She hesitated. "And by then, you'll probably be dead from it, because you're all so weak and pathetic. Useless advice for near-useless cunts.

Whatever. Onward." And she pointed her rapier down the flaming tunnels.

"My cunt has various uses," Marina said indignantly. "Not surprising your fakeass demon one doesn't." And she stalked forward, forcing Hendricks to move to stay out in front.

There was a wide chamber ahead just past a curve, and as they approached, Hendricks started to steel himself. Other things were running by on fire – dogs, cats, goats, squirrels, a Hare Krishna. The last one didn't bother him too much, but the others were a little unnerving. They made the most hideous screams as they passed, too, as though shouting pain and agony directly into his mind. It left him grimacing, and when he glanced back, he saw Arch was feeling just the same.

Hendricks stuck his head around the curve just slightly, leading with his rifle barrel in the classic "slice the pie" maneuver. As he brought it slowly around, he found himself looking at Gary, buck naked in his wheelchair, who waved. Then the next thing he saw–

Was Starling, also naked, pregnant as hell, and squatting in front of a gate that defied Hendricks's living experience with architecture and design. It was simultaneously the prettiest and yet most terrifying thing he'd ever laid eyes on. The horror wasn't because of the look of it, either. It was because it tripped some trigger buried deep inside him, one that told him to STAY THE FUCK BACK, DO NOT GO IN THERE in a way that screamed from his brain all the way to the tips of his fingers and toes.

"Whoa," Arch said, sticking his fucking head out like he wanted to get shot in the face. He wasn't even looking at the threat, he was all eyes on the gate, like it was some sort of tourist attraction cliff he wanted to snap a selfie on the edge of.

"Is amazing," Marina said after a soft gasp. "And pants-shittingly terrifying."

"Yeah," Hendricks said, focusing his scope on the pregnant woman squatting in front of the gate like she was about to take the world's biggest dump...or maybe just had, because there was a pile of something already there. He ignored her face and focused on the spot just above her nose, the gap where her eyebrows didn't quite meet. The safety was off, there was pressure at his finger, and he gave the trigger a nice, gentle press until it broke–

The Spear leapt lightly in his grip, a three-shot burst issuing forth before Arch batted the barrel down. Didn't matter; Hendricks had already blown his whole wad before the big man acted.

Also, it didn't matter because the bullets struck Starling right in the face...and hung there for a second like lead acne, three big bulbs a little bigger than eraser heads, mounted from dead center between her eyebrows and working their way up to just below where her flaming red tresses met in a light widow's peak.

"Shooting the mother of your demon baby right in the face?" Kitty's voice was laced with mock horror. "I approve, cowboy. I kinda want you to go down on me again right now after seeing that. Someone check if I'm wet."

"Well," Hendricks said, catching a scorching look from Arch and not really caring all that much, "it was worth a shot before we rushed in there and tried doing things the hard way."

Arch put a hand on his shoulder and yanked him back. "When the Duchess is approving of your actions, maybe it's time to take a pause and reconsider."

Hendricks just rolled his eyes. "You do things your way, I'm gonna do things mine. Maybe between the two of us, one of us will end her. Now...you finished with the moral lecture? Because we've still got an extreme demon to kill, and the sooner we end it, the less chance it has to grow."

"Starling is invulnerable to holy objects at the moment,"

Duncan said, "because Lucia, as the host, is being protected by everything the possessor has, including certain consecrations from blood rituals." He looked pointedly at Hendricks.

"Don't get your dick in a knot, I'm trying to fix it," Hendricks said, back to the stone archway.

"And once the baby is out?" Arch asked.

Duncan shrugged. "All bets are off, I'm guessing. The powers protecting the mother goes into...well, whatever comes out."

"And every moment that thing draws breath post-birth," Kitty said, "the stronger it gets. So stow the mercy and snuff it quick m'kay, for all our sakes?" And she winked. "But mostly mine."

Something slammed into Duncan just behind them, knocking him thirty feet into the flames climbing up the nearest wall. "Oof," Kitty said, shaking her head. "I think I just detected a domestic disturbance."

"Guthrie?" Hendricks asked, turning his weapon in that direction. He couldn't see Duncan through the curtain of flames; if the two OOCs had gone behind it, there had to be a spur off the main tunnel beneath the fiery illusion.

"Yeah," Arch said, and pushed his gun away again. "You shoot, you might hit Duncan."

Hendricks just raised an eyebrow. "You want to just let them fight it out? What if he loses?"

Arch looked him right in the eye. "What happens between them doesn't determine the fate of the world. Or if it does, it's not going to have nearly as much influence as what's happening in there." And he pointed into the room where Starling's howls once again took up, eerie and high-pitched and awful.

Hendricks nodded. He knew smart reasoning when he heard it. Or at least he did once it walked up to him and slugged him in the jaw. Whether he'd listen, even then, was a different question... "Okay." And he stepped out into the big room, not sure if he'd be ready for what he found there.

And upon reflection, once he was out...he definitely was not.

BRIAN COULD SEE the belt of ammo feeding his machine gun beginning to run low. They'd brought boxes and boxes of the stuff, had stopped using two of the machine guns after the initial volley of fire wiped out the army that had been here when they arrived, yet still – still – they were about to run out. Holy hand grenades tossed with unerring accuracy by Erin had slowed down the push being made by this seemingly inexhaustible number of demons climbing Mount Horeb, but it hadn't stopped them.

This was as close as Brian had ever imagined he'd get to filling his sister's shoes. Not her literal ones, like her high heels or something. But when demons had come to town, threatening both Midian and her husband, Alison had gone right to their dad's gun cabinet and picked out his biggest rifle – the fifty-caliber monstrosity of a Barrett. Then she'd engaged in her own private little war, providing cover fire for Hendricks and Arch, helping in her own way.

Now Brian was providing cover fire, using a fifty-caliber machine gun, no less, watching demons dissolve into bursts of dark sulfur that made his nose wrinkle, sensing that it was a matter of time before they became overrun.

Yet still he stayed. They were coming, he knew they were coming, and still he stayed.

"For you, Alison," he muttered under his breath, considering himself fortunate that even if someone could have heard him over the thunder of the machine gun (and real thunder interspersed here and there, lighting up the cloudy haze of smoke) there was no way they could hear him over the ringing in their collective ears from all the cumulative gunfire so far.

He just kept on shooting until he felt the gun go click, and the flashes at the end of the barrel come to an abrupt – and unwelcome – halt.

ARCH CAME in the room expecting real trouble. He did find trouble, but not as much as he expected.

"Losers," Hendricks said, and drilled two demons with his rifle in rapid succession. They puffed into mere sulfur and darkness, and were gone, the haze of fire around them gone so quickly they might as well not have been there. "I guess they didn't have the special protection over them." He turned his rifle to the other figure in the room, and it took Arch only a second to identify her as Darla Pike, clad in black robes that looked a little too small for her.

"Hah!" Gary Wrightson cackled. "Charmless Travolta is done *Staying Alive*, it seems."

"I surrender," Pike said with an impish smile, raising her hands up.

"I don't accept," Hendricks said, and Arch barely batted away his gun before it ripped off three shots again. They bounced off a wall and ended up harmless, but he shot an acid look at Arch. "You keep doing that. Do you not want to beat the bad guys?"

"She surrendered," Arch said testily.

"Great," Hendricks said. "You want to take her into custody? Because I don't see any cuffs on your belt, and the last thing we need is her doing us dirty while we're fighting the biggest bad that's ever walked or crawled on the face of the earth."

Arch just shook his head; his word on this was final. He

wasn't going to let Hendricks execute a woman right here, no matter what she'd done. "We've got bigger problems."

"And she's part of them," Hendricks said. "You'll see."

"Relax, boys," Kitty said, sweeping in front of them to hold the rapier up to Pike's throat, causing the woman's eyebrows to raise. "I'll watch the bitch." She swayed the rapier slightly and inclined her head toward Starling, who was still squatting in front of the portal groaning. "You get in there and do your thing."

"Be careful," Gary Wrightson called, just between Starling and the gate, sitting in his wheelchair naked as the day he was born. "I get the sense that whatever is coming out of her, it ain't coming gently."

"Get back," Starling said.

No. Not Starling. The voice wasn't right, and in the light of the flames burning along every inch of the cave surface, he could see iris and pupil, not that dusky shade she'd always possessed before. "Lucia?" Arch asked, and was answered with a groan that turned into a scream as the woman rocked back on her heels. Something was starting to emerge from her down there, and as much as Arch wanted to look away, he couldn't.

"Remember," Kitty said, just so dang helpfully, "the minute it makes it across the threshold of the gate, it's all over. So fight like your chimpy little lives depend on it. Because they do."

Arch caught movement out of the corner of his eye and saw Marina inching her way around the perimeter of the room. She was either moving to flank Lucia and the demon coming out of her, or else trying to get to Gary, and he didn't know her well enough to guess which it was.

"It needs a human sacrifice to finish things," Lucia said, voice straining like one might expect during labor.

"Nah," Kitty said. "It just wants a snack before it goes." Everyone must have turned to look at her, because she shrugged.

"What? It's not a simple door that you're walking through there. It's a conduit between states of reality. There's energy involved, it's a process, it's tiring. Oh, and it's just about to be born, which is also a process involving all those things."

"So I was supposed to be supper?" Gary sounded mildly offended. "Well, here's what I think of that." He grabbed his crotch, then left his hand there, brandishing his pecker, which just gave Arch another reason to look away.

"It's coming," Lucia said, and a dark shadow started to creep out of her. At first, Arch thought maybe it was liquid, but no – it was like a tentacle of shadow, crawling its way free from her body, writhing down to the earthen floor of the cave.

"Is this going to kill her?" Arch asked. He directed his question to Kitty, who was watching with her blade pressed against Darla Pike's throat. A little line of red was leaking its way down her long neck.

"The labor? Maybe," Kitty said. "It's hard to say since this has *never been done before*."

There was an aroma to the room and it was tickling Arch's gag reflex. He kept a firm hand on his gun as another shadowy tentacle slithered its way out of her, and her screams gave way to groans again as the labor intensity subsided. Hendricks sure wasn't laying off keeping the gun on target, though, thankfully, he seemed to be aiming between Lucia's legs instead of between her eyes.

"Lucia," Arch said, trying to go for reassuring, but probably not concealing the edge of concern undergirding his words, "you hang on, okay?"

"I don't want to die," she said, and she looked him dead in the eyes. It was all fear there, absolute terror. Arch had seen a few people who'd been in desperately over their heads in his time, but he couldn't recall anyone quite as far in over their head as this girl was.

"Good luck with that," Kitty offered.

"We're going to do everything we can for you," Arch said, easing forward. "You just get that thing out of you, then get out of the way."

"It wants out," Lucia said, straining. The poor girl was covered in sweat, muscles popping out of her neck as she strained. "It wants out so bad I think it might turn me inside out."

"That'd lead to two snacks," Kitty said. "Even better." Curse her.

"We have to save this girl," Arch said, looking right at Hendricks. Who was looking down his scope.

He seemed to realize Arch was talking to him, finally, and looked up. "Seriously? The world is about to end, and you're focused on saving the hooker rather than the world?"

"Not twenty minutes ago you were thinking harder about revenge than you were about saving the world," Arch said. He was only a few feet from Hendricks now. "You were this girl's lover–"

"I don't think I was ever this girl's lover."

"Do you not have an ounce of loyalty?" Arch asked. "Of responsibility for what you've done here? Or are you okay with using her for her body and leaving her to die to this thing?"

Hendricks hesitated. "Your point is taken." He lowered his gun just a little. "But I swear to God, Arch, your soft-heartedness is going to get us killed. We need to come at this with every bit of strength we've got. You go holding back in the fight because you're afraid she's going to get killed, you'll get us – and the world – killed in the process."

"You tell 'em, cowboy," Kitty said. "Don't be afraid to do a little murder saving the world. You certainly won't be the first."

Hendricks gave her a savage look. "That's not helping."

Arch laid a hand on Hendricks's arm. "If we do this the wrong way, I don't think we win."

Hendricks gave him a look through slitted eyes. "Go on."

"That girl is innocent," Arch said. Kitty made a terrible, throat-clearing sound. "Well, she's innocent of trying to end the universe. We murder her in the process of trying to save it, here, in this place...I don't think it ends any better for us."

"Well, I'll be a cunt," Kitty said. "You know, Bible-thumper may just be on to something there." She pushed her sword harder against Darla Pike's neck, then brought it up to brandish the scarlet-tinged blade in front of her eyes. "What do you know about this? Assuming you want to keep your head."

"I don't much care if I keep my head at this point," Pike said, grinning. "You people are fucked. And if you think I'm intimidated by the sight of my own blood...come on, I'm a woman. I've been looking at my own blood monthly for almost all my life."

"That's a yes," Kitty said, taking a step back, and seemingly great care to keep the blade between her and Darla. "Okay, new rule – no shedding innocent blood in this room. Or guilty blood, either, maybe. I don't know." Her face had paled, which was a strange thing to see from a soulless demon.

"You're such a font of helpfulness," Hendricks said between gritted teeth. "Now–"

He didn't get to finish his thought because something bowled over both he and Arch. Arch found himself flat on his back, looking up at the seemingly burning ceiling, and above him saw something black and snakelike dancing over his head.

It was the tendrils that had been wriggling their way out of Lucia. They moved quickly now, snapping the sling that had kept his rifle on him and flinging it into the walls of flames. A couple random gunshots followed, but Arch saw no one hit.

"Fucking distractions," Hendricks said, rolling to his feet. He, too, had been stripped of his rifle, and instead of going for the pistol holstered on his belt, he pulled his sword. The black tendrils waved before him.

"It's coming," Lucia said, as Arch got to his feet, his own sword now in hand as well. "Oh, God, it's coming." And sure enough, there was something emerging from her, something Arch did not care for the look of. Not at all.

DUNCAN HAD TAKEN the tackle like he'd been speared by a cruise missile traveling at a thousand feet per second. It had lifted him off his feet and carried him down a spur tunnel where the illusion of flames had vanished, and he was left in darkness, a familiar shape pressed against him as they landed in a hard roll, slamming into the earthen floor of the mine.

"Get off me," Duncan said, flipping and rolling, using a kick to separate himself from Guthrie.

He slammed into a wall, and she slammed into the one opposite him thanks to his kick. Duncan's essence swirled angrily within him, pissed at being attacked, maybe even more pissed at being shaken and then stirred by the hard landing.

"Just trying to help you separate yourself from the pack, pal," Guthrie said, straightening her skirt. Not a single strand of her hair was out of place; it was anchored by enough product to supply a New York fashion week show. "You're all in with these do-gooders now, it's too easy for you to get lost in the shuffle when we all know you've singled yourself out for special attention."

"I don't think I give a fuck about special attention anymore," Duncan said. "Misery is misery is misery, and if you get your way, I'm in for it regardless. You said so yourself."

Guthrie opened her mouth and let out a cackle. "You're starting to sound like me, Duncan. Old me, anyway. Remember when you were the quiet, stoic one, who took each setback with total equanimity?"

"I remember when I gave you word of the day toilet paper," Duncan said. "That's turned out to be an annoying mistake."

They faced off across the gap, the mine's darkness near total. Only his demon senses allowed him to see anything. Through them, though, Duncan could feel Guthrie tensing. Not in the musculature, for she had none, but across the shell, within the essence, even though he couldn't "sense" it the way he might once have.

"You're damned, Duncan," Guthrie said with glee. "Blood gets spilled on that gate, it's all over."

Duncan felt himself go still. I need to warn them, he thought, but before he could, Guthrie leapt at him again, and they began a dance that they'd avoided for nearly a century – until now.

ERIN KNEW the trouble was going to really start when they ran out of ammo for the fifty calibers and grenades. She ventured a look back at the shed, but already knew what she'd find.

Spellman's door was gone. Of fucking course. His support had already been provided, and, job fulfilled, he'd made good his exit. Now this world was entirely in their hands.

Another peal of thunder crackled somewhere beyond the smoke that ringed the mountain, that smothered Midian. The fires in the distance seemed to be growing ever nearer.

"Probably ought to move ourselves in front of the cave entrance," Micah said, picking up one of the extra MCX Spears that had been neatly laid against the shed, probably by Spellman before his exit. "They get in there and flank our folks, that's game over."

"They swamp us, they'll get in there," Lauren said, her voice tight. And all she had was a fucking squirt gun filled with holy water. Erin respected the doc, but...goddamn, why would she decide to get soft right now? Holy bullets were a hell of a lot more effective than that, especially in this fight, when they were all lined up on one side and the armies of hell were charging right at them.

"You heard him," Erin said, and started jogging over to the mine entry, just a shadowy maw in the dark. "Move your asses!"

And move they did. Double time, even. Erin would have felt a swell of pride – if she hadn't already been feeling a swell of goddamned terror at the sight of what came out of the darkness next.

HENDRICKS WAS SWEARING. Out loud, in his head, in the interstitial spaces between his thought and his reason, probably. There was no reason not to be, after all, because this whole situation was terminally, completely fucked.

He'd had his feet yanked from under him, his rifle pulled away. He'd been kept from killing Starling – Lucia, sure, but whatever, they were the same damned thing for the purposes of this exercise. Been kept from killing Darla Pike, too, and boy were they going to regret that before the end, he suspected. You didn't make demon pacts like that bitch had without getting some darkness on you, and he could smell it on her like stink on a sweaty taint.

He voiced none of these thoughts to Arch, at least not in an articulable manner, because why? The big man was in this for the morality, all the way down to the core. "The fuck, Arch," he muttered, pretty sure he wouldn't be heard.

He was heard, though. "What good does it do a man to gain the world but lose his soul?" Arch said, then glanced at him.

Yeah. That was Arch for you. The world coming to an end, and all he had was scripture, sanctimony, and a sword. Well, at least the third one should be worth something.

Lucia's slit was splitting wide now. Hendricks found it hard to believe he'd been there, done that, and this was the result: a black, many-tendriled thing that was trying to snake its way into this world. The tendrils all connected to something that was just beginning to show, and it had scales, and – as near as he could observe in the flame-lit glow – no head, as yet.

The tendrils waved and danced against the background of the fire, and it made Hendricks a little sick, a little woozy, to know he'd had a big part in this. Maybe not the biggest part, considering the thing didn't look one bit like a human, but he'd been involved in the process. He should have felt guilt. He should have felt shame.

But mostly he just felt nauseous.

"I can't believe I killed for you," Hendricks said, then looked at Mrs. Pike out of the corner of his eye. "She had me murder the shit out of your weaselly husband just so she could have his blood."

"Oh, honey," Darla Pike said. "I would have gutted him and spread his blood on her belly myself if it got me what I wanted. With my tongue, if necessary."

"That would have made things easier, I imagine," Hendricks said. "Not the tongue, obviously."

"No," Kitty said. "It had to be the father that did it." She kept her rapier pointed at Darla, but it seemed an empty threat now. "And before you say it: This isn't Vietnam. There are rules to the physical world, and semen was required. Accept no substitutions."

"I thought I was the only one willing to say the uncomfortable shit in this place," Gary called out. Still naked. Still in a wheelchair. Hendricks still wondered why he had stayed in town, given all that. "Welcome to the party, bitchnuts."

"Any chance that block surrounding the birth has given way yet?" Arch asked.

"Why?" Hendricks asked dryly. They were just holding position, waiting to see if the tentacles were going to hit them again. "You wouldn't let me shoot her before. You starting to come to reason on that prohibition?"

"I've always been reasonable about killing innocent people," Arch said, the tip of his sword waving to match the nearest tendril to him. "I'm not in favor of it."

"She's a whore!" Kitty shouted. "Not that I want you to kill her now, given the stakes. But seriously...a hooker. She's worthless, even among you pieces of cosmic flotsam."

"I don't believe that's true," Arch said, all drawn up to his full and imposing height. "I don't believe anyone is worthless, and I certainly don't believe this girl is."

"This is so inspiring I think I'm gonna puke," Kitty said.

Hendricks felt a distinct unease himself, but not for the same reason. "All right," he said, drawing an eyebrow raise from Arch. "Yeah. You got a point."

"Great," Kitty said. "Why don't you go suck each other off and leave stopping the apocalypse to those of us who aren't in the middle of a gay rapprochement." But she didn't move, either to strike down Darla, or challenge the thing that was still – gradually – pulling itself out of Lucia.

Hendricks met Arch's eyes for a long moment, and he just nodded. Arch nodded back, because at last they understood each other. He wasn't going to kill Lucia, no matter how expedient it was. And not just because it would bring about the very end of the world they were trying to prevent, probably.

It was because in all Hendricks's shitty journeys of the world, until he'd finished Mr. Pike, he'd never truly murdered a human before. Oh, sure, he'd shot some combatants in a war zone in Ramadi. But cold-bloodedly ending Pike? No matter what a piece of shit the man had been, he'd been steered to do that, and by an entity who clearly had other motives.

And what good had he done by ending Pike? None, as near as he could tell, and so much harm. Hypothetical arguments about lives he might have saved seemed pale compared to the thing that was being born now, the evil which it was giving off seemed to affect him viscerally, in the guts.

He'd fathered that. Not only by the act of using Lucia's body while Starling was driving, without concern for the girl herself, but by shepherding it through all the blocks put upon it to keep it from happening. The blood truly was on his hands.

Arch knew this. He knew it before Hendricks even wanted to admit it to himself. Somehow, killing Lucia before this thing could be born would not tip the cosmic scales in the direction he wanted them to go. It'd push them further in the direction he didn't.

Now he knew: Lucia had to live, or the world would die. It was just an unfortunate fact that she was giving birth to the worst thing in the history of the universe right now, and it was entirely possible it would kill her either in the process or shortly thereafter, just for kicks, and there might not be a damned thing they could do about it.

As if to emphasize that point, Hendricks felt his legs ripped out from beneath him once more, by another tendril he didn't even see coming, and didn't have a chance to react to. His back hit the ground hard, all the wind was knocked out of him, and he saw fucking stars.

BRIAN'S KNEES quivered as he saw the things coming up the road toward the mine's entrance. They were shrouded in the smoke that hung in the air, stood considerably taller than the tallest man, and loped like gorillas or something. They didn't just go down with one shot from the Spear, either, it took four or five or even six shots, making him wonder if he was missing due to fear.

"The fuck are those?" Erin muttered. Father Nguyen was praying softly behind her, probably because he was carrying a squirt gun.

"Don't know," Micah said, ripping off a precision shot that didn't kill one of them. "But they're big, they're tough, and they're less than a football field away. Get shooting."

Honestly, Brian was so scared that for the first time in his life he didn't take the opportunity to mention how Americans would use anything but the metric system to quantify a distance. He just took a knee, drew a bead, and kept putting rounds as on target as he could, watching them dissolve into a puff of black every once in a few shots. Not nearly as often as he needed them to.

"CAN YOU FEEL IT?" Guthrie asked in the darkness. She and Duncan had just parted. Or more accurately, thrown each other across the chamber, causing each to slam their respective shells into the implacable stone. "Can you feel it in you, Duncan? That's the rules changing."

"This isn't a game," Duncan said. He wasn't bleeding, because he couldn't. But there were definitely some spots in his shell that were wearing thin, hinting that a fissure could be coming before long with further rough treatment.

Guthrie stood with her arms spread, challenging Duncan to come at her again. She wasn't feeling what he was, almost certainly. They'd improved shells in the interval between when he'd got his and she'd been reshelled after the breaking of Lerner. "It's always been a game. We were just the losers before."

"Maybe we deserved to lose," Duncan said, getting up on a knee. "You ever contemplate that?"

Guthrie cocked her head. "You want me to pontificate?"

"Sure," Duncan said, brushing himself off. "Take a minute."

"I don't have a problem with that," Guthrie said, "for you know time is on my side." She dropped her arms. "We were ill-treated. We raised a rebellion."

"We were differently treated," Duncan said. "That's not the same."

Guthrie's eyes flashed in the darkness. "We were the disfavored children. We were reacting to injustice."

"It was never a just universe," Duncan said feeling the straining pops of his shell trying to squeeze the thinned, weakened areas back together. "But our choices made it so much worse. We were angry children, and reacted with all of the emotional stability and perspective you could expect of them. Which is to say, none."

Guthrie chuckled in the dark, a strangely shrill noise. "You wish you could go back and do it all over again. You think you'd choose differently. Well, I will say this to you: you wouldn't, unless you're a coward."

"Just older and wiser," Duncan said. "And having spent time with the so-called favored children...I don't think they got a better deal than we had. I think we were fooling ourselves because we were angry, because we listened to someone who was arrogant, and envious, and poisoned in the soul. We let it spread – no, we spread it. We took the poison into ourselves, and then we gave it to others. We, who should have known better."

"There's no going back, Duncan," Guthrie said. "You'll never be a seraphim again. You made your choices. There is no forgiveness. Not for our kind."

"That's the burden of knowledge," Duncan said, curving his neck. It popped; not a great sound. "That's why, yes, if I had it do over again, I wouldn't have done what we did. I would absolutely choose differently." He set his feet, because he knew the attack was coming, and he had a plan, albeit a weak one. "And I think you're a fool if you live as we have all these millennia and you don't think: 'I was wrong. I was an idiot. I was better off before.'"

"You are an idiot, that's true," Guthrie said, and launched herself at him. But he was ready – sort of – and he spun, clipping her, grabbing her, and then throwing himself with her into the nearest wall to continue their battle.

DARLA STARTED to move after the two boys had their legs cut out from under them. She wanted to help, to draw this thing to its natural conclusion, but she found herself facing the pointed blade of Duchess Kitty Elizabeth. The taller woman had stuck her imposing self between Darla and the trouble developing in the middle of the room. As if to punctuate the situation, Lucia screamed in pain, something Darla could easily recognize as from a contraction.

"I thought you were too scared to run me through?" Darla asked, trying to play it cool and probably coming off a little coquettish. She didn't want to fangirl, but this was Kitty Elizabeth, *the* Kitty Elizabeth. Scourge of men, scourge of hell, one-time paramour of...well...the persona being born right behind her.

Kitty offered a momentary glance at the drama behind her, so quick that Darla almost didn't catch it. "I am," she said, and lowered her sword.

"Oh, good," Darla said, taking a step forward, "because–"

Kitty slammed a fist into her sternum and sent her flying back. Darla landed hard on her ass, and, when she recovered, looked up to find Kitty looming over her, a stylish, black leather riding boot planted on her chest. She put a little weight on it, and Darla found herself screaming to match Lucia. "Why don't we wait here for the boys to finish what they're doing?" Kitty said, quite amiably. She didn't stop grinding Darla's injured sternum, though, and the pain was quite unbearable.

ARCH TOOK the hit like a tackle from a three-hundred-pound offensive lineman and went down hard. His sword skittered away, across the ground, knocked farther by tentacles of darkness he hadn't even seen coming.

His sides hurt, his back hurt, and he was left staring up at the fiery ceiling of the cavern, left with a grim sense that molten something was going to drip on him at any moment. It wouldn't, of course; he'd reconciled in his mind that the flames were not really there, but he could still smell the smoke and feel the heat.

Rolling onto his elbow, he looked up to find Hendricks bleeding from a head wound, dark crimson sliding down his temple from somewhere above his hat brim. Past that, something fuller, and larger, was finally making its way out of Lucia.

Much, much larger than should have been able to fit in that slip of a girl.

Worse than that, there appeared to be two of them. Except

that was just his bell having been rung, Arch realized, trying to push himself up and then toppling over. Hendricks made a similar effort with similar results, getting dirt all stirred up and making it cling to the blood drenching the side of his face.

"Gary Wrightson," came an awful voice from somewhere in the darkness. It was like nothing Arch had quite ever heard; echoing, terrible, it sounded like it was being projected into his very soul. "Last of his line."

"Yeah, that's me," Gary said, sitting calmly in his wheelchair, hands folded in his lap.

"No, it is not." Marina appeared out of the shadows, the fire, or just the haze in Arch's consciousness. "He is not the last of his line." She was brandishing the gun, pointing it at the scaled, leathery, shadow-clad thing that was half in Lucia, half out.

"The fuck, Marina?" Gary was staring at her, open-mouthed. But his hands hadn't moved from his willy. Why hadn't the man's hands moved?

She looked back at him. "I have been carrying your plumbing business for years through my efforts, motherfucker." She drew down on the thing, the demon thing, the evil thing, and shot at it. It made a loud noise, but seemed to have no effect but to puff away a couple of tendrils of shadow. "Now I carry your child."

Something slammed into her from the side and she went sprawling, gun knocked out of her hands as she went hard into the nearby wall. A moment of silence reigned, and then the voice said, dryly, "Or at least you did."

"You are a real fucking piece of shit," Gary said, leaning forward in his chair, hand still – why, Arch wondered, brain still knocked hazy, why did he set it there, on that, not even bothering to cover himself?

"And you are a tasty piece of meat," the voice said, for it was starting to separate from Lucia now. She was panting, and whimpering, but the worst, the largest part of it, was clearly out. "Your soul is going to wet my whistle before my journey."

It crept on toward Gary, the last bit falling out of Lucia, and she tipped over, slipping into unconsciousness, possibly dead–

And Arch couldn't get himself to stand and do a darned thing about either of them.

ANOTHER BLAST of thunder shook the earth around her, and Lauren felt the first droplets of rain coming down through the thick smoke covering Mount Horeb. The fires blazed brightly in the distance, and she could really feel the heat. How close were they? Close enough for it to feel like hell was on their heels. Or yawning into their faces, at least.

"Getting low on ammo!" Brian shouted, ejecting a magazine and throwing another one in. Lauren shuddered a little seeing it; the demons were getting close, their breath crowding in like the heat and the thunder. His vest had been weighed down with the boxy magazines only moments before. Now it was hanging loosely from his skinny frame.

Something leapt out of the darkness and smashed into Micah, bowling him over. Lauren yelped and drew a bead, squirting it with holy water. It caught immediately aflame, screamed, and writhed away. It didn't look anything approaching human, or animal-like, and the way it moved, the way it screamed, was like nails in a chalkboard pressed against her very soul.

"Medic," Micah said in a pained voice. Lauren, stirred to action by that, grabbed him by one arm while Nguyen took the other and between the two of them dragged him toward the entrance to the cave. They were almost in the mouth of it now.

"Tell me where it hurts," Lauren said, taking a knee beside

him, the flashlight hanging from her vest playing over his dark features.

"Got my leg," Micah said. There was definitely blood there, and it did not look superficial. Fortunately, it didn't look like it was torn to bits or gushing, either, so that was fortunate. "I could kill that son-in-law of mine."

"You're going to have to get in line today," Lauren said, opening the medical kit she'd strapped to her vest. Spellman had handed it to her specifically. Had he known this was going to happen, or was he just trying to generally prepare them?

Oh, who knew? And who cared at this point?

"I never should have taken pity on his dumb ass," Micah said, gritting his way through the pain. "I brought him home, did you know that? Introduced him to my daughter, like an idiot. If I hadn't, maybe the world wouldn't be ending right now."

Lauren couldn't suppress a chuckle. "I think the world would still be ending. It seems to me the plans of devils and demons don't hinge on one Marine with a tragic backstory. There were plenty of other wounded, violent men that could have been repurposed to do what Hendricks did in all this." Another peal of thunder cracked overhead, making Lauren blanch.

"Maybe," Micah said, looking up at the heavens. "The storm is just about here, though, and I don't see how we're going to make it through this."

"Just leave it to me for now," Lauren said tightly, already bandaging the wound. It was all she could do, since it seemed likely giving the growing closeness of the demon noises, this would not be the last wound she'd be addressing tonight.

GARY WATCHED the thing knock Marina sideways, watched it finish birthing itself, watched Lucia keel over, a trail of dark liquid smeared down her leg. Blood, ichor, bile, something worse – Gary didn't know. Hendricks and Arch were both down, the dumb fuckers, bowled over by the sneaking, shadowy tentacles of this evil-ass thing.

And it was evil. He could see it now, before him in its lack-of-glory. It was like nothing he'd ever laid eyes on: black, goo-like tentacles blended together with reptilian scales across a torso that seemed to be shaped like something in the insect or crustacean family, except gargantuan. How Lucia had passed that thing through her hoo-ha was a real mystery.

Then there was the face. If the rest of the construction of the thing had left any doubts that it was fucking evil, the face certainly put those out to pasture. And then shot them in the fucking head with a double barrel. It was shaded by the fires around them, that face, but there was nothing good nor noble in there, not the expression – which was haughty, malicious, and leering – nor the structure, which was like a demon, a dinosaur, and goat had gone into an orgy with the ugliest man alive, and this had been the impossible genetic result.

The face extended toward him on a long neck, but the body followed. The jaw came unhinged, and a maw presented itself with something between a smile and a hunger, ready to devour.

It was then that Gary decided the time had come to pray.

"Dear Lord," he said aloud, causing the head to hesitate in its path toward him, "bless my body, my dick, and the piss within it. Please make it holy and use it in your service."

And with that, he let loose of his bladder as the face surged forward.

The stream struck the damned devil thing squarely, and for just a second, Gary wasn't sure it was going to work like he hoped it would.

Then...it burst into flames.

Gary wasn't the sort to let up, either, once he got it going. He sprayed like a motherfucker, dousing it as much as possible, until the stream started to fall short and the flames – not at all like the ones that had been crawling over the walls and ceiling of the cave – had fully involved the thing. It spasmed and screamed, and Gary found himself rolling back to avoid the thrashing. He ignored the little bit of piss still trickling, because it seemed a trifling thing at the moment.

It screamed and it danced, that scary devil, its face and neck on fire. It was spasming, throwing its hands in all directions, when something moved beside it and Darla screamed–

"Sorry, son." Hendricks came in hard with the sword, and suddenly it was Marie fucking Antoinette time for the newborn demon. "Maybe I'll see you again on the other side."

The body stopped jerking, and the head sailed free, flying across the room to where it thumped against the wall and rolled down, coming to a stop next to Darla Pike's bare foot, where she lay. She stared at it wide-eyed, horrified, presumably because she'd just watched her demon meal ticket come to a swift end.

With a strange hiss, the body collapsed into a sulfuric burst that knocked over Hendricks and just about bowled over Gary. His nasal passages got blown open like the sulfuric version of wasabi had just passed over his tongue, and he was left retching at the smell of it.

"Is that...is that it?" Arch was wobbly, on one knee, head bobbing back and forth, a little like that thing. "Is it over?"

Gary, for his part, wasn't waiting for an answer. He was already rolling for Marina, and had nearly made it to her side when a too-damned-familiar voice cut into his very thoughts.

"No," Starling said, and he turned to find Lucia back on her feet, eyes dusky as hell again, "It is not over."

DARLA TENSED UP, and felt the poke of the blade as she stared down at the head of the creature as it turned to dust.

Yes, that vessel was dead, and it did hurt. Not quite as much as the pain in her sternum, but still. It stung a fuck lot.

But it wasn't the only vessel, obviously. Starling was standing there, wearing Lucia's skin again, and she had a clear feeling projected on her face.

And that feeling was *fury*.

Darla tried to sit up, but Kitty pushed her back down. Gently, but pushed. "Let the boys fight this one out," Kitty said with a grin.

THERE WAS NOT a hell of a lot of ground left before they'd be in the cave. That was Erin's considered stance on where they were. Demons were pressing in hard, running, slithering, and crawling up the slopes toward them. Bullets were in short supply and then, suddenly, they were out. Holy water was sprayed, and that kept them back for a short time, but everyone – human and demon alike – knew what was happening here.

The good guys were about to lose, and lose hard.

The smoke was thick, piping up the face of Mount Horeb; the fires had to be a quarter mile away or less. Erin was holding her nose, both from the smoke and the overwhelming sulfur that had been loosed in the last few minutes.

"I guess it was always going to end like this," Brian said, popping his last empty magazine and throwing it down carelessly. His bitchass would have cared more about littering in the past. Probably a pretty good mark of how fucked they were that he didn't. "We never did have much of a chance." He looked up at the heavens. "Thanks for all the help. Asshole."

That remark was greeted by another boom of thunder, and the wet slap of rain coming down in great droplets. The demons were out there, pacing just beyond the reach of the flashlights. What were they waiting for? Who knew. Not Erin, that was for sure.

"The storm is here," Micah said ominously.

All Erin knew was she was soaked in mere seconds, and her sword was the only thing in her hands as they started to rally and come up the slope again, drawing ever closer to the last remnants of the Watch.

STARLING WAS BACK IN LUCIA, and all Hendricks knew how to do was attack the problem head on. Well, sort of. She had her back to him. But the principle was the same – go right at her.

So he did, bringing his sword down in a clipping attack on the back of the girl, trying to give her a little poke in the ass with just the tip, two things that did not make him feel at all better about the numerous times he'd stuck it in the body of Lucia.

And the damned thing bounced off.

Starling spun on him, eyes dark and hideous. "She is mine," she said, and gave Hendricks a whack so hard that he flew sideways ten feet, rolling to a stop just short of the gate. Which gave him the heebie jeebies even through his five new pains. "You destroyed my vessel." She seemed to loom, like a pillar, suddenly in the center of the room. "Now I am forced to reconsider how best to approach this." She swept her gaze over the room, and Hendricks felt uncomfortable as it settled on him. "One thing is certain...I will not let go of Lucia. She is mine, body and soul–"

"What do you want for her?" Arch spoke up, standing just a little ways behind Starling. Starling did a slow turn.

"Ooh, the bidding has begun," Kitty said from across the chamber. "Watch this, sugar tits, it's going to be a real show." She made some sort of movement, and Darla Pike whimpered in pain.

Starling stared down Arch. "You."

Arch stared back. "Are you asking if I am me? Or are you asking if you can have me?"

"You...are a righteous man," Starling said. She sounded as robotic as she ever did when that entity had been at the helm. "You want to give your life for hers?"

"If that's what it takes," Arch said, hobbling forward on unsteady legs. "I'll let you kill me if you'll let Lucia live – and let her go free."

She only looked him up and down once before saying, "But I could kill you anyway. You could hardly stop me."

"Then do it," Arch said. "Just let her go." He stood there, tall and proud. "I won't fight you. I just want her to be safe."

Starling stared him down. "The world is ending, and you concern yourself with the welfare of one whore who gave herself freely to me?"

"Oh, yes, bring your innocent blood right to her," Kitty said. "That's a great idea. Remember how we were trying to keep that from happening?"

"Arch, this is bad strategy, man," Gary called. "She's knocked the fuck outta the cowboy, my girl is unconscious, and I don't know how much use you think I'm gonna be, but I'ma tell you right now that my bladder is empty, brother."

"This isn't strategy," Arch said, taking another step closer. "I am willing to give my life for Lucia's. Let the girl go – and I'll go with you."

Starling stared at him. "Where do you think I'm going?"

"You need innocent blood, don't you?" Arch asked, holding his head high. "If you kill me, it lets you go right through, doesn't it? Breaks the seal?"

Starling's eyes narrowed, and she considered the room for a moment.

"Come on," Arch said. "You know I'm the only option. You going to go with the cowboy with the guilty conscience that you already roped into a human sacrifice ritual? The man in the wheelchair that never met a swear word he didn't like to use on a random stranger?"

"I like to think every person I meet is a representation of God," Gary said. "Then I call him a fucking cunt right to his face."

"How about your ex over there?" Arch inclined his head toward Kitty. "She pure of heart?"

"Oh, my goodness, dear," Kitty said. "That's the worst rhetorical question I've ever heard asked."

"Or how about your loyal servant?" Arch took a step closer. "Does she have the blood you need to finish this thing?" He jutted his chin out at her. "I give my life for Lucia's. Take my bargain."

She only stared at him for another moment before pronouncing, "Your bargain is accepted." And she raised her hand to strike at him–

Then suddenly the world seemed to explode around Hendricks.

DUNCAN WAS FEELING THE STRAIN, and more than the strain, as he slammed into a disused segment of rail. It clipped him on the shoulder, stopping his momentum inasmuch as it caused him to flip, feet coming up over his head, back jamming into the metal and dislodging a dozen crossties.

This was what losing felt like. He could feel his shell, ready to crack, and his essence prepared to dump forth, and he knew he had nothing left to give.

"You look like you could really use a righteous instrument right about now," Guthrie said, taunting him out of the darkness. "Of course, if it's not properly insulated like your baton, it'd do just as much damage to you as to me." She loomed overhead and stomped him into the dirt again. "You ever wonder where the Office of Occultic Concordance got holy objects? Because it's kind of an interesting story–"

"Just fucking crack me already and spare me the pontificating," Duncan said. If he had blood to spit, he would have. Instead, he just watched the shadow of Guthrie as she slammed down on him again, trying her hardest to grant his wish.

"WHAT THE HELL WAS THAT...?" Kitty murmured, heel still buried painfully in Darla's chest. Something had blown up in the chamber, but being at the edge, it hadn't hit them. A cloud of dust was swirling at the center of the room, though, and Darla could not tell what had happened there.

"Darla," Kitty said, putting aside her sword to lean down, still resting enough of her weight on Darla's chest to make it feel like an elephant was sitting there, "since it's just us girls now – what did you have to do in order to get in good with your bestie over there? To get your crown, you know?"

She didn't want to answer, but the pressure and pain were horrible, and so she screamed, "I tortured and dismembered and flayed my children alive! They were just babies and I did it to them and I'm not sorry!"

The pressure receded, and so did some of the pain. Darla looked up to find Kitty staring down at her with eyebrows risen almost to the bottom of her bleached hairline. "Oh. Wow. That's too much even for me. Ugh." And she stood, removing all the pressure from Darla's chest. "You are a true piece of shit. I get selling out the world, society, a man – but torturing and dismembering your own flesh and blood?" A horrified look, which seemed extra terrible on that demonic visage, appeared. "What the fuck is wrong with you?"

"Look!" Darla had rolled to her side, pointing, now that the haze was starting to clear.

And what she saw there in the center of the room, where Arch and Starling had been only a moment before...

...Well, she almost couldn't believe it.

ARCH HAD BEEN ready for the blow when it came. Not ready for it in the sense of being prepared to counter it; how could you counter a blow from a fallen angel, one strong enough to wipe you off the planet in one proper hit?

No, he'd been ready for it in the sense of being ready for death, being ready to go, ready to sacrifice his life if it bought back Lucia's, even for a moment. He didn't know the girl's story, other than the brief outlines Lauren Darlington had hinted at, but he knew that whatever she'd done to get herself into the grip of this mess, she didn't deserve it.

So he'd stuck his chin out, offered himself, and been ready to be removed from this life. Part of him never had believed that Starling could walk through that gate, not even with her terrible new skin. He certainly didn't believe she could now that she was bereft of it, and back in Lucia. Didn't believe it for a second, otherwise why bother with all the hullaballoo of making that new body...?

The blow came at him quick, almost quicker than his eye could follow. He didn't flinch away; this was his comeuppance, his penance for not being satisfied with Alison and the life they'd made here. That was why he'd jumped so fast when Hendricks had clashed with that demon on the town square all those months ago. He wasn't Catholic, but the Prayer of St. Francis came back to him in that moment.

God, make me an instrument of your grace...

He couldn't think of anyone who needed grace more than he did. He'd led his wife into this war, had seen her killed along with their baby, and now her parents were dead, and the town she'd loved was as good as gone, too.

With grace, he'd see her again right now.

The blow connected and he didn't even feel it. Some sort of shock ran through his system, and his eyes closed. There was a momentary flash, and things went bright, like lightning had just struck beside him.

And when Arch opened his eyes...there was darkness.

But it didn't last long.

A cloud of dirt cleared from where it had been stirred up, and nothing in the room was quite as he left it. Starling was splayed out in front of him, unconscious, a little nosebleed trickling down her upper lip, eyes closed. Hendricks was dang near in the gate, curled up in the fetal position, head about three inches from touching the waving, fluttering center of it–

Arch didn't give that much thought; Hendricks would keep. Instead he dropped beside Starling, and found her warm to the touch. When her eyes fluttered, there was green in them instead of darkness, and when she breathed, it sounded like a girl, not the thing that had worn her like a skin suit. "What happened?" she asked weakly.

"The holy man here was willing to sacrifice his life for you," Kitty Elizabeth said in that annoyingly preachy tone of her. "Turns out, that has a certain power that your possessor forgot, either in her anger or greed."

Arch saw Gary across the room, leaning over in his wheelchair, checking on Marina. She seemed to be stirring, too, but was flat on her back. "Where's Starling now?" Arch asked, once he was reasonably assured that Lucia was fine, her pulse regular, though she seemed a little clammy.

Kitty hesitated. "Well...there's only a few places she could have gone. You're out, obviously. This idiot consecrated his dick earlier," and she waved the rapier at Gary, "which made all of him an instrument of you-know-who, so he's out, too."

Arch just cringed. Gary must have seen it, because he said, "What? If God made me, he made my dick, too. Seems like he didn't mind making it holy."

"I'm a poor candidate for obvious reasons," Kitty said, "and the pregnant gal with him," she waved a hand at Gary, "is hosting an innocent soul, so she's out. Which leaves..." And she nodded to Hendricks, "...Him. And..." Her eyes widened, and she looked down quickly–

Kitty was flung through the air like she'd been standing on a catapult. Arch flinched away involuntarily, and when he turned back...

...Darla Pike was wearing a look of pure spite, and her eyes were pure darkness.

DUNCAN FELT the boards at his back, felt the pain in his essence, and knew he was soon to die.

And furthermore...he wasn't sure he cared any longer.

"You could have just gone along," Guthrie said, sounding

like she was seething. "Could have folded right in line. But not you. You had to be a rebel."

Duncan snorted. "Not the first time...I rebelled. Just the first time I did so alone."

"There is no redemption for you, idiot," Guthrie said, leaning over him. She smacked him in the face, and it sent him sideways a foot, ripping a hole in the back of his jacket against the nails in the wood crossties he'd been lying on. "No forgiveness. That's the curse of us, there was never any going back. You get splashed with holy water, you burn like the rest of us. You touch a cross, you scorch. Do you not get that?" Guthrie was screaming in his face now. "Did you feel welcome in their church earlier? No, you didn't, and do you know why? Because you're fucking *unwanted*, demon, and you always will be!" She spat on him. "You are the accursed of the earth and the heavens, and that will never change! You will always be the enemy!"

She leaned in closer. "And you know what else?"

Duncan let his hand drift to the crossties, which should have bent his shoulder out of socket. "Do I even want to know?"

"You were never going to–"

Duncan brought his arm around and socked Guthrie in the side of the head, shattering a wooden tie across it. Something about the wood felt odd, but his vision was hazy, and he hammered it home again as Guthrie staggered, pasting her upside the face with it.

"You will never be loved," Guthrie said, sounding choked. "You will never be forgiven."

Duncan pulled himself to his feet, and started to swing the board at Guthrie when he realized–

It was more than one crosstie. And they were nailed together. Like a–

"Huh," Guthrie said, staring at it. "That's a–"

Duncan shoved the makeshift crucifix right into Guthrie's

face, not even hitting her with it. It rested beneath her nose for only a second before she shrieked, bright light burning from beneath her shell at the mere contact with it. Only a moment later and black flames crawled out of her face, consuming her in a burst of unholy fire as she was purged from the earth.

Staring down at the boards in his hand, Duncan couldn't quite decide if he'd just seen what he had. "Maybe," Duncan said. He didn't know if he believed in the impossible. But he was holding a cross in his hands, and it didn't burn at all. "Maybe."

"IT'S BEEN a real pleasure fighting alongside y'all," Brian said, right next to Erin's ear. They were in the tightest possible formation, all clumped up at the mouth of the mine.

"You said 'y'all,'" Lauren said with a grin. She'd patched up Micah as best as she could, and had rejoined them here on the front as the rain poured down around them. Lightning flashed again, showing the legions arrayed before them, and the crack heralded the arrival of their doom.

Thousands of demons. That's what they were facing. Enough that even if they had all the ammo in the world, they could not have held them back. Not with this few. Not against this many.

"Is it wrong," Father Nguyen said, his black hair matted down in his face by the downpour, "that I wish for a new flood? Noah could sail right here, pick us up, and off we would go. At least someone would survive what's about to happen."

Erin cocked her head; something was striking her as funny about that.

"No holding back now," Lauren said, pumping another squirt out that disappeared into the rain. "Out of holy water." She pulled off the strap of the squirt gun and hurled it at the demons. They were like sharks, circling closer, and this only pushed them back a little.

Erin blinked. That was a thought. She felt a jolt down her spine. It was an idea. No, more than an idea. It was–

"Father," she said, turning to Nguyen. "*Africa.*"

Nguyen stared at her, looking like a drowned ferret with his hair pressed down by the torrential downpour. "What?"

"Toto," Erin said, too excited to form the words. "You need to–"

"BLESS THE RAINS!" Brian shouted, getting it before she could get the words together.

Nguyen only stared blankly for a moment before he opened his mouth and bellowed, "Heavenly Father, please bless these rains and make them holy!"

The night lit up as though someone had set fire to a massive book of matches, the rain falling down upon the heads of the demon army. Every droplet seemed to make them spark, then burn, and they flared, lighting the night like a thousand fireworks. It grew in intensity, burning bright, screams and cries of the demon army as they dissolved into flames and sulfur growing and then dying in a matter of ten seconds.

"Aqua a Deo," Nguyen said, smiling into the dark as the sparks faded away. It had been like the fireworks at the end of Summer Lights festival all over again, but in January.

And then...there was silence.

Except from within the cave.

DARLA PIKE WAS DEFINITELY FEELING the burn. It was not a subtle sensation, sharing her body with one of the oldest beings in the universe. It was powerful. It was empowering. It was–

Cramped. Really, really cramped.

"You think you have beaten me," Starling said, through her lips. "I am eternal. Timeless. My plans do not fail, not forever."

Except that wasn't quite true. Darla could see that now. She could see a lot of truths, in fact, ones that previously had been concealed from her. Promises that were destined not to be kept. Ones that Darla had been counting on, dammit.

"I think you should leave," Archibald Stan said. Tall. Implacable. Foreboding, really. Starling could tear through him like–

No. She couldn't. She'd just tried, and she...she couldn't. It wasn't possible. There was a veil of protection over him that Starling couldn't defeat, no matter how hard she tried.

And...Darla could tell she would have tried. Would have walked through fire. Would have drunk acid. Would have carved her own heart out with a dull butter knife.

But none of that was possible any longer for the entity she'd come to think of as Starling. Something had happened here, just now, that broke Starling's power. There was hints of it in the rain somewhere far, far above. And the rest...

The rest of it was right here before her, in the tall, black man staring her down without fear. In the Duchess looking amused. In the man in the wheelchair who, even now, was watching as he helped his injured paramour into his lap and rolled in this direction.

"And you..." Darla stared at what Starling focused on, and in this case it was the tattered remains of the OOC, Duncan, suit all ripped to shreds, but carrying a...

...A cross?

"Your betrayal is complete," Starling said.

"Actually," Duncan said, hoisting the boards over his shoulder, "I think I've come full circle."

"And I," Darla said, somehow squeezing in to speak in her

own voice, "don't think I want to be in this particular fight any longer."

There was a moment of silence, and then Kitty belted out with a laugh. "You sold your soul and got buyer's remorse, huh, kid? Well, as they say in the biz: no take-backsies."

"Wait," Arch said, stepping closer. "Mrs. Pike?"

"It's me," Darla said, somehow struggling past the force in her body, in her mind, to speak. "Please – please, get me out of this! I regret – I'm sorry!"

"She murdered her children," Kitty said. "Just so we're clear on what she did to enter this bargain. I checked with a couple of my little whispers just now and – it was quite a scene, apparently. Viscera everywhere. Screams aplenty. Serial killers currently burning in hell shied away in disgust."

"What, are you suddenly the voice of reason?" Gary Wrightson asked, wheeling to a stop next to Arch.

"Just letting you know that what she did was so appalling that even I can't condone it," Kitty said. "And I can condone a lot. And have."

"Please," Darla said. "Save me."

Gary Wrightson looked to Arch. "You sure you want to do this again, big man?"

"Always," Arch said, standing tall.

"What if there was another way?" Wrightson asked, looking up at him. Arch just stared down at him, puzzled.

Wrightson wheeled forward, grabbed the plank of a cross out of Duncan's hand, said, "Thanks," and rolled right up to Darla. He smacked her lightly in the face and shouted, "Do you renounce Satan? And all his pomps? And all his works?"

Darla felt something swell in her just then, and suddenly she could no longer speak.

ERIN FOLLOWED the others as they trickled down into the mines, leaving only Nguyen and Micah to guard the entrance. It seemed unlikely anything was going to break through the wash; nothing was alive out there save for the surviving woods, and already the glow of the fires seemed to have diminished.

"Cold down here," Dr. Darlington said, shuffling along beside Erin.

"Doesn't help we're soaked with holy water," Brian said from her other side. "Not that I'm complaining," he added hastily.

Ahead, there were voices, and a glow. Erin turned a corner to find–

Lucia on the ground, holding her head. Hendricks, unconscious at the foot of–

"Whoa," Brian said. "Now that...has gotta be the gate to heaven."

Gary was in front of Darla Pike, Marina across his lap in his wheelchair. Pike's face was stricken with terror – and, somehow, a wooden cross that he'd planted against her cheek, mashing her nose. Kitty Elizabeth was there, too, and so was Arch. She got the feeling she'd just missed something, but she didn't care, because one thing out of all of that mess stood out to her, and she broke into a run–

Hitting her knees beside Hendricks, she shook him. There was a terrible vibe coming off that gate, something that warned her that she should not be here, that it was dangerous, that getting too close could be of great peril to her or anyone else.

"Hendricks," she said, roughing his shoulder. He did not stir.

"WHAT ARE YOU DOING?" Arch asked Gary as he shoved that wooden cross into Darla Pike's face. She started to bleed from the nose, but he couldn't see any other effect.

"Ain't you ever seen *The Exorcist?*" Gary asked.

"You need a priest to do an exorcism," Lauren Darlington said. She looked waterlogged, strands of dark hair in her eyes.

"Look, I just turned my own piss into holy water and killed a demon with it, so I'm not sure I believe that," Gary said.

Darla Pike cackled – except it wasn't her. It was a cold, mechanical sound that Arch knew was Starling.

"I own this vessel," Starling said, "body and soul, mind and spirit. As the Duchess said...no takebacks."

"This is going to be a fight," Brian said, and seemed to be looking around for something to use to hit her with.

A gunshot rang out in the confined space, making Arch flinch. It came from behind them, and Arch turned to find–

Hendricks was on his feet, pistol drawn, but it wasn't pointing at anyone. Erin was beside him, helping him by letting him lean against her. Blood still trickled from his temple down his face, and his hat was on the ground, coat flowing black all around him in the pale glow of the gate.

Darla/Starling stared at him, looking suddenly wary. "And now you."

"Go back to hell," Hendricks said, advancing on her slowly, Erin helping him every step of the way. "You failed. That body you wanted, just for this purpose? We destroyed it."

"Oh, and that army you brought, just to invade?" Brian piped up, sounding stronger than he ever did...when he wasn't stoned. "We destroyed that, too."

"I am no longer a creature of yours," Duncan said, taking back the cross from Gary and taking a step closer to Starling.

"I exorcised you from one vessel," Arch said, stepping up. "And I wouldn't mind the chance to do so from another."

"And I pissed right in your ugly hellbeast face," Gary said, with undisguised glee. "I bet they talk about that one behind your back for all eternity."

"Welcome to Midian, Tennessee," Lauren said, stepping up. "Where we take it real seriously when you mess with our town – or our people."

"Now," Erin said, helping Hendricks right up there, so they were forming a semi-circle around Darla/Starling, "as the duly chosen, acting sheriff of these parts," and her face hardened into a cold expression, "get the hell out of here."

"I am...everywhere," Starling said, dark eyes moving around them. "And I am in every one of you. You may have defeated me today, but I am eternal. And I will return."

"That's all right," Brian said. "This is the South. We have long memories." He stepped right up to her, and there was a smoldering anger in him that Arch couldn't recall seeing before, a righteous indignation that went beyond his usual obsessions of politics, or philosophy. "We will remember you. We will remember this place. And if you come back tomorrow, a year from now, or a thousand years from now, someone will be here, waiting for you. We will tell our children, and our children's children what happened here today. We will be on watch from now until the end of days, whenever that is," and he pointed, "and you are not coming to it through that fuckin' gate."

"Face it, cupcake," Kitty said, unflappably amused. "You lost the minute this thing was placed here." She waved a hand at the gate. "He knew what He was doing when He chose this spot. Knew what He was doing when He chose His fighters." She cocked a perfectly manicured eyebrow. "Knew what He was doing when He made you."

Arch watched a not-so-subtle change move over the face that had once belonged to Darla Pike. It was a look of panic, a change of the eyes to reveal the iris.

"No!" she cried. "Please! I can't – you don't know what's waiting for me down there!"

"Some of us do," Kitty Elizabeth said with a smirk. "And can I just say: well earned."

Darla Pike's face began to melt, and a hideous screaming filled the cavern. It was like a fire had begun beneath her skin, and it crawled its way down her until she was no more, though her screams seemed to echo for a few seconds longer, like a warning for any who cared to listen to it.

A few moments of silence finished with Marina's quiet voice: "Is this it? Did we win?"

"For now," Duncan said. He sounded rough, and by his clothing he had been put through the mill.

Kitty clapped her hands together once, loudly. "I gotta say, my little pigeons: well done. I really didn't see you pulling that one out, but you did. Congratulations on saving your entire universe. Also, this town. For whatever that's worth, given its current state. And its original state, frankly."

"You didn't really help much," Arch said.

"Yeah, you were kind of standing on the sidelines," Gary said. "Almost like you were hedging your bets, waiting to see who was going to win so you could throw in with them at the last possible second."

She looked right at him and winked. "Can't fool you. At least, not about this. See, the thing is – I'm on a shit list in hell, so I didn't want to go back. But if I did, because the whole world was about to be dragged into a hell state, I needed to be certain I could at least get myself a few rungs off the bottom of the ladder."

"The sense of solidarity I'm feeling with you is just breathtaking," Lauren said.

"I've never been one of you," Kitty said, drawing up to her full height, which was...imposing. Arch had never noticed her as particularly tall before, but it was like she was unfolding before them. "I am older than the earth. I was old when life began on this planet." Her voice deepened, and echoed. "I am the Duchess Katlin Elizabeth. Souls of hell bow to me, and demons of this world answer my call in humble admiration." Her eye fell upon Hendricks, where he leaned against Erin, clearly not able to take her on, with one arm or two. Though funnily enough, the shadow of her had two.

She gasped, jerking upright, arms spread wide and grandiose. Something was sticking out of the center of her chest.

Cracks began to appear in her skin like dry earth peeling. Blackness shone through, and then seemed to consume her from the inside out, and a burst of sulfur filled the air.

A makeshift cross clattered to the ground, and behind her, unflappable, stood Duncan in his tattered suit. When he had every eye, he said, "I sent her to find a more receptive audience for her bullshit monologue."

"Duncan," Hendricks said, sounding strained, "didn't you say that even threatening to kill her meant an immediate death sentence by an OOC?"

The demon just stood there for a moment. "Yeah," he said finally, and Arch could have sworn he was wearing a very slight smile, "but I'm not operating under their authority anymore...so they can go fuck themselves."

DARLA *BURNED.*

Oh, it wasn't quite fire. Wasn't quite the traditional roast that people thought of when they considered hell, but still...

Darla burned.

She stewed in the voices of her children, screaming at her. They permeated her, encompassed her, wrapped her up in agony and terror. She could feel every emotion, and it was more than feeling, it translated into a flame taken to every one of her nerve endings. Even though she didn't have them any more.

And it played like the most horrific symphony; it pitched and rose, rose and fell, so that she could never quite adjust to its horrors. Lesser or greater, she was always feeling it, and would always feel it, for all time.

She knew this, and she suffered.

And the worst part was...even if they'd won...

This was always going to be her fate.

GARY HAD EXPERIENCED QUITE ENOUGH of being underground. With Marina spread across his lap, and that gate behind him, he started to roll up the incline of the mine. Sure, his arms were tired, but he was sick of being here.

Besides, he was now an instrument of God. What was a little ramp rolling over uneven ground after that?

"Why didn't you tell me?" he asked. She was slightly limp, probably concussed. He should have Doc Darlington take a look at her once they got out of this place. Didn't stop Marina from looking over his shoulder, cradling him gently, hands on his naked flesh, as he pushed them out of there.

"I did tell you," she said. "I just did not say until moment when it mattered." She pulled back a little from her embrace so she could look him in the eye, peeled her cheek off his sweaty chest. "We were fighting apocalypse. You think this is really time for me to say, 'Hey, look at me? I have exciting, unexpected news?'" She scoffed. "I am not American woman. I will bear up until we finish dealing with the business. Then I tell you." She made a slight shrug. "Because it motivate you to live."

"It did do that," Gary said. Fuck, his arms were tired, and it was a long way out of this place. "I just want to tell you...I consider myself damn lucky to have found a woman like you. You got real steel, Marina. And guts of pure gravel. I sure do like you. A lot." He blushed.

She patted him on the chest. "You can say love."

"We didn't really say that word in my family," Gary said, still blushing.

She nodded. "But now...is new family, yes? We try to do better than was done to you, before? For...efficiency, maybe?"

"For efficiency," Gary said, with a nod of his own. He wanted to stop, to put a hand on that belly of hers. "I hope this is just the first of many. I had a pretty good-sized family before, you know."

She rested her head again on his chest, her thin little legs hanging off the side of the wheelchair, ass rubbing right on his dick. "You want to name the baby after one of your brothers?"

"Hell fucking no," Gary said. "That naming scheme thing is the biggest pile of bullshit I ever endured. I would rather have been named Sue than have my brothers get singsongy rhyming names. And poor Paul – he was always dealing with an inferiority complex. I'm fine with not naming them after my brothers or mom. Them just being here is tribute enough to the Wrightson family." He held his chin up high. "Because we go on, dammit. No matter what you throw at us, we keep going." He stopped, because his arms were screaming bloody murder from this slope, and just held fast, hands on the wheels. "Metaphorically, anyway. I just need a quick breather. Pissing in that demon's face really took it out of me."

Someone landed firm hands on the back of his chair, and he looked up to find Duncan standing over him. His wheels started turning, and he moved his hands off. "Well, well," Gary said. "You ain't got to do that, you know. I just needed a second."

"I'm happy to give you a hand," Duncan said, looking straight ahead. "If you don't mind taking one."

Gary reached up and planted his own hand on Duncan's wrist. "I'm good with taking help from you. You're a hell of a dude, Duncan."

"You're not bad yourself, Gary." Duncan seemed to be almost smiling in the darkness. He moved with self-assured, easy strides, like pushing the wheelchair with Gary and Marina in it was nothing. Probably was, to him. "Say, you don't know where I could find a job, do you? I think I just got let go from my last one."

"I find it's not wise to make dramatic career decisions in the heat of the moment," Gary said, sitting back and letting the fire in his arms fade. Just enjoying the ride. "But if at the end of this, you decide you want to do something as pedestrian as plumbing, you just let me know. I'd take you on as an apprentice in a heartbeat." And with Marina against him, he sat back to enjoy the ride.

BRIAN WATCHED Duncan push the wheelchair up the slope, Marina nestled in Gary's lap. He was about twenty paces back, maybe twenty-five, and slowing to give them room. He didn't want to feel like he was invading their space. Not just because of privacy, but because he was lost in his thoughts as well.

The comment about Duncan becoming a plumber had set his mind to spinning. It was over now. Midian was safe, he felt like whatever he had to prove, he'd proved, so...

...What the fuck was he supposed to do now?

His father was dead, his mother was dead, and so was Alison. The family business had been a grocery store – the only grocery store in town, as such–

What the fuck was he supposed to do now?

Wander back to New York? Make coffees with Heidi and

Shirley for people terminally online, forever asking for the wifi password, bus the tables in the bustling cafe while life just passed him by? What meaning did that hold for him, personally? He loved a good cup of coffee, but he was hardly obsessed with making them, and it wasn't exactly a great living.

Brian knew this much: the days of being able to sit in his room and smoke weed were definitely over. Even considering doing that left a bitter taste in his mouth, and not because of the aftertaste of his preferred sativa blend, either.

He'd never given much thought to the family business before, but now...well, he wondered if Midian was going to make it, or if it was going to become one of those ghost towns that dotted the American landscape, where all the young people left, and all the old folks stayed, and it died an inch at a time.

But this much he knew: if he could stay now, he would. Maybe he'd taken over the grocery store, rebuild it. Whatever he did, it'd be here, in Midian, for as long as he could. This was where his family had planted their roots, and he wasn't too good to take up where they'd left off. Not anymore.

"HOW ARE YOU FEELING?" Lauren asked. She was perched over Lucia, who was sitting upright, her legs spread wide, not a stitch of clothing on the poor girl.

"Like I shot a bowling ball out of my vagina as if it were a cannon," Lucia said, looking up at her. Green eyes, stunningly so. Just like when Lauren had first met her at the ER.

Lauren just stared at her for a moment. "Yep. That's how it's supposed to feel. Hendricks!" She caught sight of the cowboy out of the corner of her eye. "Give me your jacket."

He was still hanging on to Erin's arm, but let go for a

moment to peel out of the big, black coat. He tossed it at her, not moving any closer, as if he were afraid to.

"Gee, thanks," Lauren said, scrambling across the ground to retrieve it and return to Lucia. She covered the girl up, helped her into the coat, and started to turn her so that the open end faced toward a wall–

"You really think that's necessary?" Lucia asked her, eyebrow raised in amusement that pushed through the tiredness written on this girl's face. "Everyone in the room has seen my vagina at this point." She shifted uncomfortably on the rocky floor. "Hell, a whole lot of people who weren't in the room have seen my vagina, doctor. Or been in it. I don't feel now is the moment I should develop a sense of propriety."

Lauren didn't stop gently turning her, skidding her butt until her legs faced the wall. "If not now, when?"

Lucia hesitated. There was a glistening in her eyes. "You know who I am. You know what I've done."

"You're Lucia," Lauren said, taking a quick peek down there to make sure she didn't need stitches. Surprisingly, she did not. It actually looked like everything was normal, like she hadn't just experienced a birth at all. "And you helped me – helped us – save the world. Remember? You warned me that night."

Her small shoulders moved up and down in a shudder. "I didn't think that would help at all."

Lauren looked up at her, caught her. Tried to project reassurance. The way a doctor was supposed to. "It helped. In fact, it may have made the difference in all this."

Her eyes brimmed with tears. "I caused it."

"Hey," Lauren said, catching her chin with a finger. "You did not cause this." God, the girl was only a little older than Molly and she'd already been through hell. Literally. "This was fated to happen. Because someone meaner and more evil than anything we can imagine decided it was so. You got taken in by a liar, okay?"

She sniffled. "Been taken in by a few of those over the years." She looked up with blurry eyes. "What's one more?"

"Just...make this the last one. Hm?" Lauren turned to see Arch standing in front of the gate, staring at it. "Hey, Mr. Stan? Mind giving me a hand here?" She looked back at Lucia. "We're going to get you out of here." Lauren put a hand on her shoulder. Still, all she could think about was Molly, and how soon she could see her again. Surely it wouldn't be long now.

ARCH FELT himself stirred out of the silence he'd adopted while staring at the gate. "I'll be right there," he told Lauren Darlington, almost as an afterthought. Of course he'd help carry Lucia out of here. It was the least he could do for the girl after what all she'd been through.

But he wanted one last look at the gate.

"That thing..." Hendricks shuddered, only a few feet away from him. He seemed to be edging away from it, as though he couldn't stand to be in its presence.

Arch didn't have that problem at all. Oh, he knew there was something a little odd about it, knew by its mere curves and lines that it was special, not of this world...but it didn't make him want to run away.

In fact...it seemed to be asking him if he wanted to stay. Like within it waited something better, some home he couldn't recall any more, but that he'd once known. A great and wonderful home, with the aroma of dinner cooking hanging in the air, and a big, warm fire keeping the world's cold at bay.

Part of him wanted to run to it, that vision of things, but

another, smaller, voice knew that it was the end of these days if he did.

Someday, it seemed to whisper. *But not just yet.*

And the voice was – he could swear – Alison's.

That was enough for him. He turned and stooped low, picking up Lucia in his arms. Lifting her was hardly any effort at all, and she squeezed at his neck as he picked her up.

"Thank you," she whispered, her eyes glistening. "For...everything."

"It's no trouble at all," Arch said, and he meant it. Dr. Darlington walking by his side – as if he'd drop her, or as if she could catch the girl if he did – he made his way out of the room, leaving the feeling of home behind.

"HOW ARE YOU FEELING?" Erin asked. Hendricks was still leaning on her, though not as much.

They were still in the depths of the cave, though others had started to peel off and head back up. Arch had been staring at the gate until just a moment ago.

Hendricks...wasn't. He seemed to be looking everywhere but at it. Erin, for her part, was happy to look at it, but thoroughly enjoyed keeping her distance. "I'm okay," he said, in a manner that suggested, no, he wasn't. He did, however, finally shift the last of his weight off her, wobbling on his own two feet.

"What happened before we got down here?" Erin asked. She was still holding on to his arm, though barely.

Hendricks blinked a couple times, then let loose of her hand. He shuffled his way over to his hat, which was lying in the dirt, and picked it up. He didn't put it back on his head, though. "Some blustering," he said, brushing the dirt off it. "Some birthing. Which, gotta say, having only before seen it in a video in high school – I hope the real thing doesn't look like a demon birth." He shook his head. "That one's gonna stick with me for a while. If I shudder a little the next time I see you naked, I promise it's not you. It's the memory of that."

She crossed her arms over her chest, and looked down, kicking the dirt. "What makes you think there's going to be a 'next time?'"

Hendricks had paused, stooped over his sword. He looked at her for a long moment, then picked it up, brushing it off on his pants before returning it to the scabbard on his belt. "I guess I was a little presumptuous, huh? Thinking the van...that it meant something."

She just shrugged. "Your work here is done, isn't it?" She looked over at the looming entrance back to the cavern. "This was always just a stop for you, wasn't it? So...time to be getting on your way, right?" She turned back to look at him.

He stood there for a moment and now, at last, he looked at the gate. Really looked at it, long and hard, with some stripe of fear, awe, and dread all mingled up on his face. She watched him watch it, then shifted so she could look at it, a feat she managed for all of five seconds before, no, she had to look away.

Hendricks didn't, though. Not until a few seconds more had passed.

"I think," he said, face like he was coming out of a trance, "my wandering days are done."

Erin tried to figure out how to take that. Like a punch was her first instinct. "What?"

"I'm done," Hendricks said. "With the demon slaying. With the drifting." He looked...tired. "I just want to stay somewhere for a while. Sleep in the same bed. Live somewhere where I know people and they know me. Somewhere I'm...wanted." He cracked a sly smile. "Know anywhere like that?"

She held back for a moment, then got to him in two steps,

wrapping her arms around him, her skin against his dirtied up t-shirt. "I might know a place that'd have you," she said, after a long kiss. "It's kind of a fixer upper, though."

"I don't mind work," Hendricks said, then brushed his hand against his scabbard. "Long as it's less of the demon hunting variety, more of the...hell, I don't even know what I'm good at. Hanging drywall, maybe? I did that once upon a time, it was okay. Demolition, probably? I've done plenty of that."

"It just so happens there's a high demand for that around here," she said, keeping her arms wrapped around his waist. He draped his over her shoulder, and they started walking out. He did take a last look at the gate, but that was it.

"What about you?" Hendricks asked, once they were out of its light. She could see his face in the shadows, and the reflection of the brightness coming from the flashlight hanging from her vest. "You gonna be sheriff now?"

Erin made a face. "I don't think I want to be in law enforcement anymore, actually."

Now it was his turn to make a face. "You want to be, like, a housewife, then?"

She laughed. "Maybe someday. But no, not now. I just don't want to go back to patrol schedules and writing tickets. It'd feel like too much of a comedown after killing demons and saving the world. I think I just want to shift gears a bit."

"Whatever you do, I'm sure you'll be great at it," he said, and she must have raised an eyebrow or something, because he added, "because you've already proven you're great at the leading thing, and killing demons, and writing tickets." He hesitated, and she could see the mischief playing in his eyes before he added, "And the sex. You're really great at that."

"Well, that last one I'm not giving up," she said, hugging him tighter as they made their way out of the cave. "Might confine it to just one person, though."

"That'd be appreciated," he said. "I'll do the same."

"Then we have a deal," she said, though she didn't make any signal to shake on it, she felt it was implied. "Done and done." And with a nod of her head, in her opinion, it was. His, too, by the look of him. And also because he was squeezing her tight in return, and she didn't mind it a bit.

DUNCAN MADE it to the mouth of the cave, the weight of Gary and Marina in the wheelchair barely anything to him – under normal circumstances.

But these were hardly normal. His shell was battered, was near broken. These things didn't heal, either. Sure, with proper care, he could perhaps live a good many years yet without experiencing a sudden break. But one hard jarring that hit the right spot – and there were dozens now, thanks to Guthrie – and he'd be done. Pop. Sucked back to...

Well. That was a bit of a question now, wasn't it?

Rain was pouring down outside, the sky split with another bolt of blinding white, thunder rattling his shell as he came to stand just before the place where the droplets splashed.

Hendricks's father-in-law was there, back against the cave wall, looking like he might fall asleep, bandages swaddling his leg. He stared at Duncan, then the two in the wheelchair, and let his gaze slide away. Didn't say anything, either.

"Are you all right?" Nguyen asked. To Gary and Marina, naturally.

"We're fine," Gary said, his face right up next to Marina's in a nuzzle. "Just fine."

Then, he realized, Nguyen was also looking at him.

"I'm..." He stared out into the rain. It was really coming down out there.

Something came across Duncan then, a feeling he hadn't maybe ever felt. Before anyone could say anything, he leapt out into the rain–

"No!" Nguyen shouted. "It's–"

It spattered down on Duncan's head, cool and pure and fresh from the heavens. Duncan thrust his face up and let it come down, run down him, down his nose and eyes and forehead and everywhere.

"It's...holy water...?" Nguyen finished. "Or it was."

Duncan let it soak his clothes. Soak him. "Still is."

And then...he danced.

It was probably not a beautiful dance, but it was heartfelt. Because finally, finally...

Duncan was free.

HENDRICKS MADE it out of the caves only a few steps behind Arch, who was still carrying Lucia. They slowed a bit at the entry, mostly because...well...

Duncan was dancing in the rain. Which was...well, it was fucking weird, frankly. And, Hendricks had to concede, after a few moments of watching, slack-jawed, just a little bit beautiful. Which...he did not know where that came from.

"Can you set me down?" Lucia asked. Her eyes, too, were anchored on Duncan. "I'm not going to dance or anything, but I think I can stand on my own two feet."

"You just gave birth," Dr. Darlington said, in her doctor voice. Very different from how she sounded when she wasn't trying to be commanding.

"Yeah, but I don't think it was the same as a real, human one," Lucia said. "For one thing...I was only pregnant for like two months. And for another–"

"You want to walk," Darlington said, nodding in concession. "Which is not a thing a mother who just gave actual birth to a human has said, ever. Well, go on, then. Give it a try."

Hendricks watched her stand uncomfortably. Which was to say, he was uncomfortable and she was standing without trouble.

Erin still had her arms around him, and was looking up at him, watching him watch her. "Something on your mind, cowboy?"

"I think," Hendricks said, watching Lucia take a few steps on her own, "I have an apology to make." He looked down at Erin, and she nodded. Not mad, exactly, but not happy, either. It was a complex emotional state, and one that he felt was much more at home in her expression than any he could muster.

"Well," she said, turning him loose with a pat on his side, right where his ribs hurt, "you should do that, then."

"You know what's great about what I did in there?" Gary Wrightson asked. The sonofabitch was still nude, with only his girlfriend draped across his lap to hide his shame. "I'm like Ricky Bobby now: I piss excellence."

There were groans. So many groans. But Marina laughed, and that got Gary laughing.

Hendricks shuffled toward Lucia, who was standing just inside the mouth of the cave, her blazing hair being slowly doused by the spatter blowing in. She looked over at him as he approached, and he halted. She didn't show any sign of wanting to flee; in fact she didn't show much sign of recognition at all, none of the tension he might have expected from a prey animal. "Do you remember me?" he asked.

"No," she said, his coat bound tight around her; she positively disappeared in it. "I mean, I do from the time you visited me at Miss Cherry's. And I've seen you around town, but...any interactions we had...I wasn't present for, mentally. You were talking to Starling the whole time."

Hendricks found himself staring down at his boots. "I'm sorry anyway. I used you, used your body, knowing someone else was steering. And that was shitty as hell of me to do." He glanced up to see if she was taking any of this in.

She looked him over once. "I suspect I've let worse be done to my body while I was conscious."

"That doesn't absolve me of–"

"We all did terrible things here, okay?" She looked back out to the rain. "And all our terrible things combined to take us right up to the brink of the end. You did what you did and that's..." She took a deep breath. "I guess I just have a hard time getting too mad at you because Starling wasn't me. She killed people with my body, I know that now. Hurt people. And yes, it sucks ass that she used me to use you. But in my desperation, I opened the door for her. So forgive me if I don't blame you for doing what you did at her invitation...because I'm the one who invited her in to begin with."

"You cannot blame yourself," Hendricks said, still keeping his distance. "Starling was...you know what Starling was. You got deceived by a master. And you...you're what? Twenty?"

She flushed. "Eighteen."

"Oh, fuck," Hendricks said, blanching, and caught a sideways glare from Erin where she stood a small distance away, clearly listening. "Well, I'm gonna have a hell of a time forgiving myself, but look – you got snookered by an older player."

"So did you," she said. "You going to stop blaming yourself?" She shuffled back and forth uncomfortably between her bare feet, as though she was still having trouble standing. But stand she did. "The way I see it, you're...what, thirty?"

"I'm twenty-five," Hendricks said, and suddenly he felt a spear of self-consciousness. Ouch again.

Now it was Lucia's turn to blush. "Oh, fuck, I'm sorry," she said. "But the point is – there's only a few years that separate you and me. Starling...is millions of years old, I think. I got that sense, anyway, from her, and from what that crazy demon lady said before she got popped through the chest. So if you're worried about me being taken in by an old hustler, and my body being used by someone older..." She gave him a pitying look. "...I'm a lot more used to that than you are."

Hendricks felt a real burn of shame. "That doesn't make it right for me to have done it."

"I'll forgive you if you forgive me," Lucia said.

"Already done," Hendricks said. "But you don't have to–"

"Already done, too," Lucia said softly. "Whether you want it or not...you've got it. Please. I don't want to carry this – any of this – any farther. I'm carrying too much poison already." She turned her face back to the rain, and there was a slow smile spreading there. "I just want to let it all go."

Hendricks nodded slowly, able to look her in the eye, finally. All he saw there was a quiet sincerity, absent any malice at all. "Okay," he said. "You can keep the coat, by the way."

She looked down at it uncomfortably. "No, thanks, I'll get it back to you." She shrugged, almost apologetically. "It's not really my size. Or my color. Or...mine, really. I only want things that belong to me."

Hendricks looked over his shoulder at Erin, who had lost her look of malice as well. "Me too," he said, and saw her nod at his words. "Me, too." He shuffled back toward her on aching legs, and felt something slap his knee. Looking down, he almost jumped in surprise. "Gunny?"

Micah was sitting there, his leg bandaged, half-soaked, leaning against the mine's wall. "Forget about me already, shitheel?"

"Kinda," Hendricks said, squatting down next to him. "You going to be okay?"

"Doc seemed to think so," Micah said. "Told me I'd be on my

way back home in no time. Just needed to get this stitched or butterflied or something." He had beads of water across his brow, and Hendricks couldn't tell if it was sweat or rain. Landing a hand on Hendricks's shoulder, he said, "I'm glad you married my daughter now."

Hendricks looked back, and offered a pained smile to Erin before lowering his voice. "I think, I uh...I heard her in there." He watched Micah's brow furrow. "When I was next to the...the thing."

Micah stared at him long and hard. "What'd she say?"

"She said," and his voice cracked a little, "'I'll see you again.'" He felt his throat get thick, but he squeezed the words out anyway. "'But not today.'"

Micah put that hand back on his shoulder and squeezed, lowering his head so Hendricks couldn't even see the tears in the rain. But he stayed with him like that until the rumble of a car engine in the distance sounded over the falling rain.

"Someone's coming," Erin said, and he was up and at her side in a moment, pistol in hand. He had six more rounds of blessed bullets in the gun, plus another couple mags, and his sword–

"They are not your enemies, Hendricks," came a small, quiet voice from behind him.

Hendricks turned, and there in the lee of the cave, a little damp...

...was Rhea.

"Holy fuck," Gary Wrightson said. "It's the little Indian girl. How the hell did she make it through this shitshow alive? And which one of you retards brought her to this shindig?"

"I run my own schedule, Mr. Wrightson," Rhea said, pushing off the wall. She meandered over to Hendricks, taking her sweet time. "You did it. You chose the world."

"I did," Hendricks said. "And now I'm done." He put his pistol away, and started to reach for his sword to hand it to her–

"Keep it," she said. "There are more than enough holy blades now that even if that one never draws another whiff of sulfur, it's better you have it."

"Retired, huh?" Micah guffawed. "Bet you don't get a pension from that."

"I think we can come up with a small stipend while Mr. Hendricks gets back on his feet," Rhea said.

Micah just stared at her. "You gonna send him your lunch money?"

Rhea brushed past him; the rain was beginning to dwindle. The sound of engines – more than one – was clear in the air now. "I actually have a very effective crowdfunding campaign going. A lot of patrons from all over the world send me money every month. Almost all of whom have seen demons, many of them have lived in towns where hotspots have struck them." She looked down the mountain, made a show of it, as the first truck came turning the corner.

But not the last. Not by a lot.

"There are a lot of people out there who have been dispossessed by demons," Rhea said. "Who are looking for a place to...put down roots, as it were. In addition to the returning souls from your town, coming back now that the fight has been won."

"Kinda chickenshit of them," Gary said. "Maybe we don't want 'em back." He eyed the convoy working its way up the hill now. It was a motley assembly; Hendricks saw big trucks, passenger vans, even a big cargo truck.

"Hey, that's Paul," Brian said, perking right up. "Paul Cummings. He's the driver for Rogerson's." He pointed at the truck. Pretty overexcited to see a fuckin' truck. At least for a philosophy major. Who wasn't three years old.

"No, not everyone wanted to stay for the fight," Rhea said.

"But historically, few ever fight. Wars always rest on the shoulders of a few. And if you really want to rebuild your town, can you afford to turn away help?"

"Fuck," Gary said. "I guess not."

"Well," Erin said, "I guess we've got some work ahead of us." That caused an uncomfortable shuffle in the ranks. Not dissension, exactly, but some definite...discomfort.

"Let's work tomorrow," Hendricks said, looking up and seeing the sun just barely start to shine through behind the clouds and the residual smoke. Below, the wildfires were out, gone, extinguished by the driving rains. And in him, too, something had been extinguished, some burning that had carried him from New Orleans til now, and all the dark places between. "After all, we did just save the world." He felt himself crack a grin. "Any chance there might be a six-pack of Leinenkugel's anywhere in that convoy?"

EPILOGUE

WINDSWEPT

Three Months Later

Arch's coffee steamed on the table in front of him. He was sitting in one of the booths of Surrey Diner, on the square in Midian, clad in khaki pants and a button-down shirt. It was a Sunday morning in April, with spring blooms hanging on the trees in the square. Outside the window, the sun was peering down, and he could see a couple kids playing on the grass.

He could also see the place where Alison had died.

Most days, he only thought about her once or twice now. Most days, he could make it through without a racking surge of emotion threatening to bring him to his knees.

Most days. But not all of them.

He took a sip. The coffee was ripe with one cream and one Splenda, just enough sweetening to turn it from terribly bitter to mildly enjoyable. They made a strong cup here at the diner. Always had and, he figured, always would.

The bell dinged to indicate someone had entered, and Arch looked up. He half expected one of the new faces, or one of the old residents. Most of them had come creeping back in the days and weeks after the final showdown in the cave. The mill had reopened, even. FEMA funds had come pouring in unexpectedly, to help rebuild after the earthquake...according to the emergency personnel. The interstate had even reopened, after a blitzkrieg construction project to clear the fallen bridges. I-75 couldn't be closed to traffic for too long – or so the line went that they were fed.

All that bullcrap, Arch didn't believe. No one did, except the construction workers and FEMA folks. But they were mostly gone now. Now it was down to the residents, the old and new, the people who'd decided to plant their feet in Midian for one reason or another. Because they'd been born here or because they'd chosen here, it didn't seem to much matter.

Certainly none of it mattered to Arch.

An old face was the one that entered, then shuffled over to him in dress shoes that looked like they might be the best that Shoe Carnival down in Chattanooga had to offer. With a single finger held aloft to signal the waitress, Lafayette Jackson Hendricks squeezed into the booth across from Arch, putting his back to the window and letting his feet hang over the end of the bench. "What's up?"

Arch just eyed him, then took a sip. "Today's the day." When that didn't produce a reply, Arch added, "What's with the fancy getup?"

Hendricks looked down at his own button-up dress shirt and black Dockers dress pants. "Erin's got me going to church with her," he said, and then, as if to stave off any undue reply, added, "I'm still not sure what I believe, or that I believe in – well, I don't know what I believe. But I do go with her, most Sundays."

Arch raised an eyebrow. "'Most?'"

Hendricks grinned. "Some Sundays I manage to convince her that staying in bed and shouting, 'Oh, God, oh, God!" constitutes a fair expression of praise."

Arch just shook his head. However much he had changed, there were some things about the man that wouldn't move no matter what he experienced. But that struck Arch as human nature. "Other than that," he said, brushing a couple stray grains of Splenda off the table in front of him, "how is Madam Mayor?"

"Erin? She likes it a lot better than law enforcement," Hendricks said. "So far, at least. Better hours, better pay." He sat up as the waitress approached. "You know, you could still–"

"No," Arch said. Firmly. That door was closed, now.

"Hey, Hendricks," the waitress said, putting down a cup in front of him and turning the carafe up to pour in the steaming liquid. "How's it going?"

"Good, Lucia," he told the redhead, sitting a little uncomfortably compared to his previous slouching. She wasn't exactly the popping-her-gum type, but she was friendly, she was personable, and she seemed to be doing okay at it. "How are you doing?"

"Working a double today," she said, topping off Arch's cup. "To be honest," and here she put a hand on her hips, cocking them just so, and standing before them like she had a lifetime of experience, "I do think sometimes that spending five minutes an hour on my back a few times a day, and a maybe a little time on my knees, is just a little easier than sixteen hours on my feet."

Hendricks winced; Arch couldn't blame him, he did a little of the same.

"Still," she said, like she hadn't just dropped a bomb on the table, "the tips are pretty okay. You guys want to order or do you need a few minutes?"

"Not sure I'm going to eat today," Hendricks said, smiling wanly. He looked...pained.

"I'll flag you down if I want anything, Lucia," Arch said. "Thanks."

She smiled brightly, and off she went, two tables down, to banter with Ed Hornsby.

Hendricks turned to watch her, still looking quite pained. "I don't really know what to make of her, I really don't."

"That's your guilt talking," Arch said. More Splenda grains had somehow escaped his attention; must be the light. He swept them off to the floor. "She forgave you, didn't she?"

"I'm not sure she knew what she was forgiving," Hendricks said, turning back to him. "But yeah. She did."

"Then either dwell in it forever or let it go," Arch said. He didn't have much room to dwell himself. Not today.

"You're testy today," Hendricks said. "You in a hurry?"

Arch stared across the table at him for a long moment before answering. "I suppose I am."

Hendricks nodded, and fished a few singles out of his pocket. Dropping them on the table, he winced. "Leaving her singles feels a little like–"

"Dwell or drop," Arch said, putting a few dollars down himself. "Your choice." He rose to leave.

Hendricks led the way, ringing the bell as he opened the door for incoming. Arch didn't realize until he was almost there that the entrants were a triad of women – two with darkest hair, one light blond.

"Oh, hey," Hendricks said, kissing Erin as she passed. "Didn't know you were coming here for breakfast."

"Where else would we go?" Molly Darlington asked, offering him the sarcasm only a teenage girl could, especially when she thought she was responding to something stupid.

"Rogerson's? Because it's literally the only other thing in town that's open and has food."

"Now, now, Molly," Lauren Darlington said, "consider that Mr. Hendricks was once a Marine, and his diet probably included things we wouldn't commonly think of as edible."

Molly brightened. "Like crayons. I hear Marines love crayons. What's your favorite flavor? Is blue any good?"

Hendricks just smirked, taking the abuse. "You know, I'm about to be your uncle." He brushed Erin's hand, where a small diamond in a band waited on her left ring finger.

"I know!" Molly said, eyes wide with amusement. "Which is why I'm asking. For your wedding gift. Do you just want an entire box, like a smorgasbord of different flavors, or do you want a smaller selection, kind of curated–"

"I was considering what kind of graduation present I'm supposed to give a niece," Hendricks said, deeply pensive, "but I struggle with whether there's a solid difference between a favored one and a disfavored one. Anyone know the rules on that?"

"Oh, Uncle Crayons," Molly said, feigning, "you already got me the best graduation present ever when you saved me from being impregnated by a randy demon on that Ferris wheel last summer."

Laughing, the girls made their way past him – and Arch – with a flurry of kisses on the cheek, and hugs. Arch took it all in stride, and when they were out on the sidewalk he stood there a moment, letting his eyes adjust to the light.

"Feels weird to have...family," Hendricks said. He seemed to mostly be talking to himself.

"It should feel good," Arch said. There was a distinctly echoing sensation he felt inside himself.

"It does," Hendricks said, still to himself. Then he seemed to wake, and his faint smile disappeared. "Sorry."

"You don't have anything to apologize for," Arch said gently. But with a wave, he started to walk. Hendricks fell in beside him. "Where'd you park?"

"Right beside you," Hendricks said, back to smirking. It seemed his natural state these days. Well, that was fine. Hendricks was living his best life, as they said. Who could blame him? Certainly not Arch.

They made it to his car, and Hendricks went on past to his own. Arch didn't pay him any mind, he was too busy taking care getting the box out of the front seat. When he stood up with it in his hands, he found Hendricks pacing back over to him, his own arms full.

"What's this?" Arch asked.

"Just a few things to speed you on your way," Hendricks said, looking at the pile in his arms. "If you want 'em. If not...no big. You don't even need to take all of it, just pick what you want and toss the rest." He looked up. "I don't need it anymore."

Arch looked down at what he carried. It was his old, black, drover coat, his cowboy hat, a couple books that Arch recognized as demon classification tomes. It was Hendricks's collected items for demon hunting, minus his sword and his pistol. The backup knife was even there, bound inside the brim of his hat.

"If you're really going to do this," Hendricks said softly, squinting against the bright sunlight, "you ought to do it right."

"I'm going to do it," Arch said, passing the box carefully to Hendricks, and taking up the demon hunting gear in return. "Rhea says there's a hotspot going in LA right now. Expected to last a while. And there just aren't that many demon hunters left out there." He looked down at the coat, at the hat. "Someone ought to do something. Might as well be me."

"She'll help you as best she can," Hendricks said, now holding the box Arch had handed him. It was simple, white, but had some real weight to it. "But you'll mostly be on your own. It's a solitary profession."

"I could use some alone time," Arch said. "For a while, at least."

Hendricks just nodded. "Don't stay out there too long, Arch. It wears on you after a while. Hollows you out."

"I won't," Arch said. "Or at least I hope I won't. And...I'm already hollow. You ought to know that by now."

Hendricks cupped the box by his side, freeing up a hand, which he landed on Arch's wrist. "You could stay. This place – these people...they love you, Arch."

"It's not my home anymore, cowboy," Arch said. "But maybe I'll do like you have, and find my home – somewhere on down the road."

Hendricks nodded. "I hope you do. Get out there and ride the wind." Then he pulled Arch into as much of a hug as they could muster with their arms full. "Thank you. For everything. Saving my life." He pulled back, and there were little points of glistening light in the corners of his eyes. "Thank you."

Arch just nodded at the box in Hendricks's arms. "Take care of that, will you? That's plenty enough thanks for me."

He didn't remember putting the gear in the seat of his car, but it was there a few minutes later when he looked, the car rolling down Old Jackson Highway as if on autopilot. The interstate was ahead, and so was the road, and that was all he needed, for now, all he could handle.

The sheriff's department Explorer was sitting on the side of the road almost at the freeway entrance, and Arch nudged his vehicle off, failing to signal his turn as he did so. Its tires bit gravel when he pulled off, and he barely managed to slow it down without fishtailing. Bringing it around, he pulled up beside the new sheriff of Calhoun County and dropped his window.

"Howdy, Duncan," he said, looking at the former OOC. He looked good in khaki; it seemed to go well with his complexion.

"Hey, Arch." Duncan smiled at him; from his higher vehicle, he could see right into Arch's, and took note of the gear strewn on his passenger seat. "This is it, huh?"

Arch just nodded. There was a lump in his throat, though not much of one. It felt...natural to leave. "Take care of them, Duncan."

"I will," Duncan said. "Take care of yourself, Arch. And if you ever run into demon trouble you can't handle–"

Arch just nodded. "You'll be the first one I call." He did frown, though. "You ever get a cell phone? Or should I call the office?"

Duncan stared down at him placidly. "Just call my name. I'll hear you, wherever you are."

Arch stared at him. "Just...say the name Duncan, and–?"

"That's not my name," Duncan said. "Not my real one, anyway. My real name is...Sariel."

"Sariel," Arch said, and the reaction was immediate. Duncan closed his eyes, and when he opened them again, he looked right at Arch. "I won't go saying it if I don't have to."

"But if you do say it," Duncan – Sariel – said, "I'll come running. Count on that. Count on me."

"I will," Arch said. "Thank you."

He rolled up the window and got back on the road. Passing the sign that said, LEAVING CALHOUN COUNTY, he felt a little twang within, like he was leaving something important behind. Which he was; other than college, he'd never lived anywhere but Midian. This was his hometown.

Where he'd grown up.

Where he thought he'd die.

But life didn't always work out the way you planned it, did it? And this was no longer his home. And it was, as Hendricks said, time for him to ride the wind, trusting that wherever he went, he was meant to be there.

HENDRICKS TOOK the box up to the peak of Mount Horeb the next time he had an afternoon off. He didn't bring anyone with him, because they'd all been through enough of this foolishness.

No, not foolishness. That was the wrong word.

But enough funerals. They'd definitely had enough of those.

This was the last, and he was doing it all by himself. Fair or not, he'd been handed the box containing the ashes of the last of Midian's dead. The sun bore down on him from on high, and he stood upon the overlook just down from where they'd won the battle that had saved the world. Midian stretched out below, along with a black charring of woods that had burned in the fires. The rains had put paid to those, but the scars would last for decades, according to the US Forest Service.

Scars that lasted for decades? Hendricks knew a little something about that.

He hiked up to the edge, feeling a little sweat creep down his temple. He brushed it off, reminded of the blood Starling had drawn in that last fight. Scalp lacerations bled the worst; well, other than an arterial bleed. Those could kill you.

Kind of like losing family, and then the will to go on. That had certainly done it for the man whose ashes were resting in Hendricks's arms.

Hendricks paused, staring out over the Caledonia River Valley. This was as good a spot as any. He pulled open the box, and found himself looking at the tightly compressed ashes of Braeden Tarley.

"I don't know if this is what you would have wanted,"

Hendricks said, talking to the air as much as the ashes. "We had that lawyer, Lex Deivrel, do a lot of digging to figure out what the folks we've buried this last few months wanted done with their remains, their estates. And you...you're the last one. I'm sad to say we didn't even remember to get you until quite a bit later. That's on us, I guess. I hope you'll find it in yourself to forgive us."

He paused, thinking. "I wanted to do this for you because...well, we've done a lot of funerals. Too many, really. Everyone's tired of them. And I didn't know most of these folks. Didn't even really know you, if it comes to that. But I knew this – you lost people you cared about, and it ripped your damned heart out.

"Fair enough, right? Lot of that going around this town. Except you," Hendricks said, turning his eyes to the sky, wondering if somewhere, out there, Braeden Tarley might actually be able to hear him, "you picked up your wrench and you kept fighting. You didn't have to. But you did it. You lost more than almost anyone...and you kept fighting. And then you lost again...and that was it." Hendricks pulled a hand off, balancing it, so he could snap his fingers. "You lost your new girl, you lost hope...and you rode this thing right into the ground.

"I know what that feels like," Hendricks said. "And when I think about you dying in those tunnels...it could have just as easily been me. I was ready. Ready to die just to be...done." Those words tasted like ashes in his mouth, especially now. "And if I had...I wouldn't have what I do now." He rubbed his thumb's tip against the bare skin on his ring finger. It wasn't going to be bare for much longer. "So...thank you, Braeden Tarley. Thank you, to all the others who died along the way. For us. So Midian could live. So *we* could live."

He lifted up the box. "When I came to this town, it was doing what I called...riding the wind. And when I left, I figured

I'd go the exact same way." He tipped the box over, and the ashes spilled out; the winds caught them and carried them, swirling in the currents and drifting out over Midian – and beyond.

"Because of you...now I don't have to," Hendricks said, watching the ashes disappear into the distance, drifting off into forever. When they were gone, he turned and walked back to his car. Erin was waiting for him at home, and he couldn't wait to get there.

AFTERWORD

Well, that was a journey.

I started the first book of Southern Watch in July of 2013, opening the door to Midian, Tennessee, while on break from writing the two series I had already begun. It had its roots in an idea I'd had while sitting in a terminally boring summer session of American Literature class my junior year of college. It started with a simple premise: what if a black-coated, cowboy hat wearing demon hunter did battle in a small southern town? Our cultural canon is filled with lots of stories in cities; I wondered what an urban fantasy novel would look like, feel like, without the "urban" part of it.

This was my answer, and it's taken over ten years (over twenty, if you want to go back to the original origin) for me to play it all out in print. The last three books were supposed to be entitled Hallowed, Inflamed, and Windswept. There wasn't much to them, frankly; it was easy to wrap them into one because the only ideas I had were fairly simple to telescope into this one volume. I know this will still disappoint the hardcore fans of the Watch; I wish I could have done more to make this series a success, and write the full ten, but know that I'm grateful you chose to spend your time and interest on these people, on this story. I hope this ending satisfies you. It's not exactly what I planned, but here, at the end, I can safely tell you – it is everything I hoped for it to be.

If you enjoyed this, you might enjoy some of my other works. Click ahead just one more page and you'll find oh-so-many to choose from; I've written over a hundred books at this point. Anyway, in case you move on...thanks for reading.

Robert J. Crane

Other Works by Robert J. Crane

The Girl in the Box
(and Out of the Box)
Contemporary Urban Fantasy

1. Alone
2. Untouched
3. Soulless
4. Family
5. Omega
6. Broken
7. Enemies
8. Legacy
9. Destiny
10. Power
11. Limitless
12. In the Wind
13. Ruthless
14. Grounded
15. Tormented
16. Vengeful
17. Sea Change
18. Painkiller
19. Masks
20. Prisoners
21. Unyielding
22. Hollow

56. Stolen
57. Scorched Earth
58. Heart of the Storm* (Coming November 2nd, 2024!)

The Girl Who Ran Away
Contemporary Mystery Fantasy

1. Buried in Lies
2. Listening to Fear
3. Bound in Silence* (Coming in 2024!)

The Sanctuary Series
Epic Fantasy
(in best reading order)
(Series Complete)

1. Defender (Volume 1)
2. Avenger (Volume 2)
3. Champion (Volume 3)
4. Crusader (Volume 4)
5. Sanctuary Tales (Volume 4.25)
6. Thy Father's Shadow (Volume 4.5)
7. Master (Volume 5)
8. Fated in Darkness (Volume 5.5)
9. Warlord (Volume 6)
10. Heretic (Volume 7)
11. Legend (Volume 8)
12. Ghosts of Sanctuary (Volume 9)
13. Call of the Hero (Volume 10)
14. The Scourge of Despair (Volume 11)
15. Rage of the Ancients (Volume 12)

Ashes of Luukessia
A Sanctuary Trilogy
(with Michael Winstone)
(Trilogy Complete)

1. A Haven in Ash (Ashes of Luukessia #1)
2. A Respite From Storms (Ashes of Luukessia #2)
3. A Home in the Hills (Ashes of Luukessia #3)

Liars and Vampires
YA Urban Fantasy
(with Lauren Harper)

1. No One Will Believe You
2. Someone Should Save Her
3. You Can't Go Home Again
4. Lies in the Dark
5. Her Lying Days Are Done
6. Heir of the Dog
7. Hit You Where You Live
8. Her Endless Night
9. Burned Me* (Coming in 2024!)
10. Something In That Vein* (Coming in 2024!)

Southern Watch
Dark Contemporary Fantasy/Horror
(Series Complete)

1. Called
2. Depths
3. Corrupted
4. Unearthed
5. Legion

6. Starling
7. Forsaken
8. Hallowed

The Mira Brand Adventures
YA Modern Fantasy
(Series Complete)

1. The World Beneath
2. The Tide of Ages
3. The City of Lies
4. The King of the Skies
5. The Best of Us
6. We Aimless Few
7. The Gang of Legend
8. The Antecessor Conundrum

*Forthcoming, title subject to change

ACKNOWLEDGMENTS

Thanks to Lewis Moore for the edits and Jeff Bryan, for the proofing.

Thanks as always to the great Karri Klawiter of artbykarri.com for the cover.

Gracias to Tim Bischoff and Heidi Schweizer for being such diligent fans and taking an early look - and providing early feedback. You guys rock.

And thanks, too, to my family for making this all possible.

Made in the USA
Columbia, SC
11 July 2024